P9-CBC-958

JIMMY DEAN PREPARES

Also by Sam Toperoff

QUEEN OF DESIRE: MARILYN MONROE, A FICTION

JIMMY DEAN PREPARES

Sam Toperoff

Granta Books
London

Granta Publications, 2/3 Hanover Yard, Noel Road,
London N1 8BE

First published in Great Britain by Granta Books 1997

Copyright © 1997 by Sam Toperoff

Sam Toperoff has asserted his moral right under the
Copyright, Designs and Patents Act, 1988 to be identified
as author of this work.

Extract from *The Immoralist* by André Gide reprinted with the Permission of
Simon & Schuster, Translated from the French by Dorothy Bussy (London:
Cassell & Co Ltd, 1930). Extract from *The Hairy Ape* by Eugene O'Neill
from *The Collected Plays of Eugene O'Neill* (Jonathan Cape) reprinted by kind
Permission of the Estate of Eugene O'Neill and Jonathan Cape. *Rebel
Without a Cause* © 1955 Warner Bros Pictures, Inc. Renewed © 1983
Warner Bros Inc. All Rights Reserved. *The Green Pastures* © 1936 Warner
Bros Pictures, Inc. Renewed © 1963 United Artists Associated Inc. All Rights
Reserved. 'All of Me' Words and Music by Seymour Simons and Gerald
Marks © 1931, Bourne Co, USA, Reproduced by Permission of Francis Day
and Hunter Ltd, London WC2H OEA. 'Route 66' by Bobby Troupe © 1946
Edwin H Morris & Co Inc, Burke & Van Heusen Inc, USA,
Warner/Chappell Music Ltd, London W1Y 3FA, Reproduced by Permission
of International Music Publications Ltd.

All rights reserved. No reproduction, copy or transmissions of this
publication may be made without written permission. No
paragraph of this publication may be reproduced, copied or
transmitted save with written permission or in accordance with the
provisions of the Copyright Act 1956 (as amended). Any person
who does any unauthorised act in relation to this publication may
be liable to criminal prosecution and civil claims for damages.

A CIP catalogue record for this book is available
from the British Library

1 3 5 7 9 10 8 6 4 2

Typeset by M Rules
Printed and bound in Great Britain by
Mackays of Chatham plc., Kent

This is a work of fiction. The incidents as presented are wholly fictitious. If there are events described that do have some relationship to actual events in the life of James Dean, they are not descriptions of what actually happened, nor is the dialogue what was actually said. The reader should not interpret any of the material as factual.

With Faith

Contents

1.	A Matching Madness	1
2.	Manhattan Serenade	23
3.	An Actor Acts	47
4.	The Power of Yazzy	71
5.	Inner Man, Outer Man	93
6.	Mystery Prince	113
7.	The Theater of the Real – Encore	131
8.	Studio New York	155
9.	The Actor's Life for Them	181
10.	Take All of Me	203
11.	East of Warners	225
12.	Not Home at Home	249
13.	Saved by The Dream	275

1. A Matching Madness

THE HOOSIER HOTSHOTS: screenplay by Danny Gross; based on a story by Carol Kennish; lyrics and music by Gary Garnish; directed by Heinz Forsch; produced by Sol Sulloff for R.K.O.–Radio Pictures.

Bill Coles	*Roy Gillespie*
Jess Coles	*Clark Raymond*
Jugs	*Will Packer*
Catfish	*Calvin Owens*
Rufus	*Red Sonnet*

On February 15, 1948, one week after his seventeenth birthday, James went to the Fairmount Theater with Brett Collins and Jenna Craig to see Julia Misbehaves *because Jenna just loved Greer Garson. James's dream memory retains the 'B' movie from that day, about five young musicians from Indiana who call themselves the 'Hotshots'. Their country-styled music catches on with the kids and then with older people throughout the Midwest. The action follows them through their struggles to their ultimate success. It ends with the group in Hollywood, where the boys have been signed to make their first movie.*

The scene he remembers best is the one with the Hotshots piled in a jalopy heading back to Kokomo after playing at a high school dance. Bill Coles, the driver and leader of the band, is exulting to his brother and to Rufus, Catfish and Jugs jammed in the back seat with their bass fiddle, drums, and saxophone.

Bill: Whoooo-eeee. We sure were hot up there tonight. Weren't we, boys?

Jugs: They sure did love us. Sure did.

Bill: And they ought to. We're the best, aren't we?

Jugs, Rufus, and Catfish: (Chanting together) We *are* the best. We *are* the best. We *are* the best.

Jess: Simmer down, you guys. Playing this chug-a-chug-a-chug-a music for a bunch of hicks don't exactly make us number one on America's Hit Parade.

Bill: What do you mean, 'a bunch of hicks?' We're from Indiana, darn it. Folks out here may not know all about psychology and how the Stock Market works, but we sure as heck know about things like loyalty and honesty and courage. Don't forget, little brother, that the war was won by that 'bunch of hicks.' And they also know about hard work and how to grow enough food so that no American starves. So don't let me ever hear you disparaging these folks. They're the salt of the earth.

When he was eight years old, living with his father and mother in the low, Spanish-styled house in Santa Monica, James Dean found a pearl-handled revolver at the bottom of his father's clothes hamper.

For some reason he never understood, he took it to his room and placed the barrel of the gun between rounded lips and slid it into his mouth. He believed he simply wanted to taste the metal, give the projection a warm home. The smooth barrel felt rough and cold on his lips at first but it warmed quickly. It tasted of slate and smelled like carbon paper. As he looked at the cocking pin advancing toward his mouth, his eyes crossed slightly. He had no idea if the revolver was loaded or not; he pulled the trigger with his thumb.

Since that day nine years earlier, James has heard the voices of life and not-life. The voice of not-life was more seductive and consoling; its sweetness attracted him. He placed the gun in his mouth long before he ever saw it done in a movie. In this respect, art anticipated art.

He often hears the voice of not-life when he talks to Lem Craig, the young mechanic he works with at Hardy's Texaco.

*

Lem Craig passes James a pint of Three Feathers, and James forces down a burning mouthful. Late one Saturday after work, the two are driving the rutted back-roads around Fairmount. Lem's Chevy is a trash heap, full of tools and electrical wires, spare parts, magazines, flashlights, beer and whiskey bottles. 'Cigarette?' Lem points to a pack of Luckies on the dashboard. James lights one and hands the pack over. In the silence, the Chevy's headlights clarify a small bit of rural Indiana's darkness.

James wants Lem to talk about the war. 'So what was the feeling you had going ashore?'

'Mostly, I was just plain scared shitless. That's the truth of it, J.D. But there's a small part – a real quiet voice in the back of your head – that keeps saying not to worry about anything. Even dying isn't so bad; it keeps whispering that. Let me tell you, man, I wanted to follow that peaceful voice even though I knew it was the voice of dying. Maybe another time I'd have followed it, but not out there coming ashore. You needed your wits.' Lem lights his cigarette and turns north onto Route 112. 'Funny thing is, I hear that peaceful voice all the time now, and I'm really starting to believe it.'

'Still, you had to wade in, what, about 200 yards? I don't think I could have done that without pissing myself.'

'Hah. Who said I didn't?' Lem draws on his cigarette with a purpose: he squints. 'Had this buddy. His idea was to try to get over the landing ramp and onto the beach as fast as possible. Told me they'd have less chance of getting you the faster you went. He got it almost before he hit the water. Damn fool. The trick was . . .' But Lem doesn't say what the trick was.

James waits politely. 'What was the trick?'

'What trick?'

'About getting to the beach alive.'

'What makes you think I got there alive?'

'Don't jive me, Lem.'

'Big thing was finding the right rhythm – not getting in too fast, not staying in the water too long. The first wave took it bad. We all knew it would. But, believe me, kiddo, it was so damned cold, made you want to move your nuts through that water toot-sweet. But you sure as hell couldn't dawdle. I was carrying all this fucking equipment. Said to myself. "Shit, if they're piling all this on me, I might as well use it." I . . .' Lem Craig laughs from his lungs, 'I damn near came in walking behind my own pack. They told us to

4

come in staggered in waves, you know like setting up checkers. No one did it, though. I tried to line myself up right behind the guy in front of me. Most everybody did.'

The lights of a passing car reveal Lem's face, especially the protruding incisor that overlaps his front tooth and gives him a demented cast. His eyes lock on James Dean's. *Do you understand? I got myself covered behind someone else. We all did it. You would have, too.*

When Lem passes the Woolman Street turnoff, the normal way home, James senses that Lem has something in mind. Maybe it has to do with his admission of cowardice during the D-Day landing, maybe it's that lulling, seductive voice of death; whatever the reason, James is inclined to go along with whatever Lem Craig has in mind tonight.

The Chevy is moving to a part of town James has avoided since he returned to Fairmount from California. They pass the highway patrol station and the abandoned Quaker Meeting House. His first home in Fairmount lay about two miles ahead. His father sold it when the family moved to California. 'Your mom buried up there?'

James's nonchalance is forced. 'Uh huh.' The cemetery is just beyond the next stretch of woods.

'Want to stop up there?'

'You kidding?'

'How come your old man dumped you?'

'Didn't *dump* me. I went to California with him. Just didn't work out. People out there are really "different." Insincere. Rather live with my aunt 'n uncle anyway.'

'What's he do, your old man?'

'Works in a dental lab.' Actually, he runs the lab.

'Sounds like a real winner.'

'He can't help it. He's okay.' James draws deeply on the cigarette and flips it out the window.

'At a distance maybe he's okay. You miss her?'

'Not anymore. Did for a while. I'm pretty much on my own. Good thing to be.'

They are passing the cemetery gates. James has not seen his mother's grave for seven years. He had gone with Ortense and

Marcus, his aunt and uncle, on the first anniversary of Mildred's death. In the car going home Ortense said through soft tears, 'Why does He take the gentlest ones first?'

And James, then aged ten, said, 'No one gets taken unless they really want to leave.'

Aunt Ortense, his father's sister, turned around in the front seat and smacked him flush across the face with a callused palm. He never stopped loving Ortense, not even at that moment.

'Where we going, Lem?' James works at sounding unconcerned.

Lem doesn't respond for a while. 'Need someone to take a few pictures for me. You're elected, sport.'

'In the dark? Why not wait 'til daylight?'

Lem chuckles. 'Has to be at night. You'll see.'

They drive on in silence, returning to the Fairmount James knows. He lights a new cigarette. Past the high school, the police station and fire house, past the town library. Lem turns right on Quincy, and James thinks he might be going back to the gas station.

'J.D. J.D. J.D.' Lem is mulling over the sounds. 'One initial lower and you'd be "J.C." *That's* who you remind me of. Knew it was a real mysterious name.'

'That mean I'm supposed to end up crucified?'

'Just could be.' Lem Craig flashes a broad smile: James sees it distorted in the windshield.

James Dean believes this will become a crazy night, possibly dangerous. Maybe it was Lem's telling about being afraid on D-Day, maybe his strange, off-beat humor, but something in James is willing to go along with whatever Lem Craig has in mind.

And not with any great reluctance; his own embryonic madness pulled along by a greater, more cultivated lunacy.

The Chevy turns on to East Carver. Lem darkens his headlights and cruises past the bank, the market, the feed store. James turns in his seat, putting more of his back against the door; he can observe Lem Craig more completely. Touching James's arm, Lem says, 'J.D. That stuff I told you about the landing, that stays right between us in the car, okay.' Lem Craig's eyes take the expression of a stalked deer.

James's smile matches Lem's look. Nothing is said until Lem asks,

'So, these plays you're in, I sure hope it's just so you can be close to Jenna.' Jenna Craig is Lem's kid sister. James has gone out with Jenna all winter. He has given her his Fairmount 'Quakers' basketball jacket.

'No. Well, yes, I guess. But I sort of like it, too. You get to be other people. Maybe not *be* them. *Feel* like them, anyway.'

'I hope you're not going fruity on me.' Lem wiggles his fingers in an airy, butterfly gesture.

'I'm still playing basketball.' James delivers a sidelong smile to indicate he can be trusted, even though he's been in two school plays.

'Going out with Jenna tomorrow night?' Lem is casual.

'Drive-in over in Sterling. Doubling with Brett and Carrie.'

'His car or yours?'

'Don't have a car.'

'Means you get the back seat with Jenna.' Lem is smiling, his eyes are not. 'What's showing?'

'Something about zombies. Jen sort of likes being scared.'

'Better than that lovey-dovey garbage they show in town.' He makes his butterfly gesture again.

James laughs knowingly and feels dishonest doing it.

'Open the glove compartment, J.D.'

A boxy camera sits on a pile of maps.

'Know anything about photography?'

'Uh-uh.'

'That there's one of the finest cameras in the world. Got it in Düsseldorf after the war.'

'Oh.'

'Best cameras in the world, Düsseldorf. It's a Hasselblad.'

Lem has a crazy grin on his face, watching the darkened street with great interest. He turns into an alley off South Fourth, glides behind the post office, over a dirt road and onto a macadam flat in the rear of Mosbacher's Funeral Home. He cuts the motor and rolls the Chevy right up to the rear steps. 'Wait here.' He pulls his camera from the glove compartment and slides out of the car. Like a monkey in a tree, the strap of the camera in his mouth, Lem Craig mounts the railing of the building, leaps onto a drainpipe and is on the porch roof in a blink. From there to a higher, intersecting roof and inside a second-floor window. James is amazed but not particularly surprised – this is Lem Craig.

James had stood in Mosbacher's years before, a boy in his Sunday suit, hair goo-ed down, his new glasses slipping whenever he turned his head, resenting the propriety of the sorrow everyone displayed, the pats on the shoulder and the sympathetic phrases that begged the question. His mother had abandoned him; he hadn't acknowledged her right to leave. Or Winton's right to stand there looking distraught, accepting condolences as though they were personal compliments. Mildred Dean in the casket, smiling as she had never smiled in life, too contentedly, too self-satisfied. A smile that pacified most of the visitors. Prompted so many of them to say, 'She never looked more natural.' James wanted to wipe that fraudulent smile off her face and chase them all out of the place. Maybe then he could go home with his mother.

The rear door of Mosbacher's opens. A finger beckons from the slit. James obeys. The place has not changed over the years. James recalls the chemistry–lab odor. He breathes through his mouth, following Lem into the showroom, where, in the blue light filtering through the windows, he sees open caskets displayed randomly at odd angles. Lem's hand is on James's shoulder; his breath warms James's ear: 'The flash is on. Just be sure I'm in focus. You click right here.' He directs James's finger to the button.

Just as quickly as he had leapt onto the railing, Lem Craig is in a plush casket, his head resting on the satin pillow, arms crossed high on his chest. 'Go ahead. Shoot.'

Through the lens James sees an unfocused idiot face, eyes closed, tongue lolling onto the cheek, tooth protruding. He backs up a step to capture more of the casket. 'Where's the focus?'

'The lens, you turn the whole ring.'

'Hold it. Need my glasses.' James takes them from his jacket pocket. He sees how badly focused the camera had been. As clarity comes into the viewer, Lem's idiocy becomes more apparent.

'How's it look, J.D.?'

'Crazy, man.'

'Shoot it, then.'

Click!

'Another.'

Click!

'One more.' One eye open.

Click!

Lem leaps out of the coffin like a gymnast. He takes the camera. 'Now you.'

'Naw, I don't think . . .'

'I'm going to print these up myself. No one'll ever see 'em. C'mon, it'll be wild.' He pushes James toward the casket. Smiling over his shoulder, James Dean climbs into the polished coffin, into the plush satin nest. He feels a strong sense of violation, which reveals itself as blushing embarrassment. 'You look scared. No one's ever scared in there. That's the end of being scared. Forever. Shut your eyes.' James does. *Click!* 'Smile.' *Click!* 'Stick your tongue out. C'mon, it'll be cool.' James refuses. *Click!*

'Someone's sure to see those flashes, Lem.' James thinks he sees someone watching him and darts his eyes toward the window. No one. Still, he's sure he's been seen. 'Hey, man, we'd better get out of here.'

Lem doesn't want to hear. He wanders back toward the work-room, the source of the chemical stench. He passes through a hallway and the door to the embalming room. 'Hey, J.D., catch this.' He steps into the doorway behind Lem Craig. What J.D. catches is a corpse, female, around fifty, in a very large, very expensive, brass-trimmed casket. She is dressed in pink and has the cosmetic mask of life painted across her death face. James believes he knows this woman, should know her; this is Fairmount, after all. But death has made her a stranger. Artificial flowers lie on a nearby table as does gold braid, some of which has been pinned to the edge of the casket. She will be presented to relatives and friends in the morning.

James should have left at that moment, having anticipated Lem's intention. He takes a couple of steps backward. 'Just one,' Lem whispers, handing him the camera.

'That's sick.'

Lem and James Dean stare at one another. 'Listen,' Lem says, 'I'm

9

almost as dead as she is. We belong in a picture together. It's Mrs. Trasker, the bank president's wife. Used to date her daughter.'

'You're not getting in there.'

'Course not.'

Lem Craig raises Mrs. Trasker gently and gets his arm around her shoulder. Mrs. Trasker is coming back. Lem places his cheek against hers. His eyes slide sideways as though to indicate his pleasure in holding a beautiful woman. Her smile is mysterious, more than mysterious. Not his mother's smile at all.

Through the viewer James sees a pair of stupefied faces, not unlike two kids having a strip of photos taken in a booth at the bus station. The girl always has her eyes closed. *Click!*

*

The ignition button fires cleanly. The motor idles. The Chevy rolls silently out of town in the dark. The country road to the turnpike veers slightly where the farms become orchards. Where road meets turnpike, a flashing light entreats caution. Lem drives with a single finger hooked at the bottom of the wheel. The hand holding the whiskey bottle is out the window.

'Ready for an adventure, Herr Dean?'

James thinks, *What the heck did we just have?* 'Sure, Herr Craig.'

On the pike, Lem smooths the Chevy through gear changes up to 60 m.p.h. Then back down again to second. There are no lights on the turnpike to be seen before or behind. There is no reason to speak, no reason to make an admission. James says, 'My old man wants me out in California next year.'

'You goin'?'

'Maybe. To visit.'

'You didn't ask my permission.'

James looks at the burning in Lem's eyes and bites his lips. They're crawling down the road in second. Suddenly Lem hits the gas and jumps into fourth. The tires squeal.

The turnpike is arrow straight. Beams a mile or more ahead indicate an oncoming car. Lem has the Chevy at 70. 'It's a goddamned tank. Feel it grinding the road.' At a half-mile separation, Lem and the approaching driver hit low-beams. When they pass with a whoosh, Lem's at 75. 'Here's the thing. If the speedometer only goes up to 90, will the car top out at that? Or can we break the Chevy barrier? Can we? No? Yes?'

'Lem. Come on.'

'Don't trust me, J.D.?'

'Sure I do. But . . .'

The gauge needle quivers past 80, 85. The tires crackle on the concrete road, thumping rhythmically over the seams. Lem flicks off the headlights.

'Come on, Lem.' He hates that there's a whine in his voice.

The car still accelerates.

'I'm trusting you on this, J.D. Closing my eyes. You got to tell me how to steer.'

'Why'd you want to . . .?' Although the turnpike is straight, minor adjustments are necessary. 'A little left. No, no, not so much. Inch maybe. Less. Okay. Hold it there.' James waves his hand in front of Lem's face. He really cannot see. 'A touch to the right. Jesus, why are we doing this?' Far ahead, another car's lights. 'Car coming. Open your eyes.'

'That's the excitement. Hoooo-eeee!' He takes the last drink from the whiskey bottle and tosses it away. The smash cannot be heard behind them.

'Come on, turn on the headlights.'

'Don't touch those fucking lights.'

'Lem, open your eyes, for Christ's sake.'

'Make believe I just went blind and I'm trying to land a Liberator. Talk me through it.'

The road remains very straight. The cars advance, one unknowing. At about 200 feet, the oncoming car hits its horn and veers slightly aside. A thudding impact of air hits the passing vehicles. The moment should not be, but in fact is, thrilling to James Dean.

Lem Craig laughs, howling almost. The Chevy's speedometer is stuck on 90: the car vibrates on the verge of flying apart. The pitch of its engine whines like a dive bomber in a movie. It's the moment when the co-pilot is supposed to holler, 'Pull out, man, or we're a goner.'

They hurtle on and Lem says something James can't hear. 'What?'

11

'Is it up?'

Is what up? The temperature gauge? The oil pressure?

Lem's laugh is a clue: ironic, solemn, insane. James sees the shadow of the driver's erection, then more clearly the pumping hand motion. 'Got to have a hard-on, J.D. Got to.'

Lights flare ahead over a rise. The speed is breathtaking. The danger stunning. And now Lem planting the idea. James's penis throbs and pulses larger. 'Car coming. Half mile. Less maybe. You're drifting. Pull right a little, a little more. Hold that.'

Lem's fingers are climbing James's pants.

'Steady. Hold it.' The Chevy rushes toward the undiscerning, approaching car. James's erection grows. Lem has it in his fingers, squeezing and releasing the tight cloth of his pants. What surprises James is that he's not surprised; he finds Lem's touch an intrusion but not an affront.

Light from the oncoming headlights enable James to see Lem's left hand on his own cock. He has the wheel cradled between his knees. Lem's face is contorted – the upper half intent on holding his eyes closed, the lower half agonizingly on the verge of rapture.

The Chevy holds its line, although James would wish a greater separation. The cars will pass. They rush on. The other car flashes high-beams. James says nothing, does nothing. They'll pass. Lem has a firm hold of him.

The other driver leans on his horn, which increases in pitch as they pass with another thud of air that deflects the line of drive. James grabs the wheel.

'Told you not to touch that fucking wheel, J.D.'

James says nothing. He doesn't release the wheel either. Lem takes the wheel in both hands; at the same moment he eases off the gas pedal. 'Spare me small-town minds,' he screams, 'small-fucking-town-minds.'

It takes half a minute for the speed to fall below 50. Lem hands James a handkerchief.

'What's this for?'

'Wipe up that pool of piss you're sitting in.'

The lights of the Koko-Diner throw an aura in the sky far ahead. They drive toward it in silence.

There are more people in the Koko than James expected. A girl sitting at the counter smiles at him when he comes in. She's familiar and pretty: he smooths his hand over his short hair and returns the smile. But she's unfamiliar too: her print dress, blue sweater over the shoulders, her long hair are strangely old-fashioned. When he waves hello, her soft smile neither deepens nor fades.

Lem knows the waitress, a chubby woman with two pink bows in her hair. When she comes to take their orders, Lem pulls her forward and drapes his arm across her shoulder. 'Vera. This is my friend J.D.' She nods and smiles. 'My friend J.D. will be leaving us for California, Vera. A question: Do you consider this young man lucky or unlucky?'

'Real lucky.' She winks.

'You think he'll write to us folks who've been left behind?'

Vera shrugs, 'Depends.'

James winces: 'I'm not really sure I'm going.'

'I hope he don't even bother, 'cause I won't write back.'

Vera senses trouble. 'What'll you guys have?'

'Two coffees, black. Two peach pies with ice cream, vanilla.'

The soles of Vera's shoes squeal on the linoleum.

When they get ready to leave, James notices the girl at the counter is gone. He hadn't seen her leave.

In the car, they sit in silence, smoking. Lem drives slowly back toward Fairmount. James imagines Winton meeting him at the Union Station in Los Angeles, the incredible awkwardness, the swallowed words, the stammering, unaware that Lem has been speaking quietly for a while, '. . . when you get right down to it.'

'Down to what?'

'The heartland. Our nation's breadbasket, for Christ's sake. No place crazier in the world than our good ol' great Protestant plains.' Lem smiles his nuttiest smile; his tooth is accusative.

James will not refute anything Lem says now.

'I'm saying the real madmen, the roaring maniacs, the ones who kill their whole families after Thanksgiving dinner, you find them in the heart of the heartland. The guy who buries the hired man alive or bashes in the brains of newlyweds stranded in a snow-storm, them's the crazies you find only in the small towns.'

James is troubled by the cocksure matter-of-factness in Lem's tone. He says, 'There's ten times more murders in the big cities.'

Unhearing, Lem says, 'There's this Oktoberfest they have in Germany. It's just an excuse for everyone to get fall-down drunk on beer. The whole place goes sort of crazy; you can do just about anything. But it's everyone at the same time, same time every year, saying let's admit we're all a little nuts and act that way. Because we really are, you know. And when it's over, everyone goes back to behaving like they're normal. But they know deep down there's this other side too, and there's always another Oktoberfest. Met Elsa in a beer hall during Oktoberfest.'

James doesn't quite follow.

'That's the difference. Here, we got to try to be normal all the fucking time . . .'

'All of us except you.'

'. . . and if you got to work so hard to be normal every minute of every day, the craziness got no place to go. So when it does finally come out, it's like water that's been dammed up – it just bursts out.' He lowers his high-beams for an oncoming car. 'That old woman up in Grafton ground up the mailman and fed him to her cats, for Christ's sake.'

James drags deeply on the nub of a cigarette and flips it into the darkness off the turnpike. 'You trying to tell me I'll go nuts if I don't get out of here?'

Lem looks hard at James. 'Who's even talking about you, J.D.?' He sneers. Again, the dangerous silence. Lem chuckles: 'Actually, I've been thinking of leaving myself.'

'For where?'

'Back to Germany maybe. For a while I was stationed near Cologne. You know where that is?'

For some reason, James says, 'Yes.'

'There was this girl. Elsa.'

'Like the girl in *Casablanca*?'

'Her father was killed by our side in the war. That was a big problem between us.' Lem offers James a new pint of Three Feathers that's materialized from nowhere. James waves him off. He takes a long swig himself. 'Never really could overcome that. She was older than I was, too. I think she even had a kid somewhere.' He is speaking as much to remind himself as to inform James. 'In the south, I think. Munich. Where it was safer. She was a violinist. Played in a symphony orchestra they were starting up again. They used her because some of the men weren't able to play anymore. God, could she ever play that thing. You ever hear Mr. Cravitz play in the auditorium?' James nods. 'Well, she could play ten, no, twenty times better than him. She took me to concerts, operas, stuff like that. All around Cologne.'

'Maybe you should have just stayed there.'

'Couldn't. Had to get mustered out stateside. Besides, she went south to be with her kid. The kid was a big consideration for her.'

'She married now?'

'No telling. Probably. There was this one opera I saw, never will forget it.' He shakes his head and looks toward some heavenly stage. 'Knew a little German actually, but I couldn't understand a damn thing except there was this man and woman who I believe did something to make the gods angry. Maybe they were gods themselves, I don't know. It was Wagner.' Lem says the name with a 'V.' James had only heard it with a 'W.'

'In order to cheat the gods, or for some reason I never figured out, they decide to kill themselves with poison. It's not important why. Eventually they die in each other's arms, but before they do, the singing is unbelievable. And the orchestra music was something like I never heard before in my life, or could imagine. It just about pulled me up out of my seat. I mean really up. You begin to feel lighter and lighter and a part of you wants to go right up to the chandeliers. Right through the ceiling, straight on up to heaven. Makes you believe there really is a heaven. You just feel it; everything in you goes shivery and you want to soar like a bird. I swear I never in my whole life heard anything even close to it.'

'What was it called?'

'What? The opera?'

'The opera, the song, whatever.'

'Don't know the opera. Elsa called it *Liebestod*. She had an old scratchy record she played all the time. Even with the scratchiness, you had that same feeling of leaving the ground. And you know what, J.D.?' Lem Craig looks smugly over at James.

'What?'

'I bought that same record. C'mon. I want you to hear it.'

*

It's well after midnight when the Chevy rolls up the bumpy road to the Craig farmhouse. Lem makes no effort to be silent on the darkened staircase. It is hard in the dim light for James to follow Lem to his room. James is stunned when Lem turns on the light: the room is bathed in a weird red glow. It smells of chemicals, too.

It feels spooky and comfortable all at once, like living safely on the other side of normality. 'Darkroom,' Lem says, but James doesn't understand his meaning until he sees the developing equipment.

James keeps looking around Lem Craig's darkroom repeating, 'Man, this is neat.'

He anticipates the entire process of printing photographs before Lem starts to explain: it has something to do with reversing the real and the unreal, light and substance, shadow and space. That's why the ultimate reduction of the process is the negative, something that wears the exact mask of what is not.

The music from a turntable floats out of two speakers placed high on the wall. It is the slow, circular ascent to heaven Lem has just told him about. James has forgotten the name: all he remembers is it's German, *V*agner. The crystalline voice of a tenor alternates with the orchestra and a darkly timbered soprano in round after round of divine promise.

Pinned to the walls are photos of foreign buildings and landscapes, familiar Fairmount faces, cars, Hardy's Texaco, and one of Lem lying dead on a cemetery plot. Most prominent on the wall is a very large picture of a naked woman on a pale rug, holding her oversized breasts near her face: she seems about to swallow herself. James wants to look at it more than he allows Lem to know. He wonders how Mrs. Craig feels about it.

'How long have you been doing your own developing?'

Lem doesn't answer. He is leaning over the enlarger, sliding a piece of paper in the bottom and calibrating the spacing. 'You want to hit that light?'

'Sure.'

'You just set the timer and shoot this light through the negative. It kisses the paper. You get the negative of a negative, and that's a positive.'

The machine flashes on, burns brightly, and clicks off. 'That's it?'

'Pretty much all there is to it. To print it up, just slide the paper out the bottom. Be sure not to touch it. Just the edges.' Lem takes the paper from James with the flat of his hands and drops it in the developer. He wiggles it in the liquid with tongs. 'Uh-huh, lookie here. Hee-hee.' James sees nothing recognizable. Then a pair of pale gray circles – they're glasses. But the eyes, the face, remain indistinct. The ascending music and the circular movement in the developer seem to encourage greater clarity. There's the nose. Or is it? Must be. The glasses sit on it. And a beard. Very fuzzy, very curly. The clearer the print becomes, the less sense it makes, and the more Lem chuckles idiotically. 'Get it, J.D.?'

He can't say yes, so he nods and says nothing.

Lem lifts the photo out of the developer and slides it into the fixer. 'Little too dark,' he says critically. But he's smiling. 'Still don't get it?'

The glasses are the trick kind, with astonished, spiralling eyeballs glued slightly off-center. Bushy eyebrows overgrow the top rims. The nose they sit on has no bridge, doesn't narrow on top but extends down from the glasses like a hose. No lips. A chin cleft that . . . The photo still refuses to yield its mystery to James.

'It's a self-portrait. Let's see, what'll I call it?' He's moving it all sorts of ways. Suddenly, as Lem turns it in the fixer, it becomes clear. James wishes he showed less surprise. The nose is Lem Craig's penis. The brows, his pubic hair. Testicles, a chin of sorts. 'That's the way I'd look if I was a hairy Jew, right J.D.?'

'How'd you do it?'

'Easy. Just set up the camera, the lights. The angle's the important thing. Toughest part was finding the right glasses, hee-hee.'

James studies the picture when he hangs it up for drying. The penis isn't normal; it's severely discolored by something James takes to be a problem with the developing process. He starts to say something before realizing it isn't that at all – the penis itself is badly scarred as though by fire. Or it could be a birthmark.

'So what d'you think?'

'Unbelievable.' James's tone is insincere, but the music has reached a crescendo and Lem is taking another negative off the desk.

'How long would it take me to learn all this stuff?'

'When it gets under your skin, it's not even a question of learning. You just do it.'

'Cost a lot?'

'Same deal. You just go with the thing and you get what you need because you need it. Know what I'm saying?'

He's saying you don't judge something you love by work-a-day standards. The *Liebestod* heightens to non-existence, and the record clicks off.

The door handle jiggles. The door's locked. 'Keep it down, you guys.' Jenna complains from the hallway in a loud whisper.

'Told you never to bother me, didn't I?'

'I don't care what you told me. Just keep it down in there.'

'If you don't care, then go away.'

'Glad to. Just be quiet.' She leaves. James thinks he ought to go after her, say something.

'Stay. She thinks she's got the world knocked. She talks about going off to I.U. next year. Meeting some rich, dreamy guy. Major in Matrimony. Graduate. Travel. New house. The perfect life. Some chance.'

'I don't know. Jenna's sharp.'

'*Und schöne*, too. *Schöne*, that's what's going to do her in. She'll be pregnant by the end of the summer and have to force some poor sucker to support her for the rest of her life at the ripe old age of eighteen.'

James is a candidate for the 'some poor sucker' role. 'I don't know,' he says.

'But I do. I can tell things like that.'

The *Liebestod* starts again.

'I know about things like that,' Lem repeats for no reason. He places the negative in the enlarger. At the end of the process this time, his mottled penis, erect, strung with a small, bejewelled cross. A pair of hands, entwined in prayer, are placed where his testicles should be. The hands are small and delicate, not Lem's. '"Bless This House." That's a good title.'

*

The glitter of an enormous volume of stars keeps the sky from a proper midwestern darkness. On the drive-in screen a camera pans the dim hall of an archeological museum, slowly scanning the ancient Egyptian artifacts – vessels, weapons, icons. A sarcophagus bears the image of a human being with an animal's face, feathers, and feline claws. Another sarcophagus, a third, a fourth, all decorated with strange Middle-Eastern-cum-Hollywood symbols of death and regeneration.

The music, low reeds and deep strings in minor chords, builds on pauses and anticipation. It works its intentions perfectly on Jenna Craig snuggled in James's arms in the rear of Brett Collins's Ford. She notches her thumbnail with her front teeth; her other hand runs down James's jeans and grips the inside of his thigh. He's soft there.

The mummies on the screen do not move. Or do they? The camera lets the hundreds of kids in cars at the Sterling Drive-In decide for themselves. It stays on each bandaged body for an inordinately long time. James smiles at the screen, feeling untouched by the cheap effects piled up on one another, happily superior to Jenna's fright. His hand slides off her shoulder, down her upper arm. The soft texture of her sweater, the tense flesh beneath it, pleases him. He can picture his own smile and his smile intensifies.

His hand stops at her elbow. Without diverting her gaze from the screen, Jenna pulls her arm away from her body. She tenses: the gauze over their faces is stretching, stretching to bursting point. It starts to disintegrate. The dead begin to breathe. Not alive, but breathing, moving. Slowly – here, the cellos in pizzicato – they rise. Arms before them. Shuffling. Zombies.

His hand edges into the warmth of her side, fingering the waistband of her sweater, curling it up slowly and touching, finally, her taut flesh. James Dean places his lips on Jenna Craig's arched neck and offers the lightest semblance of a kiss. At no moment do her eyes leave the screen. Her quivering breath remains shallow, unsure.

James looks away from the screen and is struck by the curved rows of cars fanning out like ripples from the screen. For him there is something eerie about this silent pattern of vehicles – each isolated, self-contained – on a tarred-over Indiana cornfield. His fingers slide over Jenna's ribs as the stiff-legged zombies descend the museum steps and point themselves toward the university campus.

Below the music, and then through and above it, is the sound of shuffling feet. A methodical *shush . . . shush . . . shush* builds to a pulsing heartbeat. The dead souls, imprisoned no longer, begin to make their way toward the lights of a nearby sorority house. Whatever horrors that have been locked away for millennia are on the verge . . .

With his hand on her ribs, James can feel Jenna's intensified breathing. He moves his hand closer to her heart and feels a fluttery rhythm – a bird in a cage. This other person's life, pulsing beneath his hand, intrigues him. His fingers move upward still, touching the lower seam of her bra. The soft tightness of her breast is his goal, but his hand wanders all over. He spans the mystery of this female human being. It feels as scientific as it does sexual. Home base, however, is her nipple, the button of her desire, hard now under his circular touch.

Jenna's hand glides up and down his thigh. James spreads his legs so he will have room to swell.

The zombies are wiped off the screen with a cut to a large, cheery bedroom in the sorority house. Girls in pajamas and nighties sprawl across beds; others are smearing on face cream in front of mirrors or putting curlers in their hair. Oblivious to the death-walkers approaching, *shush, shush, shush.*

Jenna turns quickly to James for a kiss and knocks his glasses askew. She takes them off and her tongue shoots immediately into his mouth. He closes his eyes and circles and parries with his tongue. She slowly begins to pull open his fly. He feels her shudder as if chilled. James sneaks a look at her face: her eyes are searching again for the movie screen. Impulsively, James bends Jenna sideways, raises her sweater, and seeks her breast with moist lips.

The sudden light is blinding. So sudden and so intense it seems to make an explosive sound. Jenna's scream never fully materializes. James cannot see anything but a spectrum of glaring colors. He hears Brett stammer, 'Hey. What the hell? Who's . . .? Where's . . .?' Carrie kicks the speaker off the window. Everyone in the car is suddenly buttoning and zipping and tugging at clothing.

James blinks and rubs his eyes. He hears the voice before he sees the face. 'Nice to see youngsters having such a wholesome time.'

'Damn you, Lem. Why can't you just stay out of my business?' Jenna's tone is more weary than angry. 'I swear you're about as funny as . . .' She hooks her brassière. 'And I want that film or I'll tell Ma this time.'

James sees Lem Craig's face, broadened by a stupid grin, at the window, his lank hair flat across his forehead. His camera is under his chin. Lem Craig says, 'Homework, huh? Biology, seems like.'

Jenna says, 'I swear to God, you're a complete idiot.'

For James there is no doubt that Jenna's right. Lem Craig really *is* nuts, *completely* nuts. He envies Lem that completeness, for James is troubled by the knowledge that he is woefully incomplete, or, even worse, a whole bunch of personalities that don't add up to a single, complete anything, even to an idiot. And probably never will.

2. Manhattan Serenade

GOT TO SING: screenplay by Hilda and Karl Chester; lyrics and music by Reginald Holman and Fred Krusick; directed by Solomon Benisch; produced by Harvey Waltz; released by Pathé Films.

Caroline Martin..Frances Everson
Dr. Lance Gregory...Harrison Brush
Ivory Johnson.. 'Bones' Rustin
Mrs. Martin...Kay Baynter

James went to the Fairmount with his Aunt Ortense to see Got to Sing because Ortense was absolutely mad about Frances Everson, saw every movie she made. In Got to Sing Frances plays Caroline, a blind girl in a small Southern town who wants to play the piano more than anything in life. None of the town's music teachers will encourage her. An old Negro man, a gardener on a nearby estate and a former jazz musician, agrees to teach her. The girl makes remarkable progress: the surprise is that she sings even more beautifully than she plays. Ivory, the teacher, takes her to New York City, where the girl is an overnight sensation. One of her greatest admirers is Dr. Lance Gregory, a young brain surgeon who believes he can restore her eyesight with a delicate but dangerous operation.

The day the bandages come off, Caroline sees Dr. Gregory and falls instantly and completely in love.

Caroline: I . . . I don't know why I should be so blest. Why me, of all people. It's a miracle I don't . . . can't deserve. (She begins to sob.)

Dr. Gregory: (Taking her hand.) You deserve this more than anyone I know. More than . . . anyone. If it is a miracle, I think you owe it as much to this gentleman as anyone. (He motions a modest Ivory over to the bed.)

Ivory: How you doin', sweetie-bird. Told you we'd make it.

Caroline: (Looking up into his brown face with curious eyes.) Oh, Ivory, if it weren't for you, none of this would ever have happened. I don't know how to thank you for all you've done.

Ivory: All a teacher ever wants, chile, is the chance to pass on what he's learned. I'm one old man who wants to thank you for the chance to do that. (There's a tear forming in his eye.)

Mrs. Martin: You know, I think we've all had quite enough excitement for one day.

'Stop. Just hold it right there, Jim.' Miss Boyce is the only one who calls him Jim. He likes that: it sounds classy the way she says it, makes her seem different from everyone else in town. She *is* different from everyone else in town.

Miss Boyce walks slowly, thoughtfully, down the center aisle of the auditorium, looking at her own feet. She stops before the stage apron and looks suddenly to the ceiling. 'You're doing nothing more than saying the words, aren't you?'

'Well, sure, that's what the play's full of – words.' He hears the kids laugh from the darkness of the wings. James nods toward the laughter. He's seeking out Jenna Craig, but the spotlight blinds him. Miss Boyce chose to cast Jenna as Gertrude even though she tried out for Ophelia. Nora Bagley was Ophelia. Squinting into the light, James looks pleasingly perverse.

'Very cute. But if you're mouthing words, it comes out lousy Shakespeare.' She begins backing up the aisle. 'It starts whenever you forget what's going on in the story.' She expects a response. 'Doesn't it, Jim?'

Amanda Boyce knew and generally subscribed to the conventional wisdom against trying to mount a Shakespeare tragedy in high school, and especially against messing around with *Hamlet*. That was before she discovered James Dean.

'Right, Miz Boyce.' He seeks her out with narrowed eyes.

'So what exactly is happening in this scene?'

'Well, Hamlet knows he can't do it 'cause the king is right there with his back to him.'

'But?'

'But what?'

She knows he is acting like a dummy in front of the other kids and comes within a breath of throwing them all out of the auditorium. 'What does Hamlet notice about the king?'

'That he's praying.'

'And what's the significance of the praying?'

James shoves one hand in his pocket and mutters, 'He's worried that if he kills him, Claudius'll go to heaven, or his soul will, anyway, and it won't be a real revenge. It's almost like he'd be doing him a favor by knocking him off.'

'Precisely. So Hamlet sees his chance, gets all worked up and then suddenly thinks . . . What?'

'. . . Whoa, hold your horses right there, Dane.' Giggles from the darkness.

'Okay, so now let me hear at least a bit of that happening.'

In this, Amanda Boyce's second year at Fairmount teaching English and Drama, she has finally begun to feel comfortable. She'd been a drama major at I.U. and taught at Kokomo High for four years, but the year she spent in New York as an actress is what really won over the kids at Fairmount. They see her as a miraculous transformation – in, a Hoosier hick, out, a woman of the world.

He shifts his weight in the spotlight. The hand comes out of his pocket and rests on his hip. The thumb of his other hand marks the passage in the text. In the darkness at the rear of the theater, Amanda Boyce smiles. *My God, so beautiful.*

The boy's trim body, at rest until this moment, begins to animate itself, as though energy has entered it from the illumination on his face and chest. James Dean draws the light, transforms it, and gives it back – not merely a reflection – as a comforting touch across space, an offering of considered mood and thought.

The face is extraordinarily expressive although it's not particularly pliable. Expressions do not reveal themselves in the eyes alone, although the eyes are remarkable, seeming to look inward and outward at once. The extended brows, the long, malleable lips, the puckered cheeks and the clean chin – each and all express emotion and thought as though they are solving mysteries.

He's found his mood. A sneer – a decent young man trying to be sinister – sweeps over his entire face. He turns and looks over his shoulder, stage left. The alto voice is of human scale yet fills the auditorium easily, creating the impression that the more softly he speaks, the better he will be heard.

'Now might I do it pat, now 'a is a-praying, and now I'll do 't . . .' The diction is natural and clear, neither an imitation Englishman nor a midwesterner's twang. It is possible to discern, below or perhaps through Hamlet's stated intention, his distrust of himself. Two contradictory feelings at the same time. The boy's instincts encompass paradox and human complexity. It is this quality that drew Amanda Boyce to James Dean in the first place. This is the core of his talent.

'. . . a villain kills my father; and for that, I, his sole son, do this same villain send to heaven . . .' He has begun to pull an invisible sword out of its sheath.

Now Amanda Boyce senses danger in the boy; he is really capable of drawing that sword and running it into his stepfather's back. It's a quality appropriate to Hamlet, but it's also there naturally in Dean, just below the surface, a smoldering resentment against whatever it is that may be confining him. Usually it is held in check by a silent, thoughtful sweetness, the exact counterpoise to the danger. The result is a personality that can turn back on itself, full of simmering tensions and moods. Amanda Boyce is attracted to its mysterious engine.

On stage, Hamlet's mood shifts suddenly. He checks his sword, his anger. His face is transformed by an idea, a last-second realization. James sheathes the invisible sword slowly and says, 'Why, this is hire and salary, not revenge.' He has emphasized *Why* and given it a quizzical tone, as though interrogating himself.

'Hold it, Jim. "Why," isn't what turns his thoughts. It's just what catches his attention. He realizes what he has to do – or not to do, in this case – later in the line. You've got to find the pivot there. Go back to "A villain kills my father . . ."'

'A villain kills my father, and for that I, his sole son, do send this same villain to heaven. Why, *this* . . . is hire and salary, not revenge.' Having rethought the passage, Jim decides to make this the emotional turning point. He pauses slightly after the word and his face registers mild self-disapproval – *How could I have been so dense?*

She can't imagine how a kid can comprehend profound human emotion so quickly, so quietly. That knowing silence was part of his mystery, what drew people into his aura.

She loved being close to the heart of his mystery, enjoyed probing it. She was more reluctant to admit that she also wanted to shape, direct, and participate in it. 'Yes. That's the idea. The pivot's when it dawns on him that he may be doing Claudius a favor by skewering him.'

The kids laugh at 'skewering.'

'That'll be it for today. Tomorrow afternoon, we'll run – and I do mean run – through the first two acts. And, people, please try not to be joined to your scripts. Jim, would you wait a minute before you leave?'

His body sags. He shields his eyes, looks off toward Jenna, and shrugs.

'Jim. I read your short story last night. I think it's terrific. I was wondering if you'd let me print it in the *Harvest*.'

'I don't know, it was just for that assignment. The *Harvest*. I don't know.'

'If you're embarrassed, we could leave it anonymous.'

'They'll figure it out.'

'Well, think about it. I'd love to have it.'

The story appears under the name of Will Auer. Miss Boyce also changes the title from 'The Hardest Train Ride' to 'One Boy's Courage.'

ONE BOY'S COURAGE

The boy was angry without knowing exactly why. Maybe he didn't really want to let himself know what he was angry about. He was nine years old and had seen plenty of movies in which streamlined silver trains speed straight across America. In the movies passengers sipped drinks in the observation car and the desert sped by outside. They dined in beautiful restaurant cars and slept in fancy bedrooms. You never saw the train stop until it reached its destination.

The train the boy was on had none of that Hollywood stuff. Coffee and soda and sandwiches, dirty windows, double bunks in a long sleeping car, and stops in every town that had a depot. The train also carried his mother's coffin – in the baggage car, where the observation car would have been in the movies.

His mother had died suddenly in a small house in a town in the southern part of California, not far from where they make movies. She was only thirty-seven years old. The boy believed it was the train and the long monotonous trip back East that was getting on his nerves. Sometimes we don't want to admit what the real problem is. His father told him he had to be brave. But it was a very long way back to Indiana.

He had a book with him, an adventure story with a young boy and swashbuckling pirates all looking for buried treasure, but his mind wandered whenever he tried to read it. Then one night before the train pulled into Chicago, he was restless and not able to sleep in his bunk. It was hot and stuffy, his mind wouldn't be still, and he climbed down from his berth very quietly so his father couldn't hear him. He was ready for an adventure. It was very late because not a soul was visible in any of the cars he walked through. Even the porters were sound asleep sitting at tables in the dining car.

He made his way to the rear of the train, not exactly sure where he was going but somehow knowing too. He knew when he came to the baggage car – the very last one – because a sign said, 'OFFICIAL – KEEP OUT.' The door was very heavy but it was part-way open and he could move it by pushing hard against it with his shoulder. That made it feel like even more of an adventure.

Inside the baggage car the boy could see a swinging light that threw long, dark, spooky shadows against the walls. (It was pretty scary for a kid.) Two men were sitting underneath the light bulb playing cards. But they were not playing on a table or on a steamer trunk. They were playing on a polished casket. All at once the boy's anger boiled up and poured out of him. He ran out of the darkness, scaring the card players half to death. He was screaming bad words, making threats and knocking the cards off his mother's casket. He felt very brave, defending her honor against these callous strangers the way an adult who loved and respected her would have. The moment his anger boiled over and he defended her honor the boy really became a man, whether he knew it or not.

*

Mr. Ebinger drums his fingers on his desk. He knows a principal has to be talked into anything that is going to cost money. 'And we won't embarrass ourselves?'

'No, absolutely not.'

'New York for three days? Hmm.'

'Three and a half days, but they'll take their schoolwork with them. I'll watch them like a hawk.'

'A hundred and forty-five dollars: that's substantial, Miss Boyce.'

'Half of it can come out of my Drama budget, Mr. Ebinger. If we go beyond that, I'll make it up out of my own pocket.'

'No, no . . . that's very generous, but, no, we can't allow anything like that. Still, I . . .'

Amanda decides to reverse course. 'If it's going to cause this great a problem, Mr. Ebinger, why don't we just say . . .'

'And you think these kids might actually win something?'

'It's a *national* competition, sir, and there are scholarships to Columbia University. The experience would be irreplaceable for them.'

'You'll need their parents' consent,' he says and shakes his head. 'I don't know, though.' For Mr. Ebinger this is a ringing endorsement.

That was back in February. In March, Nora Bagley and Jim Dean started to prepare in earnest for the competition. On the first day, each contestant was expected to deliver a polished Shakespeare soliloquy; on the second day each would be given a speech from a modern play and half an hour to prepare it. Miss Boyce gave Nora and Jim dozens of scenes from O'Neill, Shaw, Ibsen, Wilder, and Odets on the theory that the more playwrights they knew, the more comfortable they'd be with whatever they were asked to perform.

It was probably debatable which of the girls, Nora Bagley or Jenna Craig, was actually the more deserving. Miss Boyce knew that Jenna would present too great a distraction for Jim, and it was really for him – for his future – that Amanda pushed to enter the contest in the first place. That, and the chance to see New York once again.

Two days before they were to leave Fairmount, the Bagley barn burned down. That act of fate alone did not cause Nora to withdraw. Her cow Imogene, a 4-H champion, died in the fire, and Nora was rendered helpless. Miss Boyce did not replace her with Jenna Craig.

Gossip in Fairmount. Talk – whispers, actually – of cancelling the trip rather than letting a twenty-eight-year-old divorcee accompany an eighteen-year-old boy to New York. Better opinion was that the boy had worked so hard he'd earned the chance at a New York scholarship. It didn't make sense taking that from him just because a cow got incinerated. All things considered, James was probably a heck of a lot safer with Miss Boyce than he'd be with Mr. Whittle, the previous drama teacher.

*

At the Pennsylvania Station, Amanda Boyce walks with an authority James had never seen before, up from the platform, through the concourse, and out onto the street. It's past midnight. James cannot quite keep up with her. A light rain polishes the streets. With a no-nonsense gesture, Amanda Boyce hails a taxi. James Dean, bleary-eyed from the trip, sees Manhattan's colors blur into a wash of neons and drenched reflections. He hears her say to the driver, 'Hotel Dixie.' He's surprised when she doesn't add, 'Please.'

'Dixie. Gotcha.'

'It's right in the heart of the theater district,' she explains to Jim. She might as well be speaking Romanian.

The Dixie's main entrance is on 42nd Street, half a block from

Times Square, but the driver takes them to the rear entrance on 43rd. Jim doesn't know this and is disappointed – looking at it, it could even be a hotel in Indianapolis. The doorman is a large, glistening Negro, liveried in maroon and gold. He reaches for their bags, but Amanda smiles sweetly and clutches her valise. 'We're perfectly fine.' The bright lights, the opulent reflections of polished brass in the revolving door, give James a hopeful feeling which is bolstered by the burgundy carpets and golden frames inside, the burnished hues of the registration counter. The Dixie is respectable, but barely so. James doesn't notice the tarnish, the taint, or the prostitutes.

Amanda Boyce rejects the assistance of a bellhop, a small man in his sixties.

'It's hotel policy, madame,' the desk clerk insists.

'I've been coming here for years,' she counters, 'and haven't needed any help yet. Thanks.' She takes their keys and strides off toward the elevator. In the mirror, James sees the bellhop touch the tip of his tongue to his nose and make an obscene hand gesture.

Their rooms are across the hall on the ninth floor. Hers overlooks 43rd Street, his is over an air shaft: his large window faces another large window with the shade drawn.

'It's late,' she tells him standing in his doorway. 'We've got to be up there by eleven. Meet you at breakfast in the dining room at eight. We'll go over your lines in the morning. It's important to get a good night's sleep. Try.' She winks and blows her displaced, bewildered Indiana boy a kiss.

'But,' his face clouds over, 'I don't have an alarm.'

'Just phone the desk. They'll wake you up. Any time you'd like, just tell them.'

'Oh.' He's not sure he understands.

Jim sits on his bed in his underwear, staring at the phone. He doesn't want to think he's afraid. The written instructions are clear but he imagines the obscene old bellhop taking his call. He dials zero and hears electronic buzzing. 'Main desk.' Nasally.

'I'd like to be waked up tomorrow morning, please.'

'And what time, sir?'

'Oh, around seven.'

'And the room?'

He doesn't know and begins to panic until he sees his key on the table. 'It's 912.'

'Right. Nine-twelve at 7 A.M. Anything else?'

'That'll be it. Thanks a lot.' A rush of satisfaction sweeps over him. He doesn't really believe it will work, but at least he's done the citified thing. He swings into bed and shuts the light. The sheets are cold, almost damp. The room is not dark, not Indiana dark: light from the city seeps in through every crack. The very air in New York must hold a residual glow.

*

Even as he stands in the wings of the compact, wood-panelled Memorial Theater, James cannot expunge the memory of the subway ride up from Times Square. Three or four times he made eye contact with someone and was about to break into his winning Fairmount grin, but each time the other eyes just burned back in challenge. James looked away, confused and angry with himself at having backed down.

He is the seventh of forty-three contestants, most of whom Miss Boyce determines have come from New York, Boston, Philadelphia, and Washington. One girl is from Chicago. Amanda sits two rows behind the three judges. Two of them are women who scribble continually on notepads. The third is a tall man with a goatee.

In the wings, Jim glances at his lines, looks away and goes blank, finds a familiar phrase and starts to build on that. He is not nervous as much as displaced. *What the hell am I doing here?* He smiles a wondering smile and almost laughs. *They can kill you, but they can't eat you.* That's something his mother used to say all the time: he hadn't fully understood it until now.

On stage, a boy, not five feet tall, is mopping up King Lear's mad scene. If it's too ambitious to offer *Hamlet*, Amanda thinks, it's got to be absolutely insane to do *Lear*. The boy has a strong New York accent made ludicrous by an overlay of British pretension. The kicker is his shape. He's not only chubby: he has a stomach below his belt that looks exactly like a rump. Since he also has no ass to speak of, it's as though his top has been twisted half a turn from his bottom. She thinks she sees the goateed judge fighting mightily to hold back laughter.

Finally, in breathless assertiveness, the lumpy Lear stretches to his full stature and declares that he is 'every inch a king.' Amanda Boyce sees the bearded judge's body quiver and go rigid.

'Next contestant. James Dean, Fairmount, Illinois.'

'Indiana, ma'am.' He is walking toward the spotlight like himself. Not like the self that pumps gas and cleans up at the Texaco station on Saturdays, or the one that races his Whizzer on the quarry road, or even the self that can hit nine out of ten foul shots almost every time. It's the self that lives in the spotlight on stage and is ready to skirt the borders of failure and humiliation. The self that lives with a queasy warmth in the pit of its stomach and an incredible alertness in its mind that races ahead of words and actions, that can see all sorts of dramatic possibilities just before they develop, the self that nevertheless draws everything from a calm, confident center in his chest, his heart maybe, and infuses his totality with a curious charm that he offers confidently to the darkness.

James Dean feels all this without knowing quite what has triggered it or how it will allow him to project. Whatever the feeling is, or its mysterious source, it enables him to not worry about trying to be impressive – or, for that matter, trying to accomplish particular effects. It simply liberates him, frees him to play Shakespeare's music and dance into Hamlet's personality. But he can't be certain it will be with him so many miles from Fairmount, in such a strange place where even smiles are provocative.

'Performing?'

'Yes, ma'am.'

'What will you be performing, Mr. Dean?'

'Oh. *Hamlet*. Act 3, scene 2. The speech to the actors.'

'Well then, Mr. Dean.'

Jim zips open his jacket and tosses it onto the stage behind him. He wears tight black pants and black shoes. The sleeves of his white T-shirt are rolled to the shoulder. Amanda Boyce stops breathing; he had a perfectly fine dress shirt on when they left the hotel. He takes almost no time to prepare the mood, but it is perfect when he begins – urgent, instructive, conspiratorial. 'Speak the speech, I pray you, as I pronounc'd it to you, trippingly on the tongue; but if you mouth it, as many of our players do, I had as lief the town-crier spoke my lines . . .' The familiar words flow from the boy, made almost unfamiliar by an utter spontaneity in the delivery. *Almost* unfamiliar, but still assuredly, familiarly Shakespeare: there's a charge of tension in Jim's approach, the too-well-known pulling against the unknowable.

It seems as though he's moving around the stage: in fact, he never moves more than a step in any direction. James Dean's Hamlet has a proprietary pride in the play he's written for the traveling players: he wants it acted well, not only to trap Claudius into a confession but because, well, because he's proud of his words. '. . . for anything so o'erdone is from the purpose of playing, whose end, both at the first and now, was and is to hold, as 'twere, the mirror up to nature . . .' Hamlet smiles to himself, pleased with his own brilliance as a director.

Jim touches his lips. Here comes another thought, '. . . now, this overdone, or come tardy off, though it make the unskillful laugh, cannot but make the judicious grieve . . .'

Amanda Boyce doesn't have much to compare Jim to except his other performances. She has seen him almost as good but never any better and has a sudden urge to embrace her work in progress. Could she possibly be wrong? Isn't this an extraordinary talent?

'. . . that's villainous and shows a most pitiful ambition in the fool that uses it.' Jim stops to be sure that's all Hamlet wants to say to this churl. He begins to add something then thinks better of it. With a wave of his hand, he says, 'Go, make you ready.' He holds his position: it's not clear that he's finished.

Amanda has noticed the two female judges scribbling throughout his performance. That offends her. The tall man seems exceptionally alert. It is hard to evaluate the judges' reactions without seeing their faces.

'Thank you, Mr. Dean. Be sure you consult the schedule for tomorrow.'

'Thank you, ma'am.' Jim does a childish bow – Amanda winces – and picks his jacket up off the floor with the same sweeping motion.

'We'll take ten minutes, people. Miss Ellowitz, Radcliffe Prep, you'll be up when we return.'

In the hallway, Miss Boyce embraces Jim tightly. She kisses each cheek. 'You were won-der-ful.'

'Really? No kidding?'

'Really, no kidding. Except for the dumb bow. And why'd you wear your underwear?'

'I agree. Wonderful. Indeed.' The voice comes from over Miss Boyce's shoulder. She turns and sees the bearded judge approaching with his hand extended. 'Professor McCauley Quirk. I just wanted to tell you how much I admired your performance, Mr. Dean. Great understanding from one so young. A true pleasure.'

'Well, thank you. Thanks a lot.'

'Probably I shouldn't be telling you. It is, after all, a contest, and we still have a long way to go. You know how these things are.'

This confuses Jim. Amanda says, 'How kind.'

'I simply wanted to encourage you, win or lose, to please, please carry on. I'd like you to get in touch with me when it's over, regardless of what happens. Unfortunately, I don't have a card with me, so I've written down my address and telephone number.' The folded sheet of paper is intercepted by Miss Boyce. 'And I *do* look forward to seeing your contemporary piece tomorrow.'

'Thanks a lot for the kind words,' Jim says. 'I look forward to it, too. I think.' He manages to look humble and confident at once. When the professor excuses himself, Amanda hooks Jim's arm and exults, 'One down, one to go. C'mon.'

On the subway downtown, Jim shouts a whisper into her ear: 'What'd he mean, "You know how these things are?"'

She cups his ear. 'Just that he can't guarantee anything. He's only one judge. But he was saying that if it was up to him, you'd be it. But, heck, we both knew that back home.' She squeezes his knee for emphasis and makes him squirm.

*

As they climb the subway steps near Columbia for the second day's competition, James notices a man descending, about to toss away a newly lit cigarette. Jim, extending a hand, asks, 'You don't mind, do you?' The man grimaces then smiles, admiring the kid's nerve. He hands James the cigarette. 'Thanks, mister, you saved my life.'

He takes a long, slow draw, inhaling deeply. Amanda looks on with disapproval. 'That's not appropriate, Jim.'

'I was dying for one, Amanda. Haven't had a cigarette for two days.'

They walk in silence toward the theater building: there is space for two people to walk between them.

Each contestant is given a script at random, differentiated only by male and female parts. Each student will have thirty minutes in isolation to study the speech. The script can be referred to when the role is performed on stage. The order will be alphabetical, as it was for the Shakespeare.

Amanda takes a seat in the audience not far from Professor Quirk but this time where she can see the faces of the other judges as well. He nods at her reassuringly. She is not reassured. The luck of the draw means everything here. Amanda Boyce closes her eyes and crosses her fingers. It's too late to do any good, he's already studying whatever role fate has written for him.

Fate does not treat yesterday's Lear very kindly. Today he is Yank, the 'Hairy Ape' of O'Neill's play. Poor kid. He's supposed to be a sub-human required to stoke the furnace of a great ocean liner. The undersized actor doesn't know whether to play him as Irish or German and opts for something in the middle. This is no Ape: this is a sweet, soft kid trying to sound like a tough guy. He's required to say, 'I'm de ting in gold dat makes it money! And I'm what makes iron into steel! Steel dat stands for de whole ting! And I'm steel – steel – steel! Steel dat stands for de whole ting!' His decision to add realism by shovelling coal into the furnace in cadence to his lines is not a good one. Yesterday a half-assed King, today an ape in rhyme.

'Thank you, Mr. Cianelli. Next, please. James Dean.'

Jim walks out on stage carrying a metal folding chair. Amanda worries he'll be punished for having props. Where the hell did he get it anyway? She notices one of the women judges whisper in the other's ear. Amanda wants to tap her hard on the head with her program.

He takes a moment to find the spotlight and look out into the darkness. 'Any time you wish, young man.'

Jim takes the words literally: he gathers himself much more slowly. Amanda is taken, as always, by his presence, and today, even more so, by his beauty. He opens the chair, takes off his shoe and pulls a handkerchief out of his pocket. He sets his foot on the chair, the shoe on his knee, and begins polishing it with the handkerchief. *What the hell is he doing up there? What play is this anyway?* Amanda shifts sideways in her seat – it is her skeptical position.

He is looking up at someone close by. It can only be a girl, a girl he adores. 'There'll always be barriers between us as long as we stay in this house.' There is a delicate mixture of hopelessness and resignation in the line. His voice has the rhythms, vaguely suggested, of someone not American but without the conscious touch of a foreign accent. *What is it? Chekhov? Ibsen?*

'There's the past and there's the Count.' Jim looks respectfully at the shoe he's polishing, imagining a boot. 'I've never met anyone I had such respect for. When I see his gloves lying on a chair, I feel small – when I hear that bell up there ring, I jump like a skittish horse – and when I look at his boots . . . I feel like bowing.' He holds the shoe up like a trophy, showing it proudly to the young woman, to . . . *Ah, that's it.* Miss Julie, *Strindberg. I didn't give him any Strindberg, damn it.* Amanda turns forward and puts her chin on the back of the seat in front of her. Jim's character, she can't remember his name, the servant, he does indeed respect his master . . . and despises him as well. Resents all the things he cannot have. The Count's daughter Julie included.

'Superstitions and prejudices we learned as children – but they can easily be forgotten. If I can just get to another country, a republic, people will . . .' Jim adds . . . 'To America perhaps . . . people will . . .' Here James Dean pauses and turns away from Julie to the audience, allowing his understanding of character to reveal itself: '. . . people will bow and scrape when they see my livery – bow and scrape, you hear, not me!' This servant, given power over others, would be an absolute bastard. The young actor has everyone in the room in his power.

'I wasn't born to cringe.' He spits on the boot and polishes.

'I wasn't born to cringe.' He spits and polishes. In the text the phrase is not repeated. 'I. Wasn't. Born. To. Cringe.' He spits at the audience.

There's a long moment before James breaks character and says, 'That's it. That's the speech.' Someone in the darkness claps loudly twice. James sits down, puts on his shoe and carries the chair off stage.

Amanda Boyce's mouth is open. She almost forgets to rush to the hallway to tell him how he did. But how *did* he do? Brilliantly, of course. But too daring for them? Truth was, it was almost too daring for her.

In the hallway she throws her arms around him and squeezes very hard. 'Strindberg. How did you know Strindberg?'

'I knew, I just knew how a guy like that would feel. Was I a little too . . .? I decided, heck, it's New York, why not take a chance. It was a lot longer, but I felt that was a great place to stop. What'd you think? Really?'

'One thing I will say, James Dean, there's nothing ordinary about you. And you're right, this *is* New York, why *not* take the chance.'

'Yoo-hoo, Mr. Dean.' Waving from the doorway and approaching was Professor Quirk. 'I can't really say anything, but brilliant, Mr. Dean, brilliant. Of course, spitting won't endear you, but even had you danced the 'Dying Swan' up there, it wouldn't have mattered. Here, I found a card. More official looking.' He smiles and hands it to Jim. 'I probably shouldn't be telling you this, but I plan to put all my support behind you for the prize.'

Jim flushes. Amanda squeezes his arm.

'It won't do very much good. I'm afraid. I'm sure to be outvoted.'

Amanda and Jim look at each other and then at the Professor with non-comprehension.

'I want you, Mr. Dean, to try to cushion yourself for a bitter reality. Perhaps you can receive an honorable mention or something equivalent. But that's of no import. Something can surely be arranged if you wish to attend the School of Drama here. There are other grants, smaller scholarships, lots of compensatory . . .' Other possibilities are indicated with a wave of his hand.

'Why can't I win?'

'Because we live in a very imperfect world, young man.'

Amanda steps forward. She's angry. 'I think Jim deserves a some-what better answer than that.'

'Yes. Of course he does.' He takes a deep breath. 'There are, I am afraid, other considerations, political ones, schools that have sent students here for years and haven't even gotten an honorable men-tion. Reciprocal considerations for all sorts of things done or not done in the past. People are owed certain favors. It's as simple and depressing as that. But none of this should matter a whit where your future is concerned, Mr. Dean.'

'You mean this whole deal has been fixed from the start?'

'That's a bit harsh, and, as I've said, as far as you're concerned . . .'

'You can't be pulling that kind of stuff on people, Mr . . .?' He looks for the card and can't find it. 'You can't be playing fast and loose with other people's hopes. That's worse than . . .' He can't think quickly enough of exactly what it's worse than, but he says, 'teasing dumb animals, or something.' He turns away from the hand the professor has held out since offering him the card. 'You people ought to be ashamed of yourselves, pulling a stunt like this.'

Amanda Boyce runs after James Dean, turning back just once to see Professor Quirk standing helplessly with his hands offering nothing.

On the subway, Amanda finally says, 'All that really matters is that you were the best.'

James glares at her.

'You-were-the-best. Say, "I know it."'

He shakes his head.

'Say it.' She tickles him.

He says, '"You-were-the-best."'

'Say, "I-was-the-best."'

'All right. "I-was-the best."'

'Now say, "Therefore a celebration is in order." Say it.'

'"Therefore a celebration is in order." Are you serious? Where?'

'You'll see.'

The emotional exhaustion of their effort and the taint of Dr. Quirk's words have taken the heart out of both of them. Nevertheless, Amanda will have her celebration.

Her reward is intended to be Sardi's. She had been there twice when she lived in New York. The walls of caricatures of everyone who has ever been anyone in American theater are what she wants Jim to see. But Sardi's is not to be. Amanda is told by the *maître d'*, a man even smaller than the tiny Lear but genuinely aristocratic, there would be no tables available for the foreseeable future. Amanda motions to numerous empty tables visible from the alcove. 'Reserved, I'm afraid, madam.' He looks all the while with great disdain at Jim's windbreaker.

Yet another setback. She takes her student's arm and walks him out on 44th Street. 'Don't worry. I know a place. A lot less fancy and even better for our budget. Friendlier too.' The Backstage Deli, just off Broadway, is about the size of the office at the Texaco Station. There is an open table for two in the rear, near the restrooms. As they make their way back, trying to avoid brushing other diners and tables, Jim says, 'It's like a subway for eating.' But his words are swallowed in the general clamor.

The place also has its share of autographed pictures, as many, in fact, as the walls can hold. Near their table, Amanda points out Ray Bolger, Billy Rose, Olsen and Johnson, Bea Lillie, Katherine Cornell, Irving Berlin. James knows Bolger from *The Wizard of Oz* and nobody else. 'All the others are just as famous.' She explains who they are. While doing so, Amanda searches for someone else he might know. 'There. You must know her from the movies.' She tries not to point.

Jim squints at the wall. 'Which one? Next to that guy with the bald head?'

'Holding the little dog.'

He looks without recognition.

'Ethel Barrymore.'

The name means nothing. 'I guess I'm hopeless, huh?'

'No, just disgustingly young.'

Eventually a flat-footed waiter moves painfully toward them. 'It's a sandwich place,' Amanda warns. She orders first. 'Corned beef on rye with coleslaw and Russian dressing.'

Again Jim has no idea what language he's heard.

'To drink, what?'

'Cream soda.'

'And you?'

'I think I'll have a roast beef sandwich on white bread, please. And what flavors of pop do you have?'

'Pop?'

'He means soda.'

The flavors come by too fast to catch. Jim says, 'Coca-Cola.' The waiter starts to shuffle away. 'And could I have mayonnaise on my sandwich.'

The waiter looks sickened. 'Mayo, we don't serve. Mustard, ketchup's on the table.'

Jim is bewildered.

Amanda explains. 'This is a kosher restaurant, Jim.' His confusion deepens. 'Jewish people only eat certain kinds of food. It's called being kosher. They don't have dairy products with their meats.'

Jim's confusion becomes perplexity. He simply cannot believe it. 'No dairy?'

'That's right. And no pork either.' His perplexity is now disdain. 'There are more things in heaven and earth, James Dean, than are dreamt of in your philosophy.'

Jim mutters, 'No dairy and no pork. Good thing there aren't more of 'em. Those Jews would put the whole Midwest right out of business.' He punctuates his joke with a serious face.

After their sandwiches, they walk wearily back to the Dixie, past dozens of theaters. Amanda indicates the marquees, the names and photographs of the stars. 'Someday, that'll be you.'

'Are you kidding?' New York seems to him the least hospitable place in the world.

'Where do you think those people come from, Mars?'

'They sure don't come from Fairmount, Indiana.'

She seals his lips with her finger. Her finger is slow to pull away.

The sun has left the streets of Manhattan and is visible only as reflection on the tallest buildings. It has gotten chilly. Amanda and Jim walk slowly back to the Dixie holding hands: he is smiling with sad satisfaction. The clasp of hands is tight, binding their consolation.

*

Twenty minutes later, when he taps on 913, she says, 'Go away unless you're the Prince of Denmark.'

He's amazed by her response. ''Tis none other, madame.' If he is Hamlet, who must she be?

'Then enter, fair prince.' The lights are off. Amanda Boyce is on her bed still dressed. Her short, dark hair frames her pale face propped on double pillows. 'Believe it or not, it was more exhausting for me, watching, hoping you'd do well, than it was for you up there acting. You don't believe that, do you?' She pats the edge of the bed for him to sit.

'Probably.' He sits. 'You know what I'm dying for?'

She can't help being coy. 'Hmmmm, let me guess.'

'A cigarette.'

'Worst thing for your throat.'

'Can't help it. I'm hooked on smoking.'

'Get unhooked.' She takes his hand in both of hers and examines it carefully – fingernails, knuckles, the veins along the back, the blond hair, and, finally, the long, slender palm – as though it will reveal the mystery of his talent.

Each knows instinctively not to speak again in the darkening room. A rhythmic pulse, a feeling if not quite a sound, comes from the street below, or the floor, or the coursing of bloods. She looks into a boy's face and sees the man he will be. Jim Dean at thirty.

He sees the expressions of a person he's never seen before. People should not be so alone as this woman has been. Her eyes have never looked so deep. His eyes indicate an intense curiosity. A word, any word, will break the mood, alter the emotional direction. It is a pulsing silence.

She brushes his face with the back of her hand. The rough texture of what appears to be baby smooth surprises her. She could almost cry at the tenderness of the moment. He would like to touch her small, round lips. There are two rhythms now: the pulse beneath, and their breathing.

She places his fingers on the lowest button of her blouse and wills him to open it with a tightening of her eyebrows. She closes her eyes and feels his fingers twist the button free. James Dean's hand is cold on Amanda Boyce's skin. She is certain she will know when to stop exploring this sweet, consoling intimacy.

James traces circles on her stomach, larger and larger figure eights. Their eyes are locked. Her smile is modest, balanced between approval and concern. His lips are questioning. He opens the next button. Her breath is almost a soft moan.

Now the boy's circling fingers brush the bottom of her brassière. Amanda opens the top button of her blouse. She is certain she'll know when to stop, even while realizing the beat of desire is more insistent than any resolve she can muster.

Jim, mouth closed, unsmiling, undoes the two remaining buttons. Amanda Boyce's blouse falls open. He knows to span the bottom of her bra and pull the snug garment up and over her swollen breasts. Unaware, he moistens his lips as he looks at her. Full breasts pulling to each side, nipples and circles as dark as her lips. She breathes a moan when he leans down to kiss her breasts lightly.

Amanda closes her eyes. *This is not a boy.*

At the same moment she kisses his neck, his lips begin to draw at her nipple. The moist suction on her breast is arousing and disturbing. She reaches for his zipper. She fumbles it open and wishes his stiffening penis can be extracted with more grace. It cannot. He has to assist her. She may have heard him chuckle.

Touching him, she feels it harden rapidly. She wants to see it in her hand. Perhaps then she will stop. 'Oh, God,' she whispers. It is fuller than her ex-husband's: it is beautiful. She considers the extension of this marvelous boy. 'Sweet Jesus.'

Never in Fairmount. Not even in Indianapolis. But New York is foreign territory, another planet almost. Conventional restraints are downright stupid. This is a cruel, thoughtless place where people need each other desperately. Amidst their Manhattan suffering, even while afire, Amanda is aware of consequences. Fairmount, Indiana, consequences. 'I can't do this.'

His face wrinkles.

'I just can't risk something like this, Jim.' Should she have said 'We'?

He says, 'I won't . . . you know . . . stay in . . .'

She holds his face. There is pain, briefly, but there is also his beautiful face beaming down with pleasure and expectation. She begins to move gently, passing the slow rhythm to him. He laughs like a teenager. She stops him with a frown. Her hand rests on the back of his head: his hair is silken, softer than her own. His lithe, hairless body is roped with elongated sinews. There are beauty marks on his chest: he is flawless. He does not smell of maleness: she doesn't believe he ever will. So sweet a body, she wants to cry.

A crease forms on his brow, a twitch flickers on his lips.

Amanda pulls away and feels James Dean leave her. The loss is momentarily disheartening, but imperative. 'We just can't.'

It looks as though he won't say anything. He says, 'I understand.'

'No you don't. Come here.' She rolls out from under him and pushes him on his side. Her head is at his waist. Her tongue flicks his stomach. And lower. Then he feels the wet warmth of her mouth on his penis, her tongue circling its surface. She stops suddenly and says like a teacher, 'Try not to like this too much. Some men become obsessed with it and never learn about the rest of lovemaking.' He knows she's talking about her ex-husband. Then she places him in her lips and moves her head as though nodding deliberately.

At the gas station Lem Craig is always talking about this. James has listened and said nothing. Now he knows. He won't say anything, though. But how is it possible not to like this too much?

When he slips across the hallway back to his room, he catches his breath, thinking he has seen someone, just briefly, a girl in a flowered dress, a pale sweater sitting on her shoulders. She is, and as quickly, is not at the end of the hall near the elevator bank. He wonders if he's been seen. Then, if he's really seen anyone at all. It doesn't matter. New York City is light years from Fairmount, Indiana.

3. An Actor Acts

THE MAGIC BOOK: screenplay by Serge and Monica Ladinsky based on a Persian fairytale translated by Horton Guy; cinematography by Franz Kliest; art direction by Philip Console; musical direction by Oren Classman; directed by Walter Beeson; a First National production and release.

Caliph	Hershel Vetti
Princess Fatima	Chloë Crane
Abdul the Camel Boy	Brand Cobbett
Abdul's Father	Akim Brandov
Sharif	Guy Garrick
Emir of Cairo	Farley Plumb
Ali Baba	Gregory Marchet
Sorceress	Ursula Flair
Genie	Tunch Calderon

James went to the Fairmount alone to see The Magic Book. He'd overheard Brett Collins's little sister telling her friends about it. He was way too old for the Genie exploding out of his bottle, the magic carpet rides, labyrinthine passageways, and collapsing mountains. He sat alone along the wall in the balcony. He loved The Magic Book.

When the Genie comes out of his bottle, the Book of the Future tumbles out with him. Whoever has that book knows what will happen *in life and profit enormously from that foreknowledge. All the powerful forces in the Empire vie for its possession, but it is Abdul the blind Bedouin boy who comes upon it in the desert. He has no idea what purpose the book can have: he admires it purely as an object, touching it seemingly with sensitive fingers, placing it against his face and smiling.*

When, in turn, the Sharif, Ali Baba, and the Emir try to take the volume from Abdul, he thwarts each of their attempts.

In his father's tent, Abdul tells of his love for the book:

Abdul: It is difficult to explain, father, but when I hold this book, a peace comes over me, a peace even deeper than a cool sunset upon the desert.

Father: Some would find it strange that a blind boy treasures a book he cannot read.

Abdul: True. I may seem to be the fool. But in my heart I believe that some day I shall know everything that is on its pages.

Father: How shall that be, my son?

Abdul: What is written cannot really change the direction of our lives. Our lives themselves are the true prophecies to which all words must finally conform.

Unbeknowst to Abdul, his father has read the final pages in Abdul's book. He knows the boy shall see one day and marry the Caliph's daughter, but he opts not to tell his son of what is written.

During dinner, Ortense tells Marcus, 'Jimboy says he'd like to do some traveling this summer. My brother's invited him out there. The Collins boy's thinking about selling his car. Don't see why we can't help him out with that.' She is looking the whole time at James not at Marcus.

Marcus cannot cut through his roast beef. He picks the piece up in his fingers and tears the gristle away with his teeth. 'Sorry, folks. Sometimes crudity is the politest way with tough meat. That '39 Ford? I believe it was his daddy's car way back when. First-rate man with a machine, Lorne Collins. First-rate. Sure. We could help out with that. How much he askin'?'

'Hundred and a quarter. But I've got most of it put away. It's not for you to . . .' James indicates the end of his thought with a circular wave of his fork. It's a gesture he's taken from Marcus.

'Don't be saying such fool things,' Ortense warns, spooning more mashed potatoes onto her husband's plate.

'How many miles she got on her?'

'Around a hundred ten, fifteen. Comes out I'm paying him 'bout a dollar each thousand miles.'

'I've seen those things go to two hundred, two fifty easy if they're lubed up properly and oil's changed regular. Sure, we can help you out with it. That mean you'll be giving up the Whizzer?'

'Like to hold onto her. She'll be a classic cycle some day, like a Perfecta or a Gem.'

'Been thinking of New York, too.' He speaks slowly and narrows his eyes at his aunt.

Marcus says, 'Shoo. Damned near forgot. That teacher of yours came by yesterday. Wanted to drop something off for you. Told her you'd be at the garage, but she said she was heading home. Said she wasn't going to be around for graduation and there was something she wanted you to have. A package. Pretty little thing, ain't she?'

'Shame on you, Marcus. What'd she drop off?'

'Drop off what?'

'I swear, you're losing your marbles. The package. For Jimboy.'

'Left it in the barn. Top of the milking machine. I'll get it when I load the night feed.'

'Deuce you will.' Ortense stands and takes her shawl off a peg by the kitchen door.

'I'll go, Ten-ten.'

'You two finish up. I'd welcome a stroll. That way, you can start to clean up.'

Marcus talks about Brett's Ford. James really doesn't listen. He is concerned over what the package might be, whether he could open it in front of his aunt and uncle. They leave silences between the scrape of knives on plates.

Ortense returns holding what appears to be something the size of a book. A book eases his concern a little. But what book? 'Isn't that woman sweet to have thought of you before she left? All the things she must have on her mind these days.' She hands him the parcel. 'Such lovely wrapping.' The colors are of fall – rust orange and burnt gold – not of summer. 'What do you suppose it is?'

'You're not getting me to open it.'

'A present. We open presents in this house, don't we Marcus?'

Her husband nods.

'It's a graduation present, and I'm not officially graduated yet.'

'Heck,' Marcus says, 'less than a week away.'

'Nope,' James says with a pout. It's a gesture close to acquiescence.

Marcus guffaws: 'It isn't one of those dirty books from New York, is it?'

That's precisely what James worries it might be. He looks for help to his aunt.

She picks up a dishtowel.

'Okay,' James mumbles. 'I'll open it.'

'Good. I'll get the pudding.'

Marcus props his elbows on the table, getting ready for something to tease the boy about.

James shakes his head. 'You two are really something, you know that?'

Ortense says, 'Here. Use a sharp knife. It's such beautiful paper, I'll find a use for it.' Drying the knife with her towel, she hands it delicately to James, who begins to score the sealing tape with care. He peels the paper off like an old skin. It is indeed a book. An old book. The binding on the spine is worn. Some of the pages are yellowed, a few dog-ears torn away. Marcus is very much drawn to it because of its age. It is *An Actor Prepares* by Konstantin Stanislavsky. On a card stuck inside the cover, Amanda Boyce has written: 'Dear Jim – There is a whole new way of acting beginning all over the world. It will sweep away everything before it. This will help you be part of it. All the best, Amanda.'

On the title page is a scrawled message in a tiny, precise hand. The ink has paled. An illegible name and date underscore the sentences. James cannot make sense of a single word. He goes to the sideboard for his glasses. Marcus pulls the book closer and runs his fingers over the strange words as though to understand them by touch. 'It's not English. I know English, and that's not a word of English.'

'Well, it's awful nice of Miss Boyce to encourage you like that. There's a person who believes in you, Jimboy.'

He doesn't hear, so absorbed is James in trying to make sense of the unintelligible script. He opens the book randomly and reads fragments: '. . . must not imagine the emotions . . . not only appear to be an old man or woman . . . we have had enough of the theater of sleight of hand . . .' James Dean doesn't know he has received a treasure.

'You have to write her a "thank you" note tonight, Jimboy.'

'Uh-huh.' He continues reading phrases.

Marcus taps his finger emphatically. 'Nope, that's not English. The letters are completely different from English.'

*

Ortense laughs when there's nothing really funny being said. As they leave the long road that cuts through the Wanamaker farm and take a right onto County 633 headed south, Marcus slows and points to Hardy's Texaco, where two cars wait at the pumps unattended. 'Miss you there already, Jimbo,' Marcus says over his shoulder. Ortense laughs. Nervousness, of course.

She laughs again when James, in the back seat, says, 'And, no, I didn't forget my hairbrush, comb, toothbrush, toothpaste, nail clippers, shoe brush, scissors. Anything you can think of, Ten-ten, I didn't forget it.'

'Don't really need much out there,' Marcus says. 'I'm surprised they even bother to wear clothes.' Ortense doesn't laugh.

James watches the lush fields roll past his window, blur and clear and drift away. He does not allow a sense of loss to take hold. His uncle wise-cracks: his aunt cackles. The Winslow car heads toward Indianapolis. When he sees a string of Burma Shave signs, he feels a longing in his stomach: 'A LOVELY WOMAN . . . WOULD RATHER BE . . . SPEARED . . . THAN BE ASSAULTED . . . BY A STUBBY . . . BEARD.' His chest tightens when they pass an announcement: 'LEAVING GRANT COUNTY.' The pang confirms to James that this has indeed been his home.

James hasn't been to Indianapolis since his trip to New York with Miss Boyce. He thinks fleetingly about those offers to go to Columbia University, which had remained an option until a week ago when he left Professor Quirk's final letter unanswered. His hand on his plaid suitcase moves reflexively to the bulge that is *An Actor Prepares*: he has vowed to read it on the train.

There are no seasons at somber Market Square Station: it is eternally cold and bleak. For James it is a neutral place, a starting point only, a prelude to possibilities. Small groups of people wait at mid-station for the liner to Chicago. The same train will take him on to California.

Marcus shifts from foot to foot, an impatient gesture he adopts during those rare moments he must stand without something to do. Ortense picks non-existent pieces of lint off James's jacket, as though trying to collect tiny particles of the boy she loves. They speak in brief phrases amid lots of long pauses. 'You'll write.'

'Sure will.'

'They eat different out there.'

'Not that different, Marcus.'

Ortense brushes his shoulders. 'Remember. Winton tries best he can. The man deserves a chance.'

James says to Marcus, 'The Whizzer, keep an eye on it for me.'

The station-master announces the imminent arrival of the *Sun Chief*, and James suddenly recalls the sun in California. It's a different, unmitigated sun: it warms you outward from the bones.

*

James opens the book at random a few minutes out of Indianapolis and reads, 'Someone comes to an acting studio with his mind still clothed in the rags of prejudice he has acquired in his environment. Or he may possess the precious germ of creative art, but it is smothered by layers of incidental personal flaws from which he has to be set free.'

James is stopped short: he touches the page with his fingers as though identifying a rarity. His mouth has formed a small 'o.' He reads those sentences again. For some reason, these words speak to him as no words in any book he's ever read. This author, this – he turns to the cover to check: he says the name to himself stressing the wrong syllable – this Stanislavsky knows something about him he hadn't even recognized in himself. He automatically thinks of Amanda Boyce. He should have seen her before she left, should have offered to help her move. Maybe he can still get in touch.

He flips to the first page and is stunned by the opening sentence. 'It is not accident that brings people together in art.' The idea, the tone, has rare power and seems to lodge behind his eyes. He gets the eerie feeling that someone in the swaying car is watching him; he looks around slyly while reaching into his coat pocket for his glasses. He spies no one.

He reads it again. 'It is not accident that brings people together in art. They come together because some of them are anxious to share their experiences with their fellow artists, while others, finding it impossible to stand still, want to move forward because their inner powers grow stronger and develop, and search for new ways in which to express themselves in creative action. It is these things that have brought us together now.' The direct address pops his head back.

James senses himself to be in the presence of a powerful enchanter. 'Brought *us* together now!' The sentence has the power of a prophecy fulfilled, as though this Stanislavsky, whoever he is, wherever he is, cast this message in a bottle that was destined to find no one but James Byron Dean. Spooky. And somehow Amanda Boyce knew this.

Something transforming is happening to him. Something restrictive is about to be loosed, a liberating spirit about to be freed. It's all very vague, but it's very real to James. He does not immediately accept the fact that a book can have such powerful effects. He attributes some of it to the lengthening distance between himself and Fairmount. Perhaps it's both that and the book. Yes, most likely both. But that book.

In the comfortable but isolated world of Fairmount, Indiana, in which James had been 'clothed in rags' during his formative years, idealism was not held to be a virtue. Far from it. It was thought to be dangerously high on the scale of human expectation and, therefore, potentially harmful. It was deemed far wiser to hover near to the middle ground of values and hope for decency and occasional flashes of goodness while keeping one foot firmly planted in the cynic's camp as a hedge against disappointment. Indiana soil had to be worked too damned hard to expect dreams to flourish in the real world.

And here's this wild man from – James turns back to the title page where he reads 'Translated from the Russian' – here's this wild Russian rhapsodizing about a quest for love and beauty and personal fulfillment through the haze of something he calls 'a life in art.' *A life in art*, the phrase resonates in James, and just in case it's missed, Stanislavsky sounds it on almost every page. Living such a life, an actor, properly trained of course, can reach into himself and find the means to understand the emotions required to play *any human being in the world*. All possibilities exist for the courageous actor willing to risk everything for *a life in art*. How that phrase beckons James Dean.

Now he remembers his mother being chided at Dean family affairs as a dreamer. Good-natured teasing mostly, but there was an edge to it that suggested something more serious. Only Ortense defended her sister-in-law. Mildred's capacity to dream was treated like an inherent character weakness. Flights of fancy were all right for a girl: a grown woman had better be more practical, for her family's sake. The non-dreamers seemed to take pleasure in distancing Mildred from themselves. James hadn't realized until this moment the extent to which his mother had been isolated in the family.

Mildred Dean accepted the family's attitude good-naturedly, she thought ostracism a small price to pay for perceiving the world so differently from them. And there was a rather significant consolation: she knew her son was exactly like herself. In him, if she had her way – and that was always her unshakable intention – all divergence from the conventional would be encouraged; celebrated even. Her son would have a life of dreams, and dreams would be most diligently pursued. *A life in art.* One subverted dreamer was enough in the family.

James knows he'll have to get in touch with Amanda Boyce somehow. She'll have some ideas about how to proceed.

The *Sun Chief* encounters dark clouds and thundershowers east of Chicago. Intently reading the chapter on 'The Proper Apprenticeship,' he doesn't bother to notice the skies. In Chicago, where the train empties during a forty-five-minute stopover, he pores over 'Being Part of the Ensemble' in the gloom. Normally a slow reader, James's eyes race ahead of his brain. One idea after another, chapter after chapter, astonishes him. For example: all acting, Stanislavsky proclaims, begins with breathing, the common denominator of all rhythmic action and the key to stage movement and pacing in a role. Breathing. All preparation for a role begins with the state of rest. James leans back, closes his eyes, and listens to himself breathe for a long while, considering for the first time in his life the mystery of the respiratory system. A serious student must also observe carefully the breathing of people in various states of activity.

The would-be actor, James is told, must develop his body and learn to control it absolutely, must be able to isolate and master the various muscle groups. At the same time, he must avoid at all costs the falsity of external gestures and the danger of being petty and vain among the other actors. He should attempt to develop the rare amalgam of joy and seriousness as he approaches his daily tasks with others from the ensemble.

James is enthralled by the difficulties Stanislavsky presents; every challenge excites him. James doesn't look up again until the train pulls into Springfield. He doesn't know if he's in Illinois or Missouri. It's late afternoon. He doesn't know he's starved.

Aunt Ortense has packed sandwiches and plenty of fruit. James devours the ham and cheese while reading; the mayonnaise that fringes his mouth is mostly washed away by the juice of a peach. He wipes off the rest with the back of his hand. A passing porter stops and says, 'Young feller, let there be light.' James blinks, uncomprehending. 'You're reading in the dark.'

'Oh. Sure. Thanks.' He flips the switch and there is light on the page; he is surprised by how dark it has gotten. He blinks and starts the chapter on the importance of paying careful attention to all human behavior, trying to understand the sources of action in order to be able to reproduce not only the action but its emotional currents. There is nothing James cannot understand as he reads: some of it he feels he'd already known without realizing it. Such discoveries deepen the book's mystery, his kinship with this unknown Russian.

James stands and spots the conductor near the end of the car talking to a porter. He approaches them and waits while the conductor finishes a story about a particularly irksome passenger. James files the behavior away as subject matter. 'Excuse me, sir. What's our next stopover?'

'Kansas City.' The conductor checks his watch: 'Be there in about fifty minutes or so.'

'Will it be possible to mail a letter there?'

'Heck, we'll be there long enough to send off a letter and get it answered.'

James withdraws a single sheet of letter paper from his writing kit. He searches the kit, but his pen isn't there. He notices a fountain pen in the jacket pocket hanging alongside the businessman facing him. 'Excuse me, sir. Wonder if I might borrow your pen for a few minutes.' He'd have noticed the neck muscles tighten even before he'd read Stanislavsky; now, however, everything registers – the catch in the breath, the cock of the head, the averted eyes. The face never unsmiles, but the man's unwillingness is palpable. 'I, uh. Pen. Not sure it's got ink.'

'Oh. Thanks, anyway.' James takes his battered suitcase down from the overhead rack and opens it on the floor. Everyone watching shifts uncomfortably. James fishes through and around clothing and books and toilet articles. It's there, stuck in a ball of socks. He shows it proudly and offers one of his truest smiles. 'Guess I got lucky.'

Ortense will do anything he asks, but for the first time in a good, long while he doesn't take her reliability for granted.

Dear Ten-ten,

Guess you think I must have got really homesick really fast. I'm not even in California yet – haven't even gotten to Kansas City, and already I'm writing you a letter. Don't know, maybe I am – homesick, that is. But I just discovered that I have to ask you for a favor. I need Miss Boyce's address in New York City. I never thanked her for giving me that book about acting. It's pretty important. You can probably get her address from Mrs. Knight where she (Miss Boyce)used to live. Or from the post office because they are probably forwarding her mail to New York. I wouldn't ask you to do this favor for me if it wasn't important – it won't be a waste of your time. If you would send the address to me at Winton's, I'd appreciate it. As soon as possible, okay?

So far the trip is going real good. I'm reading that book and learning a lot about acting. The people on the train are really interesting. It's something to see how grand America is. Best to Marcus. Ate the sandwiches – they were Ten-ten good.

Yours truly,
Jimboy

Everyone watches as he folds the page in thirds and addresses the envelope. He's enormously pleased with himself.

When the train stops in Kansas City, James buys a stamp at a newspaper stand and mails his letter at the station post office. He feels confident: he makes this the first independent action of his new life in art.

Much to the annoyance of those trying to sleep, James remains awake reading *An Actor Prepares*. It is well past midnight when he finishes. Even after he's closed the book, he sits in the lamplight considering what he's read, and then reconsidering. Eventually he darkens the lamp but does not sleep. He dreams.

Where exactly does the balance change? After Flagstaff but before the California border, James's sense of well-being, which he had been certain would buoy him up for the rest of his natural life, begins to fade a little. Maybe it was the businessman announcing after Prescott, 'I won't feel like myself again till we get under that good ol' California sun.' It's something his father might have said. Winton would probably have been the same way about the fountain pen, too. Maybe it was thinking of Winton Dean that began to deflate him. James hadn't really considered his father during most of the trip, not even bothered to factor him into the new equation of his life in art, his life as an actor.

As the train approaches Los Angeles, James begins to consider how to accommodate his father without letting the new dream slip away. James knows what happens to him in Winton's presence, the paralysis, the contrariness, the anger, the disgust. Around Winton he could never be, as Stanislavsky advises, 'his best, most open and attuned self.' Years of resentment have produced an automatic scowl whenever Winton Dean is the subject of his thoughts, a resentment that has come to take on a life of its own, one that no longer needs his justification.

In Winton's presence James's breathing changes, his facial muscles tense, his eyes burn unforgivingly, he struggles against allowing sarcasm to color every word. *Maybe*, he tells himself, *if I saw him as someone to study, someone I might play someday, I wouldn't get so damned* . . . He can't label exactly how he might not get.

He also knows he has Winton Dean where he wants him, feeling so guilty about some unknowable sin, so defensive he'll agree to almost anything James wants. There's a part of the son who'd really like the man to slap him down; but a deeper part enjoys the silent, punishing power he has over his father.

The *Sun Chief* winds cautiously down through the dusty Santa Ana hills and rolls tediously across the San Bernadino Valley, eventually clacking like a freight through East Los Angeles and Huntington Park. It broils in the midday sun. None of the terrain looks even distantly familiar to James because he doesn't allow it to.

Even before he had left Fairmount and read *An Actor Prepares*, James resolved to try to get out on his own as soon as he could. Now there's an imperative to establish his independence even faster: it gives him the feeling that he has already begun to compose his new life.

Other passengers are taking down their bags and beginning to crowd the aisles. James decides to bide his time. He leans against the window seeking Winton among the crowd waiting to greet the *Sun Chief*. James believes he recognizes his father before he actually sees him. He accurately anticipates the blue suit and red tie before there is the blue suit and red tie. The man is square-shouldered and stiff-limbed, older-looking than his age by at least ten years; his lips are pursed, giving the leathery, credulous face its only expression. His clipped, light-brown hair is parted so neatly it makes him look brittle and manufactured. James shakes his head and smiles.

They stand facing one another. The sun glares pitilessly off James's glasses. Not a word is exchanged. Winton touches the sleeves of his son's jacket. They are the same height exactly. Their shoulders square in the same way, heads at the same incline. Winton looks like an older, better-baked version of the son. James, of course, never acknowledges any similarities.

Winton reaches for James's suitcase, but his son draws it away. So as not to seem too rude, he says, 'It's fine.' They do not touch –

Winton's fear of a rebuff activates James's aversion. The dry air crackles.

Winton takes out a pocket watch. 'Really something, isn't it? Travels across the entire country and gets here less than a minute off schedule.'

It's been almost nine years and Winton's first comment is about railroad scheduling. 'Yup . Sure is something, this modern world of ours.' James smiles in spite of his resolve.

'It really *is* like a miracle.' Winton's voice breaks and squeaks. He reaches again for James's valise, and James lets him take it. Winton wants to smooth down James's matted hair. He refrains. 'Been here half an hour waiting. Thought it was possible it could come in early.'

'They're fine and send their best.'

The confusion James intends creeps across Winton's face slowly. He stops walking.

James says over his shoulder, 'Marcus, Ortense. They're fine, they send their best.'

'Oh, I know. Talked to her last night. It's this way.' He points to the parking lot.

'Still the Ford?' An unnecessary question.

'Still and always. I'm a Ford man, born and bred. Son, you know that.'

From behind, James observes Winton's walk; how stiff, deliberate and biting it is. James knows the old car will sparkle like no other in the lot. It does. Winton, expecting a compliment on his Ford, opens the trunk. James looks up at the hard sun, exhales, and gets in the passenger side.

It isn't easy for Winton to speak as he drives, so intense is his concentration and care in traffic. That's fine with James, who has taken off his jacket and rolled up his shirtsleeves. He puts his arm out the window and feels the sun sting his skin. He doesn't intend to speak and is surprised by his own voice: 'Got a notion about what I'd like to do while I'm out here.' He gives Winton a chance to respond, but he's unsure if his father, intent on the changing traffic lights, has heard him. Problem with his hearing maybe.

At the lights, Winton hits the brakes and says, 'Rhea has a real nice dinner planned. Pork roast.' He looks over and smiles quickly, proud of having remembered one of his son's favorite meals.

James has not even considered Winton's wife, his stepmother, for God's sake. He laughs his soft, rusty-gate laugh. It's hard for him to stay angry when the bombardment of such bizarre things – a reclaimed father, a brand-new, never-seen mother, the car he played in as a child, pork roast, a dizzying sun, this crazy traffic in Los Angeles – is so extreme.

'Peewee'll be glad to see you.'

Peewee? Jesus Christ, Peewee. 'He still alive?'

'Alive? He's in his prime, son. You should hear him chatter on. He's got a welcoming speech for you.'

James adds one more senseless item to the list – a ten-year-old parakeet.

'Pork roast, Jimbo.' Winton shakes his son's shoulder. His smile is the bravest he can muster.

'Sure. Pork roast.' James closes his eyes, licks his lips, and rubs his stomach. He sniffs. The sour smell he's always associated with his father is not in the car.

*

August 28, 1949

Dear Jim:

It was so good to get your letter – for lots of reasons but mostly because you really seem to have discovered what you feel you must do with your life (acting of course). If *An Actor Prepares* opens your eyes, I couldn't be more proud. Jim, I've always believed you were one of the special ones – nothing would have been sadder than if someone with your gift hadn't found the best – no, the *only* – means to express it. With the commitment you convey in your letter and the kind of training you now know you want, nothing can keep you from becoming a wonderful actor. It probably won't be easy – the actor's life never is – but when you discover the path, the only thing to do is follow it. Remember, nothing is ever sadder than the words, 'It might have been.')

About myself – well, I'm studying. A good studio in Greenwich Village – The Actors' Ensemble. We do new plays, one-acts mostly; we play to audiences on weekends, so something's cooking all the time. I audition for everything listed in Equity from ingénues to the old nurse in *Romeo and Juliet* (got a call-back on that, so keep your fingers crossed). What has everyone here hoping are all the plays they're putting on for television. I've been on an *I Remember Mama* and twice on *New York Stories*. (You didn't see them by any chance? Of course not.) Television drama could be the best thing that's ever happened to an actor – even the commercials get you seen. Oh yes, be sure to learn to sing and dance – that's one of the first things they ask you here. I always say yes, but I have no idea how I'd do if I actually had to perform. All right, I think.

In answer to your questions, I talked to some actors and teachers here who know something about Method teachers and the L.A. scene. One reason it's taken me so long to respond is that the information wasn't easy to come by. Among the people who seemed to know the most, three names kept coming up – oh, one other thing, you should know that no two teachers teach the Method in the same way, there's lots of variation, but I'll bet you knew that already.

Anyway, the most respected three seem to be:

1. Zabor Konrad, 'Studio Konrady.' They say he's good, but he only deals with actors with some professional experience (no problem there, you just do what any actor worth his salt does, you lie about your experience). He stresses the psychology of a character. They also say he can be a little expensive.

2. Martin Goldglass. He teaches most of the acting courses at U.C.L.A., but they think he also gives private lessons. A friend tells me he's a genius with beginning actors. He was in the original Group Theatre with Odets and Kazan and the Adlers and Strasberg; went to Hollywood with John Garfield. He plays character parts in all the Garfield movies and lots of others. You've probably seen him.

3. 'Acting and Actors,' Ellen Janus and Serge Strangoff.

They tell me he's hard to understand but was a member of the Moscow Art Theatre, where he knew all the greats including Stanislavsky himself. Ellen is his wife, and she makes sure the students get what he's got to offer. You have to audition for Strangoff, maybe for the other ones too.

(I don't have addresses for any of these, but you shouldn't have any trouble finding them in the phone book. Wish I could help you make the choice, but I'm sure you'll know soon enough which one is right for you.)

I never told you, but it was that trip to New York last year that put the bug in my head to follow my own dream again. I realized, seeing you on that stage, I wanted a life up there more than anything, and if I didn't do it soon, I might never do it. So I want you to know, young Mr. Dean, how important you've been in my life.

I'm glad you now have my address. My phone number is GR3-3422. So there's no reason for you to be a stranger since I'm really interested in how things go for you out there.

One piece of advice – what would a letter from 'an older woman' be without a final word of wisdom? – start to think of yourself as an actor. If someone asks you, tell them you're an actor because you are what you think you are, and the more you hear yourself say it, the sooner you'll really believe it.

Well, that's it from this end. Break a leg, Jim Dean.

Lovingly,
Amanda

P.S. Oh, God, the most important thing. I changed my name! I'm called Amanda *Archer* now. The day I changed it, I got a part on *Suspense*, so I think it's lucky.

A.

James reads the letter quickly, and then again more carefully. He's got something real. Names of real people, real decisions to be made, a real course of action to follow. A practical, professional response from very far away; it reinforces the uplifting feeling that he has indeed embarked on an acting career.

He turns to the part of the letter that lists possible teachers. He invents them in his mind, their faces, their personalities. He imagines Serge Strangoff's voice; it's the same as the one that echoes off the pages of *An Actor Prepares.* Strangoff is his choice.

James is given the number of 'Acting and Actors' by the information operator. When he dials it, he is cheerfully informed by another operator that the number has been disconnected.

'Theater Arts Department.' It's a girl's voice, cold and uninspired.

'Uh, Martin, uh . . .' he forgets the name, '. . . uh, Glass . . . gold.'

She sighs. 'You mean Professor *Gold*glass.'

'Sorry, I'm having trouble with my glasses.' He waits for her to be amused. She isn't. 'Is he there?'

'Doubt it.' The pause indicates she might be checking. 'No, he's not in today.'

'Well, when can I get him?'

'Wouldn't bother if I were you.'

'Why not?'

'He never answers the phone. You sound cute, are you?'

'Yes. I'm very cute. Extremely cute. So how can a cute guy like me get to talk to him?'

'If you're honest-to-God really cute, I'll tell you.'

'I *am* honest-to-God really cute.'

'Who do you look like?'

James tries to think. 'You know Jeff Chandler?'

'Ye-es.'

'I get mistaken for him all the time. Except my hair's a little curlier.'

'Curlier! That's not possible.'

'But it's true.'

'He has office hours tomorrow at eleven. My name's Allison. I'll be in the main office. And I look like Martha Scott.'

'Hey, I think we were in a movie together. I was an Indian brave. You were the school marm.'

'Did you die?'

'Right in your arms.'

*

James knows this face. He's seen it overblown on the drive-in screen back home. It's off-putting to see it worn, human-sized, on a total stranger. Jenna would have recognized the name. She memorized all the picture credits. If you said Martin Goldglass to her, she'd have said, 'The little guy who strangles Raymond Massey in *Assignment Berlin*.' James still wouldn't have recognized the reference until Jenna described the movie's plot and zeroed in on the murder scene. James thought Jenna's memory remarkable.

Professor Goldglass, backlighted by a morning sun, tilts in his chair with his heels on the edge of the desk. A blue beret falls rakishly over one eyebrow. A full mustache and short gray goatee frame a stubby black cigar. If he senses James's presence, he doesn't acknowledge it, and apparently doesn't intend to. He reads a newspaper pleated lengthwise. James can see it clearly enough to realize he cannot understand the printed text. The *Racing Form*. James waits an inordinately long while to be noticed. He isn't.

''Scuse me. Professor?'

Goldglass doesn't respond.

James steps back to check the name on the door. He clears his throat.

'You won't go away, will you?' The gravelly voice is as familiar as the face, and as uncanny.

'I guess not.'

'What's your lucky number?'

'Nine.' James doesn't have a lucky number. Nine is Lem Craig's.

Goldglass studies the page and mutters, 'A switch to Longden today.' He shakes the newspaper. 'Possibility. Can you believe I'm reduced to playing lucky numbers?' He asks the question of the ceiling.

James doesn't know if he's expected to comment. He doesn't.

'Hoosier Holiday.' The Professor circles the name. 'Five-to-one.'

James blurts, '*I'm* a Hoosier. Fairmount, Indiana.'

'Did you know Hoosier Holiday was running today?'

'How would I know that?'

Goldglass snaps his fingers and points at James's chest. Then with the same finger, he dials the telephone. He stares at Hoosier

Holiday's recent form, looking for a mathematical justification. 'Gabe. Marty. The feature at Santa Anita. The nine horse, Hoosier Holiday. Yeah. A little bird just told me. Ten bucks across the board. I know that. Yes, I know it is, but I'm good for thirty bucks, for Christ's sake. Don't worry, I'll worry for both of us.' While Gabe is talking, Goldglass signals James to take a seat. 'Worse comes to worst. Gabe, you can have my other kneecap. Bless you, too, my *landsman*.'

Goldglass hangs up the phone and shakes his head. 'So, kid, what can I . . .?' He notices *An Actor Prepares* cradled in James's hand. He takes his feet off the desk and reaches out for the book, his face softened by memories of a time when his own copy was his most precious possession. Opening to the title page, Martin Goldglass whistles. 'My God, look at this! It's signed.'

James comes around the desk and begins to understand as he watches Goldglass poke at the signature. 'See. *Konstantin Stanislavsky*. This Russian phrase, what's it mean? This could be valuable.' He's far more excited than when he discovered Hoosier Holiday.

'I have no idea what it means. I didn't even know it was signed.'

'Listen, I'd like to have a picture taken of this page. Get it translated, but I'll have to keep it for a while. Okay?'

James shows reluctance, but he also realizes it means he'll get to see Goldglass again.

'I won't let anything happen to it. I know it's sacred stuff.'

'Sure. I guess so.' He has no idea that Goldglass has assumed him to be a matriculating student at the university.

Leafing through: 'You must carry this around with you to impress people, or do you actually read it?'

'Read it five times.' An untruth.

'So. What's the best thing in here?' He waggles the book.

James knows this is a critical question, a test. 'I guess how important it is to observe people. How every detail can tell you something important about them.'

'Tell me, what's the thing that would reveal something important about me?'

This one's even more critical. James must decide quickly exactly how honest to be. 'Well, that you're from New York.'

'So how? The way I bite off certain words?'

'More from the way you move parts of your sentences around. You drop phrases in at the beginning and at the end. And the way you use your hands for emphasis.'

'But that's just business. You really think *those* are the things that disclose basic character?'

James needs time to think. 'No, not really.'

'What, then?'

He's being pushed to a deeper truth, but it's something that might offend Goldglass. 'The "K"s, the "M"s, most all your consonant sounds, they're all just a little off. It's the thing that gives you a unique way of talking and makes people notice. It's probably a real good mannerism for the movies.' He takes a breath. 'But I think maybe you had to learn to say those sounds when you were a kid.' He'd rather not continue.

Goldglass indicates more with beckoning fingers.

James remembers the Stanislavsky dictum 'Acting is Risking' and says, 'I'd say there was some sort of speech impediment you had to overcome. That would be the real key to the character, so if I was playing you, I'd . . .' He lets the sentence trail off.

Martin Goldglass narrows his eyes at James and taps his fingers on the edge of his desk. 'They must be starting to grow some real wise-asses in Indiana. What brought you out to California?'

'My father lives out here.'

'Good reason to head East. Better yet the North Pole. Answer me this: If you were playing a woman, what one thing would you want to know about her life?'

James doesn't think, rather he isn't aware he's thinking: 'Only one thing?'

'One thing.'

'I guess I'd want to know what it feels like when . . . she has her time.'

Goldglass looks puzzled.

'That's what we call it back home.'

Goldglass winks. 'Got it. You know what I was thinking just the other day? How ideal it would be to live half your life as a man and the other half as a woman. You'd see some incredible performances then, let me tell you.'

James doesn't know what to say.

'Anything else you want to tell me about what you learned from Stanislavsky?'

'I like the part where he says you've got to develop all your intellect, learn everything in every field. It's an impossible thing, but I really dig that idea. I've started taking books out of the library on history. I realize I don't know doodley-squat.'

'Stop it, kid, you're killing me.' Goldglass leafs through the book. 'When I first got my hands on this, I felt like that too. It was like, as they say, the scales fell away from my eyes. So you win. What's your pleasure?'

'I'd like to get into your acting workshop.'

'Which one. Intermediate or Advanced?'

James isn't ready for this option. 'Both.'

'That proves you're not from Indiana.'

'I've got to make up for lost time.'

'Lost time? Hell, you're just a twit. You've got all the time in the world.'

James shakes his head emphatically. 'No. I should have started years ago.'

'What have you done?'

James sags. 'High school plays. But I won a contest in New York, at Columbia University.' Untruth.

'Don't say. So what's your name?'

'Jimmy Dean.' At that moment, it becomes his California name.

'Jimmy Dean. Why should I teach you what I know? I show you the secrets and you go out, get your hair streaked blond, your eyebrows dyed, and strike poses and I'd just be giving Sam Goldwyn another pretty boy to sell to all the Fairfields in America.'

'Fair*mount*. And I'm not a pretty boy.' James takes off his glasses and tilts his head. He relaxes his right eye in such a way that it falls out of balance in his face. He begins to look marginally normal; as the eye falls further, his tongue reaches toward his chin. His breathing becomes labored. He's starting to look like an imbecile. It's a trick he'd done for the other kids since eighth grade, long before he read about independent muscle control or a life in art.

'I get it. The Advanced is at 7 P.M., Thursdays.'

James keeps going. The imbecile falls to his knees, his hands locked in pleading.

'And for what it's worth, you were right. They operated on it when I was a kid. A harelip. That's why I grew the mustache. You got an ear. Did you happen to see Clift in *The Search*?'

James has only a vague sense that 'Clift' is an actor. He assumes *The Search* is a movie. He has no idea that both had been nominated for Academy Awards earlier that year. If he says he's seen the film, he runs the risk of getting caught in a lie: if he admits he hasn't, can he be taken seriously as an actor? 'He did such really interesting stuff.'

'How about the German accent? It wasn't too heavy for you?'

'No. I thought it was just right. Except maybe once or twice when he got excited.'

Goldglass looks at James and flicks at his beard with his thumb as though re-evaluating him. 'Didn't have a German accent. Better see it before you show up on Thursday.'

'I will. I promise.'

'Don't promise. Do it.'

*

That afternoon James scours the newspaper trying to find a theater where *The Search* is playing. It's at the Granada in Inglewood. If he offers to take Rhea, his father, who hates movies, will lend him the Ford. James Dean and his stepmother go to the movies together after an early dinner.

Montgomery Clift is an American soldier in Germany just after the war, trying to find the parents of displaced children. He's looking for the mother of one boy in particular: every lead ends in failure. At one point Clift and the boy are sitting by a river and the boy wonders if his mother is really alive, if she misses him. Clift explains that his mother is out there somewhere missing her son as badly as he misses her. 'Your mother. She loves you. She loves you always.' That reading, that last word, Clift delivers in a most surprising manner: he elongates the word and breaks it in the middle – 'all-*ways.*' Meaning the mother loves her child constantly and in every which way a mother can love.

Clift's performance confuses James. It doesn't seem like movie acting. Clift's idiosyncratic cadences baffle him; the rhythms make him uncomfortable. There's never the sense that Clift is repeating lines he's read in a script, and James gets itchy during the pauses, anxious over the uncertainties that play across Clift's face. It will take a while for James to realize he's seen something special.

When the lights come up, Rhea is dabbing her eye with a hankie. Her other hand is resting over her heart. She says, 'I feel I've been with them.'

James doesn't understand.

*

James has no way of knowing the result of the feature race at Santa Anita. Hoosier Holiday broke from the outside, got to the lead at the turn, and won going away by five lengths. Marty Goldglass paid $12.80 to win, $6.20 to place, and $3.60 to show. He won $83, which his bookie deducted from his $825 debt.

4. The Power of Yazzy

SANDY: original screenplay by Alan Sprewell; cinematography by Luge Gainert; art direction by Karl Gadeles; costumes by Edith Reade; directed by Sterling Dane; produced by Paul S. Grosse for U-A.

Sandy Johnson	*Peggy Fiske*
Harley Burgess II	*Ronald Tyler*
Harley Burgess	*Irving Davies*
Madeline Burgess	*Fay Watts*
Mandy Johnson	*Brenda Nix*
Sheriff Carleton	*Clem Craven*
'Bump' Kelly	*Clyde Donnell*

James saw Sandy *with Rhea in the Granada Theater on Santa Monica Boulevard. It was a Sunday evening in January 1950.*

Harley Burgess II, scion of a Southern textile family, falls in love with the daughter of the family's dark-skinned cook. Sandy, her daughter, is an octoroon. Against his parent's objections, young Harley pursues Sandy. Similarly, Mandy Johnson's attempts to cool her daughter's ardor are unsuccessful. When Sandy refuses to stop seeing his son, the father decides to have her secretly taken out of town. The men hired for the job accidentally kill Harley II.

In the film's only love scene, young Harley's lips approach Sandy's but never actually touch on camera. Leading up to that forbidden moment, young Harley has said to her, 'We live for the present, not the past or the future. And we live for ourselves, not for our parents or our parents' parents.'

Sandy: 'Course you can say that. You don't have to wear your history smack all over your face.

Harley: (He flashes his profile.) Are you kidding? This nose has been in the Burgess family for centuries.

Sandy: Guess it matters just what sort of history it is then.

Harley: History is bunkum.

Sandy: Not when history's written in dusky tones.

Harley: If this is history . . . (He runs a finger down her forehead, over her nose, stopping at her full lips.) . . . then history can be a very beautiful thing. (Their lips approach.)

James leans back in his chair and glares out across the desk from under a dangerous brow. His face fragments itself – eyes flaring, lips thinning, cheeks and chin uncertain. His complex reaction gives existence to an unseen antagonist. James looks straight up and takes a deep breath. A slow smile cracks his face. It is self-mocking, a wry awareness of a great cosmic joke working on him. He tries one last time to be reasonable: 'Trel flob. Po neuva nuvva slar-grue. Lewn hally a gram, ay flennack gloo wappy quin fort. Mal . . . slok . . . breniflan . . . woo . . .'

'That's fine, Jimmy. God help me, when I hear gibberish long enough, I begin to get a sense that even real words are nothing but empty sounds.' Goldglass, pulling at his goatee, comes toward the low stage: he's talking to sixteen students sprawled on the carpeted floor of his Advanced Acting class. 'Hate to admit it, but it sounds like gibberish is your native tongue. Okay, so what's the situation he was trying to show?'

A tan blonde girl Jimmy has had his eye on for a while says, 'Well, I get the impression he's gotten in some sort of trouble, maybe at school or something and is trying to talk his way out of it. And it's not working out so well for him.'

'I think,' says an Asian boy, 'he's asking someone important for something and it's not going so good.'

'Could be on target. Jimmy, what's the situation? In English, please.'

'Chan has it pretty right. I was in a bank . . .'

'*A* bank? Just *any* bank?' Goldglass raises his eyebrows to his beret.

'Actually it was the First Guarantee Trust in Fairmount, Indiana.'

'And?'

'I was talking to Mr. Marvin J. Kyle, vice-president and senior loan officer. He wants to repossess my '47 Buick.'

'What color?'

'Dark green.'

'There. That's the point, my little chickadees. You've got to be as specific as possible in your mind: believe it or not, so much of what's planted in your mind gets conveyed just because it's there. Of course, our avid Mr. Dean didn't want to leave anything to the imagination. That explains the cigarette behind the ear, the pack rolled in his sleeve.'

'Well, I figured . . .' He looks charmingly foolish. 'Figured the kid wouldn't know how to dress or even how to act when he gets to the bank. Either he didn't know or didn't want to do what he has to do to impress Kyle.'

'You see, take the language away, in fact more than away – turn it to gibberish – and see what you can do with what's left. It's the sort of exercise that takes a while before it begins to help you. At first, all you're thinking about is coming up with crazy sounds, so you can't really develop pacing and movement and reaction the way you will after you get the hang of it. It feels terribly unnatural, but trust me, you'll get the hang of it, even if you're not a native speaker like Dean here.'

Jimmy bows like a child and says, 'Gazornin fleep.'

'I first saw it done in a Stella Adler workshop. She said it was important because it mirrored the process of learning to absorb a text so well you can actually forget the words completely, at least consciously. She swore to us that someday we'd get so good the author's words would simply be there for us, exactly the way they are for people in everyday life. You want the truth? I'm still waiting for it to happen to me.'

Jimmy blurts, 'I got the feeling. Not for long, just in flashes, that I'd be able to know exactly what to say and do.' His eyes enlarge. 'It was kinda spooky, like acting and really being in the situation at the same time.'

'Jeesus, an exercise that could really work. I'll be damned.'

For weeks the lithe, mocha-skinned girl in the rear of the studio had tried to talk to Jimmy after class. Tonight she vows to approach him. But Jimmy is out the door chasing down Goldglass before Eusabia Gomez can get close.

Goldglass is placing his key in the office door when Jimmy runs up from behind. 'Got a minute, Marty?'

'Nothing cosmic, okay?'

'It's just that you haven't told me much about my work. I'm not in this class to get a grade. I'm in it . . .'

Goldglass unlocks the door and indicates *sit*. 'I know why you're here, Jimmy. And it would be a waste of time to tell you what you already know. You're good, that's a given. Seems to me, though, you've forgotten your Stanislavsky.'

Jimmy closes his eyes. No need for Goldglass to say the word. James knows it – the ego . . . the ego . . . the ego.

'I love the way you move on a stage. The warp of your body. Everything crooked, almost like you can't do anything straight. It's powerful stuff, expressive, lots of tension . . .'

James feels a tingling in his chest. The ego . . . the ego.

He always knows when a *but* is coming. '. . . but what you do instinctively isn't where you should be concentrating. That's just piling gold on gold.' The ego chill comes again. 'You can use some movement work. I'll call some friends. What you really need is dance. Voice training.'

Jimmy does a slow soft-shoe while seated and chants: 'Isn't it a lovely day for a walk in the rain . . .'

'Nothing trains you for movement like dance, nothing improves general tone and timbre more than singing. That's what I think you need. What do you think?'

'How much is all this gonna cost?'

'Money a big problem?'

'I have some saved. My old man'll lend the rest, I guess. It's just that I'd rather not take anything from him.'

'It won't be cheap – these are good people – but they're not going to sock it to you either. They're well worth their hire, believe me. It's your choice, kiddo, but the way I see it, what you'd be buying is time. You're going to need this training eventually, so the real choice is now or later. Begin it now and that means you'll be able to start working that much sooner.'

Until he hears the word, James had forgotten that being a *working* actor was actually the end result of this learning.

'Look, I'll find out what it'll cost. Then you decide. I'm just telling you it's what you could use. If you want me to tell you that you were good tonight, okay, you sure were. But you should have seen Jules do that same exercise when he was a kid. ("Jules" was Garfield to Goldglass.) Or what Clift would do with it. Remember, acting's exactly like the fight game, there's always someone tougher out there trying to climb over you. You're better off if you measure yourself against the best there is. No matter how good you were tonight, you're still going to have to pay your fare on the bus.'

'I have the car.' James stands. 'Guess you know best, Doc.'

'Guess?'

'Maybe I'd have more confidence if you ever got around to giving my Stanislavsky back.'

'Sorry, kid. I've got it right by the front door, I swear. I keep forgetting the damn thing.'

James is reaching for the doorknob. 'Sigmund's lace hankie.'

Goldglass screws up his face.

'Don't you remember the Freud story you told? The woman patient who left her handkerchief, her glasses case, something, every time she came to his office. How she always sort of forgot it on purpose.'

'Good try. Dead wrong. I want to return your book.'

In the hallway, leaning against the wall, her textbooks pressed against her chest: Eusabia Gomez.

'You waiting to see Professor Goldglass?' James asks. He sees a dark-skinned girl: he does not realize she's gorgeous.

'No.' A blush splashes her face. 'I sort of wanted to talk to you.' Her voice is unsteady, dry, the rhythms of Mexico.

Jimmy's charm clicks on like a thermostat. 'Well, I sort of wanted to talk to you, too.' He isn't completely sure this girl is in the workshop. She is his exact height. Their eyes are level. Hers are remarkable – almond-shaped with large rounded irises so dark and liquid it is virtually impossible for a man to look into them without feeling a touch of vertigo. In Jimmy's case, the sudden imbalance is combined with feelings of sorrow and protectiveness. His arm wants to wrap itself around her shoulders. He says nothing. Eusabia Gomez says nothing. She knows she should smile but her lips only waver. He knows he should speak but doesn't.

Without a word, they begin to stroll along the hallway toward the door. Each mind is racing through possibilities. They speak at the exact same moment and do not understand each other. Eusabia has said, 'I have no idea how to do . . .' Jimmy said, 'I guess you haven't done your . . .' They stop. At the doorway, James makes a sweeping 'after you' gesture.

Eusabia smiles and says, 'I see how you do the exercises and I swear I want to quit acting.'

'Come on, don't say that.'

'It's true. I do them dozens of times in my apartment and I know they just don't work.'

'So we'll make them work.' James offers his hand as though to seal a bargain.

Eusabia is confused but takes his hand and smiles. She is a deep well with dark, dark waters.

'Tell you what. Why don't we come in early and we'll practice before class?'

Her face becomes pinched, pained. 'Ohhhh, I can't. I work until 6:30. I just barely make it here on time.'

'Then, okay, we'll get together somewhere else. After class? Weekends?'

Her body sags. 'I've got to get home right after class.' She checks her watch. 'If I don't catch the bus, my brother . . .'

'I'll drive you home.'

'You don't have to.'

'I know I don't *have* to. Want to. We can talk about the exercises in the car.' He realizes he does not know her name and expresses this with a shoulder hunch.

She smiles beautifully: 'Yazzy.'

'Yazzy?'

'Eusabia, but they've always called me Yazzy.' Her accent – with stresses slightly different from the expected and the rolling 'R's – fascinates him.

'Yazzy. Mmmm. It's different. Exotic sounding. You won't have to change your name for the show business.' He's already begun to copy her speech patterns. It's not outright mimicry, but it isn't completely unconscious either. 'Where d'you live?'

She sags. 'Alhambra.' She makes it sound like an unlikely destination, as though she knows it's far out of Jimmy's way. It's true. Yazzy lives well past East Los Angeles, Jimmy due west.

'Great. Gives us lots of time to talk.'

Winton waits up on nights he's lent his jewel to his son. He's already begun to listen for the motor's hum in the driveway.

In the parking lot, Yazzy Gomez approaches the gleaming black car as though it's sanctified. Her eyes and lips round. A slight rush of air, not quite a gasp, is her comment.

'I'm looking to trade her in,' Jimmy lies. 'I keep her in good shape, but that new Chevy convertible, you seen it?'

Yazzy shakes her head.

'That's the dream car of dream cars, the dreeee-eem car.'

Yazzy slides in reverently.

James puts his glasses on and becomes studious-looking. 'So where to?'

Her face clouds over. She has no idea. 'I . . . I take the bus. I only know the way the bus goes.'

Jimmy laughs a true laugh and shakes his head. 'Tell you what, we'll wait at the bus stop and follow it to Alhambra.'

'But I change at Crenshaw.'

'How about I take Wilshire for as long as it's familiar to you?' She looks as though a great responsibility has been placed on her shoulders. 'No problem, Miss Yazzy. I'll find Alhambra one way or t'other.' He steals little looks at her as he drives east, but her concern never leaves. She's beautiful now.

'Acting.'

The word confuses her.

'How come you're interested in acting?'

'I can't explain. I feel free when I'm acting sometimes.'

'Becoming someone else?'

'A little bit of that.' She wants to say more. James lets it happen. 'It's my brother – the problem.'

'Are all actors' relatives horses' asses? My old man wants me to be a lawyer. A lawyer. Says it's exactly like acting except that it's steadier and it pays better.' Jimmy shakes his head and runs his hand through his hair.

'I'm supposed to become a nurse.' At a red light, they turn and look at each other for a long while. He has an urge to kiss her. She could be kissed. The light changes.

'That's a tough deal. What're you going to do?'

'I'm not sure. That's why I have to know if I can make it.'

He doesn't want to upset her, so he checks his first impulse. 'You know, I don't think it really works that way, Yazzy. I mean being careful, measuring this against that. Acting is just something you *got* to do. The more you're willing to go against your brother, the more it means you believe you're an actor. I mean, it's only your brother. It's not like it's your old man or something like that.'

'That's easy for you to say. You've got talent just dripping off you. Everyone can see it.'

'C'mon.'

'There's Crenshaw.' She points. He loves the slow liquidity of her movement. 'That's my bus, if you want to drop me off.' She looks over at him. He has a sudden urge to squeeze her very hard.

'Are you kidding? I've got to convince you not to give up the dream.' That's not what happens, though. After he angles over to Sunset Boulevard and east onto Mission Road, there is silence in the car. Eusabia Gomez has the sharp feeling she will never become an actress. And James begins to doubt he has any future with Yazzy.

The houses on the other side of Lincoln Park catch his eye. They're generally smaller than any he's seen, rundown and cramped into tight rows on streets laid out in a grid. Cars in various states of disrepair sit in driveways: more serviceable cars are on the street. 'It's right up there,' she says. He hears the quiver in her words. 'The corner's fine.'

He loves her voice. 'I've come all this way. I'll take you home.'

'No. This is fine. Really.'

People are clustered under street lamps; more shadowy figures are sitting on the steps. There is a sense of subdued gaiety. Talking, drinking, singing. Alhambra smells very different from Santa Monica, and it's not just the absence of sea air. Cooking oil , meat frying, simmering sauces – Alhambra smells like a kitchen to Jimmy.

Yazzy has opened her door a crack to keep James from turning into her street. She looks frightened.

'So when are we going to work on those exercises?'

She goes tense and doesn't answer. James observes a man approaching through the window on her side. Not yet a whole man, just the lower torso clothed in shiny black pants and a gold cummerbund. A hand holds a guitar case. Jimmy lowers his head and sees a ruffled shirt front and gold neckerchief. A face, dark and wide and frowning. Yazzy's brother?

Yazzy is quickly out the door without a look or a word back to James. He can see her approach the man. James hears him speak harshly in a language he assumes is Spanish. James does not hear Yazzy answer. She runs past him down the street. James starts to get out of the car, but the man is speaking to him through the window. 'Just leave the girl alone, Chico. I don't ever want to see this car in the neighborhood again. And I sure don't want to see your face.' The scar along his cheekbone gives him a sinister look.

It's the wrong place to make a stand. It's not even wise to try to explain, but Jimmy says, 'We're in the same class. I was just giving her a ride home.'

'Fuck "the same class." She don't need no rides. You just ride yourself the fuck out of here.'

'We were talking about acting.'

'Look, shithead, you get rolling or we hang you up from that telephone pole.' The *we* has an immediate effect. Jimmy starts to speak, sees the scar highlighted by the street lamp, and fires his motor. He'd like to burst away from the curb. The Ford races, lurches, and dies. He's in the wrong gear. So much for bravado. As he drives off, he sees the man in the silly costume watching him. He holds his guitar case away from his body.

James anticipates the sickening feeling; he doesn't expect it so soon. The throbbing hollow in the pit of his stomach, the metallic taste in his mouth, signs of pure cowardice. He knows leaving was a reasonable thing to do under the circumstances. That doesn't matter – what matters is he'd been chased off without putting up a fight.

He drives almost two miles before he realizes he's driving further east. The road begins to wind into the foothills. He pulls off the road on a curve and looks back toward the lights of Los Angeles. He knows he must return to that neighborhood, not only to claim Yazzy Gomez but to try and purge the shame he feels. The guy with the guitar has to be confronted. James's upper lip is wet with perspiration.

Before he does anything, he must talk to Yazzy. At school. He drives south to the San Bernadino freeway and then west back to downtown Los Angeles. His dialogue with himself occasionally drifts from pure thought to actual voices in his head. He's intensely alive for almost an hour.

As he pulls into the driveway of his father's stucco house, he notices the reading light in the front parlor. *Winton, you sure do have a knack.* The best strategy: in quickly and up the stairs. Quickly is the problem: there is no way to keep the blinds on the front door from slamming behind him.

It's not the blinds that undo him. It's Peewee the parakeet, still uncovered, suddenly screaming the greeting James had been trying to teach him for weeks. 'Hel-lo, Jim-bo. Jim-bo, Hel-lo. Eeeeeee.' Winton didn't need the bird or the blinds: there was no way the boy was getting past him tonight. He's in the doorway before Jimmy toes the first step.

'You're late tonight.'

'Had to drive someone home.' James hands Winton the keys. 'Other side of L.A.'

'Good that you're making friends.' James doesn't acknowledge that he's been spoken to. Winton slaps his leg with his newspaper. 'You able to give me a minute?'

The son exhales loudly, his body sags, a gesture that's always been very effective in making the father uncomfortable. It works yet again – Winston takes a step back and clears his throat. But he also adds, 'There are some things got to be settled.'

'Sure.' Grudgingly.

Winton sits on the divan. James leans against the molding of the archway.

'It's got to be real hard for you without a car of your own.' He waits for confirmation and gets a shrug. 'I told you I'd be more than glad to advance you the money to buy something decent.' In his son's eyes Winton looks shrivelled and loveless.

'I'd just as soon earn the money.'

'And you would be. Earning the money, that is. Just that you'd have the transportation while you were repaying me.'

'You worry that much when I've got the Ford?'

'Not me. It's more Rhea.' A slight untruth.

'Jesus, it's two nights a week.'

'Still. It'd be better all around if you had your own means. I heard about a pretty good job available. A car would help you get around.'

James Dean shrugs.

'I spoke to one of the owners at the lab. There's a chance for something regular, five days a week, and the possibility of making some decent money.'

The dance lessons, the voice lessons: yes, he's going to need more. 'Not at the lab. I couldn't handle that.'

'No. The fellow I spoke to is connected to the Los Angeles Museum of Modern Art.' He says the title with reverence. 'It's yours if you want it.'

'Doing what? Sponging down the naked statues?'

Winton appears to wince. 'Not letting people touch the paintings.'

James squeezes his closed eyes into the bridge of his nose. Some things you just can't argue with. The image of Yazzy's brother leaning into the car passes behind his eyes. He wants to slow things down. When he's acting, he controls the pace of events; in the world he always feels pushed too fast. 'Sure. Sounds good. Anything else?'

Winton looks up into his son's eyes and sees insolence. 'Been thinking about school at all?'

'I'm going to school.'

'I mean enrolling, working toward a degree.'

'Becoming a mouthpiece, you mean.'

'Becoming . . .' It's Winton's turn to sigh. 'Listen, son, the world was here long before you were, and it runs a certain way. It doesn't make exceptions for people like us. We've got to obey the rules of the game. And rule number one is that the world gives you nothing lest you earn it. You got to be able to supply food, clothing, and shelter for yourself and your family. That's the economic reality of living anywhere in this world. Why you think it doesn't apply to you is something I can't comprehend.'

The words *people like us* spill over and over. They begin to ring in his ears.

'Acting on stage, it's something you like to do. All well and good. I'm glad you have an activity you can enjoy so much. But, my God, Jimbo, didn't you ever hear about the difference between vocation and *a*vocation, between what you do for pleasure and do to earn a living? You like acting on a stage, and there's nothing wrong with that – as an avocation. But in the real world you've got to have a practical way to earn a living. At the very least you should have some profession the world values, if not as your first choice, then as a back-up in case the acting doesn't work out the way you hope.'

James sees more clearly than ever that the differences between them are purely a matter of temperament, and are unbridgeable precisely for that reason. They share none of the same premises about their lives. They should never be lumped together as *people like us*. 'I think sometimes that maybe I got switched in the hospital or something. I swear. We have nothing in common.' A comic observation because they look so much alike. James suddenly implores: 'Don't you see that if you believe in back-ups, or in what-am-I-going-to-do-in-case-of-this-or-that, then you might as well hang 'em right up because you don't really believe in anything. And you sure as heck don't believe in yourself or in risking everything for what you *do* believe in. I'm going to be an actor. That's it. Period. If I fail, they'll have to kill me and then they'll have to eat me, 'cause I won't ever walk away and go shopping around for the next best thing.'

Winton gestures toward Los Angeles. 'I'm just telling you how things are out there. You've always been headstrong, and I just don't want to see you do something stupid with your life.'

Their voices have stayed under control while getting louder. The effect is a mad rationality. James doesn't want to invoke his mother's name: it just sort of happens. He pushes himself away from the wall and mutters, 'She'd have understood how things are.'

Winton shouts. 'Your mother would have felt exactly as I do.' He feels suddenly self-conscious or perhaps conscious of Rhea listening. He whispers coarsely, 'She had a practical side to her, too. She knew the value of a practical education. We always talked about your going to college. Always.'

'Mom would have believed in me if I told her this is what I wanted for myself. Man alive, she'd have been right with me, pushing me even, if I ever began to lose heart. And you know she would. I'm going to bed.'

'We haven't settled this thing.'

'What thing? If I'm going to become a lawyer?'

'The job. The car.'

'I told you, sure.'

Another father would have touched his boy at that moment. Either to shake him or slap him, to tousle his hair or to put him in a headlock. A dozen different ways to make contact, each with a different but perfectly acceptable way of indicating a resolution. Winton Dean cannot. James Dean would not have known how to respond. Neither one of them knows if Winton Dean truly wants to connect with his only son.

James takes the stairs three at a time. Winton puts the cover on Peewee the parakeet.

*

Of all the possibilities he had considered during the week, the one James never imagined was that Yazzy Gomez would not have come to the workshop. He gets there early so he can talk to her, find out more about her life in Alhambra, about the forces that seemed to be oppressing her. To provide the sharing of personal fears on which friendships can be built. Yazzy didn't come early.

James is just off stage left doing his stretches and his breathing: it's a spot from which he can see the door. Other students drift in and pair off to practice their gibberish exercises. Murmurs in the studio build to a soft roar. Still no Yazzy.

After class begins, Jimmy has trouble concentrating on his exercises. She's not there. Is she all right? Will she be there next week? He resolves to go looking for her after class.

He clearly remembers Mission Road and going beyond Lincoln Park. That's when all the streets begin to look alike. He'll try them all if he has to, but he starts by parking near a corner that seems the most familiar. He asks a group of kids sitting on the curb where the girl called Yazzy lives. Giggling and shrugging. 'Yazzy. Her brother plays the guitar. He dresses up sometimes.'

A girl in a black silk blouse and white shorts points further down the street and ducks her face between her knees.

On a stoop in front of a four-storey brick building, people are talking, listening to a Spanish radio station, a few boys play catch with a pink ball, girls jump rope, some of the older kids are practicing mambo steps. James feels his heart beating as he approaches the crowd. Movement and conversation slow and stop. ''Scuse me. I'm looking for a girl called Yazzy.'

The reaction isn't too different from the kids on the curb. Giggles. Silence. Embarrassment. But no response.

'I go to school with her. I got to see her.'

'Yazzy Gomez. Next house. Second floor.' A heavy woman standing in the doorway points with a broom.

'Thanks a lot. *Muchas gracias*.' They titter. He hears them mocking his speech as he walks toward the clapboard next door. A pale light glows in two upstairs windows. James listens to the voice – the voice with his voice – that talks to him in times like these: *Just do it. By stages. Up the stairs. Knock on the door. Get through it. One step . . . and one step . . .* His intention is not to take Yazzy out of there, although he's going to give it a try. He simply has to undo last week's humiliation. Knocking on the door and just asking for Yazzy would accomplish that.

The front door is partly open. Steep stairs rise from obscurity into greater obscurity. The voice reminds. *Got to do it. One step . . . and one . . .* Of course he'll do it. He's already started up the stairs. The intense drama of the situation is not wasted on him. He thinks fleetingly about knocking on the door and talking gibberish with a Spanish accent. He smiles and snorts a laugh. A good sign.

At the top of the stairs, it takes a long moment for his eyes to acclimatize themselves to the darkness. He cannot find a name. There is none. He must knock on a door that may or may not belong to Eusabia Gomez. There's no need to run his fingers through his hair before he knocks, but he does. No need to practice his best smile either.

He hears a man's voice coming from a distant room. The response, also in Spanish, comes from closer: a woman's voice, deeper, more sensual than Yazzy's. He assumes it's her parents. A favorable thing: he's good with older people. He readies his charm and knocks cleanly on the door three times.

There's no response. He knocks louder. The man's voice resonates against the door from afar. *Abri a puerta.*

No tengo traje.

Es Olgarita.

The door swings open. A woman stands before him. In a brassière and half-slip. The two gawk at one another: no words, no movement. She has recognized him immediately; he is unsure, or chooses to be. She is fuller of body than Yazzy; her loose hair falls over her shoulders in lines very different from Yazzy; she does not have Yazzy's modesty. Her expression – a mix of embarrassment, fear, disgust – gives her away.

Jimmy says, 'Yazzy?' He can see the man he thought was her brother reflected in a mirror on the wall beyond her. On a bed completely naked pulling on a bottle of beer. His legs are crossed at the ankles. His cock, round as a potato, rests against his thigh.

She sees James looking past her and closes the door until just her nose and an eye are revealed. 'I can't talk,' she whispers.

He whispers too, but irritably: 'What the hell are you doing to me?'

'To you. Nothing. I can't talk.' She halves the opening.

'Come to class next week.'

'I'll try.'

'Come.'

'Okay.'

'Promise.'

'I'll come.'

He burns his eyes into hers.

'I will come.'

His eyes have become accustomed to the dark: he sees the man in an undershirt and boxer shorts standing at the foot of the stairs. James must descend to another confrontation. The man says sarcastically, 'Lookin' for someone?'

'Found them. No problem.'

'You know those locos?' He motions upstairs.

He'd like to get by. ''Scuse me.' The man refuses to yield: 'You tell 'em it's disgusting. An' we're gonna do something about it.'

'How's about moving?' Jimmy feels the beginning of rage stoking up in his stomach. His fists start to close.

The man backs into his doorway. 'Everybody wants them out. Dirty the place up for decent people, living like that.'

James wants to ask, *Like what?* He doesn't want to know *Like what?* He hears a woman's voice from within the apartment, elaborate curses in Spanish directed upstairs.

Immediately after class the following week, Jimmy looks for Goldglass in his office. If he hadn't, Goldglass would have been looking for him. 'What the hell got into your head tonight?' Goldglass could have said the same thing without conveying quite so much disappointment.

Jimmy opts to play dumb. 'I need some more work on the accent is all.'

'I'm not talking about your goddamned accent. I'm talking about trying to get your head out of your ass. I'm talking about *preparing* Sir Anthony Absolute and not just reading his fucking speeches. Once upon a time there was a book called *An Actor Prepares*. Remember?'

'You're right, you're right.'

'So what, what?'

'What I told you about.' He proceeds to tell Goldglass the story of the Yazzy mystery from the first meeting in the hallway outside this office to the cryptic encounter in the dark through a partly opened door. He includes all the salient details – the scarred man with the guitar, his shame at being chased away, the astonishing difference in Yazzy's appearance, that same guy on the bed naked, the downstairs neighbor.

'So?'

'So what should I do about it?'

'What the hell am I, the Answer Man?'

James stands, hurt by the sarcasm.

'What's the thing that bugs you most, that she's not the nice girl you thought she was or that she just might be *shtupping* her own brother? And what attracts you most? The come-on, the lies, or the incest?' The word disgusts him, an observation Goldglass doesn't miss. 'You've fallen into a weird situation. You've got to ask yourself what you really want the truth to be: that he's not really her brother or that he is? It's for you to figure out.'

James imagines the uncertain, demure girl he drove to Alhambra: replaces the image with the ripe woman in the doorway, the valley between her breasts burned in his memory. The menacing man on the bed. His fat cock.

'Listen, kid, sometimes I forget just how young you are. Doesn't mean you don't owe me one. And I want to see it next week. Right out there in the studio.'

'You got it.' His enthusiasm is hollow.

'I'd like you to play a scene. Something different, maybe European. Let's say Ibsen's *The Wild Duck*.'

'I'll give it my best shot.' Hollow still.

Goldglass thinks to say *Promise?* but checks himself.

*

The car is an old Hudson. Winton's choice; the best deal around, given the fact he wants to buy quickly. In excellent condition inside and out, a little less than 43,000 miles on the odometer, the Hudson had belonged to a retired railroad man who had died two weeks earlier. His wife hopes for $150. Winton says, 'Right here and now. No need to talk or bargain. I'll give you $110 cash.' He produces a roll of bills from his pants pocket. She looks into her hands folded in her lap and nods. James watches with pursed lips but never says a word: he is becoming a very good observer of need, desire and compliance. Stanislavsky would have been proud. Perhaps he is simply destined to own a Hudson. When he's behind the wheel, he can't help thinking about Lem Craig, to whom he still hasn't written.

The understanding is that Winton will take half the cost of the car from James's savings, the rest to be paid out weekly from his museum job. When James offers his father $55 at dinner that night, Winton won't take it. The experimenting Peewee chatters 'Hel-lo, Jim-bo' in slightly different voices and rhythms. Rhea, smiling broadly and serving food in a most subdued manner, acts as a silent but integral part of her husband's generosity.

Winton, raising a glass of soda water, offers, 'A boy's first car is an important thing. You could call it an honest-to-God rite of passage.' It's his best joke in a long time and he repeats 'Rite-of-*passage*, get it?' Rhea looks at him as though he were a dickens.

James raises his glass of tap water as if to recognize the toast and accept the bequest. But he has not actually said the words, 'Thank you.'

*

His reasons for going back to the apartment yet again couldn't be explained very clearly. It's just something he feels, a constant unease in his stomach. He decides to go late on a Saturday night – the 'brother' might be working. She might be alone.

He believes he can find the street and the house easily. He's wrong and has to circle the streets of Alhambra searching for the small apartment house with its celebrants on the front porch. Because he's coming from a different direction, he almost drives past: he's fortunate to hear a *jota* that gets his attention.

Lights in the house next door are burning on both floors. The upstairs lights are paler. It makes him feel she really is alone.

There's no reason for silence but he closes the car door quietly and walks over the pavement on the balls of his feet. Breath quivers in his chest: he is intensely alive. He hasn't the faintest idea of what he'll say to her and prefers it that way.

A shrill voice is flying out of the downstairs window, its anger mellowed by the music in the air. James believes he can understand this language if he wills it. He could be Mexican, Spanish, anything: he's an actor after all, the ultimate shape changer.

He doesn't see the man sitting on the front steps until a cigarette lights the darkness. Same undershirt, same man, same brow-beating from the shrill voice within.

The man's eyes narrow as James approaches. He does not give way as James moves past. James brushes his arm with the screen door.

Again the steep stairway. Again the unknowable. Again the taste of danger. He climbs deliberately and raps on the door with a single knuckle. He hears soft music inside turn softer. Then in a flash he knows what will happen. She will come with him, they'll find some place to live, as she did with the guitarist. He raps again.

The door opens slowly. He sees her eyes, her fright. James feels faint with possibilities. The door stops at exactly the moment he hears the catch in her breath. She is wearing a flowered kimono. She whispers, 'N-o-o-o.'

He says, 'Yazzy.' In the name there is a plea: *Explain to me. Make me understand.*

'I couldn't . . . I don't . . . it's so mixed up.'

'Is he here?'

'Coming back soon.'

'Let me in. A minute. I can help.'

Eusabia Gomez snuffs a cruel laugh and repeats, '. . . help,' but she does open the door and steps backward against the kitchen table. He wants to embrace her – one animal protecting another. She shies, unworthy of protection.

'Tell me. You want to stay with him?'

'I've been with him.'

'Who is he?'

'I told you.'

'Your brother?'

'Half.'

James is confused, absolutely unable to fathom the concept of a half brother, unwilling to work out the details. 'You want to stay with him?'

Yazzy begins to laugh, confusing him more: it is her way of

crying. She turns away. A muscle in her back is pulsing. He reaches out to touch the quiver beneath the floral pattern. He will not be able to remember if he actually touched Yazzy or not.

The voice behind him is melodic with sarcasm. 'You don't stop, do you, Chico? We'll have to heat up some *tortillas* for this boy, won't we?'

Yazzy sees him first and reaches in front of James, shielding him with her palms.

'We don't have to have any trouble,' Jimmy says. He's gone to a slight defensive crouch, hands low, fingers spread.

'Throwing you down the stairs won't be any trouble, Chico. It'll be a pleasure.'

What would Lem do? Rush him. Come in low. Try to take the breath out of him against the wall. 'Listen, we could sit down and talk . . .'

'*No hablamos Gringo aqui.*' Even his scar is smiling.

Yazzy says, 'Ramon, no.' She sees his arm moving behind his back.

Jimmy says, while indicating passivity by easing his body, 'Come on, *amigo*, there's no reason for . . .' Then in a blink he's lunging forward, low but balanced, as though coming in for an open-field tackle. The runner isn't there. He has quickly darted to the side and delivered a sharp kick to Jimmy's ribs. James is crumpled, breathless against the kitchen wall. Yazzy's screams come to him from a great distance.

James is on the floor, completely disoriented, being rolled over, and over. He pushes aside chairs and the table. He grasps the door jamb with all his might and has his hands torn away. Now he's being stood on his feet. His mind wants to throw a punch but it's impossible: instead, he gets hit in the stomach and loses all breath. He is sucking air like a beached fish. He hears laughter and crying. Again he is stood up. He sees the glint of light on metal. A cool slash. Then he's tumbling through the air, striking an elbow, a knee, his head. Landing in a heap at the bottom of the stairs.

He sees faces. The neighbor in his underwear. A woman, his wife, her hair in ringlets pressed against her head by a net. James wants to speak but there is no breath. He gasps, 'I'm okay . . . I'm okay' half a dozen times before he hears the voice.

With more awkwardness than pain he tries to right himself on the stairs. 'I'm okay.' Then he and the neighbors see the T-shirt pooling. The woman howls. The shirt is blotting blood above and below the long slit across his abdomen. The blood runs off his jeans and begins to puddle on the carpet.

In the ambulance, the pressure clamps stop the flow. The gash is not deep. He sits with his knees up to his chest. An attendant says, 'You got lucky.'

Jimmy snorts.

'Really. He didn't get any muscle, none of the organs. It's more like a shaving cut a few feet below the chin.'

'That's real funny.'

The attendant shows a clipboard: 'Who should we contact? Family? I need a name?'

James blinks and says, 'Mr. Martin Goldglass. He's in the book.'

*

In the hospital emergency room, he sees, swimmingly, a variety of victims of Saturday mishap and malevolence. He fastens on a young woman who is not injured, her hair in a bun, a knowing smile on her serious face. He has the distinct feeling he's seen her before but isn't sure where: he believes she is here to reassure him, to assist his recovery. The dress, the flowered print: he has seen it before. He closes his eyes and half expects her to disappear when they reopen. She is still there, though, smiling encouragement.

5. Inner Man, Outer Man

THE MOON AND SIXPENCE: adapted from W. Somerset Maugham's novel by Albert Lewin; directed by Mr. Lewin; presented by David L. Loew-Albert Lewin, Inc., and released through United Artists.

Charles Strickland	*George Sanders*
Geoffrey Wolfe	*Herbert Marshall*
Dirk Stroeve	*Steve Geray*
Blanche Stroeve	*Doris Dudley*
Captain Nichols	*Eric Blore*
Dr. Coutras	*Albert Basserman*
Mrs. Strickland	*Molly Lamont*
Ata	*Elena Verdugo*

When he heard that The Moon and Sixpence *was about Paul Gauguin, James drove to the Granada expecting to learn about a painter Amanda Boyce had mentioned admiringly. The movie confused him. The main character wasn't French at all, but an English painter named Charles Strickland. James didn't know that the movie was only loosely based on Gauguin's life.*

In the scene that left the deepest impression on him, the movie's narrator, Geoffrey Wolfe, interviews Dirk Stroeve, a second-rate painter whose wife, Blanche, has been seduced by Strickland. The wife eventually commits suicide. Stroeve tells Wolfe of seeing Strickland's nude painting of his wife.

Stroeve: I don't know what happened to me. I was just going to make a great hole in his picture, I had my arm ready for the blow, when suddenly I seemed to see it.

Wolfe: See what?

Stroeve: The picture. It was a work of art. I couldn't, wouldn't touch it. I was afraid . . . It was a great, wonderful picture. I was seized with awe. I had nearly committed a dreadful crime. I moved a little to see it better and . . . I shuddered.

J ames walks the salons of the Los Angeles Museum of Modern Art slowly, painstakingly. Not so much because of the wound across his stomach, but because of the adhesive tape on his skin and the tightness of the gauze wrap that starts just below his nipples and runs down to his hips. He's only missed three days of work.

He swings his legs, stiff at the knee, in small arcs from the hip joint, just allowing the soles of shiny black shoes to slide over polished oak parquet. The shuffling movement produces a faint, rhythmic *shush, shush, shush*.

This frailty is new to him. Ankle and knee injuries when he was playing ball in Fairmount weren't comparable; the stomach, he has come to realize, drives everything. As he moves tenderly from room to room, he's unaware the walk is a kind of rehearsal. He'll use it in his movies to give the impression of extreme vulnerability.

The job requires him to move steadily from the 'Pre-Impressionists' all the way through a salon labeled 'Our Contemporaries.' If there are any people lingering in a gallery he's to stop and look at them with a friendly wariness. The most important requirement is just to be seen to be watching. He gets to practice expressions that range from imperious to suspicious. Other than the walk and the facial expressions, he doesn't think much about acting; he doesn't think at all about the surprising colors and forms of modern painting or its connection with the acting revolution. He simply shuffles through the museum for fifty minutes of each hour trying not to think at all, and rests on the sofa in the Employees Lounge for the other ten.

When he complained to Goldglass about the boredom, the mentor huffed. 'Boring? Are you kidding? Art galleries are the best, the absolute best place, bar none, to pick up women. Great women too – deep and soulful – more than a twit like you could possibly handle. And he says "boring."'

'Maybe, but they make me wear this goopy-looking uniform and cap.'

'Even better. It gives you something to play against.'

James made a few attempts with girls in 'Dada and Cubism' without success. He attributed his failure to the costume rather than his surreal ignorance about the paintings.

Since his first week on the job, however, only one painting has drawn his attention. It is in the small, out of the way 'Expressionist' salon. He knows 'Expressionism' is also a movement in drama but isn't exactly sure what. He keeps meaning to ask Goldglass about it. And keeps forgetting.

The painting is dark: in black, grays, browns and dark blues with thin highlight lines in white. It was done with a heavy hand; the glistening paint thickly applied. The plaque alongside reads '*Inner Man, Outer Man*, 1934: Emile Voltanz (1898–1943?). Hungarian. Oil on canvas. 35″ × 27½″.' It is the only painting by Voltanz in the museum.

James *shushes* over to it now, as he often does on his first tour of the day. He knows it well, yet every time he stops he notices something new. The brush strokes are thick and wide, almost grotesque. A man's round face and upper torso – brown, but he could be of any race, or the composite of all races – form the center of the canvas. This morning James makes something of the fact that the painted body ends in the precise place where he'd been slashed. On the head, the casually painted outline of a Chinese peasant hat. Yet the figure is Caucasian. James wonders if a Chinaman or an African would see the painting in the same way. The face reveals nothing specific because the features are so artlessly rendered, a child's idea of 'A Man.'

Slightly off-center and within the outline is another man – rather, another version of the same man; less brusque, better but still not cleanly articulated. Without resorting to obvious color contrasts, the artist has managed to make the inner figure the photographic negative of the outer, yet both men are dark. On the left side, the outline of the inner man bursts through the boundary of the outer; where it is exposed to the world, it goes soft; the paint mixes and thins, color dissipates.

Maybe he's a little woozy because of the pain, but as he stares at *Inner Man, Outer Man* the figures begin to change places. Inner Man begins to expand and pulse to the limit of the Outer Man. At the limit the outlines blur, but the inner grows beyond the outer. *Optical illusion*, James thinks. *Like 'which line is longer?' Switching places because I'm looking too hard.* He reaches to his breast pocket for his glasses: they're back in the lounge.

James moves away from the painting, and the Inner Man shrinks back inside where he belongs. A young woman, her hair in a page-boy, walking noiselessly on tiptoe in high-heeled shoes, brushes against him as he backs away from the painting. ''Scuse me,' he says without looking. When he takes his eyes off the churning portrait, he sees a wisp of her floral skirt trailing out of the salon. He takes a quick step in that direction and feels a stab of pain; he looks back over his shoulder at *Inner Man, Outer Man*. James glides again toward the painting and the captive form begins to push to the boundary again. Shaking his head, James tips his cap back like a wise-guy cab driver. He slides backward slowly and the Inner Man begins to recede. *Get back where you belong.* He's spoken out and surprised an elderly couple just entering the salon. They stop and watch him in silence.

James shuffles forward and backward, narrowing and widening his eyes. At a distance of about fifteen feet, each figure seems to be in its proper place. He backs away once again: *Jesus, look at that, will you.* The couple look at the muttering guard, at the object of his fascination, at each other.

At a certain point, try as he might to differentiate, James sees a single, thickly outlined, primitive figure – a simple man, age indeterminable. He's almost backed right into the couple, who unlink their arms and scurry aside.

'Sorry. I swear I must've looked at that painting a hundred times and I never . . .' He shakes his head in disbelief.

The woman's smile is neighborly, hoping to convey her support. Her husband's brow is furled with concern.

James takes it as a sign of interest and says to him, 'That painting changes, really changes. It looks like one man now, doesn't it?'

The man doesn't take his eyes off James and says, 'We didn't come to make trouble.'

'Just walk toward it slowly and you'll see it's really two men, one inside the other.'

The wife tugs on her husband's arm. 'There's supposed to be a Braque in the next room, Frank.' They exit on tiptoe.

James works his way not quite painlessly back through the salons toward the entrance.

In the lobby, a large class of ten-year-olds brings a sinking feeling to his tightly bound stomach. He'll have to watch them for the entire tour. There goes his break.

He walks over to Clara Dompf, cheerful, chubby Clara, who sells the tickets, guides the groups through the museum and runs the souvenir shop. She's just about to tinkle her bell and start the children on the first gallery: drawings by Ingres and David. 'One minute, Clara. Do we have anything on Voltanz?'

The boy has never before asked her anything related to art. His most frequent request is, 'I'd like to go out and get some ciga-rettes.'

He amplifies: 'The guy who painted one man inside the other?' He tilts his head toward the Expressionist room.

'Emile Voltanz!' She corrects his pronunciation, 'No, we haven't any material. But there is a biography in the catalog.'

'Could I have a look at it?'

'Not right now, James. I have to . . .'

'Do me a favor, Clara. I'll get 'em ready to go.' He sweeps an arm toward her office while taking a step toward the kids. 'Looky here, chilluns.' It's a phrase Ortense always used when Marcus and Jimboy were bickering. 'Y'all have this great big glorious opportunity today. And I'm here to help make sure you get the absolute most of it.' He captures their attention with the volume of voice, its off-beat rhythms, and spooky-looking eyes. 'You're in eleventh grade, right?'

The kids giggle and yell, 'Nooooo! Fifth.'

'Fifth? I can't believe it. None of you act like fifth-grade cock-a-mamies.' They giggle at the word. 'Fifth grade? Can't believe it. I first came to this museum when I was in fifth grade myself, and you know what . . .?' He lowers his voice by degrees until it's barely audible. He creates Montgomery Clift pauses and tensions. 'In every single room here there is one picture that has magical powers. No, I'm not kidding. I won't tell you which ones they are. But if you look carefully and the room is quiet, you'll be able to feel which picture has the power. You'll know because it will hold your eyes. You won't be able to look away even if you want to.' He goes googly-eyed and the kids wail with exaggerated laughter. 'But . . . when I first came here with my class, I didn't believe the pictures could have that kind of power. And you know why? Because I didn't respect them enough. And do you know what else? I was . . .' He leaves the sentence full of expectation. '. . . punished.' He repeats, 'Yes, punished. A terrible, terrible punishment.'

'What was the punishment?' a girl asks.

'I was never allowed to go home . . . been here for fifty-seven years.' His raised eyebrows ask, *What do you think of that?*

They're confused, don't know what to think.

Clara hands James the catalog and leads the children off as fast as possible.

Sitting propped on a sofa in the lounge, James finds a disappointing black and white photograph of Voltanz's painting on page seventy-two. Below, this biographical paragraph: 'Born the son of a Jewish intellectual in the Pest section of the Hungarian capital, Voltanz opted for the Bohemian life. Fueled apparently by the revolutionary ideas sweeping the Slavic world, he left his university studies abruptly and threw himself passionately into his painting. Without formal training, he was nevertheless quickly accepted by artists in Paris and Berlin. He was said to have a severe stutter and, as a result, rarely spoke in public; his diaries, however, are replete with effective descriptions of the artistic process and the life of the artist in the modern world. His work was often a powerful influence on other artists, Malevich and Nolde, in particular. He is said to have perished in Dachau in 1943, but absolute proof of his demise has not been established.'

James lets out a whistle, more air than tone. There is more, a description of *Inner Man, Outer Man,* apparently from Voltanz's diary: 'Every year we spend on this earth inevitably creates a greater distance between the public person – the one who shops for groceries, takes the bus to work, speaks on the telephone, goes to the cinema with a friend – and the person within – the one with whom, all life long, we communicate our fears, our needs, our aspirations. Permitting the separation between the public self and the private is the worst sort of self-deceit. It is the artist's task to give the inner self public expression. When one chooses (as though we ever *choose* our original path!) a life in art, one does no less than pledge to bare the secrets of the deepest soul . . .'

James runs his finger back over the sentence. There it is, the phrase, Stanislavsky's phrase – 'a life in art.' He mutters Stanislavsky's opening sentence: 'It is not an accident that brings people together in art.' Nor is it an accident that today he is reading a dead man's words about the actor's greatest challenge, how to bring the inner man to a theater full of people with only the outer man's techniques. No, this can't possibly be an accident. This is design.

He reads on, confident he will be shown a way: '. . . secrets of the private soul. But are these secrets individual idiosyncrasies or matters of wider and deeper significance? They are both. If we dare to share the secrets of our private hearts, no matter how perverse they may seem, we inevitably discover a matching human sympathy. (In this way I have made my closest friends in life and art.) Dare to reveal the private self that other people choose to isolate and keep hidden and you suddenly discover a veritable army of similar hidden selves in others. This is the world's best kept secret.

'In *Inner Man, Outer Man* I have attempted to project the process – requiring more bare courage than intellect – by which the two selves can become unified. Truth is the harmony. I cannot tell if I have succeeded. I must say in candor, that to produce my desired theme, I have resorted to a *trompe-l'œil.* There ought be no flummery or trickery in the transforming personality. This work gives me hope that in time I shall achieve a purity in technique to match the purity of my intent. Even fakery to achieve a higher good is to be despised. Emile Voltanz, Berlin, 1935.'

Without knowing what *trompe-l'œil* means, James understands the statement of Voltanz to constitute a troubling discovery. Since there are no accidents in art, even his being wounded is part of the conjunction of positive events.

It is time to get to his feet, or try to. The pain of the cut feels old: the throb of a hot liquid cooling. The sting of the adhesive is sharper than the wound, an insult to the outer man.

He runs his middle finger lightly over the wound and reaches for a cigarette he doesn't have. His thoughts run to Yazzy's brother, lover. *Probably just trying to help bring out my inner man.* He eases back on the sofa. The pain is approaching a perversely pleasant level.

With hungry eyes, unaware that his chest is heaving, he searches the text for some nourishing phrases . . . *more bare courage than intellect.* Even though he is in fact brave, he believes himself wanting in courage. *Truth is the harmony* . . . When you're so involved with techniques – the gibberish exercises, isolation and cooperation of body parts, the inanimate object and animal drills – where then is the core of character, the rock-bottom truth of personality? . . . *can be no trickery in the transforming personality.* A trickster, a conjurer only, a player of games, a theatrical con-man. And finally the crusher: *Fakery to achieve a higher good is to be despised.*

He's worked himself into a depressed state plenty of times before. Now, though, he is forced to smile and then chuckle at his extreme physical and emotional despair.

At this precise moment in the Employees Lounge of the Los Angeles Museum of Modern Art, James Dean has forgotten he is an actor. An easy thing to do because he hasn't acted a complete role in more than a year. If he could only act, he'd have a chance to bring his inner self into some sort of harmony with his outer; if not that, he'd at least have the chance to introduce the one to the other.

He hadn't performed in public. That's why his life was without risk and constructive terror, without focus and the right sort of self-love.

*

'I am not working for my own sake. Far from it. It is my life's mission that is in my thoughts night and day.' He sits on a stool near the edge of the low stage, working with his fingers as though pulling a photograph through developing solution.

Goldglass, as Gregers, stands stage left and just a bit behind James. He says, 'What mission?'

James closes his eyes and tips his head to a portrait of his father, which he believes – knows – is actually there: 'The old man with the silver hair . . .'

Goldglass runs his finger over the script line: '. . . but what exactly do you think you can do for him?'

Hjalmar laughs soundlessly at himself. He does not look at Gregers: 'I can resurrect his respect for himself by once again raising the name of Ekdal to fame and honor.'

'So that is your life's mission.'

Hjalmar the photographer is completely absorbed in his emerging photograph and responds absently: 'Yes. I will rescue that shipwrecked man. For he was shipwrecked the moment the storm broke. During those terrible inquiries he was not himself. The pistol over yonder . . .' James does not look at it, but it is there, '. . . the one we use to shoot rabbits with – it has played its part in the tragedy of the Ekdal family.'

'The pistol? Really?'

James, now utterly absorbed in his work, mumbles, 'When sentence had been pronounced and he was to be confined – he had that pistol in his hand –'

'He tried to –'

James pulls his photograph out of the liquid. He says nothing.

Not everyone in the class had read *The Wild Duck*. Some didn't even know they were watching Ibsen. Dean had not only read the play twice, he'd read *Hedda Gabler* and *An Enemy of the People* as well as a new biography. (One line unlocked Hjalmar's character for him: 'Take the vital lie away from the average man, and you take his happiness, too.') He thinks of it before he looks toward Goldglass. 'Yes, but didn't dare. He was a coward. So much of a wreck, so spiritually ruined was he already then. Can you understand it? He, an officer, the killer of nine bears, descended from two lieutenant colonels . . . can you understand it, Gregers?'

'I can indeed.'

'Not I – But the pistol came to figure in our family chronicle a second time . . .' Hjalmar pauses. His non-existent photograph is ready. He removes it carefully and places it in the fixer. 'When he had begun to wear the garb of gray and sat there behind bolt and bar – oh those were terrible days for me, believe me.' (James has said the words in such a way it is almost impossible for a viewer not to think, ' *You? What about old Ekdal?*) 'I kept the shades down on both windows . . .' He moves the photograph gently in the fixer, '. . . it seemed to me that all of existence ought to come to a standstill, as during an eclipse of the sun.'

'I felt that way when my mother died.'

For the first time during the entire scene, James looks directly at Goldglass: 'In such an hour Hjalmar Ekdal turned the pistol against himself –'

Goldglass registers genuine surprise: 'You too were thinking of –'

'Yes.'

'But you did not pull the trigger?'

'No.' James shakes his head like a man who recognizes a great mistake and turns back to his photograph. 'In the decisive moment I won a victory over myself. I remained alive. Take my word for it: it requires courage to go on living . . .' He pulls his photograph out of the liquid and examines it critically.

The scene is over.

Most of the students have no idea what they've just seen – the power of its emotion or its message. A scene that might never be played quite as well again. After a curious silence, a few hands clap uncertainly.

Marty Goldglass approaches the stage and stands with his fingertips on James's shoulder. His large body is limp; his eyes are moist. The tip of his tongue wanders over his mustache, finding the notch left by the operation that mended his hare lip. James is close enough to smell an odor of musk coming off the perspiring Goldglass; his own T-shirt is soaked through as well.

The first tear rolls off Goldglass's cheek into the gray hair on his chin. He cries soundlessly, delicately; his chest and shoulders tremble. The reaction is not performance, or not only performance: James senses a touch of embarrassment in Goldglass. Goldglass whispers, 'Kid, you're some piece of work.'

'Get out.'

'Someone compliments you, you say "thanks."'

'Thanks.'

Goldglass turns to the students, eyes puffy, cheeks glistening: 'Let's just leave it there. Next week we can talk about this.' His voice is rheumy, 'Or not.' He tucks his script under his arm and lets his other hand wave the class off and fall limply to his side.

'You old enough to drink?'

'They didn't pay much mind to age in Indiana.'

Goldglass blinks and pushes his tongue in his cheek – his imitation of a hick: 'Shoot, here in Indiana we drink our corn-licker at ten and git married at twelve. Even collect our Social Security at thirty-five. Yuck-a-yuck-a-yuck. Why don't I meet you over at Fredo's. Twenty minutes. Know the place?'

'Across from the parking lot?'

'Right.'

'See you there.'

*

Someone had loaded up the same song on the jukebox. Before Goldglass arrived, James heard Nat Cole sing 'Nature Boy' five times.

'So what'll you have?' Goldglass continues to whisper.

James isn't sure. 'Something with soda water.'

In a surprising voice shift, Goldglass bellows to the bar, 'Neddy. Four Roses and soda. And the regular.'

The waitress brings the drinks. James's highball is pale amber in a tall glass. Goldglass holds a double Scotch in front of his eyes and says, *L'Chaim.*' He draws the top off vacuum-fashion.

'I'd feel better if this scene was scripted because I'm lousy at true confessions. I need someone smarter – Odets maybe – to put the right words in my mouth.' Goldglass is turning his glass on the table as though to leave an imprint in the wood. 'I probably even need stage cues to do it right. "Old man, mawkish, head down, searches for words. Toys with glass. Can't look student in the eye. Self-conscious about what he's got to say, knowing it applies more to himself than to student . . ."'

'But student, refusing to make things easy for old man, remains silent . . .'

'"Old man stands, exits stage left." How'd you like that?'

James zips his lips closed and smiles teasingly with his eyes.

'I wish you wouldn't pull crap like that, this is going to be tough enough.' Stuck with his self-imposed silence, Dean places both hands over his heart and opens them like butterfly wings. 'Some of the stuff I've been doing, I didn't even realize I was doing it. No, that's not it. Listen, that was great Ibsen tonight, moments anyway. Not just good, great. I knew you had something, Jimmy. I just didn't know it was *that* good.' He holds his arms wide as though embracing the world.

James dips his head. Goldglass throws down the rest of his drink, Dean sips his.

'What I'm really trying to say is, I've done you wrong, chile, and feel really rotten about it.'

James is confused but stays silent and attentive.

'These months, I could have done so much more.' He looks at the black-and-white T.V. behind the bar. It's a war movie. He recognizes John Hodiak. 'Much more. I knew you had stuff to work with, and I knew you were teachable as hell. I just let you drift out there.' He looks into the ceiling lights. 'I just let you drift and I don't know why I let you do it.'

James leaves the silence. That much he's learned from Goldglass: holes are not the absence of dramatic action, they intensify it.

'I've never felt threatened by talent. Never thought I could be. I guess none of us is as immune as we think we are – about anything. Stella told me there were two kinds of teachers – the ones who want students to succeed, the ones who, deep down, really don't. Drink up.' He flashes two fingers at the bar. 'And a bowl of ice, Neddy.' Jimmy picks up his glass and forces a long sip.

105

'Back then, I had no idea what she actually meant – a teacher not wanting his students to succeed. Who ever heard of such a thing? She told me about her mother teaching her how to iron when she was a little girl. At first her mother would show her and explain. Then, every time she got stuck, or even hesitated, her mother would always take the iron from her and do it herself. Stella said she never forgot that. Her mother swore she wanted her to be able to iron, but every time she took the ironing away. Stella said she thought it had to do with being afraid of making her daughter independent. With you, I told myself I didn't want to rush you along. Didn't want to give you a big head too young. Delusionary crap like that.'

The waitress brings the drinks and ice, takes away a dollar in quarters and an empty shot glass.

'I guess you could say that until tonight I never even let you have the iron in the first place. Maybe because you scared me. Who knows? Jealousy? Maybe it's age – you're so fucking young.' Goldglass picks up an ice cube and rubs it over his face.

'Don't worry, Marty. You're teaching me to iron just fine.'

'Ain't you sweet.' Goldglass leans across the table and pulls the boy's head down. Jimmy feels the pinch on his abdomen.

'You know Kazan once played Hjalmar on Broadway?' Although he's heard the name often, Jimmy doesn't really know who Kazan is and doesn't ask. 'Didn't actually see it, heard about it, though. I played Gregers in The Group with Jules. Odets was in the audience that night. He told us we got Ibsen's sense of fatalism perfect.'

Goldglass closes his eyes to make his memory more vivid: 'We were on cloud nine and a half. Not just that night – for months. I think that's when I believed I could be a real actor. I mean a *real* actor.' He gulps half his drink and begins to speak before he swallows. 'And Jules. My God, unbelievable. He's never done anything out here that could touch that night. Un-be-lievable. Not to compare you. He was after something completely different, something more sentimental. Not a question of better, just different. Jesus, we were so young.'

James allows Goldglass's feelings to range.

'Jules just signed to do a movie with Warners. Threw me a bone. He plays a psychopathic murderer; I get to play his father – his *dead*

father. A few flashbacks. Don't get me wrong, I'm grateful. Haven't
worked in nine, ten months. Maybe that's why I've been such a
horse's ass lately. Who knows?'

He considers, and forgives himself. 'Tell me, how the hell did you
figure out Hjalmar? You do it purposely? Or just stumble on it?'

'It was there, wasn't it, Marty? So why not just give me credit for
being smart.'

'You *are* smart. Smarter than I figured.'

'Marty, tell me how to get better.'

'Time. Time'll get you better. Work'll get you better.'

'Don't have a lot of time. Every day is a goodbye.'

'Well . . .' He does a timeless shrug.

'No, come on.'

'Tonight, good as it was, here's something to think about. This
Hjalmar at this stage of the play is one of those self-pitying guys,
completely absorbed in what he does, what he feels, what he needs –
you know the type? And that's pretty much how you played him.
Fine. But he's a smart son of a bitch too, a deceiver. So let him be a
little more aware of Gregers, even if it's only to see how Gregers is
taking it all. More glances over, fewer pauses, more ambiguity in the
words: that's it, a little more double meanings.'

'Like Clift?'

'Sure, why not like Clift? Gestures, thought processes, a personal
history, the works.'

'And?'

'That's about it.'

'And?'

'It's something you don't have any control over. Like I said, time
might take care of it.'

'Marty, *and?*'

'Your face. You're too damn pretty. You got to grow some character lines or something. At the very least try to be as expressive as
you can more of the time. It's when you hit certain poses that there's
a problem.'

'Maybe I should try to find ugly pills or something.'

'That's not a bad idea.' This time when he orders drinks, Marty's
voice hits a gravelly spot. 'Over here again, Ned.' He points to

107

Jimmy's drinks, one unfinished, the other untouched. James shakes his head. 'A double, Ned.' His voice is huskier, the cadence slower, the words have become more distinct. 'The worst thing about that guilt I told you I felt . . . I hated even thinking about it . . .' He stops. Exhales.

James raises his eyebrows.

'I even thought maybe . . . if you were a Jewish kid from New York, I'd have worked harder with you.' His eyes seek out Dean's.

'But, Marty, I *am* Jewish.' Said with such natural honesty a small puzzlement paints Goldglass's face. 'Yeah. We were the only Jews in Fairmount. Maybe all of Indiana. My uncle ran the only kosher deli in the state.' Goldglass's grin turns crooked. 'I'm not kidding. They ran us out finally when they discovered that we turned all the stale doughnuts into bagels.'

'Don't say. You know, I remember reading about that in *Life* magazine. That was *your* family? Jewish, huh – I guess that explains why you can't drink.' Marty's third glass is almost empty. James sips his first drink. 'Back in New York,' Goldglass recollects, 'we were all Jews. Those who weren't were Socialists, so it all came to the same thing.' James can see memory soften Marty's features and color the heavy voice. 'All we were going to do was change the freaking world and do it through the theater. Hah. Look at us now. Scattered to the winds. Someone waves a check in our direction, and there goes the unity, the pledges and promises. All for sale. Scattered to the winds.'

The tone is confessional. James feels the same intense curiosity he felt when Lem told him about covering up at the Normandy landing. Martin Goldglass is crying softly and touching his face with ice. James sees the bartender looking over and reads his expression to mean, *He's at it again.*

'Stella sat me down once – I couldn't have been much older than you – and gave me the pep talk I should have given you a long time ago.' His breath begins to catch in his chest. 'I'm going to need some time, kid. Why don't you go take a piss or something.'

When James returns to the table, Marty is sliding the back of his hands over his cheeks. 'What's a matter, never seen a crying jag before? Basically, Jews are nothing *but* crying jags.'

'Indiana Jews must be different.'

'Fun-ny. Anyway, I thought of one thing I could do. Odets is out here. He's writing dialogue for Jules's film. I'll see him, tell him about you. Maybe he can help get you a little something. Right now, you're better than ninety percent of what's out here.'

'Only ninety?'

'Ninety-five. Trouble is, I know what he'll say.'

It's Goldglass who leaves the hole, forcing James to ask 'What's that?'

'It's what I'd tell you too. He'll say, "If the kid's got talent, get him out of here. Get him to New York, where he can become a real actor instead of trying to become a star." It's good advice, too. Get out of here, get some New York credits and get yourself discovered – un-covered, re-covered, re-upholstered, resurrected, whatever. Go east young man and re-invent yourself.'

The word, the idea, sticks in James's consciousness: *Re-invent yourself. Inner Man, become Outer Man.*

Goldglass drinks from an empty glass. 'That's how it works in this crazy business. You got to get as far away from Hollywood as you can to get them interested back here. You can't really be any good if you come up and knock on their door. They've got to pluck you from distant shores, that's how they can prove how smart and hard-working they are.' He blows out his breath. 'He was a real piece of work on stage, you should have seen him. Raw emotion. Men wanted to fight him. Women would rub their cheeks on his thigh.' A part of James hopes he will cry again, just so he can study the facial changes. Goldglass grinds the glass into the table. No tears come. 'And whatever he did, you believed him. You know why?'

'Because he believed himself.'

Goldglass is surprised. 'Exactly. The kid who took your heart and gave it back just before the final curtain. Made it so you absolutely understood someone else's life. What a piece of work.' He picks his teeth with his thumbnail and flutters his eyes. 'So special he was. And not just him, it was the idea that held us all together, the risking, the being more alive than any of us had ever been.'

James doesn't understand so much as sense Goldglass's Golden Age. 'You're lucky you had that.'

'Maybe it's not supposed to last. Maybe having had it once in your life is enough. So many people haven't the slightest idea of what's possible. But it would have been nice for the world to have known what he could really do, not just this tough-kid-fights-his-way-to-top-of-heap garbage he makes over and over again for Warners. You know, you can't even tell what he is – a Wop, a Kike, a Greek or a Mexican–what?'

He must ask an embarrassing question: 'Who's that, Marty?'

'Jesus. You really are a hick. Garfield. Named himself after a fucking president.'

'Oh.' James leaves a respectful pause. 'Any chance we could play another scene?'

'A scene every week if you want to. Who gives a shit? Are you gonna touch that drink?' James shakes his head. Marty downs it steadily, like medicine. 'No doubt about it, got to get more Jews in my classes.'

'Why not just circumcise the ones you got now?'

Goldglass's laugh comes from the lowest register. 'So if you're Jewish, how come you didn't use your *kupf* when you took up with your Chiquita Banana?'

'I got the idea from the Old Testament, from King David.'

'What are you telling me?'

'Didn't he have something going with Bathsheba? And wasn't she a Chiquita? Same thing.'

'Still, if memory serves, it isn't David who gets knifed in *la bonza.*'

'But that story isn't over, Marty.' James looks for a long while into Goldglass's eyes. He doesn't blink.

Goldglass enunciates his advice: 'The smart thing is to stay away from those people.'

'Older man conveys life's wisdom to callow youth.'

'No, it's more like, "Older man thinks youth is fucking idiot about women."'

'Maybe, but I've got to get a piece of him, Marty. It's important.' Again the implacable gaze. Goldglass senses the fire in the boy's belly. Jules twenty years ago.

'There are parts of you amaze me. Quiet, nice manners, polite, twangy, down-home style. So I figure you're tried and true and four-square. Then you come up with the kosher deli and stuff that throws me. Now you're talking about getting even like you're a gunsel in a "B" flick at R.K.O. I don't now . . .'

'I guess there are more things in heaven and earth than are dreamt of in your philosophy, Goldglass.'

'Mus' be. Just watch your ass, kiddo. I'd hate to see you get messed over again . . .'

'It's okay, Marty. I've got a "B" flick, R.K.O. revenge all cooked up.'

'Still. Be careful. You need a ride home?'

'Got a car.'

'How about you give *me* a ride home then?' His small eyes shine.

James looks at him, considering his state of drunkenness and sentimental mood. 'Not tonight, Marty.'

6. Mystery Prince

THREE LIVES TO LIVE: screenplay by Adrian Rogash; based on a short story by Gary Ackermann; directed by Leslie Cobbell; produced by Dayton W. French for Republic Pictures.

Jason Davis (Jack DeVane)	*Edmund O'Bannon*
Greta Davis	*Lee Henry*
Kathy Davis	*Zoe Klinger*
Roscoe Davis	*Rory Kilty*
Kitty Hoyle	*Florence Cates*
Bat Masterson	*Kenneth Forrest*
Wild Bill Hickock	*Bryon Beman*
Starr Haller	*Irene Tracy*
Teddy Roosevelt	*Theodore Hodge*

James saw Three Lives to Live *in 1951 on television,* The Late, Late Show, *which he watched in a stupor in his father's house in Santa Monica. At the time he thought the plot was very dumb: Jason Davis, an accountant and good family man survives an earthquake in San Francisco at the turn of the century and decides to let everyone think he's been killed in the rubble. He slips away and takes another, more adventurous identity. As Jack DeVane, he becomes a cowboy, finds his way into the Texas Rangers, captures the Dalton Gang, and finally is befriended by young Teddy Roosevelt on a buffalo hunting expedition in Colorado.*

DeVane fights with the Rough Riders at San Juan Hill where, with his unit, he is cut off from the main force. The group suffers a direct hit from a Cuban cannon; DeVane is knocked unconscious and all of his comrades are killed. When he comes around and discovers what has happened, he is very upset, but he also realizes that he has an opportunity to change his identity once again.

He looks about the devastation and begins to rummage through the pockets of one of the dead. His off-camera voice reflects his thoughts:

DeVane: How come devastation also brings opportunity? I feel crummy about it, but it's true. I get a one-in-a-million chance to completely change my life from dull and predictable to free and adventurous. And now I get the chance to change it again. But the big question now is what kind of life do I really want to live?

Kathy Davis: (Daughter, superimposed) When all the other kids talk about their fathers, I get this shivery feeling, and I wish I could just disappear.

Roscoe Davis: (Son, superimposed) My dad must have been very brave. He died saving lots of other people when that building caved in.

DeVane: (Voice only) Could I just go back to being the same old person I was before?

Roscoe: Sure you could, Dad. We'd all be together, the way it used to be.

DeVane: (Considering) If I decide to go back to that life, will it really be the same as before? (Answering) Maybe it would be the same, but in a different way. If I write the word 'dull' and erase it and write 'exciting' in its place, no one can ever read 'dull.' But if I erase 'exciting' and write 'dull' again, I'll know it isn't the same old 'dull.' I'll always know the difference.

'You, Tommy. When he holds that big bottle up, bend way over backwards, way back, stunned like it's giving off lethal radiation or something.'

'It's Jimmy.'

'What's Jimmy?'

'My name, it's Jimmy.'

'Tommy, Jimmy, what's the difference . . . Listen, just lean back like the others so it looks like Pepsi is the most explosive thing since Nagasaki. Okay. Let's try it again. Starting spots. Cue the music. And girls, remember you're cheerleaders, for Christ sake, and Pepsi's the star of the team. You know what you'd like to do for the star, don't you, girls?'

The three co-eds – the young one and the ones who look young – glance at each other, pull down their Pepsi sweaters and throw out their chests. Jimmy, in a football uniform, and a guy in a basketball outfit take their marks and get down on one knee facing the camera. They smile like jackasses. That leaves the fellow with the Pepsi-Cola megaphone, the one who does the flips, between the two athletes a little further upstage.

'Okay, let's do it.' On cue, the girls will bounce in from off-camera, high kicking, and do a P-E-P-S-I-C-O-L-A cheer. The megaphone man joins them on the second cheer. Jimmy is to look at the girls adoringly, eyes sending sparkles in all directions. He's nothing but cute. Then they all freeze. The megaphone man does a forward sault in the air, then a backward one and tosses the megaphone aloft. All the kids follow its above-camera flight open-mouthed. What comes down is not the megaphone but a huge bottle of Pepsi, caught by the megaphone man. Eyes bug out of heads, mouths open even wider.

Jimmy eyes the immense Pepsi, then one of the young-looking cheerleaders. They jitterbug cheek-to-cheek, as do the basketball player and the young cheerleader, all without taking their eyes off the great bottle. They lip-sync 'Pepsi-Cola hits the spot, twelve full ounces that's a lot, twice as much for a nickel, too – Pepsi-Cola is the drink for you.'

They all come together in a tight tableau. The Pepsi is thrust toward the camera lens: the dancers freeze and bend over backward as though irradiated, smiles frozen on their faces from their hairlines to their chins. The wound across James's stomach has almost mended, but he's bound himself tightly in order to be able to go all out: he never expected anything as physical as this. That's why his smile is so crazy looking.

They've run through the routine fifteen times. The sixteenth is about as good as the previous six or seven. Probably about as good as it's going to get. The director says, 'We go on in half an hour. Get off your feet. Be back on your marks in ten. We'll do one more run-through. Then we go live. Not to worry, live is just like any other run-through except with about five million people watching. And don't drink any of this piss during the break, we wouldn't want to up-chuck on a national hookup, would we, boys and girls?'

During the break, Jimmy grabs a cup of coffee and moves off to one of the dressing rooms. Most of the other dancers are on the telephone, reminding relatives and agents to be sure to watch. Getting his feet up on a chair relieves the pressure on his stomach. It's hard to get comfortable in his football uniform, but he is starting to relax with a Zen breathing exercise: he imagines air being pulled slowly into his body through every pore. A voice startles him: 'I knew I knew you. From somewhere. But I couldn't figure where. Then I got it.' It's the truly young cheerleader, stepping into the dressing room. 'Two years ago, remember?' Although she's only about nineteen, her voice is unpleasantly nasal and metallic, a sharp contrast to her cheerleader innocence. 'Then it came to me. Bang, just like that. Guess where?'

James's impulse is to say something sarcastic, but he checks himself. He smiles his first smile of the day, 'Let's see. It wasn't at the Eisenhower Inaugural, was it? No, no. A Lifebuoy commercial?'

'Never did any Lifebuoys. Give you a hint. It was in New York City.'

Now he's intrigued. 'Only been there once.' He slides his feet off the chair and offers it as a seat. 'It'd have to be at Columbia University, the auditions.'

She takes the chair, sits and crosses beautifully muscled legs. 'Yup. I was on right after you both times. Did you know that?'

'Nope.'

'Well, I was. I saw you, and you were unbelievable. I didn't even want to go on when I saw your Hamlet. Gawd. I did a Cordelia. You didn't see it, did you?'

'No. I left soon as I was done. I guess I should have stayed.'

'So how come you're out here now? I mean, how come you're here dancing instead of being at Columbia?'

He does his slow smile. 'How come *you're* here dancing instead of being at Columbia?'

She puts her hand over her mouth. 'You mean you didn't win!'

Jimmy mimics her gesture and voice: 'You mean *you* didn't . . .'

'C'mon. I can't believe it. I can't believe you didn't win. You were so . . .'

'. . . un-be-*leev*-able.'

They laugh.

'I'm serious. How come you're out here?'

'I'm an actor, although you couldn't tell from this.' Jimmy plucks at his Pepsi jersey.

'Twenty-five bucks for half a day's work, don't knock it.'

Jimmy was getting thirty-five. 'And you? How come you're out here?'

'Me? Well, I sure as hell wasn't going to make it as any Cordelia. So I took a look at myself and decided I'd become a star instead.'

'Cut out all the trivial stuff and go right for the pot of gold?'

'Sure, why not. If the camera loves you, you pass GO and collect your studio contract. Don't you read the magazines? And it just so happens . . .' Here, she sweeps up her hair and strikes a sexy pose. '. . . the camera is absolutely ma-a-a-ad about me.'

Jimmy looks at her closely, trying not to laugh. She's a conventionally pretty blonde girl. The heavy pancake and Betty Hutton hairstyle give her the unreal look of a Kewpie doll. The long, straight line of her nose gives her an aristocratic air that is comic in context. 'You're sure of that?'

'Of what?'

'That the camera is ma-a-a-ad about you.'

'I'm positive. The way it works is the camera sweeps over a whole bunch of faces, in a crowd scene let's say, but there's always one that jumps out on the screen like . . . like somebody winning at Bingo.'

'And your face is Bingo?'

'It will be when I get the chance.'

'And what about my face?' He strikes a John Barrymore, great profile pose.

'It's not the same thing for you. You see, I can sing and dance, and do impersonations. You can't see my figure under this sweater, but, believe me, I've got no worries there.'

'You can't see my figure either.'

She doesn't skip a beat. 'When I get tested, I'll give them exactly what they want. My only problem is hanging in there until the break comes, but I don't have a single doubt that I'll make it.'

Jimmy's smile builds to a chuckle.

'You laughing?'

'No, absolutely not. Just happy. You make me feel good. Your confidence is catching.'

'I'd worry about you, though. You're a real actor. That's why I'm surprised you're not in New York. Don't you know that's where they look for actors? You think anyone'll notice you in this thing?' She scrunches up her face doubtfully; her nose doesn't wrinkle. 'Never. But there's a chance they'll notice me. That's the only reason I do these things.'

'And the twenty-five bucks.'

'Girl's got to keep herself in hose. You know, I can't remember your name.'

'It's Jimmy Dean when I'm dancing.'

'Yeah, I remember.' She offers her hand daintily. 'I'm Eve Edel, whatever I'm doing.' She whispers, 'I was Evelyn Edelstein back in New York.'

He whispers back, 'I won't tell a living soul.'

There's activity out in the hallway. 'Okay you people, let's get back on our marks. Happy faces. No grumps, we're going live, remember.'

Jimmy stands and stretches. He spreads his arms wide and then high. 'Strange business. Got to do Pepsi in order to do Shakespeare.'

She stands and stretches: 'You just don't seem made for this business.'

'How's that?'

'You act too nice. Out here they take nice for being mopey, and no one's gonna hire a mope.'

'I'm a mope?'

'No. *I* don't think you're a mope, but you act too nice.'

'If you could see my figure under this jersey, you'd see I'm not a mope.'

She misses the point and doesn't give it a second thought. 'You can't act so nice out here. It's like when you walk into a drugstore, you got to act like it's *your* drugstore, even if you only have enough money to buy an ice-cream cone, it's *your* drugstore. Confidence, I'm talking about. These people out here, they can sense when you've got it and when you don't. If you don't, they won't take you seriously.'

'And they won't take me seriously because I'm a mope.'

'I didn't mean you *were* a mope, I said you should act . . .'

'. . . like I own the drugstore.'

'Not just the drugstore but the whole damn town. Let's say you walk into a casting director's office. What does he see? A nice kid who wants a part. Ninety million other nice kids have already walked into that office. Deep in his heart he really *wants* to say no. So you got to turn the situation around, make him think that you're not like any other actor who's ever walked into that office.'

The director shouts, 'Hurry, people. Take your marks.'

Jimmy whispers to Eve Edel, 'And you learn to be that way in drugstores?' His eyes are laughing.

'You can. Yes.'

'How about after this we go to a drugstore? To rehearse. I'll buy you an ice-cream cone.'

*

Jimmy gives the idea of becoming someone else lots of thought, especially during his long, solitary tours of the museum. Every time he passes *Inner Man, Outer Man* he, and not the painting, is the subject of examination. He accepts Goldglass's professional judgment that he has to become someone else to be allowed to reveal his own deepest self. Eve Edel's advice reverberates too. So he must re-invent himself. But how? Into what? And where?

He knows he cannot re-invent himself in Santa Monica. Not only because the place holds no magic and because it belongs to Winton Dean. But mostly because that's where he is. Jimmy knows that if he is going to transform himself, it can't be done *here*: it's got to be done *there*.

In legend, the royal son has to disappear, to be lost, even feared dead, in order to come back some day and reclaim his princely birthright. The Prince has to go far away in order to find the proper path home, to discover and to be discovered. Strange as that seems, Jimmy knows from his acting intuitions that paradox is the key; truths are often revealed by their opposites. New York has always been the perfect place to get lost – and to be found.

Who is a much tougher question to deal with than *where*. If he has to invent a persona, how can he be sure he will select the right one, the one that will attract and intrigue, that will please and impel? He can't be.

At first, he imagines he could select a new personality the way someone selects new clothes: picking and choosing from actors he admires. He loves William Powell's breezy charm, Gable's powerful sense of himself. Jimmy Stewart's Midwestern hopefulness. Maybe, for a while, he can dress himself in borrowed clothes. Somehow, though, the pants wouldn't go with the shirt, and neither would go with the sweater and socks. Used clothes won't make an authentic man.

Even though he doesn't expect Eve to have any practical ideas on the subject, he enjoys hearing her talk about show business. He takes her to Googie's on the only date they will ever have, but he waits until the dessert to say, 'Did you have anything in mind when you talked about New York?'

'Uh-huh.' She's spooning chocolate pudding. 'But before that, you should change your name.'

'Change my name – isn't that a little extreme?' He's surprised that the idea offends him. It shouldn't because shedding Winton's name is the next best thing to shedding Winton.

'It wasn't hard for me. I hated who I was.'

James is peeling the skin off his pudding. 'But what if you don't, say, really hate yourself?'

'Well, maybe not *hated* myself, but not really being wild about who I was.' She's stirring her coffee. 'Prob-ab-ly because I was some-one else's idea of who I should be. I had to get myself back, to invent the person I was always meant to be . . . Eve Edel.' She speeds and slows her words as she talks and thinks and sips.

Invent. Goldglass's word. 'I don't get it.'

'I just wasn't who *I* wanted to be. I was my mother's idea of who I should be. Get it?'

'No, not really.'

'See, she really loved Lynn Fontanne, worshipped Lynn Fontanne, so guess what?' She lowers her voice an octave. 'I was sup-posed to be the second coming of Lynn Fontanne. I was gonna emote all over the place and ring every bell in the class-i-cal actresses' repertoire, all in perfect diction, on the leg-it-ee-mate stage. Six nights a week and two matinées. Nuts to that, I said. Not right away, mind you, but when I began to figure out who I wasn't. And I sure as hell wasn't Lynn Fontanne. I had a nose out to here and a body Lynne Fontanne would kill for. What I really loved to do was look at myself dancing in the mirrors at the studio. That's who I really was. After I got my nose straightened, I knew for sure that I could be whoever I wanted to be.'

'But who to be. Isn't that really the rub?'

'You already know, really. Sort of. Deep down. Don't you?'

James doesn't.

'I know what we'll do. We'll go back to my place. I'll put on my music and dance for you. You'll get all inspired. Then we'll screw. I'll bet a dollar to a doughnut before the sun comes up you'll know who you want to be.'

'Or who I *don't* want to be.' James is dead certain the enigma of personality will not be revealed to him by Eve's dancing or her athleticism. As for screwing her, he's turned off because she used the term so boldly. Eve Edel frightens James Dean.

Before she gets out of the car, she kisses him on the cheek and says, 'When you really know how to handle yourself in a Hollywood drugstore, Jimmy Dean, give me a call.'

He senses that the spirit of the invented personality has to be present before any of the various parts can fall into place. Change the inner man's character and the outer man's behavior would follow. He spends more time than ever contemplating Voltanz's painting.

Years later, he would tell an interviewer from *Life*: 'I've always wanted to be a painter. Like Gauguin or Emile Voltanz. I mean, if I weren't an actor, I'd be a painter because I love the silence of the medium. Everything that happens – the color, the forms – comes straight from the brain to the canvas. It has the power of immediacy, yet every time you see it, it's different and you must re-evaluate it every single time, like your own life.' There were times when he liked to hear himself expound on life and art. He knew he was full of bull, but he wanted to sound thoughtful, sensitive, artistic. This was a year or so after he had re-invented himself.

*

One afternoon, while gazing at the painting, James notices that the heart of the inner man is blurred, ambiguous, unreadable. Mysterious. Mystery, he realizes, is the crucial ingredient. Doesn't the missing prince, when he is rediscovered, have something alien, something unknowable about him? Strange speech? Peculiar, unpredictable behavior? A hidden wound? Isn't this what makes him curiously attractive? He immediately thinks of Montgomery Clift.

But there is no need to think of someone else as an example.

James Dean has always had a sense of mystery within and about himself. In Fairmount, he never felt more estranged from himself than when he hung out with regular kids, when he went to Stetler's for malts, to dances after ball games. It was a real effort to be one of those kids for more than three or four days at a stretch. An effort that wearied him. That's why he always hungered to be by himself after he had been with them too much. The way he felt on stage, even the very first time he tried out; his attraction to Lem Craig's craziness; being with Amanda Boyce in New York – these attested to the un-regular about him.

The princely wound was crucial. No, not the long scar across his stomach. Rather, the mother untimely taken from the sensitive nine-year-old boy, the never-healing injury, the loss. The mystery mother, long disappeared, promises made and forever left unful-filled, the doomed search for completion – these are inexplicable sorrows, an ever-fresh wound, this is a life in art.

Mildred Dean is the unknowable in himself, an attractive force toward which James is turned and drawn continually. If mystery is an element of love, James loves the mother in himself.

For more than an hour each day he stands in front of Zoltanz's painting attempting to redefine himself. The process is not, he is certain, anything as complex and slippery as re-invention. He con-jures images of Mildred Wilson from photographs, and clearer ones from memory and the clearest of all from his imagination. More often than not they are pictures of Mildred as a girl, about his own age, a few years before she agreed to marry Winton Dean. Her hair touches the shoulders of her flowered dress, the even curls along her forehead are almost too perfect. Mildred's smile is not his but could be: her eyes have the same oblique way of looking aside and inward. He wants to carry this girl's books, take her for a malt and to the hop, picnic with her on Crump's Hill – most of all, just talk to her about their lives.

When Mildred appears to him as his mother, she is still girlish. Only her clothing has changed, her manner. She's preparing break-fast or darning socks or hanging out the wash. (He never actually saw her darning socks.) He can neither conjure nor extract a voice from Mildred Wilson or Mildred Dean. She cannot, will not speak

123

to him; her eyes seek contact but in an indirect, mystifying way. Her silence is a continuing temptation.

So silence, too, must be part of what he will project into his persona. And appropriately so. There can be no true mystery without silence. In his acting, isn't it natural for him to leave inordinately long silences to draw the audience and the other players to the words, to the revelation of his character's deepest self? Shouldn't the mythic adventurer leave unexplained the details of his disappearance to all but his true love?

With a start James realizes for the first time since her death that Mildred sometimes called him 'Bonnie Jamie' in honor of Prince James. The remembrance is further proof that this is not re-invention: this is self-discovery of the deepest sort. He thought he had fathomed *Inner Man, Outer Man* before; he must have been a fool. The painting he now sees surely is the best, the truest pathway to the singular, authentic James Byron Dean.

It would require lots of refining, but through the process of honest self-deception, Jimmy Dean has actually started to re-invent himself. Of course, he still has to develop and perfect an appropriate style, a rhythm, a movement, and a look to go with the emerging personality. But these are essentially the sorts of decisions an actor has to make about a character, stage choices – the unfinished business of an unfinished person.

Eventually, his inner pain and mystery will be suggested by the way he carries his body – tenderly, guardedly, as though parts of him are so brittle he might break. A deep, unspecific pain is revealed by a tautness around the eyes and the mouth.

The power of silence will be reinforced by a slow, tight, asymmetrical smile, as self-mocking and ironic as it is appreciative. It gives the impression that, for some inexplicable reason, James Dean doesn't deserve to be fully happy, an impression that will make a great many women want to provide happiness. The speech rhythms of the new man, which he practices in his car and while walking through the museum, isn't totally different from the old one: he finds himself speaking more with his eyes closed, a dangerous practice on the freeway.

In time James Dean will become the embodiment of a great

mystery, one that draws both men and women by the power of his belief in it. He intends to spend a lifetime perfecting the mysterious within himself and bringing the mysteries of the roles he will play to the consciousness of others. James can hardly wait to get off to New York and try on his brand-new self.

*

He takes the steps slowly, with satisfaction. He's smiling. Yet scared, too. The smile is very tight across his lower lip. Every time he's come up these stairs, he has come away humiliated. Or worse. He intends this to be the last time. The downstairs neighbor rolls his eyes when he sees the gringo kid coming yet again.

Halfway up, Jimmy stops and touches the gun in his belt. It is Winton's .38. James has had it for a week without his father seeming to miss it. He will clean it in his room later tonight and put it back in Winton's closet in the morning; Winton will never know.

An urge to check the cartridge chamber one more time builds in his chest, just to be sure it's properly loaded. *Don't be an idiot.* He'd already checked it a dozen times. Sunday he'd fired it at the range, perfect every time. *If you don't want to do it, turn around now. Otherwise, get on with it.*

He sees his tennis shoes toe each step on the way up, exactly as an overhead camera might film his advance in a Hitchcock movie. He's glad a part of him remains detached, watching: he'll have a better chance of staying in control. The dialogue? It'll depend on the reactions he gets. Even his opening depends on who answers the door, and how.

At the top landing, he combs his fingers through his hair and pushes his glasses snug. The pistol catches on a belt loop as he withdraws it. He chuckles and shakes his head; he can't believe he's actually going through with this. It's a revenge that would have almost been satisfying enough in the contemplation. He chuckles and shakes his head. *Sheeee-it, you're a fucking looney, J.D., you know that?* Lem Craig talking to him. He takes the capsule out of his shirt pocket and puts it in his mouth behind his back teeth.

The soft tap-tap-tap on the door with the muzzle of the gun

sounds like rolling thunder to him. He can hear a chair move in the kitchen, the clink of a plate, words muttered in Spanish, a glass set down on the sink, more words in Spanish, a breathy laugh. His hearing is, for some reason, remarkably acute. Muffled steps behind the door. The knob turns slowly. No backing away now. Whoever it may be – Yazzy or the brother – there will be a .38 aimed at chest level. Jimmy licks his lips; he's going to have to speak. The door flies open. It's the brother.

He sees Jimmy only as a blur behind the barrel of a gun. There is no fear on his face, only concern.

Jimmy says. '*Buenas noches, amigo.*' It is not one of the lines he had rehearsed.

Since he can see only one of the brother's hands, he motions with the gun for the other hand to become visible and says, '*Dos, dos manos.* Wouldn't want that knife coming out again, *Chico.*' The packet in his mouth makes him slur his words somewhat: if he seems a little drunk so much the better.

The brother puts his hands up to about shoulder level and says, 'No knife, brother. No knife. Just don't get excited, man.' He is nervous enough now to embolden Jimmy.

James's words come easily and they thrill him: 'What'd you think, you could just cut someone up and not have to pay for it? Or that I'd call the cops? Lodge a complaint? Shit, man. The only question tonight is am I gonna just take a piece of you or all of you.' On the word *all,* his eyes bulge with insane intensity. God, this is sweet.

It is the smile around the eyes that troubles the Mexican most. In Spanish he thinks, *I could take the gun away.* But there is a good deal of uncertainty in the statement.

Time has slowed. Space condenses. James sees the brown face before him with incredible clarity: the pores, the shaving nicks, the striations of the scar on the cheek are all in sharp focus. He sees other scars too, small ones across each eyebrow, on the neck just below the ear, at the edge of a nostril. This is a remarkable face, James realizes. Yazzy's brother's eyes and lips convey a profound sadness. James feels a rush of admiration for such a face, and a pang distantly akin to affection. A complication that can only make the scene play splendidly.

James can read the eyes and beyond the eyes to the thoughts. 'Talk to me, Chico. You talked so good the first time, when I was in the car. You talked so good when I came last time. So talk to me now. Any language. I'll understand. Talk nice to me, talk nice and maybe I'll put this away.' His smile belies the possibility.

Yazzy's slow, soft voice comes out of the bedroom: 'Don't do a stupid thing, Jimmy. You could mess up your whole life with this.' Wearing a lace slip, the womanly girl appears and moves behind her brotherly lover. She is calm, her hair is down, her body careless. 'What Ramon did to you was stupid, cruel, Jimmy. I have cried through the nights over what he did to you, Jimmy. But if you shoot him, everything will be lost. Everything for you, lost. Don't be crazy.'

James notices a large Madonna on a shelf near the hallway; it wasn't there before. There are candles circling it, an altarpiece in the kitchen. On the kitchen table, the guitar rests on its side, poised for a song. The name 'Ramon' is painted elaborately on the guitar, a blue dahlia is woven into the strings.

Jimmy says to Yazzy, as though she were a bad boy's mother, 'What he did to me, he has to pay for.' No sooner has he heard his words than he wishes he had the line back to do over – no, another line entirely, something like, 'You're probably right, but I've come too far already.' No, not that either.

'You have nothing to prove to anyone, Jimmy. Not to me, not to yourself. You are beyond any doubt a man. A man proves nothing by using crazy violence.'

How come she's got all the good lines? 'What an actress you're going to be, Yazzy. It's in you. You should never, never quit.' His eyes are mad yet knowing: he must turn up the madness in order to finish the scene correctly. 'I want a serenade. I want you to serenade me, Chico. Pick up the guitar and serenade me. Remember what you're playing for, so make it real pretty. I hope you know "Estrelita."' He has no idea why he chose that song; he waggles the gun to get Ramon to pick up the instrument.

'I don't know.'

'Sing for your supper, Ramon, boy.'

'I don't . . .'

127

Jimmy aims the gun at the hallway mirror that shows the disarray in the bedroom. He squeezes, and a sharp crack unlike the sound the gun made at the range pierces the room. The mirror does not shatter: the Madonna's head explodes, two of her candles fall to the floor.

Yazzy has her hands on her cheeks, her mouth in a silent howl. Ramon is very close to fright now as Jimmy aims at the guitar. Jimmy's eyes are crazed. He considers an insane laugh. The shot snaps the stem of the guitar and sends the instrument whirling to the floor. Jimmy suddenly looks worried and frowns: he wants to suggest confusion – *Hey, where am I, what am I doing here?*

When he points the gun at Ramon again, true fear is in his victim's eyes. No more words necessary. As he slowly turns the muzzle away from Ramon and toward his own mouth, he sees a confusion building beneath the fear. He also sees Yazzy agape with frozen panic. He opens his lips and places the muzzle well into his mouth. He does not remember putting his father's pistol in his mouth when he was eight years old. The third shot is set; he must be careful not to scorch his throat. He wears an idiot's grin, a simple satisfaction at his R.K.O. revenge. It is almost achieved. *Keep the muzzle down, against the packet. The eyes, everything's in the eyes. No more words. You've forced me to do this. My death is on your . . .*

The shot is not as sharp as the previous two. He bites down on the pouch and sprays scarlet in all directions while tumbling backward and rolling loudly down the stairs, losing his glasses. He hears Yazzy scream and Ramon yelp.

When he hits the bottom landing, the stricken face of the neighbor appears to him upside down, inches from his own face. Jimmy winks and spits out the empty blood pouch. The face blurs as he somersaults to his feet and leaps out the door, down the steps and rushes across the street to his car. His heart is pounding: his cackling laugh harmonizes with its beat. He tosses the .38 on the front seat and takes a steadying breath before turning the key. As the car begins to roll down the street, James Dean lets out a tremendous whoop.

On the way back to Santa Monica, he pulls off the highway onto a stretch of farmland. His breath is still quick and shallow. He shakes his head and says, 'Damn!' For the longest time, he just keeps shaking his head and saying 'Damn!'

He realizes a little sadly that there's really no one he can tell this to. He looks at his face in the narrow mirror, the blood has spattered his cheek and chin and shirt. He can't help snorting and saying 'Damn! Damn! Damn!' The only possible person would be Lem Craig.

He turns suddenly, sensing someone in the back seat – the girl in the flowered dress. No one.

7. The Theater of the Real – Encore

Marty Goldglass took Chan, Jimmy, the blonde girl, and a couple of other kids to hear The Bobby Troup Trio at Le Jazz Cool in Hollywood. During the breaks Troup, who knew Goldglass, came over to the table to schmooze, especially with the blonde. It was the first time James had heard 'Route Sixty-Six,' and he requested that Troup play it in every set. During the last set Troup let Jimmy sit in on bongos. 'Route Sixty-Six': lyrics and music by Bob Troup:

If you ever plan to motor west—
Travel my way, take the highway that's the best.
Get your kicks on Route Sixty-Six!

It winds from Chicago to L.A.
More than two thousand miles all the way.
Get your kicks on Route Sixty-Six!

Now you go thru Saint Loo-ey and Joplin, Missouri,
Oklahoma City is mighty pretty;
You'll see Amarillo; Gallup, New Mexico;
Flagstaff, Arizona; Don't forget Winona;
Kingman, Barstow, San Bernadino.

Won't you get hip to this timely tip;
When you make that California trip –
Get your kicks on Route Sixty-Six!

It's Rhea he begins to miss first, even before Goldglass, even before he's gotten outside the city limits. He recalls her quick yet modest bird-movements, her chirpy desire to keep things running smoothly in Winton's house, her marvelous gift to him on his twentieth birthday – a packet of twenty tickets to the Granada in downtown Santa Monica.

After seeing Clift in *The Search*, they began to go to the movies together every few weeks. Although they didn't usually speak very much, they were comfortable with one another: eventually they went to the Granada most Wednesday evenings and Sunday afternoons. The difference between movies and films hadn't yet become a distinction, and Rhea kept being surprised at how real the movies were at the Granada, especially the ones in Italian and French.

Winton hated theaters: 'Walking into a big dark place, sitting down next to a perfect stranger, that's something I could never understand. And when I was a boy, those places were filthy. Still are, most likely.' Then he mumbled something about frivolity and having chores and wasting time and life being much more serious back in Indiana.

In the car coming home from the Granada, Rhea sometimes talked smartly about the movie they shad seen, about the characters' choices and what befell them. James remembers her saying, 'You know, sometimes it doesn't seem like what happens is their fault, but mostly it is.' Rhea Dean understood serious movies as she understood human consequences, but this side of her only came out in the car rides home. James would only say what was necessary to keep Rhea talking. In the house this woman devoted herself to anticipating Winton Dean's every whim. James never could figure that out and quickly stopped trying.

Now, on his way out of town, James passes the Valencia Theatre on Compton Boulevard and remembers driving way over there with Rhea to see *La Grande Illusion*. Rhea had seen it with her first husband and gushed to Jimmy about Erich von Stroheim's performance, how rotten he was and how nobody ever could take off a pair of gloves as menacingly as he did. James had never heard of Von Stroheim or Jean Renoir, the director; he did know Henri Renoir's name from the museum but never made the connection. The movie had made a profound impression, but as he drives eastward he recalls more vividly the young woman who sat on the other side of Rhea, a woman in a print dress, a light sweater over her shoulders, a bemused and knowing look on her face, as though she held a secret about James that no one else knew. Even during the film he kept glancing at her to catch her reactions: they were consistently ambiguous, puzzling. When the lights came up after *FIN*, he leaned forward to smile his most winning smile at her, but she was gone.

He has left twelve unused Granada tickets on the kitchen table with a note to his stepmother:

Dear Rhea –
    I'm going to want to see the stubs to all these as proof that you kept going to the movies without me. When I see you again, we'll talk about movies, movies, movies. I miss you already.

                                    Jimmy

Other than lifting Peewee's cover at 2 A.M. for a fast 'S'long my feathered friend,' the note is his only farewell to California. In essence, Jimmy Dean has snuck out of the movie capital of the world in the middle of the night.

*

He doesn't need a map to find Route 66 and certainly not after he picks it up in San Bernadino, but he has taken the Rand McNally out of Winton's car. As he stretches over to put it in his glove compartment, his hand touches something cold and hard. Jimmy slows the Hudson and pulls off the road. The .38! Winton's gun. *How in the world!* He'd put it back in Winton's closet, oiled and wiped down. *Did he know I was . . .Impossible.* James takes it in his hand and feels its chill certainty. *How could he know I was leaving . . .* James shakes his head in wonderment.

The pistol is the protection he'll need on the drive cross-country. More than protection – assurance. Power runs up his arm from the smooth play of the trigger, up the arm, through the nervous system to the very cortex of the brain. With this in his hand he senses the power of a playwright – a director, at least – the power to shape himself into any damn thing he wishes. *But how could Winton have known?*

He switches on the radio, which works rarely: a loose tube or wire he could easily locate and repair if he wanted to. The light brightens the dial, the radio hums to life, and a few words of a preacher's sermon ring in the car. James turns the dial and the radio goes dark, silent.

Hours later, after he's moved on into Arizona, he takes the gun from the glove compartment just to feel its potency again. Its heft brings back memories of that scarred brown face, of the comic perfection of his revenge. But he feels little of its pleasure. Where there had been satisfaction, he now tastes bitterness.

He curls the gun into his hand and looks in the rearview mirror at an approaching car. Closing one eye to draw a proper bead on the target, James lets the driver overtake him and makes a kid's sound of a gun firing. Nothingness at the flex of a finger. The passing driver doesn't slump and career off the road: rather, he pulls past the Hudson and skirts off into the distance. James's next victim is an oncoming driver, an innocent dot on the horizon who has no idea he has only seconds left on earth. James says, while there is still considerable separation, 'You didn't listen to me, Tony. You never listen to me. Why is that, Tony? I'm the kind of man, when I tell you to do something, you should listen. Tony, Tony. Maybe in another situation. I'd let this go with a warning, but with the Tucci boys moving into the business, I can't afford to look like I'm . . . Don't start bawling. For Christ's sake, that only makes it worse . . .' The passing driver, seeing the momentary glint of sunlight on metal, couldn't possibly imagine a gun, although that's exactly what it looks like.

James stops at a lunch counter gas station in Adorn, Arizona, because he likes the name of the town so much, not because he's particularly hungry. He believes he can cross America and not eat at all, if he has to. He does need gas though, and there's a pump out front.

Just for the hell of it – and also to experience the actual feeling – he sticks the .38 into the waistband of his corduroys and pulls his shirt out over the bulge. He imagines himself a convict in the 1 A.M. movie. Bogart maybe, or a wary cowboy heading east with his bankroll – Clift, perhaps. Stanislavsky would have understood his making theater out of reality.

While engaging the short-order cook, Dean learns that the town is called *A*-dorn and that it probably won't even exist in ten years. 'Big drilling company made a huge strike 'bout fifteen miles up the road. That'll finish this place, as if it weren't finished already. Just forgot to bury it.'

'Don't say,' James says.

'Do say.'

Back in the car, James likes the feel of the .38 against his crotch, his amusing, cross-country companion. It doesn't occur to him to check the gun for bullets. When he finally does, it is late twilight. The chamber holds six shells. Winton had reloaded it. *My God, I could have killed someone! I could have killed myself!*

The thrill of danger averted pulses in his jaw, and James drives on for hours. He has switched on the radio without realizing that's what he's done. The dial lights up and stays lit. Music. A small combo playing 'Accentuate the Positive.' James thinks it's a record but a voice says, 'Folks, you're listening to the swinging music of Bobby Troup coming to you from the lounge of the beautiful Wilshire Plaza Hotel in downtown Los Angeles. And for his next number, Bobby and the boys will play an original Troup composition, "Route Sixty-Six." Hit it, fellas.'

James stares at the radio. He's never accepted the notion of pure coincidence, if coincidence is nothing more than the accidental conjunction of unlikelies. Once while doing his Math homework with the radio on, the announcer said, '*The Shores of Tripoli* will be the feature movie at the Fairmount Theater this weekend.'

'No it won't,' James said to the radio, 'it's *Flying Tigers*.'

And the announcer said, 'I'm sorry, I've made a mistake. The feature's going to be "*The Flying Tigers*."'

James has believed in various forms of telepathy ever since. He thinks it's a key element in his acting.

After playing an instrumental chorus of 'Route Sixty-Six,' the composer himself starts to sing: 'If you ever plan to motor west . . . Travel my way, take the highway that's the best . . . Get your kicks on Route Sixty-Six . . .'

When the song ends, there's the applause of a few people trying to sound like many. The announcer starts to speak and the radio cuts out. James smiles, convinced he is being watched, protected in some way or other.

Eventually, he pulls onto a path that leads behind a Lucky Strikes billboard only a few miles from the New Mexico border. He locks himself in the car, cracks the windows and curls up on the Hudson's spacious rear seat. The pistol is on the floor within easy reach.

Wakened by the early light but more by the sense he's being stared at, James smiles at a green lizard that's flat against the window. 'Mornin', pardner. Feel like headin' off to Broadway? Great parts for reptiles this season.' The lizard tongues the air and scurries off over the Hudson.

The day is extraordinarily clear, the sort of atmospheric clarity that back in Indiana sometimes bodes dangerous weather: thunder- and hail-storms, cyclones. Jimmy takes the beautiful weather as nothing other than beautiful weather, a sign of good luck. He can see great distances with wonderful definition. Buttes and mountains loom impressively to his left. The azure sky carries a few small, isolated clouds. It is terribly hot. He's forgotten about the gun.

The bullet-straight road lulls him into a restful, driving ease, one hand on the wheel, the other along the top of the front seat. For diversion he raises his sunglasses occasionally. The broken white lines on the road begin to whisper in his ears, like the softest tap on a bass. *Dip . . . dip . . . dip . . . dip.* Then a slightly stronger pulse on the second and fourth *dips*. Then a distinct accent on the second, a pulse on the fourth – the road is syncopating under him.

James drives – he has no idea how long for – in a state of half-dream. For a while he imagines himself on his bike back in Fairmount coming down Cemetery Hill at a great clip. Then his pants cuff catches in the chain and the wheel locks. He is going to flip over. He sees the gravelly road coming up to meet him, sees it with the same preternatural clarity with which he observes the New Mexico landscape. He holds his hands out to meet the road. And at that moment . . . snaps out of his driving trance.

His first instinct is to check the highway and wonder how long he'd been away, but his next is to realize he's just discovered something important about acting – something he'd already known but hadn't truly felt. He may have imagined the fall from his bike, but he was actually about to feel the meaty part of his hands scraping the road surface, actually about to feel the gravel bite and rough-off the skin of his hand. He looks down at his hand, where his palm meets his wrist and starts once again to sense the old, childhood abrasion returning. It is exactly as Stanislavsky promised; he could recreate any and all tactile sensations.

James is somehow more fully attuned to possibilities when hurtling through space. It occurs to him that maybe everybody is. It happened on the train to California; it happened when he was on his Whizzer in the countryside around Fairmount; and it's happening now as his Hudson speeds into the sun.

Perhaps he'd eventually have come to this connection between image and sensation had he stayed put back in Santa Monica. But he doubts it. There is something about movement, rapid movement, that transforms restlessness into quest. It's a bit of a paradox, but just about everything important in his life seems to be a paradox. He sings, 'Just let the wheels roll and spin, spin, spin your troubles away. Spin, spin, spin all your troubles ay-way, ay-way, ay-way, ay-men.' Dip *dip*, dip *dip*, dip *dip*.

But why? Why when he's in motion? *Maybe you just catch up to yourself on the move. The nomads knew it. The no . . . mads had . . .*

it. The road carries the beat up through the steering wheel, slapping hard on *no . . .* and *had.* 'Ha-a-a-a-d it. The no-oh-oh-mads ha-a-a-a-d it.' For the next mile or two, or three, he replaces 'nomads' with 'monads' and 'gonads.' There's a good deal of bluff and self-delusion and just plain inanity in his song of the open road. Then the rhythmic silence.

A common mistake. Travel isn't distance — it's time. New York. Three thousand miles. Tells you nothing. New York in five, six days, that's a week's worth of thinking, a week of invention. You'll be different, got to be. Not just a week older, an America older. He likes that idea and smiles. 'I could *be* America by the time I get to New York. The way nomads *are* the land.'

Another long silence ends with James speaking silliness in murmurs: 'Wander. Wonder. Some deal. Wonder why. Wander why. Seek. Seek and ye shall . . . Oh ye, oh ye of little faith. Wander, wander 'til you find the way. Ah, there's the rub. Way. The way. Find your way. Way. Way.' The simple sound has a power. James sets his lips as though to whistle. He begins to voice the 'W' in the lowest register. He's read enough Zen to be charmed by its otherworldly spirit, but that was before he realized the mystery could be his stock in trade in New York. 'W-w-w-w-w-w-w . . .' In its depths, he can feel his chest vibrating. The circle of his lips slowly widens into a smile and the changing sound starts to come from the nose, the whole head: 'A-a-a-a-a-a-a . . .' His breath seems endless. He's read about monks who can breathe and expel sound continually and believes he too could learn to do it. Never has sound — sub-sound, vibrations of sound, overtones — come so effortlessly. By frowning and thrusting his lower teeth forward, 'A-a-a-a-a-a . . .' blends to 'Y-y-y-y-y-y . . .' to 'O-o-o-o-o-o . . .' to 'O-m-m-m-m-m-m.'

The long journey through sound and grimace leaves him physically satisfied. He feels he's made a marvelous discovery about himself without knowing quite what it is. He is his own way: he is the wayfarer. The passage and the passenger. One. He feels he is Zenmaster of the open road.

*

The Hudson hums and vibrates. The driver, numbed by monotony, dizzied by hunger and thirst, conjures up a universe of constructive diversions. The car is a one-man acting workshop where James explores the memory-limits of touch, taste and smell. Stanislavsky's sense memories, he discovers, must be plumbed in stages, like going down a mineshaft: concentration is the descending elevator.

As he becomes more expert in calling forth touch, the other senses follow. He smells Marcus's field horse Ginger, a strong, damp musk that catches in the back of his throat. He can hear the barn door creak, furniture crack in the middle of the night; he can remember the exact grinding of gears on the Whizzer, the smell of an oil change, flies buzzing, pots rattling, a shovel biting into cold earth, a shoe hitting the floor, cows' tails swishing – not merely sounds re-created but true sounds from a true past.

In the car's drone James, by degrees, brings himself to feel his first dog, a big mutt named Chipper. To touch his ears – there are scabs at the base – James roughs him under the chin, throws an arm around his neck and rolls him over on the rug. He feels the rug, as well, its straight bristles abrasive to his knees and elbows.

With concentrated effort, he can bring into the car almost any sense experience. The more recent things are more difficult to summon for some reason. The cold nozzle of the gas pump at Hardy's Texaco, the bales of hay hoisted to the loft of Marcus Winslow's barn, the muffled sound and waxy smell of the modern art museum, these took far more effort and came imperfectly.

That evening, James has driven over 900 miles, all the while exploring and reaching deeper levels of recall. It comes to him eventually – much longer than it should have taken – to apply the same technique to things he hadn't yet done, to form the essential bond an actor must make between imagination and possibility. Suddenly Yazzy Gomez is right in front of him. He can see her face more clearly than he ever has: it is the later, sensual, womanly face, not the coy girl from the workshop. Her long neck is muscular, her jaw tightly flexed; the nostrils flare, the eyes bite, the eyebrows arch. He reaches out a hand to brush the cheek with his knuckles, and he feels a skin he has never actually touched. He brings her face closer and can see the silky down above her lip, on the neck below her ear; the microscopic pores on her cheeks and forehead are an attractive curiosity. She is corporeal. He can feel the muscles on her neck tighten as he draws her to him with both hands. In his thumbs he can feel the pulsing of blood through her temples. He can, he is sure, pierce the skin with his imagination and explore arteries, muscle tissue, the neural system. He could know this face, the organism beneath the facade, the invisible spirit of this person, thoroughly. There is no limit to the probe of his imagination. He believes he could, if he wished . . .

Even he, who could conjure up continual wakefulness, must finally go to sleep.

*

Only a few minutes on the road again. What makes him look into his empty right hand? Yazzy's face from last night? That German music Lem used to play? The Hudson veers off the highway, almost hitting a painted boulder, but James swings the wheel back just in time. Instead of being scared, he feels invincible.

He reaches across the floor behind him, groping for the gun. He doesn't need it, not with the power of his new-found imagination. In his empty hand, he tries to regain the feel of its old comfort, the confidence of a .38: the weight is there but not the true touch of the metal, the reassuring configuration of his hand and fingers. The more he tries, the less convinced he is that he's actually holding the pistol. He sweeps the floor in the rear with searching fingers.

At the same moment he sees two guys on the side of the road ahead. Hitchhikers. Someone to talk to. Not a bad idea. He slows for a closer look. The tall one has a scraggly beard and a mattress roll high on his back. His hair is red. He looks a little like Lem Craig. The short one wears a black baseball cap; his foot is on a bulging duffel bag: he's the one who's edged out into the road with his thumb up and a broad, hopeful smile on his tanned face.

James drives by. Then he brakes. Maybe because he's been thinking about Lem. He backs the Hudson through its own dust. The short one is at the window before the car comes to a stop. He's wearing sunglasses like James's but darker: he hadn't been wearing them a few seconds before. 'Hi,' he says too cheerfully, 'how far you goin' this mo'nin', my man?'

'All the way, my man.'

'Europe?' The tan face, agelessly smooth, is very serious, then it cracks. 'It's a joke, a joke. Actually we're headin' for Arkansas but anywhere east of here would sure be swell. Got stuck here last night.'

'Tulsa's about as close as I'm gonna get.'

'Hell, Tulsa'd be real fine.'

James remembers his gun. 'Hold it. Don't get in yet, got to make a little room in the back.'

'Don't you trouble yourself. We'll just . . .'

James is already out of the car and pulling a carton of his books across the floor of the back seat. While he's bent over, he fans his hand under the driver's seat and touches the gun. He slips it into his waistband and pulls his shirt over it. The touch of the pistol encourages him again, but it doesn't quite cancel the impulse that tells him he shouldn't have stopped for these guys. There's an acid taste in his mouth.

The tall redhead gets in the rear seat with his sleeping roll piled on one of James's cartons and the duffel bag sitting upright in the middle of the seat like an attentive army dog.

'That there's Cool,' says the spokesman, sprawled in the passenger seat. 'Not that he is cool, or anything like that, heh, heh. It's just what folks call him. Right. Cool?'

Not a word. Cool is somewhat wall-eyed and lantern-jawed.

James nods into the rear view mirror. 'Howdy, Cool.'

Cools blinks a response. He may also have nodded. James realizes that up close he looks nothing at all like Lem Craig.

'Actually it's honestly his real name. His last name is Coolidge. So guess his first name.'

'Calvin?'

'Throw in the cards, we got a winner.'

'It didn't take a genius.'

'Name's Orson. Taggart. Good t' meetcha.' He tilts his cap back on his head and offers his hand. James shakes it. It's reptile cold.

'Got an uncle named Orson.' It's not true but it seems dramatically right for James to say so. 'My name's Lem.'

'Lem what?'

'Craig. Lem Craig.'

Orson offers his hand again. 'Nice name Lem Craig. Kinda rolls. We been picked up last night by some guy had a name we couldn't hardly pronounce. A Jew name of some kind. Took us into Arizona. He pissed Cool off. Said he was going to Amarillo but he stranded us back there all night. He shouldn't of did that. Where you from, Lem?'

'Minnesota.'

'Where 'bouts in Minnesota?'

'Duluth.' He had no idea he was going to say that until he heard the word.

'I'll say this, Lem, you sure came along just in time. We must be two of the ugliest fuckers in the world, all the vehicles passed us by already this morning.'

'How long you been waiting?'

'How long you reckon, Cool? Two, three hours?'

In the mirror James sees Cool scanning the prairie, as insensate as the duffel bag.

'No telling,' says Orson, 'but it was l-o-o-o-o-n-g. And cold. Even trucks shunned us, and those guys are usually dying for some companionship. Dying to talk. Want a little blast, Lem?'

James shrugs, uncomprehending.

'Red whiskey?'

'No, no thanks.'

Orson snaps his finger and reaches back over his shoulder. Cool slips a pint out of the duffel and passes it forward. The smell sickens James: he realizes he's not eaten for a day and a half. He hears Orson's esophagus open and close, open and close. 'Ooooo-eeee.' Orson rubs the back of his hand wetly over his lips. 'That's the stuff. Here go.' He passes the bottle to the back seat. Cool drinks silently.

James is glad he'd checked the chamber of the .38.

Orson starts to snore. Cool examines the horizon. Tucumcari comes and goes. James listens to the motor for signs of trouble: there are none.

'You fellas going home or something?' The question is addressed matter-of-factly to Cool in the mirror.

It's the sleeping Orson who answers: 'We're in the services.'

'Services? Which ones?'

"Army. We're in the army. Headin' back to camp.'

'Which camp?'

'Fort Ord.'

'Isn't that back in California?'

'Right. We're transferrin' to Fort Stills, I think it is. Arkansas. Got the transfer orders somewhere.'

'How long you in for?'

'Forever, man. We like it so much, heh, heh. Right, Cool?' No response from the rear.

Their lies annoy James. His own, after all, are benign, plausible, defensive. The only connection these two have with the army is that they've probably deserted it. James takes his right hand off the steering wheel and rests it on the pistol.

'So where you headin' in this big fancy car.'

'Fancy? Hah! Wish it was. It's just wheels, all the wheels I can afford. Nothing fancy about it.'

'Just smokin' you a little, Lem boy. Way I look at it, anyone got any kind of wheels is doin' all right compared to us, right Cool? So where you headed, Lem ol' boy?'

'Can't rightly say.' The role is building slowly in his mind, being shaped from scraps of words, half-formed ideas and feelings. He's made a mistake picking up these two, no doubt about it. His only real choice is how and when to get rid of them. If he waits for them to make a move, if he only reacts, they'll have the drop on him.

'Remember the good ol' days, Cool? When we were footloose and fancy free? Got to hand it to you, Lem, you're not wasting your youth like some of us did. You're getting to see America the right way. What you got in them cartons?'

'Might look like I'm sight-seeing. I can assure you I'm not.' The lie, the bluff, is poised. 'I've got a specific destination.'

'So where's that?'

'Love to be able to tell you. Just can't say.' The smile he shows Orson is slow and enigmatic and hard.

Orson's smooth face wrinkles for the first time. Cool's head comes forward and looks to Orson for help. Orson says, 'Can't say? Whatdaya mean, "Can't say"?'

'Mean I'm not allowed to say. They'd hang my ass if word ever got out and they traced it back to me.' He knows he ought not be doing this again so soon after the Ramon bluff. He feels as though he's type-casting himself permanently. He also can't resist.

The ominous 'theys' had done their work. Orson is thinking. 'You on the run or something?' Then, with a sweet and obvious innocence in his voice: 'You steal something, maybe something valuable?'

'Hah. Steal? No, man, not steal. Hell, sometimes I wish I *was* a crook. I'm just a regular working stiff. I'm one of the good guys.' James Dean cannot resist the temptation to go to the edge: 'Government man.'

Orson Taggart jerks involuntarily.

'Probably shouldn't admit it. You fellas know why they call it the Secret Service?' No reaction. 'Because there aren't any secrets about you when you're in it. Can't get away with anything whatsoever. They watch me like a hawk, coast to coast. Might even have a man behind that billboard. Wouldn't be at all surprised.' He points with his chin to a huge picture of a shiny pair of shoes and a tin of Shinola shoe polish. Cool watches the billboard passing with his mouth open. 'That's the part of this damn job drives me crazy. I hate being spied on all the time.'

'How's come you picked us up then?'

'It's not like I'm always out rounding up public enemies or something. Heck, I still need someone to talk to, don't I?'

'Guess so.' Orson is clearly troubled. James sees his upper lip protrude more than its natural set, a sign that Orson has plunged himself deep in thought.

James probably won't even have to flash the pistol to get rid of these two.

Orson Taggart barks, 'Holy shit, Cool. Know what we did? We left the damn green bag back there.'

James sees Cool's face break into confused pieces: 'Green? Bag?' This is the moment James's theater of the real becomes pure pleasure.

'The little canvas one. We got our Fort Stills orders in there.'

'Orders? Green bag?'

Orson looks mean. 'Yeah. Orders. You got to let us out, Lem. We can't afford to lose that bag.'

'I'll just turn around up ahead.' He slows. 'Get you back there in no time.'

'No, no. You can just drop us off.'

'Least I can do is get you to that flashing light back a mile or so. You're sure to pick up a ride back there.'

'Right, right. Drop us there then. It ain't like we don't appreciate . . . We do, don't we, Cool?'

'What green bag?'

James swings a wide turn onto both shoulders of the road. He's heading back toward the Shinola sign. 'Worst part of this job is being spied on all the time. Really tees me off that they don't trust us at headquarters.' The Shinola sign comes into view. 'Betcha anything they really do have a lookout behind that sign.' His voice is flat and vague sounding, and his words are unconnected, adrift. His smile is like Cool's, unfocused.

It is not actually necessary to flash the gun, the scene has already been played out, but James can't resist the dramatic excess. He justifies his next action by telling himself it's a comedy. 'Lean back, Orson. I want to send my boss a message.' He slows the car down to a roll and brings the gun out of his waistband and points it just below Orson's chin at the billboard.

Orson says, 'Hey, Lem, watch that thing.'

'Don't worry, Orson. It's not you pisses me off. It's them.' His sunglasses reflect off Orson's. He shouts: 'Why can't you guys ever trust me?'

'Don't fire, for God's sake, you could kill the guy.'

'So what? He's got no family.' James has no idea where in the world that line came from or what it could possibly mean.

'Don't, don't do it!'

James shouts again at the billboard. 'Will you bastards ever leave me alone?' The pistol's blast kicks against his thumb: a puff of white comes off the bottom of the billboard. His second shot hits the Shinola can.

'Jesus. Let's get outa here.'

James drives to the crossroads.

'Grab those bags, Cool. We're gettin' out right here. We don't want to slow Lem up.' Orson opens the door while the car is still moving. Cool's confusion is memorable.

When James tells the story years later, he'll make Orson and Cool overtly evil and dangerous. He'll say he saw a shiv sticking out of Cool's duffel, a straight razor in Orson's breast pocket. By degrees he'll come to believe they had actually threatened him in some real way and that he'd saved himself purely by performance. 'Let me tell you how acting once saved my life,' is how he'll introduce the story. He'll never tell the Ramon 'suicide' and Secret Service stories to the same people. It would have made him seem too one-dimensional as an actor. He'll never quite have the stomach to tell anyone about the rest of his trip east.

*

After dispatching Orson and Cool, he drives through another day and night. He tells himself he has to make the Missouri border before going to sleep. A crazy, arbitrary decision, not even a decision, an order he gives himself, just to see if he can actually obey himself. Marcus used to say, 'Dumb's dumb and stubborn's stubborn even if things manage to work out. And J.D.'s got a stubborn dumb streak in him wider'n I ever saw. Good thing the boy was born lucky.'

In his mind's eye now, Jimmy sees Marcus: hand up at his neck, long chin moving sideways like a pendulum, but smiling the whole time. Being critical of the boy was something he only really took seriously when Jimboy treated Ortense rudely.

'Boy's got spunk, like his mother,' was what Ortense usually said in James's defense no matter what the misdeed. Although – or perhaps because – his mind is abuzz with sleeplessness and road hypnosis, his power as a conjurer remains heightened. He recalls conversations around the dinner table with precise gestures and smells and sounds and tastes. Speeding through the darkness, he reaches further back in memory. He is three or four perhaps, and he can see, or almost see, a rubber-wheeled derrick on a hard wooden step: it is black with gold lettering – B. & O. RAILROAD. A child's toy but remarkably realistic in all its details. He is near the top of a staircase: it might be the old house in Santa Monica before the steps were carpeted. Just above his toy he can see a narrow pair of black shoes, stockinged legs, the hem of a flowered dress.

Then he is falling. The woman shouts, 'Jamie, Jamie!' She screams for Winton, but her voice trails off amidst the toppling plunge. Stabs of pain in his ankle, his foot. Terror and tears. The woman cradles him at the bottom of the stairs. Where the toy has pierced the skin on the back of his hand, the woman is drawing the blood into her mouth. She is rocking him. 'It's nothing,' a man's voice says. 'A little Mercurochrome.' He is in his mother's arms; she sucks and coos.

He holds his hand close to his face, hoping to see the pale scar that's more memory than trace. It is too dark on the road. James suddenly realizes he's been driving non-consciously for . . . how long he has no idea. The realization causes him to shake. He should pull over for a while. He chooses to drive on.

In the recesses of self, in the stomach, the cave of personality, disappointment begins to stir. He knows this sensation: never when anyone else is around, never when he has to perform is it there. But on rare occasions, and only when he is isolated and weary, after he has thought about his mother or heard his father's voice at a distance. It isn't petulance or simple anger: nor is it directed at Winton. It is a bitter, sinking feeling very close to disgust, prompted by an irrational, profound unworthiness.

He remembers Jenna Craig unhooking her bra in the small group of trees on her father's furthest section. She was – is – chewing gum. Her slim white, pink-tipped breasts are the most beautiful gifts in the world. Driving in his car, James rubs his penis through his pants. He paid homage to her then and tries to reproduce the feeling now, but his cock does not respond. Despair is stronger than desire.

His hand is holding the pistol. He doesn't remember placing it there. He opens the chamber. Four bullets left. He fires two shots into the darkness. He whirls the chamber and pulls the trigger.

CLICK. Again he spins the chamber and fires. CLICK. He smiles as though he's proven something.

He opens the chamber and tilts the gun into his lap. Two bullets tumble out. Paying little attention to the undeviating road, he places them back in randomly and whirls the chamber. The taste of the warm muzzle in his mouth reminds him more of an old bar magnet he had as a kid than the last time he placed this gun in his mouth. The metal moistens his lips: the center of the earth might taste this way. Saliva fills his mouth. He pulls the gun out and spits into the darkness.

The day before his fourteenth birthday, he went to a Saturday matinée at the Fairmount with Jenna. The feature was an ice-skating movie with Sonja Henie. He hated it. He never forgot the other one, though. Only its title is vague. He remembers it as *Russian Roulette* but also knows it's not that. Alan Ladd was in it. For a whole year he walked like Alan Ladd, a stiff-backed, cock-of-the-walk strut.

In the movie Ladd is told by a brain specialist that he has no more than six months to live. He doesn't want to leave his wife and children impoverished. They're poor because he's gambled away their modest savings. He boards a freighter to Port Said where he finds himself in one last game, the game of his life, playing Russian roulette with a small man in a fez who could be but is not Peter Lorre. A dozen utterly decadent spectators have put up thousands of dollars to watch one of the two men blow his brains out. Ladd, because his days are numbered, doesn't really have much to lose. He behaves with cool whimsicality. If he happens to survive, he intends to send his winnings back to his family in the States.

Another small, dark man of indeterminable ancestry, dressed like a croupier, holds the pistol for all present to see: the music, a repetition of three descending notes, echoes through the theater. He places it on the table between the two competitors. Ladd and the Levantine will take turns placing the muzzle to their temples. What Ladd doesn't know is that his opponent has the uncanny ability to count the clicks of the spinning chamber. He can tell when the deadly chamber is in firing position, another significant advantage.

James's memory of the scene is remarkably clear. He can recall – or at least simulate – the dialogue, which he does aloud as he drives.

Ladd: 'I've met guys like you before. Even been a little like you myself. Thought I could figure out all the odds and beat the game. Hah, hah. Well, good luck, Abdul. Right now you're thinking – one bullet, six chambers, a one-in-six chance. Very logical. But dead wrong. Life's always a fifty-fifty gamble, my friend. A bullet's got your name written on it or it doesn't. Fifty-fifty. Simple as that.'

The whole screen is Ladd's face, lighted from below, a wisp of his blond hair falls across his forehead. His face has grown a shady stubble. The shadows in the window behind reach like bent fingers: Port Said is indeed an ominous place. The smooth-faced man in the fez is lighted the same way. He draws on a long cigarette holder clamped between his teeth. He smiles continually.

Abdul: 'I respect all men with the courage to play this game, my friend. (This last is said sarcastically.) Compared to us, even those who venture their wealth risk very little in the end. (He sneers at the rich speculators, who are paying a great deal to be entertained.) It is only you and I who truly deserve to be called men. Should we draw straws to determine who will spin first?'

Ladd chuckles and says: 'I'm a very impatient man, Abdul. So let me begin the party.' He reaches for the gun.

There's a murmur in the dimly lit room: a great deal of tension pulses through the theater. The croupier picks up the gun in white-gloved hands – a tight shot – opens the chamber, shows it to the entire room and places a single silver bullet in the aperture. He hands it to Ladd, who gives the well-oiled cylinder a long spin. The extended clacking sound in the Fairmount is hypnotizing. Silence. Ladd puts the gun to his head. The camera shows his eyes. Smiling sadly, no trace of fear.

James cannot look. He hears a loud click and the exhalation of everyone in the theater.

The pistol is cleared and reloaded by the white-gloved hands. When the cheat spins, his eyes reflect his intense concentration. He's counting and finally doesn't like what he has heard. He spins again and pulls the trigger quickly on an empty chamber.

The gamblers ante up for another round and occupy themselves negotiating further bets on the outcome.

Ladd: 'Why do I have the feeling, Abdul, that your odds are always a little better than mine? But never mind. As I've said, in the end it's always fifty-fifty, no better, no worse!'

Again the pistol clicks at his temple. Again the crowd in the Fairmount exhales.

Abdul: 'Mr. White, you are either one of the bravest men I have ever known or one of the biggest fools.'

Abdul spins and listens: he smiles as the pistol makes its empty, hollow sound. The onlookers ante up and wager yet again. If Ladd were to win, unlikely as it is, he might even be able to afford the long-shot brain operation that could give him a second chance, a second chance with his wife and family. Ironically, gambling could offer him a second life.

The tension in the Fairmount is stifling.

Ladd: 'The best thing about this game, Abdul, is that there is always a winner and a loser. Never any ties. It cannot be called on account of darkness or rain. It is always winner takes all: loser, loses all.'

There's a tear in the corner of Ladd's eye. Very faintly at first and then more clearly on his forehead, we see his wife emerging. She's spooning cereal to a kid in a highchair. A daughter at the table is putting jam on toast. The tear rolls down his cheek. Ladd whispers: 'So long, old girl.' James looks away again. The gun fires on an empty chamber. A whoosh of relief in the Fairmount.

Abdul: 'For a Westerner, you have much of the fatalist about you, Mr. White. But we in the East know that what is fated must eventually occur. We call it kismet.'

Just as Abdul's spin of the chamber settles, a fat man – a Turkish Bey or a Moroccan sheik – a man the camera has focused on each time the ante was raised, lets out a loud rumbling sneeze. The surprise of it startles the Fairmount audience: more importantly, it has broken Abdul's concentration. He has lost count and cannot be sure of the bullet's position. He begins to perspire; his eyes dart cunningly.

Abdul: 'I wish to have a new bullet placed in the chamber.'

The croupier begins to come forward. The Bey stops him with a bamboo cane.

Bey: 'No. We have paid to see what kismet has decreed. No one may touch the pistol.'

An extreme close-up of Abdul's dark face. He is sweating profusely. His narrowing eyes search for a way out. He looks into the crowd: there is no sympathy for him there. No way out, he must face the situation. He spins the chamber once again to relieve his nervousness.

Abdul: 'You have said that each attempt is an even chance – life or death. But that cannot be. One bullet, six chambers. One-in-six, not fifty-fifty, Mr. White. Five more chances for hope than for despair. Those are promising odds, are they not?'

His hand trembles slightly as he raises the pistol.

The camera is on Alan Ladd smiling ruefully and nodding. When the expected shot comes, it still scares the wits out of everyone in the theater. Jenna Craig gasps. James puts his arm around her for the first time.

The highway sweeps to the right. The night is dark, his headlights are more like probes in the mist than beacons. It is after 3 A.M. and James Dean's body is electric with exhaustion and loathing. In his gun: two bullets, four empty chambers. Four lives, two deaths. He doesn't have to do this, but under the strange circumstances there doesn't seem to be any compelling reason not to. He puts the .38 to his head.

He feels her presence before he smells her sweetness. In the back seat, the woman, his guardian angel of the flowered dress. He feels her hand on his wrist, pulling, urging the pistol away from his temple. 'Why?' he says. If she'd have spoken, he'd have stopped. At the sound of his voice, her presence wavers. Slowly, she yields. 'Always fifty-fifty, Abdul, no better, no worse,' he says.

His finger squeezes the play out of the trigger. *No, no. Stupid.* He turns the pistol out the window and fires into the darkness. His hand jumps at the CRACK and recoil. One bullet left.

James Dean doesn't want to die. He wants to live. 'That's the point, Abdul,' he says. 'I want to earn the right to live. To prove myself worthy of the wonderful gift.' He is beyond exhaustion.

The barrel is at his temple. James again squeezes the play out of the trigger. His elbow is shaking. He closes his eyes. He can hear the action in the gun – springs and gears – tightening. Hears the hammer striking the head of the chamber with the emphatic ring of YES.

He has an erection.

*

When he calls Amanda in New York to tell her he's heading east, she's encouraging. Rather, her words are encouraging. Her voice is flat, without affection. He wants to hear her say, 'Oh great, you can stay with me.'

She doesn't, so he has to say. 'I'm going to need a place to stay.'

'That might be a bit of a problem, Jim. But if worse comes to worst, I can put you up for a while.'

'I have a little money saved. I can pay . . .'

'It's not that. Rooms are rare as hen's teeth. Let me ask around. I'm sure some of my friends could use a wholesome, reliable Indiana youth to share expenses with.' James feels insulted. 'How long before you get here?'

'Dunno. Two, three days. I'm near Moline. Might stop at Fairmount on the way. Haven't decided, though.'

'Listen, if you do stop, maybe you could pick up some stuff I've got stashed there.'

'Then I'll stop.'

'No, not on my account. It's not *that* important.'

'I will.'

'No, don't. Just be sure to call before you get here. At least a day ahead, okay?'

'Sure.'

'It will be good to see you again, Jim. Really. It will.'

'Same here.'

As the Hudson hums north of Evansville, a surprise visit to Marcus and Ortense seems attractive to him. He imagines Ortense flapping and whooping around the kitchen. Marcus admonishing him for 'most near giving the poor woman a heart attack.' Too good a scene to pass up. But if he doesn't turn north by the time he reaches Bloomington, he'll probably not go home.

In the booth of a diner just west of Bloomington, he flips a quarter. Heads, north to Fairmount; tails, straight on through to New York. He tosses and traps the coin on the yellow formica. *Fairmount.* While walking out to the car, he wonders if the quarter would come up heads again: he's looking for confirmation. He tries a second toss. Again heads. He flips it again. Heads. Three in a row. He changes quarters. Six more times he tosses – nine times in a row it's heads. Fairmount.

Not until the tenth toss does it come up tails. James convinces himself something bad is brewing in Fairmount. He accepts only the last toss as true.

*

The Hudson starts burning oil in Ohio and the problem worsens by Erie, Pennsylvania, but it's not so bad that he has to do anything about it other than drive slower and top up the oil every five hours.

He sees his first Klein Brothers Army-Navy billboard about twenty miles west of Scranton. There are two more signs before the town itself beckons. On the road his urge to visit Klein's has become irresistible. He will buy most of his New York wardrobe here – the pea coat, the denim shirts and dungarees, the fatigue cap. Across Potts Street, at Wanda's Music, he buys the bongos he believes will add a defining touch to his creation.

8. Studio New York

THE GREEN PASTURES: an adaptation of Marc Connelly's play which was suggested by Roark Bradford's stories, 'Ol' Man Adam An' His Chillun''; screenplay by Mr. Connelly and Sheridan Gibney; choral music arranged and conducted by Hall Johnson; directed by Marc Connelly and William Keighley; a Warner Brothers production.

De Lawd	*Rex Ingram*
Gabriel	*Oscar Polk*
Noah	*Eddie Anderson*
Mr. Dashee	*George Reed*
Archangel	*Abraham Gleaves*
Adam	*Rex Ingram*
Eve	*Myrtle Anderson*
Cain	*Al Stokes*
Isaac	*George Reed*
Jacob	*Ivory Williams*
Aaron	*David Bethea*

Hall Johnson Choir

In June 1952, James saw the film revival of Green Pastures *with his roommate Enoch Moss at the Thalia Theater on Broadway. (Thalia was the Greek muse of comedy, but James did not yet know that.)*

James knew the script by heart, having cued Enoch for a month.

Enoch planned to audition for the role of Gabriel in an upcoming stage revival.

James doesn't have a favorite scene: he enjoys the entire thing. Because he is going to try out for Lee Strasberg at the Actors Studio the following week, these lines between Moses, who is about to confront the Pharaoh, and De Lawd, take on heightened significance.

Moses: Me? I'm gonter be a tricker?

Lawd: Dat's right.

Moses: An' do magic? Lawd, my mouth ain't got de quick talk to go wid it.

Lawd: It'll come to you.

Moses: Is I goin' wid a circus?

Lawd: Yo' is goin' down into Egypt, Moses, and lead my people out of bondage. To do dat I'm gonter make you de bes' tricker in de worl'.

Moses: Egypt! You know I killed a man dere, Lawd. Won't dey kill me?

Lawd: Not when dey see yo' tricks. You ain't skeered, is you?

Moses: No, suh, Lawd.

Lawd: Den yere's what I'm gonter do. Yo' people is my chillun, Moses. I'm sick and tired o' de way ol' King Pharaoh is treatin' dem, so I'se gonter take dem away, and yo' gonter lead dem. You gonter lead 'em out of Egypt an' across de river Jordan. It's gonter take a long time, and you ain't goin' on no excursion train. Yo' gonter wukk awful hard for somethin' yo' goin' to fin' when de trip's over.

The boy had come to Strasberg recommended, not highly recommended, but recommended nonetheless. The note to Strasberg from Odets contains three tepid sentences. Marty Goldglass's letter is certainly better than having walked in off the street. Strasberg has read it and put it in his pocket.

'You have something to show me? Something prepared?' Strasberg's speech rhythms confuse Dean. He isn't sure for a moment that he's been asked a question.

When he does understand, he nods vigorously and then stops, suddenly aware of appearing too eager. He looks at his hands in his lap and says quietly, 'Sure do, sir.' That may have been too corn pone, so he looks directly at Strasberg and says, 'Yes I do.'

Strasberg rolls his hands over each other as though winding yarn. 'So?'

'I'm prepared to do plenty.'

'Namely?'

'Well. Lots of things. I can do O'Neill. Odets. Something from Williams. Wilder.'

Lee Strasberg's small face clenches in distaste. 'Oy. If I have to sit through one more simpering *Our Town*, I'll puke.' As a rule Strasberg never lets a potential student choose his own audition role. 'How are you on the Russians?'

James's face puzzles. 'I do, a little, but . . .'

'Why, *but*? What, *but*?'

'I haven't really prepared . . .'

'*Cherry Orchard.*'

This could be a question but it also has the power of a command. James is confused and the faint taste of disappointment comes to the back of his tongue. 'What about *The Cherry Orchard*?'

'I haven't seen a first-rate Lopakhin in God knows how long. Any speech you'd like, but something where Lopakhin alters the direction of the dramatic line.'

James nods in agreement as he says, 'But I don't . . . I haven't really . . .' He supposes he'll have a day or two to prepare something.

'There's a bookstore, Fischer's, on Eighth Avenue. You can get the play there. Right nearby, on the corner of 51st, is the Bohemia Cafeteria, they'll let you sit forever over a cup of coffee. You can do your preparation.' Strasberg often chases a young actor out of the studio in search of a text and a place to prepare – it's part of being Strasberg. 'Something extended, something revealing of the character. We'll say, back here, three o'clock.' Strasberg moves his hand as though tossing away some pennies. James is dismissed, but it's Strasberg who leaves.

At first he's confused. Then he's thrilled. This is the tough New York of his fantasies. This is truly the theater. A life in art. He's got an hour and twenty minutes to prepare a scene. Without a word he stands, smiles, and runs up the short aisle and out of the Actors Studio. He holds his glasses in his teeth as he sprints through the crowds on Eighth Avenue. His pea coat is open. His mind is racing well ahead of him. He's read the play once before but now it escapes him completely. A stimulating confusion.

Because he can't find Fischer's on Eighth Avenue, he circles and whirls in the street. *Where? Where?* He asks a cop and is told, 'Up near 53rd. Two, three stores from the corner.'

'Great. Thanks a lot.'

He bursts into Fischer's, breathless, and tells the girl at the counter, 'Miss, I need a *Cherry Orchard.*'

The man she's waiting on says, 'You're making preserves or something? Wait your turn.'

'I really got to have a Chekhov. No kidding.'

Jimmy fails to notice that the girl could pass for his sister. While she hands the customer his change, she says to James, 'New or used?'

'Anything. I just need it in a hurry.'

'Drama is along the rear wall. Starts on the left. It's alphabetical.' Her accent is clearly Midwestern.

'Would you be able to get it for me? Please? I've only got about an hour to read it.'

The girl and the customer shrug at each other. The customer says, 'In a drugstore I might understand. But an emergency Chekhov?' He shakes his head and moves toward the door.

'Used?' she asks as she goes to find the volume.

'Sure. Fine.'

She returns with two *Cherry Orchard*s, a thin, worn hardbound edition and a used paperback. 'Which one?'

'What's the difference?'

'The hard cover's a quarter more.'

'I mean, are they the same?'

'Different translations. This one . . .' – she waves the paperback – '. . . has some biographical material in the back.'

'I'll take that one, then. How much?'

'Thirty-five.'

He's confused. *Thirty-five what?*

She says, 'Thirty-five cents. A quarter and a dime, three dimes and a nickle, seven nickles . . .'

He realizes as he glances through it, he'd prefer a fresh, unmarked copy, but he doesn't want to waste any more time. The girl offers her freshest smile; if James notices, it doesn't register.

*

He grabs an open booth in the rear of the Bohemia and places his pea coat across the opposite seat so he won't be bothered. His black coffee steams, his cigarette smoke wreaths him. He loves the tension, the urgency, of acting on demand. *Can you do it at the snap of a finger? O.K., show me!* Loves the pressurized New Yorkness of it all.

When he played basketball back in Fairmount, Mr. Grumman, the coach, always wanted James to have the ball in the closing seconds of a tight game. James is at his best under pressure.

159

He flips the opening pages to the cast of characters. The play starts coming back to him. He would read it because Stanislavsky described the Moscow Art Theater production so glowingly. He remembers that the characters in the play all look out at the cherry orchard of the failing estate and each sees something different, something other than cherry trees in blossom. They see their own lives mostly. Their disappointments. More often, their failures. But not Yermolai Lopakhin. On the list of characters, Lopakhin is simply referred to as 'a businessman.' James recalls that when he talks about the orchard, it is always as valuable real estate.

He flips to the material in the back, to a page headed 'Correspondences.' It is a letter: a young Stanislavsky to Chekhov. There are no coincidences in art.

15 January 1904

Most Respected Author:

Already I have devoted a great many minutes trying to decide on the appropriate salutation for this letter from an humble actor you cannot know. (I shall not mention the hours spent in husbanding the temerity to pen these words.)

Our little acting company has just returned from a four-month tour of the Provinces, where we performed *The Cherry Orchard, Ivanov, Three Sisters,* and *The Seagull* to audiences of all social classes. Surely there have been finer performances of these plays, but I doubt if there have been audiences as hungry for the life's nourishment that are the themes of your thoughtful dramas.

When one selects a life in art (although I suspect our art, in truth, actually selects us), it is with the intent of offering something of substance to our fellow man. Your words, your vision, your consolations constitute a great human contribution not only to Russians, but to actors and audiences the world over.

It is with a desire to shape my own art in a similar fashion that I must ask you a crucial question: Is it inborn personality that impels your characters forward or is it your understanding of social and psychological forces? No sooner have I written my query than I realize I have asked such a generalized question there is no way for you to respond except in kind (and, I fear, you will have thought me so great a fool you may not bother to respond at all).

Allow me to be more specific: I have a relative who shall remain nameless (rather, for the sake of dramatic interest, let me call him Uncle Vanya). Vanya is one of the most charming men I know, possessed of a high degree of animal attraction that draws both men and women to his glow almost in spite of themselves. I, if truth be told, have often found myself under his powerful spell.

This man is thoughtful and courteous (perhaps the two qualities are really one); he is attentive, sympathetic, and liberal with his time and sentiment – a gentleman I have always admired greatly. (Please bear with my seeming irrelevancies just a bit longer, sir.)

Imagine my amazement when I discovered, quite by accident, that he owes virtually every shop-keeper and artisan in town considerable sums of money – and has for a very long while. Add to this the perplexing discovery of mine that he has absolutely no intention of paying them! He – and our whole family by extension – is despised by most of the people who live there.

Here is my question then – to which I suspect I know the answer and may be seeking only corroboration – Can my Uncle Vanya be both persons at the same time; notably, a thoughtful and sincere human being as well as a cunning fraud? Or must he be one or the other at heart, with an artificial second personality as a counterpoise?

These are crucial questions for me as I attempt, as a thoughtful, modern actor, to prepare the roles that you and the handful of playwrights at the highest level of human understanding have created. At hand for me is nothing less than the ability to depict human behavior most accurately. Are we essentially one personality with many facets or multiple personalities adhering to a central core? This is the mystery that perplexes me as an artist.

I hope you'll esteem my query worthy of a response, as well as accepting fond wishes on your natal day from a lowly player.

I remain your distant but profound admirer and a laborer in the vineyard of modern theater.

Konstantin Stanislavsky

He wants to re-read the letter, study it, memorize parts of it, but this is not the time. It is enough for now that the words are before him, that he feels the spirit of Stanislavsky watching over him.

He places the book face down on the table and recalls Stanislavsky's words about characterization in *An Actor Prepares*: 'A role is not words uttered by a character. It is first and foremost a function of a greater whole, a thread in the tapestry known as drama. What role do you play and how do you play it? Ah, there is where you must determine what design the author of the work intended for the entire tapestry.'

Lopakhin's age is not specifically mentioned but there are strong indications that he is in middle age. More importantly, James remembers that early in the action, Lopakhin describes himself. He turns to the second page and reads Lopakhin's first extended speech: 'My father hit me in the face and made my nose bleed . . . Liubov Andryeevna – she was still young and slender then – brought me in and took me to the washstand in this very room, the nursery it was then. "Don't cry, little peasant," she said, "it'll be better before you're old enough to get married" . . . "Little peasant" . . . She was right enough, my father was a peasant. Yet here I am – all dressed up in a white waistcoat and brown shoes . . . But you can't make a silk purse out of a sow's ear. I am rich . . . but anyone can see I'm just a peasant.'

Since Liubov Andryeevna is now the impoverished widow Lopakhin is trying to aid, he's probably a man in his fifties. James considers Lopakhin's body. *Stiff and self-conscious. Lopakhin will hold himself* . . . No, he won't be concerned about the body. That is, not play the body consciously. *Find the man, act the man, his history, and the body will be there automatically. Or enough of it will be.* James takes a deep inhalation of his cigarette and a sip of coffee. *If there's a Lopakhin in me, the voice will be his voice. No imitation Russian, no fake English. Play it American, just get the feelings right.* He checks his watch – 2:09 – there's time.

An old woman, powdered as pale as Emmett Kelly and reeking of lavender, pushes his coat into the corner and sits down opposite him. For a moment, James thinks it's a joke. There are plenty of other seats. She pulls out her hat pin with great care and places a veiled black cloche on the table alongside his coffee cup.

'My jacket?'

She looks around, oblivious. Her smile is blurry, her lips are crimson. Her eyebrows rise high on a comic face. She starts to open her purse.

'You can't sit here.'

She appears hurt.

He explains slowly. 'I'm already sitting at this table.'

'Me too.'

James grunts and leans across the table for his coat. He moves to a seat near a large window. On the street he sees the familiar woman in the flowered dress. Her hair is cut very short. She glances at him and they exchange smiles. He signals her to come in. She shakes her head modestly. He goes to the door, but she is not to be seen. Then he remembers: Stanislavsky played Lopakhin. He will be following in the master's footsteps. He remembers also what Stanislavsky said about the play.

'Cherry Orchard' is a drama about time. About history and weak people who are caught in its grip. Such people are the lost ones, the ones who are left behind. But they have no alternative, since the past and its sentimental memories hold them in thrall. James is buoyed now by possibility. His imagination has finally come fully alive. *Trapped in time. Stultified. Everything they do is an effort. Their movements. Breathing, even. Wounded people. Except for Lopakhin. He is free from tradition. Free to shape his own future, the future of Russia. But here, in the midst of these shabby aristocrats, he is inhibited.* Even as he imagines Lopakhin's reserved, tense posture, James's body has become rigid, his breathing shallow. *Lopakhin's deepest wound is the memory of his peasant roots.* James touches his stomach.

Now he need only find the appropriate lines. Starting from the last page he flips forward, stopping at any lengthy speech by

Lopakhin. There really aren't enough to sustain a scene. And nothing especially dramatic. Not until he comes to the place where Lopakhin describes what must be done with the cherry orchard in order to save the Ranyevskaia estate. But what drama can James work into a business proposal?

He flips the pages again to make sure he hasn't missed any other important speeches. A Negro boy with a filthy washcloth lifts his coffee cup and swabs the table. James says, 'Thanks.'

The boy says, 'It ain't raining either.' Which makes no sense. 'Whatcha reading?'

James tips the cover to show the title.

'Awfully skinny for a whole book.'

'It's a play.'

'Didn't know they put plays out in books. Thought they just said them on a stage.'

'And the actors just get out there and make up the words as they go along?'

'Never thought about it, but yeah, I guess that's what I thought.'

James thinks about it now. Immediately he knows he owes this kid something. *The day is magical.* 'What's your name?'

'Jerome. What's yours?'

'Jimmy.' He offers his hand emphatically, like a salesman. They shake. 'I've got to finish this thing. Got an audition in . . .' He checks his watch. 'If it all works out, you'll be seeing a lot of me in here.'

'No I won't.'

'I'll stop in a lot.'

'You might be here, but I won't. This is my last day. I quit this place.' He leaves to wet down the next table.

Lopakhin's longest speech is directed to Liubov Andryeevna, the sentimental spendthrift widow whose land he is trying to save. James closes his eyes and sees himself on stage. He is looking out on an orchard ripe with pink blossoms. It is the first truly warm day in April. James no longer sees himself: he sees only what Lopakhin sees, the trees.

The blossoms blow lightly in the breeze. Small birds flit from tree to tree. Lopakhin has seen this orchard all his life. As a youth

Lopakhin's father toiled for Liubov Andryeevna's family. Each summer his relatives picked the apples, ate them, squeezed them for cider and dried them in the sun for a winter treat. That was before his father became a free man and learned about the power of money, something the Ranyevskaia family always scorned, and as a result, something they have allowed to slip away.

Glasses, James thinks. *Glasses to start with, as though he's the only one who can really see the orchard for what it is – profit. When Liubov Andryeevna rebuffs him, then perhaps he'll take them off.*

He runs through his lines looking for a clinching idea, what Goldglass used to call a character hook, memorizing at the same time. On a second reading, he finds his hook in an aside that Lopakhin uses for emphasis. '. . . if you advertise now, I'm prepared to stake any amount you like you won't have a spot of land unoccupied by the autumn.' From the very beginning of the play when he tells that tender story about the beautiful, young Liubov Andryeevna washing his bloody nose, Lopakhin has made it appear that his only motive in advising her to cut down the orchard and sell off small parcels is sentiment. The words 'stake any amount' give James the idea that profit is Lopakhin's deepest motivation.

*

At five to three James re-enters the Actors Studio's small theater and takes a seat near the front. Lee Strasberg is sitting in his usual mid-aisle seat, watching workmen remove the first row of seats so that the stage can be made to thrust even further into audience. He stands and walks right past James on his way backstage. James waits with increasing impatience, unaware that this too is part of the trial. Strasberg doesn't return. At 3:20 James goes to find him. No one backstage seems to know where Strasberg has gone. James feels his confidence ebbing as he returns to the theater and takes a seat near the one Strasberg has vacated.

'Whenever you're ready, young man,' a dry voice says from the rear.

'Been ready,' James mumbles without turning around.

'Could you fellows hold it for a minute or two? This young man would like to develop a scene.' The workmen back away from their demolition and crouch below the lip of the stage. 'Whenever you're ready.'

'Whenever,' James murmurs sarcastically and pushes himself out of his seat. 'A minute or two.' It's an easy leap to the stage. The house lights are on. He can see Strasberg sitting with a woman in the back row. Three others, arriving students presumably, are scattered in other seats. The workmen are looking straight up at him, with the expressions of tough kids at a puppet show. James is unready, thrown somewhat by the treatment he's getting.

From the rear Strasberg says, 'It's a great deal of trouble setting up lights, so why don't you just play it as is.'

'You said whenever I was ready?'

'Of course. I don't want to rush you.'

Trying to make this place his own, James slowly folds his pea coat on a table stage left. He is trying to stretch the time he has, to find his deepest concentration. He is wearing a maroon turtleneck shirt and pale dungarees. He walks around the stage in a great circle. His thought is not about Stanislavsky or Chekhov or even Lopakhin. He is thinking about Jerome, putting in his last day at the Bohemia Cafeteria. Jerome takes him back to the moment when he reminded himself that words must come from the character not from the playwright. Lopakhin is a smooth operator, James decides then. Smart and cunning as only a clever peasant can be. These thoughts take time, he gives them time. He waits for the chain of final understanding to form link by link. Inner man and outer man must be in something approximating harmony.

Strasberg has no way of knowing if this is posturing or legitimate preparation: either way he thinks, 'Kid has balls.' He's on the verge of saying something about the delay, when the boy's relaxed body begins to tighten, as though it is preparing to ward off a blow of some sort.

James remembers the Stanislavsky dictate that all character develops from breathing. He slows his respiration, lets it become a labor by degrees. Here is a man who no longer does physical work. A soft wheeze seems to come on its own. His chest heaves; the lower lip rounds with each exhalation. His eyebrows almost cover the eyes, which are peering out with puzzlement at something familiar. Strasberg knows the boy is no longer preparing. Lopakhin gazes through the window into the orchard. He sighs and slowly removes his glasses. He almost drops them and places them on again. He backs away from the window clumsily. Acting, fine thoughtful acting without yet uttering a word.

Strasberg scrutinizes the body, its tension is Lopakhin's, not the preposterous stiffness of a twenty-year-old trying to be middle-aged. As Dean projects it, middle age is suggested through facial gesture, and when he finally speaks it is through a voice that has spent the better part of a lifetime wheedling and cajoling. The boy has authority. Lopakhin lifts his glasses off one ear and then the other; he pulls his hand slowly over his face, as though what he has to say might be grudging and unpleasant. 'I feel I'd like to tell you something nice, something jolly.' James glances quickly at his pocket watch and looks again out to the orchard. 'I'll have to go in a moment, there's no time to talk. However, I could tell you in a few words. You know, of course, that your cherry orchard is going to be sold to pay your debts. The auction is to take place on the twenty-second of August, but there's no need for you to worry.'

He looks at Liubov Andryeevna indirectly. For the briefest of moments, James peeks at the others in the room; he smiles again at her. 'You can sleep in peace, my dear; there's a way out. This is my plan.' He pauses and takes a deep breath; his hands appear to hold something of great weight. 'Please listen carefully. Your estate is only twenty miles from town, and the railroad line is not far away. Now . . . if your cherry orchard . . .' He gestures behind him with a wave of dismissal. '. . . and the lands along the river are divided into plots and leased out for summer residences you'll have a yearly income of at least twenty-five thousand rubles.' His smile is triumphant. He drops the weighty object at her feet. Although nothing has changed on stage, James somehow creates the impression that he is bathed in light. The workmen are riveted by the young player.

Strasberg, remembering when he played Liubov Andryeevna's brother Gayev, says, 'But what nonsense!'

James turns toward Gayev in the rear, glares, smiles insincerely and returns to the sister: 'You'll charge the tenants at least twenty-five rubles per year for a plot of one acre and if you advertise now . . .' Lopakhin stops short, aware that he is talking to children as far as business is concerned. 'But, of course, the place will have to be cleaned up, put in order. For instance, all the old outbuildings will have to be pulled down, as well as this house which is no good to anybody. The old cherry orchard should be cut down, too.'

Strasberg says, 'Cut down? My dear man, forgive me, you don't seem to understand. If there's one thing interesting, one thing really outstanding in the whole country, it's our cherry orchard.'

Dean's Lopakhin wants to bark a response but habit overwhelms impulse. He walks over to the window and scrutinizes the blossoming trees. 'The only outstanding thing about this orchard is that it's very large. It only produces a crop every other year, and then there's nobody to buy it.'

Smiling and remembering, Strasberg says, 'This orchard is actually mentioned in the *Encyclopedia*.'

Lopakhin nods and checks his watch again: 'If you can't think clearly about it, or come to a decision, the cherry orchard and the whole estate as well will be sold by auction. You must decide. There's no other way out, I assure you. There is . . . no . . . other . . . way . . . out.' Lopakhin is not smug; his certainty, rather, is offered as a profitable gift to an old friend.

'This is the first time, I must say . . .' James is confused. Gayev does not have another line here.

Strasberg says again, 'The first time, young man, I've seen a Lopakhin who is more of a hustler than a would-be gentleman.' The intimacy in his voice encourages James. 'Come up. We'll talk.'

James jumps off the stage, past the spellbound workmen, up the aisle.

Strasberg says, 'Paula, my wife.'

She doesn't offer a hand, so James bends and says, 'Ma'am.' Exactly as he would have back in Fairmount; it's the same 'Ma'am' he used to offer Miss Mavis Flagg and her mother every Saturday morning at Hardy's Texaco.

'You've played Lopakhin before?' Paula asks.

'No, never.'

'You first saw the lines, when?'

He looks over at Lee. 'Read it once a couple of years ago. Your husband sent me out for a copy of the play about an hour ago. It was only a couple of speeches, and I'm sort of good memorizing lines.'

She elongates her face and flutters her eyes.

'Lines,' Lee Strasberg repeats, 'lines are the least of it, Mr. Dean.' Although he had politely minimized Paula Strasberg's compliment, it bothers James that Strasberg seems to be minimizing it too. 'Acting is here and here and here.' He points between his eyes, at his heart, and to his testicles. 'You've got two out of three already. The third we will develop.'

James wants to know which of the three he lacks, but all he can hear is the future tense.

Strasberg says, 'Dean, I'd like you to hone that same scene for the group tomorrow. We're meeting at 5:30. I'll do a more definitive critique then.' James doesn't know the world 'critique,' but he figures it out well enough. 'You know,' Lee says to Paula, 'we don't do enough Chekhov.'

She is busy considering Jimmy. Her gaze has made him very self-conscious; as a result, his smile wavers and his eyes look askance. His is the most remarkable face she's seen on a young actor – wholesome, tender, sweet and malleable enough to undercut, even to betray, those very qualities. A face that can reflect thought processes that are different from what it actually reveals, and eyes that express thoughts even as they are being shaped. A complex, mysterious face. A close-up camera would never tire of that face.

In an off-hand way Strasberg says, 'You are aware of our fee scale?'

He hadn't considered that. 'I can handle it.'

As he walks toward the stage to retrieve his coat, the carpenters look at him with continued awe. He tips an invisible cap toward them. They smile back, a little afraid of his potency.

James takes the steps up to street level three at a time. The sun has come out. He spreads his arms and takes a few running strides, then leaps, intending to pirouette but thinking better of it in mid-air. He lands and continues running, his fists thrust deep into the pockets of his jacket.

Jimmy Dean Prepares

Back in the Actors Studio theater, Paula Strasberg says to her husband, 'That *punim* is movies without a shadow of a doubt.'

Jimmy lopes in a release of energy, a celebration in motion down Broadway with no specific thought of where he is going other than the general direction – downtown. Toward the Village, toward Amanda's apartment. Or his own. Wherever.

He expects to tire; if he does, he'll grab a bus at a convenient corner. But he gets a second wind and continues running past the downtown subway at 34th Street. He has become his own downtown local, running in place when he's stopped briefly by a traffic light every fourth or fifth block. A strange aura of happiness emanates from him; it is taken as normal street insanity by those who notice. To one woman who stares at him a bit too long, he says, 'I'm an actor, a real actor.' She says, 'And I'm a Rockette.' James yucks and runs off.

Past 23rd Street, across 14th, and over toward Sixth Avenue. Near Washington Square Park the expressions on the faces begin to mirror his own. More alert than uptown, more expressive, far less conventional, that is to say nuttier. He turns left on Bleecker and stops running. Rather than walking a few more yards up to Mercer Street, to the apartment, James goes into Sal's Pizza just to share the news. Sal is tossing dough up in the air. 'They took me, Sal. I'm in.'

Sal hasn't the slightest idea what James is talking about. His single eyebrow rises, his face clouds. His assumption is the kid has been drafted. 'Better you than Vinnie.' Vinnie is his son.

'Acting school, Sal, I got into acting school.'

'Schools for acting? A new rip-off.'

James goes out the side door, the Mercer Street exit, and up the steps of the first brownstone. He bounds up to the second floor, expecting to find the door to the apartment partly open, drawing some of the heat from the radiator in the hallway. He expects to see Enoch, script in hand, working on his Gabriel in the full-length mirror. But the door is locked.

James coughs and jiggles his key in the lock long enough to give Enoch and whoever might be with him time to get ready for an intruder. The place is empty. James calls into the bathroom. No one. His elation begins to melt, leaving a residue of sadness on his face.

170

He dials Amanda's number. He senses her presence and expects her to pick up after each ring. Her phone rings twelve times. He hangs up momentarily and dials 'O'. 'Operator, I'd like to place a long distance call, person-to-person. Los Angeles, California. Mr. Martin Gold-glass from James Dean. The number is AL 7–7337.' *What time is it in California?*

While the phone is ringing, he anticipates the operator's words. Sure enough, they come: 'I'm sorry, sir. That number does not answer.'

'Thanks a lot, operator. Could I tell *you* some good news?'

'I'm not allowed to personalize, sir.'

'I just wanted to tell someone that I've been blind from birth and about fifteen minutes ago I fell to my knees and prayed for the first time in my life. You won't believe this but I saw a flash of light and now I'm able to see. Able to see. I can dial a phone. Operator, it's a miracle.'

'I'm very pleased for you, sir.'

'Thanks, and God bless you, operator.'

He takes off his coat and lays down on Enoch's bed. Then he moves to the mirror. 'You did it, man. You really did it.' He swells his chest and bends his taut body right and left. Then he strikes the Charles Atlas muscle-man pose that's on the back of movie magazines. He shifts into a boxer's stance and begins to shadowbox in slow motion. Admiring what he sees, James moves closer to the mirror and sways into an unhurried dance. A life in art, he tells himself, sometimes demands unabashed self-love. The dance becomes sensual and he opens his belt and the top button on his dungarees.

The record on Enoch's machine is perfect, Duke Ellington's 'The Mooch.' The muted, quavering trumpet calls to the willowy reeds and Jimmy Dean's narcissistic dance begins in earnest. He drapes his shoulders with his hands and draws them down his arms to his elbows: his shirt comes out of his pants and he pulls it up and over his head. He traces circles around his nipples with his thumbs.

The erection that was in the back of his mind while he was running in midtown starts with a quick spasm, like a hiccup from his testicles. James rubs one hand over the lump in his jeans; with the other hand he lowers the zipper tantalizingly. The grinding rhythm of the Ellington band, its slow, surprising syncopation, arouses him further still. So does the fact that Enoch might walk in at any moment.

Lock the damned door. Go into the bathroom. He does neither. He pulls open his fly and draws his stout cock through the leg of his shorts. He strums himself in the mirror to the slow slap of the rhythm section. Teasingly, 'The Mooch' builds to a driving crescendo; in the mirror he becomes the helpless creature he loves beyond all his other selves.

The creature's eyes are unfocused, a thin line of spittle glistens in the corner of a half-open mouth. The body begins to curl like a question mark: his right hand pulses on a rose-tipped penis that approaches orgasm. He wants to come before the record ends – he must come – and begins to grunt with each firm stroke. In the mirror is a sinewy animal.

James imagines himself on stage at the Actors Studio. A shiver starts at his thigh and runs up to his lower back. 'The Mooch' slows toward a final sigh. He is looking down at his hand on his cock; he looks up at the image of his fist on himself, and that does it. The shiver becomes a shudder from his knees to his shoulders. *Ahhh, ye-essssss.*

The trumpet wails on the last, extended note. James squeezes his penis tip to keep his semen from spilling. His breathing is labored; he feels the familiar despondency begin, the sinking feeling. In the mirror, he looks brutish, pathetic. And now he must waddle to the bathroom and clean up the mess.

*

When Enoch invites him, Jimmy isn't wild about the idea: 'Oh no, not a night with thespians, agents, and other assorted show folk.'

'What the hell are *you*?' says Enoch, placing a card on his bare knee. 'Here's the address. You never been to an address as turned out as that before. Nine o'clock. Be there.'

The party is in honor of Enoch Moss. He landed Gabriel in *Green Pastures*, beating out dozens of other Negro actors who auditioned for it. He's been guaranteed thirty-six weeks, plenty of cause to celebrate.

'Enoch, man, I'm working tonight.'

'You caught your thumb in a door, don't you remember? Can't carry a tray. So who's calling in hurt? You or me?'

'I'll take off early, okay? I need the bread this week.'

'Just be there, that's all.' Enoch clenches a huge fist under James's nose.

'It's done.'

Just for the hell of it, James rolls a wad of surgical tape on his left thumb while he's riding uptown on the Lexington line after work. He's not sure exactly where Beekman Place is, but a liveried door-man tells him, 'Y' keep walkin' east. Just afore y' slip into the river, yer there.'

He gets to the address a few minutes before midnight. He's stopped by the doorman, who calls upstairs for clearance and then salutes the late-comer. In the old brass elevator he remembers how much he hates walking into parties.

Big-band music blares out on the eighth floor. The door to 8B is open a crack. He pushes it open a little more. A large, high-ceilinged living room; blue smoke hugs the molding. Sleeping and stunned people are stretched out on the parquet, oblivious to 'Peanut Vendor' blaring on the phonograph. The acrid sweetness of reefers. The room is basically unfurnished. No rugs, no chairs or sofas, no tables, no lamps, just a glaring overhead bulb, no pictures on the walls, a large, bare room on Beekman Place populated with dead drunks and reefer rats. Jimmy likes what he sees.

He hears conversation coming from the bedroom, picks an empty glass off the floor and pours himself a splash of gin. Figuring he has some catching up to do, he downs it at a gulp. The burn runs from his mouth to his belly. He pours himself two splashes more and steps toward the bedroom door. The room is edged with people leaning against the walls, mostly actor friends of Enoch and Amanda. The conversation is actually a monologue, propagated by a barrel-chested young man in a pin-striped suit-vest – he wears bright-red suspenders over the vest – holding, in one large fist, a wooden soda-fountain chair by the base of one of its legs. His striped shirt, his arm, his face, his hair, even the vest itself, are bathed in perspiration. James has walked in on a test of strength.

It is a competition because Enoch, too, is drenched in sweat. It is hard for James to imagine anyone who could out-muscle Enoch, but this guy is holding the chair at arm's length without a quaver and checking his watch. 'That's why I came to New York in the first place,' he says with a slightly clenched voice. 'If I stay in Pittsburgh, it's the mill, the tavern, a kid with a Slovak girl, hunting season, and then if you're lucky, the mill, the tavern, the Slovak girl . . . all over again. The only way my old man ever knew he was really alive was when a slag cart rolled over his foot and crippled him. By my count, Enoch, four minutes, thirty seconds.'

Enoch, taking a moment to sip from an empty glass, says, 'Didn't give it my best shot.'

'Bullshit, man. Ground rules were one try apiece.' The strong man shows two rows of perfect teeth. 'So one day I look at myself – of course, I realize I got to get out – and I say "What the hell you got to sell anyone?" I mean, what have I got that the world would want to pay me for? I can't sing. I can't dance. God knows, I can't act. I'm not gorgeous or anywhere near athletic enough. In my heart I know the answer even before I ask the damn question. The answer is I'm smart about people and I've got big nuts – bigger nuts than smarts. I also noticed that people who have real talent usually don't have the same smarts. So it hits me, go to New York and sell other people's talent.' Again the flicker of perfect teeth. He checks his watch. 'Five minutes-fifty-five, Enoch. Two more minutes and I gotcha.' He winks disgustingly.

Amanda sees Jimmy standing in the doorway and tips her glass in his direction. He offers his bandaged thumb.

The bedroom, James observes, contains a mattress, a telephone, a green desk lamp, all on the floor, nothing more. James wants to look into the closet, he's sure it's full of fine business suits.

'I just never figured there'd be so many people here as smart and ballsy as I was. So then I said to myself, "You gotta find something that'll make you different from the rest of them. Something that sets you apart." And you know what I came up with?'

'Red suspenders,' a small black woman says. It gets a laugh.

'Mock, you poor under-represented wretches.'

'An address,' James says. Everyone turns to him then.

'Give that man a cigar,' the lifter says. 'Took all my money and put down three months' rent on this place even before I had a decent suit. Why? Because I hand out my card and right away they see I'm somebody. Must know his business they say to themselves, he's got an office on Beekman Place. That's why I get clients, calls from producers, and, bingo, I'm established in New York City, two years away from Steeltown.'

'Problem is, Hal,' says Enoch, 'you ain't living a hell of a lot better'n the folks in Pittsburgh.'

'Got you your gig, didn't I?'

'But even I live better'n you do, man.'

'Then show you're grateful. Give me twenty percent, maybe then I can buy myself some silverware.'

'What'll you buy first?' Amanda asks.

'A spoon. Go right out and buy myself a spoon.'

'You've figured out the order?'

'Sure have.' A slight quiver in the chair. 'A spoon, you can use the edge to cut with and it can scoop stuff like a fork. Fork comes next for sticking. Knives are last. You'd be surprised how little stuff is really necessary.' He looks at his watch: he's about to beat Enoch's time. 'The address is everything. The business itself isn't any different than I thought it'd be back in Pittsburgh, easier even. At the heart of it all, you just have to be ruthless, right, Amanda?'

She doesn't answer. Hal's standing, moving toward the window. The chair is wobbling but he's beaten Enoch's time. He slides the window open from the bottom and a cold rush of air enters the room. Hal goes to his knees: he looks like a performer on the Ed Sullivan Show.

Hal maneuvers the chair through the window. James is fascinated.

Enoch says, 'Watch it, man. That could get away from you.'

'Someone could be down there,' the black woman says.

Hal says, 'Trying to show you, Mr. Moss, why you got yourself the best agent in this damned town. Why? Because I don't give a shit. I can't be bluffed. I go eyeball to eyeball with some lawyer, Hal Simmons doesn't blink. If I have to, I could drop this thing without a second thought.'

No one wants to say anything for fear it will provoke him. But the chair is wavering dangerously. Finally, Enoch says. 'We all know you'd do it, Hal. You don't have to prove anything to anyone in this room.'

'Damn right. I got no scruples about anything.'

James has no idea if Hal will drop the chair or not. He looks on smiling with tight lips, a look of expectation in his eyes.

Enoch says, 'You'll only have to buy a new one, Hal.'

'If I don't drop it, pal, you won't know for sure that I could really do it.'

'Are you kidding? No one in this room doubts you're capable . . . doubts that for a minute.'

'I'm going to drop it.' His upper arm is shaking violently.

Enoch says, 'No you're not. We're on the eighth floor. You could kill somebody.' He is speaking with the cold precision of a school teacher.

'Oh, no. There it goes. Hah, hah, hah, heeeeee.' Slowly, Hal Simmons leans out the window and looks below. Then he gets to one knee and brings the chair back into the room.

There is relief. No one says anything.

'C'mon,' Hal bubbles, 'this is a celebration. *Green Pastures*, remember? It'll run forever. Drinks are on the producers.'

Everyone moves toward the doorway. Only James notices Amanda drifting toward the chair. She tests it, trying to hoist it with two hands on one leg. Impossible. With each hand on a leg, it comes off the floor unevenly. James sees her carry the chair to the window and dip it through the opening. A few of the others see amazement building on James's face and turn to the window. Amanda pulls her empty arms into the room, a smirk on her face; at the same moment a shattering crack is heard on the pavement. Amanda shrugs: 'It's a ruthless business.' She chuckles.

In the street: whistles, car horns, a crowd gathering. A chair has exploded.

Amanda and James leave the party together, headed downtown in a taxi. In the back of the cab, Amanda says, 'So how do you like working with Strasberg?'

He smiles coyly. 'He pushes you around a lot. But you learn and I like that.'

'That cigarette behind your ear. Is that you or are you working on a character?'

'Why's it important?'

'It isn't particularly. It's just that when you lit up at the party, I saw you take one out of the pack. So what's with the one behind the ear?'

'One's for smoking, one's for asking.'

'Asking?'

'You asked me about it, didn't you? It's my asking cigarette. Now can I ask *you* a question? How come you dumped the chair?'

It's Amanda's turn to be coy: 'Just wanted to call that phoney's bluff.'

It's 2 A.M. and the piano player at Barnaby's is actually playing 'Melancholy Baby.' Amanda has wanted and has not wanted some time alone with James ever since he'd come to New York.

His nose touches the rim of his beer mug: 'Won't he get pissed you did that?'

'Who cares?'

'Isn't he your agent?'

'Not at all. He's strictly interested in heavy hitters.'

'You're not a heavy hitter?'

'Hal doesn't think so. But he'd like to represent you.'

'I'm a heavy hitter?'

'Jim, don't be dense. Christ.'

He inscribes small circles on the bar with his mug. 'Hee, hee.'

'Everyone knows you're the new talent at Strasberg's. And the real reason Hal had Enoch bring you was to get your attention. Wise up.' James looks at her, perplexed, then with disbelief. He shakes his head. Amanda nods assertively, 'Yes.'

James sips his beer.

'I only wanted . . .' She stops in mid-sentence and looks at the ceiling. 'God. I *hate* confessionals. Listen, I know I haven't done all I could have for you here.' He lays his head on his hands and looks at her sidewise. She slaps him softly: 'Oh, come on, don't play dumb. I hate that.'

He allows his tongue to loll out of his mouth. He places his fist inside the back of his sweater forming a small hump. Quasimodo. 'Esm'alda. Esm'alda no like-a me. I want protect-a her. No hurt, no hurt.'

'Don't, Jim. It's serious. I've hated the way I behaved.'

'Poor baby.' More drunkenly than he intends.

'I really could have done a little more when you got here.'

He says to the passing bartender, 'Why are my friends always apologizing to me?'

'Don't knock it, it beats having to apologize to them. But she, *she*, could apologize to me 'til the cows come home.' He winks lewdly.

'You've got to let me get this off my chest, Jim.'

At the word 'chest,' the passing bartender backtracks and stands in front of them again. He touches her hand and says, 'I'm just moonlighting, my child. I'm really a priest, and I do hear confessions.'

Amanda picks up their drinks and moves to a booth. The piano man is playing a lush 'Stardust.'

'Not that I'm ashamed of anything . . . anything we did.' Her eyes belie the statement. 'New York, it was touching and really very beautiful.' Now they completely refute the words. 'I wouldn't have changed that for all the world.' Utterly untrue.

James says, 'It was no big deal. Not anymore. It wasn't just you, you know.'

'That's not what I'm trying to say, damn it. That's not what turned me against you.'

'Against?' He draws back.

'No, not "against," that was wrong. But not being as much of a friend as I should have been.'

'Hell, you got me the names of teachers in L.A. A place to stay here. Leads on jobs and schools. Introductions, tryouts. No, you sure aren't much of a friend.'

'I did things, yes, but not with my whole heart in it. I did them because I knew you and have always believed in your talent. But I was jealous of you, Jim. Maybe not when I was the teacher and you

178

were the student. But once we were just two actors in New York looking for work, it wasn't the same.'

'I didn't ever see it.'

'Jealousy isn't that controllable.'

'No. I do love you, Amanda.' He doesn't believe this, but his face is convincing. Because he wants it to be.

'You're sweet. I just wanted to get it off my chest.' She takes a deep breath and sips her highball. 'I don't for the life of me see how Enoch handles it so well.'

'Handles what?'

'Being jealous.'

'Jealous? He's got real work, a great Broadway role. I'm the one should be jealous.'

'But he wanted the Actors Studio in the worst way. Twice he read for Strasberg. Last year and this spring.'

'He never said a word.'

'That's Enoch.'

A memory of Enoch rehearsing *Othello*, James cueing him, flares into his memory. The virtuoso voice could, by turns, rattle windows and then lilt a babe to sleep. It doesn't seem right; fair is what he means. 'Least he's working now.' James gulps down his beer.

The pianist is playing for himself. A medley. Cole Porter. Kern. Gershwin.

Amanda stands. 'Come on. Walk me home.'

'No. No, I'll just put this place to bed tonight.'

'Come on, Jimboy.' For the first time ever she uses the name Tenten calls him.

'I have to do some thinking.'

She kisses his forehead. He squeezes her hand around her keys. He watches her walk bravely toward the door and into the red glare of Greenwich Avenue.

The pianist plays 'Miss Otis Regrets.' James walks over to the piano. The olive-skinned young man sings, '. . . regrets she's unable to lunch today, Jimmy.'

James responds melodically, 'Such a shame, Clyde.'

Clyde slides over on his stool, making room at the bass end. He pauses so that James can find an appropriate chord. And another. They sing the end in mock sadness, a wavering harmony. 'Miss Otis regrets she's unable to lunch today.'

James's right hand clutches Clyde's waist. The new song is 'Ten Cents a Dance.' The music rolls out in sheets. Jimmy and Clyde swaying to its pendular rhythm.

James looks over his shoulder and is not at all surprised to see a woman at the bar watching him intently. Not surprised that she looks a little older, and that her print dress is a little more out of style. He wishes she was smiling.

9. The Actor's Life for Them

CITY FOR CONQUEST: screenplay by John Wexley; based on the novel by Aben Kandel; produced and directed by Anatole Litvak for Warner Brothers.

Danny Kenny	*James Cagney*
Peggy Nash	*Ann Sheridan*
'Old Timer'	*Frank Craven*
Scotty MacPherson	*Donald Crisp*
'Mutt'	*Frank McHugh*
Eddie Kenny	*Arthur Kennedy*
'Pinky'	*George Tobias*
'Googi'	*Elia Kazan*

James remembers going to Sunday movie matinées with his mother almost every week when they lived in California. He remembers most vividly her anticipation at seeing The Women. *After they had seen the coming attraction, Mildred put her arm around her son's shoulder and said, 'I've been waiting for this one forever. You'll love it, Jamie.' James didn't believe that: from the trailer he could tell it was a dull ladies' movie.*

In February 1941, weeks before his ninth birthday, Mildred took her son to see The Women. *The second feature was* City for Conquest. *It was the first time James Dean ever saw James Cagney, and he loved the cock-of-the-walk manner: the head waggle, the chin thrust, the don't-give-a-damn delivery. James walked like Cagney for months.*

Although James forgot the name of the film, he remembers some of the dialogue, parts of the scene where his manager asks Cagney to throw a fight because if he takes a blow to the head he's liable to go blind. Cagney needs the money to send his little brother to music school.

The setting is the locker room of Stillman's Gym. Cagney is on the rubbing table; Donald Crisp, his manager, rubs his chest:

Scotty: It's rotten, what I got to ask you, kid. But you got to fall down early tonight. Maybe it's not honest, but that's been the way of the world since the serpent's been selling apples. One more fall won't even make a ripple.

Danny: I ain't in the ripple business, Scotty, and I ain't in the apple business either. I'm in the fight game, where everyone's against you. I thought at least you were on my side.

Scotty: I'm on *our* side, and if you take one in that eye, you'll never see that girl of yours again.

Danny: Yeah, well, when that bell rings, I'm a fighter, not a blind fighter, an honest fighter tryin' his best to win.

Scotty: Fine, but don't hold that right up high. I'd hate to become a guide dog.

Danny: Ah, don't be so glum. You only live once, and whoever said you paid to see the whole show.

'Where the hell have you been? I've called you all morning, every hour.' It's Amanda. Her incipient good news pulses under her accusatory tone.

'Over in the Brooklyn Navy Yard. Finally found what I want to do with my life, my true calling. I'm serious. I've decided to become a welder.'

Amanda is the only person on earth who can always spot a James Dean put-on. 'Oh, that's great. I knew it was only a matter of time. I'm happy for you. Welders get to wear masks, don't they? So people won't have to look at that face of yours all the time.'

'Welders don't usually have such pain-in-the-ass friends either.'

'Listen. Are you sitting down?'

'No. But I'll make room to pass out on the floor.'

'Not a bad idea. There's an audition for the role of a lifetime if you want it. I've put in a plug for you and they're interested. It's *The Immoralist*. Gide. Broadway.'

Jimmy knocks the phone against the table and stomps on the carpet to create the sound of a body hitting the floor.

'It's the Arab boy. An unbelievable part.'

Silence.

'Do you know the story? The Arab kid's at the heart of everything. They're predisposed to give you a look if . . .' She can see him smiling. He does not speak. 'Have you read the novel?' Silence. 'Didn't think so. It's by Gide. G-I-D-E. Go out and get it right away. Jim? Come on, don't be childish.' Silence. 'Anyway, they'll want to talk to you about some stuff before you read. The producer's French. They've already done the show in Paris. Jim?' Continued silence. 'Listen, if you don't answer me, I'm not going to tell you the other piece of news.' James doesn't answer. Amanda hangs up.

James dials her number slowly, savoring the forthcoming pleasure.

She lets the phone ring four times. 'Amanda.' His voice is fresh. 'It's Jimmy. 'S'up, babe?'

'You know something? You're not funny.'

'There are indeed some who are deeply offended by my pitiful attempts at levity, but Allah has written . . .' His voice is nasal with exotic rhythms and unusual inflections. It is supposed to sound like an Arab speaking English, and it does in a forced way. It echoes Sabu the Elephant Boy. 'Strange things have been happening, my dear Miss Archer. I have been asleep and in my dream I have heard your voice telling me there is famous news for me. I was awakened from my slumber by an urgent mantra – *Call Amanda, Call Amanda, Call Amanda.* Can my dream really have been a foretelling? Tell me. Tell me what cosmic force beckons.'

'Do you have any idea what a jerk you are?'

'Jerk. Verb transitive. To move suddenly causing a spasmodic twisting or pulling and pushing that . . .'

'The second thing can be wonderful too. A "Philco Playhouse."' She waits for James to indicate some excitement.

'Gee, that's great. What is it?'

'It's a fight story. Hal Simmons told me about it weeks ago. He sent me the script yesterday: I've got it in my hand. I'll send it over. Basically a two character piece. A young, up-and-coming white fighter and an old black champ on his way out. A few teaspoons *Golden Boy* with a smattering of *Body and Soul*. It's *schmaltzy* but really not too bad. Great scene for you at the end.'

'What're the chances?'

'That's the good part. Hal wants the part of the champ for Enoch. He'd like to package it.'

'Meaning?'

'Simply that if they want Enoch, they've got to take you. And the part's a natural for Enoch, especially with some of his credits.'

'And I'm what, chopped liver?'

'You didn't let me finish. Hal's been talking to the director about you for weeks. An Actors Studio credential goes a long way. It's a perfect spot for the two of you, and I'm sure they'll go for it when you guys read for them.'

James recovers his phony accent: 'Oh, may Allah be praised for allowing me to have such a glorious representative as yourself.'

'So why not send me ten percent? Actually, you may have to work out some sort of deal with Hal. I can't believe he's doing all of this out of the goodness of his heart.'

'Maybe I can buy him some forks and spoons. With all my heart, Amanda I want to . . .'

Amanda places the receiver on the cradle very carefully. Until he asks a question, Jimmy has no idea that he has been talking to no one for quite a while. When he dials her number again there is no answer.

*

The Gide novel puzzles him. Each sentence is perfectly clear, but as they accumulate in paragraphs and pages, they veer and whirl in his head. There is something going on in the story he can never quite grasp. He is more than confused, he is perplexed, almost troubled.

Michel, the first-person narrator, is a pedagogue, a scholar of dead cultures and dead languages. But his conflicted emotions confuse James Dean and so does the strange illness that robs him of breath and energy while he and his young wife, Marceline, visit Tunisia. Why, for example, does Michel begin to shake his torpor when he is surrounded by beautiful young Arab boys in a small village outside Tunis? And why does Marceline come down with the same strange illness as Michel regains his health? Why does Marceline lose their baby prematurely? Everything is so damned vague and without clear paths of cause and effect.

And how the hell can you put on a play about a young married man loving a boy – even for a New York audience, even if the man *is* French, and even if they only touch one another playfully? That's the problem for him: in the novel nothing is really explicit, things just sort of happen. But in some strange way, when they do happen, James realizes that his intuition has anticipated them. That, too, is what bewilders him about *The Immoralist.* And why he's reading it again in bed on a beautiful Sunday morning.

He puts the beer bottle to his lips and re-reads Gide's preface. He discovers something important right off the bat: Gide refers to his story as a 'drama.' He writes, 'If certain distinguished minds have chosen to regard this drama as no more than the account of a strange case, and its hero as a sick man . . . that is the fault of the author – though he has put into this book all his passion, all his tears, and all his care.'

James looks at the ceiling and closes his eyes. The word 'illness' comes to him. The word 'deviate.' He thinks about illness and that leads him to consider the isolation that serious illness brings. Isolation and separation. The ultimate separation of feelings and actions, inner man and outer man. Michel acts on his feelings, and when he does he grows stronger. When he does not, when he cannot, he is weakened.

During his first reading, James was not absolutely sure just which Arab boy he would play, there were quite a few: but it becomes clear that he will be Moktir, the least trustworthy and most attractive of the village urchins. What exactly does Michel see in him? What secret signals does Moktir send?

James skips ahead to the scene his instinct told him was important the first time. He takes another pull at the beer bottle and reads Michel's description: 'I was standing near the fire, both elbows on the mantel in front of a book in which I appeared to be absorbed, but I could see reflected in the glass the movements of the child behind me. A curiosity I could not quite account for made me follow his every movement. Moktir did not know he was being observed, and thought I was deep in my book. I saw him stealthily approach a table on which Marceline had put down, beside some sewing, a pair of tiny scissors, which he furtively snatched up and in a single gesture stuffed into his *bournous.* My heart pounded a moment, but the most prudent rationalization could not produce in me the slightest feeling of disgust. Quite the contrary, I could not manage to convince myself that the feeling which filled me at that moment was anything but amusement, but delight. When I had given Moktir all the time he needed to rob me properly, I turned toward him again and spoke to him as if nothing had happened . . . From that day on, Moktir became my favorite.'

If he can comprehend what is really happening during the moment when their eyes meet, he will understand the motivation he will need to play Moktir. He reads the paragraph again. He can see the blocking on stage – the mirror will have to be large, very promi-nent, so the audience, too, can be part of the spying. Moktir glances around a room more richly furnished than any he has ever inhab-ited. His eyes dart everywhere. He saunters to the desk: he has his pick of valuables. But his trophy must be something small, some-thing silvery. The audience watches Michel watching Moktir . . . James closes his eyes and smiles to himself: *This is one hell of a moment*! He wishes he had a working script and could get right to the scene.

His hair will be blackened and well oiled, sideburns long and pointed, the skin darkly burnished, very white teeth bared from time to time to indicate the healthy carnivore in the boy in a thread-bare *bournous*. Even that robe, soiled by the street though it is, will be worn with ease and comfort. James's imagination can see it all. And especially the moment, the theft, the betrayal that becomes the basis for Michel's affection.

James imagines himself on stage as Moktir scans the desk. There are pens, a letter opener, paper weights, a magnifying glass. What to take? The silver scissors – he has seen Marceline with them: they are *hers*. That's the point. James hovers over the desk in his imagination. All Moktir's thought has gone into what item to take: once he decides, however, it will be done deftly and without another moment's consideration, just like that. At the very moment the scis-sors have been placed inside the robe, Moktir raises his head to discover that all has been seen.

What to do? This will be his telling moment. So, what to do?

If the scissors were Michel's, James reasons, *they would be his to lose, but they are Marceline's, so Michel, as her husband, ought to come to her defense. It is important to see if he will. Moktir must wait, a look of insolence: no, a look of unsure, growing defiance on his face.*

Seconds go by. The audience must feel the weight of the time passing. Moktir begins to smile, slowly acknowledging the complicity between them. It is not a smile of triumph or even of immunity; it is a smile indicating that, as unlikely as it may seem, the Frenchman and the Arab boy are joined by a secret sin.

James imagines his own face as Moktir's. In his silent heart James understands complicity, he admits the pleasure that only the secret soul of a sinner can share with another sinner. *Jesus, Lem Craig could have written this.* Moktir makes himself a little taller, as though to assert a certain equality with Michel. His eyes dare Michel but they also question. *Are you going to risk our love over a pair of her scissors?*

The ambiguity of the novel, a source of upset on first reading, intrigues him now. In that extended moment during which betrayer and betrayed – corrupter and corrupted – search one another's face, all moral lines blur to extinction. It does not matter who initiates, who responds, who uses whom – the sharing of what the world calls sin is a dangerous but extremely liberating bond. During that moment, corruption hangs in the air like a miasma, and Michel becomes healthier as he breathes it.

James thinks back to Lem touching him in the death-defying car ride. Of his accepting the touch. Lem's glance, suggesting that he is only doing what James has wished silently. Of course, Lem had initiated everything, but by saying nothing, by accepting the initial touch in silence, James signalled his assent. The world might call it complicity; really it is a silent accord. James understands Michel. James understands André Gide.

He cannot wait to see a script, to read for the role. He wants to call Amanda and tell her how he can taste Moktir, but she's already done everything she can; it's up to him to get the part. He is excited, alive with anticipation, and at the same time strangely hollow.

*

The American adaptor of Gide's novel, Augustus Goetz, lets James know, even as they are shaking hands, that nothing will be decided today. He uses the word 'preliminary' three times in his first few sentences. This is hard for James to swallow since everyone on Broadway knows they've already cast Louis Jourdan as Michel and Geraldine Page as Marceline. The Royale Theatre has been booked for February 8th, only eight weeks away. If they don't find their Moktir, they don't have a show.

James is tempted to tell this to Mr. Goetz. Instead, he says, 'I am Moktir.'

Daniel Mann, the director, smiles indulgently. 'I have had more than a dozen young actors tell me the same thing.'

'But you didn't believe them.'

Mann's eyebrow arches. 'This you know for a fact?'

'Would you be talking to me if you had your Moktir?'

'We could be touching all the bases, just to be sure we already have the *best* Moktir available.'

'Forgive me if I'm . . .' He doesn't find the proper word. 'But I didn't say I was "the best Moktir available." I said, "I am Moktir." I didn't mean I could convince you I was him. I mean, I *am* Moktir.'

'Funny, you don't look like an Arab.' A few people nearby snicker.

James brushes the wisecrack aside. His eyes hold Mann's eyes as Moktir's will hold Michel's in that mirror for eight performances a week. The two stare at one another. Nothing is said for a long while. 'You see, I understand unspoken, dangerous agreements. I understand the language of complicity. That is why I am Moktir.' James's smile becomes Moktir's smirk.

The writer pulls his chair closer to the table. The director draws away and crosses his legs. James and the director never unlock their eyes.

'If you have a script, I'd like to do the scene where I steal Marceline's scissors.'

'Katy, can you please find a script for Mr. Dean?'

*

Weekday afternoons at 4:30, Amanda Archer is Princess Ravi-Hashi on the kids T.V. show *It's Time For Jasper*. That means a sequinned sari and veil, gaudy costume jewelry, dark body makeup, a red dot on her forehead, and an arhythmic baby voice that is required to say two or three times on each show, 'At your dees-po-sal, oh might-tee Jaspar.' After which she is required to step through a puff of studio smoke, go into an elaborate bow, and perform a small magic trick with plates or pigeons or brass rings. Then she starts Jasper and the kids on their next adventure. Every third or fourth episode she actually enters the story line and uses her supernatural powers to get Jasper out of some jam or other. James usually watches the show while he gets ready to go to work. Amanda's legs look very fine in her transparent tulle pantaloons whenever she steps out of her sari.

Saturday mornings at nine o'clock, she is endowed with even more occult powers as Wanda in *Wanda Wonder Witch*. She's a feisty but charming crone who inhabits a cave crammed full of cotton-candy spiders' webs and rubber creepy-crawlies, home to the hag who introduces ancient Max Fleischer cartoons. Gaggles of birthday kids visit her cave each Saturday morning; Wanda gives them cheesy toys in return for their cooperation. Some of the children are petri-fied by the camera, some are cute, a few are brazen; Amanda has a real knack for handling each type, although there's always the odd kid who has to be led off the set in near hysteria – that's the show's real attraction. No one can tell that Wanda and Princess Ravi-Hashi are the same person.

Amanda's T.V. schedule enables her to audition for almost every-thing that comes up – Broadway, off-Broadway, nighttime T.V. – but she is usually only seriously considered for a role until her tele-vision identities are discovered. She makes more than $250 a week, some of which has gone to subsidize Enoch, Jimmy, and plenty of other young actors when they hit hard times. She attends two acting classes and still performs regularly in experimental one-acts in the East Village.

As God's right hand in *Green Pastures*, Enoch Moss earns $57.75 a week. The show has run for more than six months and there's talk about it eventually going on a national tour. James makes $23.50 waiting tables at La Bella Vista, plus tips that occasionally put him in Enoch's income bracket. If he arrives at work early enough, he can eat in the kitchen.

Amanda Archer often imagines that some of the folks back home are laughing at the collapse of her dreams of being a serious Broadway actress. In actual fact, those few people back in Bloomington and Kokomo, even in Fairmount, who know her as Amanda Boyce consider her remarkably successful. Heck, she's on the T.V. almost every single day.

James and Enoch are aware of how embarrassed Amanda is by the roles she plays on television. But knowing this hasn't kept them from ribbing her wickedly sometimes. Just last week James asked her with mock seriousness if Wanda was going to audition for Ibsen's *Ghosts*. She saw him wink at Enoch; the wink galled her more than anything else. She bolted out of their apartment. James has since apologized. Amanda said she ought to be a better sport.

*

They call themselves 'The Energines.' It's an inside joke no one gets, which pleases them immensely. Energine is a spot remover that claims to get out 'The darkest, most persistent stains.' Their opening skit is a patter dance to 'I've Got You Under My Skin,' during which Enoch applies more and more white powder to his face every time he slips offstage. He becomes paler as the number goes on.

The Energines meet at Amanda's place informally every two or three weeks. What had started off as a lark, Enoch's idea to put together a three-person revue – song, dance, mime, impersonation – has become a more serious lark every time they get together. Their sessions usually start with Jimmy doing his goofy teenager into the telephone: 'Amanda, I just had this tee-rific idea. How's about we put on some sort of show?'

'Golly 'n gosh, that *is* a great idea. Aunt Bea's got all those old costumes up in the attic. And we can use the ol' barn for a theater. Heck. It's been abandoned fer years.'

'Swell. My uncle's got all those chairs he never rented. And that Negro jazz band plays pretty fine, toe-tappin' music.'

'Right. And Granny'll be glad to print up the announcements, real official-lookin' tickets and everything.'

'Know what we're missin', though?'

'No, what?'

'Talent.'

Long pause. 'Gee. I never thought of that. But maybe we don't actually need very much talent iffen we're real sincere.'

'You know something – you're right. I was worried there for a minute. I'll be right over.'

The best idea for the Energines had been Amanda's. In her and James's years of training in the Method, the ability to improvise in any situation had been developed and refined, so she thought they'd be able to ask members of the audience to set the situation, the characters, the location: then she and Jimmy and Enoch could just run with it, making sure to keep it full of surprises and funny turns. It might be risky, but it would always be fresh and exciting, and since the audience had helped create it, they'd be rooting for it to work. She also believed that with enough experience, they'd develop some basic plot switches to help them work their way around any dead-ends. The key was the intuitive interplay of the actors, and the three of them had indeed developed the uncanny ability to anticipate one another's intentions and actions. They practice their improvisations everywhere.

Jimmy and Enoch are taking Amanda, fresh from her Wanda show, to the Waldorf Deli for brunch. Walking crosstown on 56th Street on Saturday morning, on the corner of Seventh Avenue, very near Carnegie Hall, waiting for a traffic light to change, Jimmy says, 'How about this one? A couple. They're newlyweds. In Manhattan for their honeymoon.'

'From Indiana,' Amanda says.

'Fairmount.' James pats her shoulder.

'Right. She starts shouting for a cop because someone's stolen her pocketbook.'

The light changes. They start to cross arm in arm. Enoch says, 'The husband catches up with the thief down the block. They start fighting over the pocketbook.'

'Right,' says Jimmy. 'Energine switch, though.' He winks archly. They all smile.

Amanda hands Enoch her pocketbook and the two men move thirty or forty yards further down the street. Amanda waits until they are in position before she yells, 'Oh, no. Oh God, no. Help.' Then much louder with complete conviction and a hint of terror in her voice: 'God, help. Help him. He-elp.' A circle forms quickly around her, close but still an arm's length away. Amanda is red faced: tears run down her cheeks. She wails, 'Help him. He'll be killed.' A muscle stands out on her neck, a vein pulses on her forehead. She sweeps her arm toward 56th Street and howls, 'My husband, help him. Please.'

At first no one notices the struggle down the street. Two men, one large and black, the other, smaller and white, locked in bear hugs. They slam against the parked cars.

A traffic patrolman on 57th has noticed the tumult and run down to help. He's overweight, ruddy, freckled, and, as luck would have it, with the thick brogue of a character actor. 'Back off a bi', won'tcha, folks? S'problem here?'

Amanda's in a tizzy, her cries turned to breathy hiccups. 'There . . . there . . . he stole purse . . . my husband . . . help . . . don't let him get hurt . . . please.' She turns and points to the two men in the street, still grappling against the cars. Enoch lifts James way off the ground, twisting him both ways and depositing him on the hood of a big, shiny Cadillac. James, for his part, hangs on to Enoch, and to Amanda's handbag for all he's worth. Crowds have gathered on both sides of the street to watch the brawl.

A driver, a hairy man in his undershirt, jumps down from the cab of a cement truck and tries to grab Enoch around the waist. A newspaper boy drops his papers and goes for Enoch's legs, pinioning his ankles. Enoch can't get away even if he breaks Jimmy's hold. He hangs on to James now for protection.

The cop runs toward the fray, his nightstick held out like a lance. The purse snatcher is pretty much under control. He places his nightstick across Enoch's windpipe and says into his ear, 'Let's keep this civil, eh, Sambo. Just ease't off if yer don' wanna be suckin' breat' trew a hole in yer neck.'

Enoch, wishing he'd never gotten himself into this, lets his body go limp. He releases Jimmy and the handbag. James slides off the car's hood and slumps forward. His smile expresses gratefulness that justice has been done this time. He holds the handbag against his stomach and breathes deeply. 'Thanks a lot, officer. Don't know how much longer I could have . . .'

A few burly men, the cement-truck driver most prominent, have pinned Enoch against the car. The policeman is frisking him for a weapon. Enoch tries to speak: 'Officer. I don't think you should let . . .' He's shaken silent by the men holding him and by the nightstick brought up under his chin again.

'Officer, I'd like to see if my wife's okay.' James motions up the block. 'I think she's worried about me.'

'Don't let him take . . .' The cop has the stick at Enoch's mouth and is threatening those magnificent teeth. No one in the crowd has recognized De Lawd's archangel. No one has recognized Wanda the Witch or Ravi-Hashi. No one could possibly have recognized James Dean.

'Officer, I'll be with my wife.'

'Be sure t' stay wit' her. I'm goin' t' be needin' a statement.'

'Absolutely. And thanks, everybody, for your help. They say New York is a cold place, but when I get back home, I'm going to tell them what it's really like.'

The crowd beams. James makes his way back toward Amanda. Some people shake his hand.

When the officer is satisfied that his perpetrator has no weapon, he sticks a cuff on one wrist and leads him off toward the corner. 'I'll be wagerin' t' is won't be yer first visit t' ta midtown precin't.'

'Officer. This is the first time I've ever . . .' Enoch is yanked silent once again.

Amanda is surrounded and consoled by women. She's biting on her knuckles. She looks at the oncoming policeman and his captive with a mixture of confusion and relief. She runs toward the black man with her arms out. The cop tries to ward her off.

'Oh, Quentin,' she coos, a loving expression lighting her face.

The cop is confused, his face painfully contorted.

'Reba, Reba,' Enoch intones in his richest bass.

Since they hadn't picked names in advance, Amanda almost breaks up at 'Reba,' but she leaps into his arms, kissing all the black skin in sight.

The crowd is confused. The cop steps as far away as his grip on Enoch's handcuffs permits. His mouth is wide open.

Enoch holds Amanda in his free arm consolingly: 'It's okay, hon. It's okay.'

'You're all right. Oh Quentin, I was so worried.'

'I think he got away, though.' Enoch sneers at the cop.

'Doesn't matter, sweetheart. I have all our money pinned in my bra. All that matters is you're all right. Oh, my darling.'

Dozens of faces are frozen, as though a foul human odor emanates from the steam-pipes beneath the street.

The cop refuses to accept the obvious: 'You know t'is man?'

'He's my husband, officer. Quentin Darrow. We're on our honeymoon. That disgusting little man grabbed my bag when we crossed the street. Quentin went after him. I was so worried. Thank God.'

'That's what I was trying to tell you. But you wouldn't . . .' Instinctively once again, the cop is inclined to shut the black man up with his nightstick but he cannot. 'Why'd you let that guy get away?'

'I just figured . . .' He looks into the crowd for corroboration. Many are nodding, '. . . t'at since he was . . .'

'It doesn't matter. My Quentin's all right, and that's all that really counts.' She kisses and kisses and the foul-smell look turns to revulsion.

Enoch says, 'If you'd take off these . . .' He raises his wrist to show the cuffs.

The cop has no choice, even though he and most of the crowd believe a far greater crime has been committed, one for which these two ought to be hauled off, locked up, and have the key thrown away on them. He takes off the cuffs. The officer addresses himself to Amanda as he takes out a black pad from inside his bulky jacket. 'Yer goin' t' hafta come down t' ta precinct t' lodge a complaint, t' give us a description.'

'Don't think that's possible for us, officer,' Amanda says. 'He doesn't seem to have gotten anything of value, and Quentin's all right. I just want to go back to the hotel room with my big, sweet, husband.' She goes up on tiptoe and gives Enoch a bite on the neck.

Enoch tilts her face up and kisses her fully on the lips. 'Officer, we'd just as soon go back to the hotel and get cosy.'

195

The cop, far redder than he was when he arrived, slaps his book closed. 'Just as well wit' me.'

Enoch makes himself appear simple: 'If we did press charges, would we have to say you had the guy but let him go?'

'Anyone would a made ta same mistake.'

'You know what he looks like, then,' Amanda says. 'Kind of short and skinny. Runty looking. Light-brown hair, crew cut. Dungarees, black sneakers. Caucasian.' Her eyes flare on that final word.

The cop salutes and walks away.

Enoch Moss and Amanda Archer hook arms and walk eastward on 56th. Eyes follow them for about half a block. They'll meet James at the deli.

Jimmy holds the handbag aloft like a trophy. They don't say a word when they meet: they just laugh, James in his aspirated, voiceless hiss, shaking his head helplessly in triumph and disbelief. The actor's life for them.

*

The cue card reads – GUNNER: LISTEN, YOU'VE GOT TO HANG ON, COLEY. THE DOC WILL BE HERE SOON. DON'T GIVE UP. WE'RE SO CLOSE, COLEY.

James says: 'Listen, man. You hang on. Coley? You hang on. Doc'll be back here any minute. Listen to me now, damn you, don't give up, man. You're almost there, don't you see?' Jimmy says his lines with alternating tenderness and anger, and without a glance at the card not five feet beyond Enoch's sweat-bathed head.

James and Enoch have played this scene in the apartment every day for three weeks, have played it through four rewrites and half a dozen name changes. At the same time, he is in rehearsal for *The Immoralist*. Enoch is still in *Green Pastures*. They are living their Golden Age.

Tears fall from James's chin onto Enoch's glistening shoulder, where they pool and run into his armpit. The black man he has just beaten senseless in the ring is the man who's taught him everything he knows about the fight game, and a lot more.

The small part of James that is not being Gunner Hansen

observes Enoch's face more intensely than he ever has before. The open pores, individual hairs, the narrow scar, the range of dark color, like ripening fruit, on the jaw and forehead. It is at this moment, under the blazing T.V. lights, the most marvelous face he has ever seen. Gunner Hansen, James's other self, is not aware of its beauty, only of its honor, its valor, its integrity.

'Why didn't you fall, Coley? Why didn't you just go down?' James isn't looking at him now but staring high on the wall of the sordid locker room behind Coley Lewis. The director has cut from a tight shot of Jimmy to a two-shot of both actors bathed in a circle of light from a bare bulb overhead. 'All you had to do was fall, damn it. Just fall. Second round, you could have gone down. Or let me peck at that cut till they stopped it, maybe the fifth or sixth. But this, Coley. Why'd you make me do this to you?'

The questions asked of the unconscious man are hopeless and hollow, but Coley Lewis stirs slightly on the rubbing table. The taped hand that hangs limply off the table twitches. Cut to a close-up of the black fighter's moist face. Enoch's head, which is propped on a boxing glove, wobbles sideways and his eyebrows try to pull dead eyes awake. The lashes flicker.

The close shot on Jimmy's face is, at first, out of focus and then only softly so. It is Coley's consciousness returning. The outline sharpens. As Gunner becomes aware that Coley is coming around, he reacts not as though his prayer has been answered but as if he's just heard a really sweet joke. 'Don't you say it, Coley. Don't you dare say it.'

'Don't . . . don't say . . . what?'

'Don't say, "Where am I?"'

Coley blinks and looks around the locker room. 'I know where I am. Just don't know how the heck I got here.' Enoch's voice is too wonderful for television, a resonant bass that's too big, too theatrical. And his diction is too fine; when he slips into the least bit of dialect, it sounds unnatural. Enoch Moss is always Othello at heart; fortunately, his inherent nobility makes him effective in the role of Coley Lewis.

'Wish't I could say I knocked you out, man. I didn't. You just went down coming out of your corner.'

'What round?' Enoch asks the question with surprising intensity. 'Ninth.'

Coley Lewis relaxes and smiles to himself. He shakes his head and says, 'I did it. I got over. Thank you, Lord.'

Gunner is very confused. 'What you mean, Coley?'

'Never mind, kid. Maybe some day I'll explain it all to you.'

The doctor comes galumphing through the door: 'Ambulance'll be here any . . . Well, I'll be chucked. Welcome back to the land of the living, Coley.' James is beaming as though somewhat responsible for Coley's revival.

'Doc, I've got to get out of . . .' Coley tries to get up, feels a stab of pain in his head, and gets woozy. He slumps back on the table.

'Not so fast, Champ. You took a pretty good licking from this here young feller.' The doctor hovers over Coley, examining the pupils of his eyes with his small flashlight.

Gunner backs away and asks, 'No problem, is there, Doc?'

'Oh, no. No. But I want this old boy in the hospital. A precaution. Just as a . . . precaution. Where *is* that ambulance?' The doctor exits.

Coley motions Gunner closer. The camera slides in very tight. 'If anything happens to me, kid, I want you to get my money – five grand – from Benito. And make sure it gets to Ginny. All five grand.'

'Don't be dumb. You'll be around to get the money yourself.'

'Promise me!' Enoch's dark, fluid eyes melt into a million T.V. screens.

'I promise, Coley. I promise you.' Jimmy's smile is uncertain, confused. The camera lingers on it.

The screens fade to black. There's a self-conscious silence on the studio floor. A filmed commercial for the entire line of Philco consoles runs for one minute and twenty seconds. Enoch takes a sip of water and allows the makeup girl to take some of the shine off his cheeks and forehead. Jimmy walks to the corner of the set, making sure with a threatening scowl that no one will approach him.

The director's voice comes onto the floor from above, like God's. Disembodied, insincere. 'So far, so good. Eight more minutes and we're out clean. Places everyone.'

The announcer says, 'And now back to the final act of tonight's "Philco Playhouse." *Fight Of His Life* starring Enoch Moss and James Dean.'

Even though the stage manager beckons madly, James returns to his mark only seconds before the red light of the two-shot camera goes on. He is 'gathered up' and restored emotionally for the expenditure he has to make.

'I don't get it, Coley. All those times you told me, "When the end comes, get that big pay day and get the hell out."' The cue card says: GET THE HECK OUT. James has almost said, 'Get the fuck out.'

'Yeah, well, sometimes you can't always practice what you preach.'

'You knew this was it. There was no way you could beat me. Not these days, anyway. Ten years ago, sure, but not tonight, Coley. You knew that.' James stops as though he's forgotten his lines. He hasn't. He's thinking. Rather, Gunner is thinking. It's an unfamiliar process that's reflected on Gunner's not-too-bright face. Just off camera, the floor manager is circling his finger madly. James won't speed up. 'Why you son of a gun. I get it. You must have bet some real money on this fight. Must have bet you could go eight rounds, right?'

'Don't underestimate yourself, kid. Benito said I couldn't even last six. Double or nothing. If I went six, I'd get the five thousand. If I didn't, I'd get a big zero.'

'Why didn't you say something to me, man. I'd have carried you easy for six. Then, piff, I tap you in the seventh, you fall down and win the deed to the chicken farm.'

'You don't get it, kid. Sure I wanted the farm, wanted it bad all my life, but I'm also an honest fighter. I guess some habits are hard to shake.'

'Almost a *dead* honest fighter.'

'Almost, but I did it, Gunner. I did it. I beat the game in the end, didn't I? Ginny and I'll have that little place in the Poconos. And you have to admit, I got to you pretty good in the first round, didn't I?'

James puts a taped hand up to his own jaw. 'You're still pretty sneaky for an old codger.' He thinks again. 'One question, though. Near the end of the eighth I hit you that hook to the side of the head. I never hit anyone a shot like that in my life. I saw you quiver like a goose. Saw your eyes go back in your head.' A siren sounds distantly, the ambulance drawing nearer to the arena. 'Almost swallowed your mouthpiece. Every guy I ever hit nearly that hard went down and stayed down. I could see you wanted to go down too. How come you didn't? You already had your chicken farm.'

'I remember that shot. Wish I could forget it, but don't be getting too proud, Gunner. Kid Larkin hit me a shot back in '39 even harder, and I stayed in there and beat him. But I haven't been hit like that since . . .' Coley Lewis stops speaking and stares beyond James, beyond the camera. An enormous, abstracting pain is taking control of his head. Enoch's face folds in on itself in creases and furrows that release him. '. . . you can't fall . . . not as long as you got any control . . . not as long as you're an honest . . .' He brings a quivering hand up to his pulsing temple. '. . . not as long as you've got a shred of . . .'

'A shred of what, Coley? A shred of what?'

The black body heaves, the face contorts.

James cradles Enoch in his arms. 'A shred of what, Coley? What?'

The doctor and two ambulance attendants burst in. The doctor can't pry Gunner away from Coley and awkwardly looks for signs of life in the man Gunner clutches. He looks over at the attendants and shakes his head.

A close-up of Enoch's peaceful face in Jimmy's arms. 'A shred of what, Coley? Tell me.' Jimmy leans in and plants a soft kiss on Enoch's forehead. There is no kiss in the script. There is, in fact, a T.V. prohibition against men kissing under any circumstances. A white man's lips touching a black man's skin is beyond prohibition. There is a silent gasp in the studio.

Amazingly, Enoch does not alter his death-mask: he had sensed something in James's touch, the undertone of voice, sensed just this possibility moments before he felt James's breath so close. James's grasp is much tighter, more desperate by far than during any of their rehearsals.

The tracking camera draws back to show the embrace. The other actors look on comfortably. Death is present. So is something ineffable and much more daunting.

A muffled ring bell begins to toll slowly. The credits start to crawl up the screen. At the tenth gong, with Gunner rocking Enoch gently in his arms, all the studio screens go to black. James holds Enoch. The studio is silent. James, purged of all emotion, releases Enoch. He believes he has got the scene exactly right.

*

Almost 900 letters – most of which were far more vehement and less literate – were received by local stations, the NBC network, and the Philco Corporation. As a result of the telecast, twenty-two NBC affiliates, the great majority in the deep South, refused to carry the 'Philco Playhouse' for the remainder of the season.

November 29, 1952

Mr. Thurman M. Philcox
President, Philco Corporation
c/o National Broadcasting Company
30 Rockefeller Center
New York City, New York

Dear Mr. Philcox:

As one who has never before written to someone of your stature, sir, I must tell you in no uncertain terms how offended I, members of my family, and everyone I have spoken to are, by the drama presented on last Sunday's (November 23, 1952) 'Philco Playhouse.'

Let me say that my family and I have watched each of your company's presentations loyally and with great anticipation ever since we purchased our first television set, which was a Philco console model. The thoughtful quality of the scripts and the general excellence of the acting rarely failed to impart satisfaction or to stimulate positive discussion.

It is television's ability to provide large numbers of citizens with inexpensive, high-quality entertainments. In so doing, you, who put your name to the creation of such entertainment, have an important responsibility to the public as well:

namely, to avoid subjects and material the general public would find odious and offensive. The concluding moments of last Sunday's drama about the two prize-fighters (I am unable to recollect its title) exceeded any imaginable limit of acceptable taste.

I am a librarian but I can assure you, sir, I am neither a prude nor someone so illiberal as to feel prejudicial about individuals of the Negro race. I remain offended and personally insulted by what I saw, so I am sending copies of this letter to the President of the National Broadcasting Company as well as to the president of my local station in Indianapolis, my Congressman and Senators.

Since I am powerless to censor the emissions that cross my television screen and must rely on 'the powers that be' to demonstrate intelligent judgment, be informed that I shall never again purchase a Philco product and shall be rather outspoken about the matter to friends and acquaintances.

Respectfully,

Mrs. Marion Kartch
Head Librarian
Folksville, Indiana

*

While Moktir is looking insolently at Marcel in the mirror, Elia Kazan, sitting in the fifth row, is looking intently at James Dean. There is a quality of dramatic manipulation he doesn't quite trust. He believes it is not only the actor's reading of the character: it may be something in Dean himself. But he sees enormous possibilities as well.

10. Take All of Me

A STREETCAR NAMED DESIRE: screenplay by Tennessee Williams; adapted by Oscar Saul from the play by Mr. Williams; directed by Elia Kazan; produced by Charles K. Feldman; presented by Warner Brothers Pictures.

Blanche du Bois	*Vivien Leigh*
Stanley Kowalski	*Marlon Brando*
Stella Kowalski	*Kim Hunter*
Mitch	*Karl Malden*
Steve	*Rudy Bond*
Pablo	*Nick Dennis*
Eunice	*Peg Hillias*

'Apparently Mr. Brando has found the need to return in order to blow some creative air through his brain – the smog out there makes you stupid.' This was how Strasberg prepared his students for Brando's return to the Actors Studio. Brando played a scene from Death of a Salesman: *he was Biff to Strasberg's Willie Loman. It wasn't his acting that caused the knots in Jimmy's stomach, not the words, the facial expressions, the gestures, it was the palpable danger that smoldered beneath. Brando had been criticized by some as playing Stanley Kowalski too broadly on the stage in 1947, and Jimmy welcomed the criticism without ever seeing the performance. He realized, while watching the scene, that the*

breadth was indeed there, but always below, hidden, the explosive fuel in the basement.

Jimmy didn't want to see the movie version of Streetcar. *He simply had to. He saw it with Amanda and Enoch at the Trans-Lux on 14th Street a year after it premiered at the Warner Theater.*

From the moment Stanley appears late in scene one, Jimmy knows he is about to see a performance that will turn him inside out with envy. Later in the film, when Stanley exposes Blanche as a liar to her sister Stella, James realizes he must re-dedicate himself as an actor.

Stanley: Which brings us to Lie Number Two.

Stella: I don't want to hear any more!

Stanley: She's not going back to teach school! In fact I am willing to bet you that she never had no idea of returning to Laurel! She didn't resign temporarily from the high school because of her nerves! No, siree, Bob! She didn't. They kicked her out of that high school before the spring term ended – and I hate to tell you the reason that step was taken! A seventeen-year-old boy – she'd gotten mixed up with!

Blanche: (Singing from behind the bathroom door) It's a Barnum and Bailey world. Just as phony as it can be –

Amanda has stopped breathing. James only sees the welling satisfaction of Stanley Kowalski: the bully finally has the power to destroy Blanche du Bois. Brando's Kowalski is vindicating himself for every slight he's ever received in his life, especially from women, and doing it with a mean pleasure.

'You think I don't know how the system works? There ain't enough chauffeur and butler roles in all the studios combined.' There's a taut control in Enoch's voice partly because he has to drive his words into the bathroom and through the spray of the shower.

'No, man, I'm telling you.' Jimmy sends his words into the living room. 'I've got 'em by the balls now. There's no way I'm letting go.'

'How come I haven't heard them hollering "Uncle"?'

''Cause first I'm going to give 'em a chance. I ain't started squeezing yet.' James likes that retort and chuckles, his face turned right into the force of the water. He turns off the tap and sheds water with a violent quiver that runs down from his head. As he steps out of the shower, steam comes off his body. Water beads on his sinewy back, a rivulet forms on his chest and runs over the ripples of his stomach. 'Once I get out there and they get a look at what they're going to have to deal with, Jack Warner'll . . .' He rubs a clear circle into the foggy mirror and flashes his teeth at himself. '. . . Jack Warner'll say, "Jimmy, I only want to keep you happy. Just tell me what you want, and it's yours." And I'll say, "Look, Jack, it's simple. You need good actors. I know good actors. There's this guy back in New York who'll blow your mind. I've worked with him, and he's absolutely incredible." And Jack'll say, "Jimmy, Jimmy, Jimmy. You know I want you to be happy, just tell me what to do." And I'll say, "Why not fly my friend out here for a test?" And Jack'll say, "If that's what you want, Jimmy, you got it. What's this phenom's name?" And I'll say, "His name's Enoch Moss, and he doesn't play butlers or chauffeurs." And Jack'll say, "Enoch Moss. Holy shit. I've been trying to get him out here for years. If you can help, I'll sign him immediately. We've got a project that'll be perfect for you and Moss."'

'Could only be *Robinson Crusoe*.'

'And I'll say, "Bring him out and sign him then, but we don't do *Robinson Crusoe*." And Jack'll say, "It's a great script about two Army buddies. You'll both win Oscars." I'll say, "Great, send Enoch the script." He'll say, "Will do. And thanks a lot for delivering Moss. I owe you one." And I'll say. "No sweat, Jack. This one's on me."'

James takes a yellow towel and holds it around his midriff as he steps out of the bathroom.

Enoch is on the sofabed, posed like a reclining warrior on the Elgin Marbles. His head is propped on a relaxed arm: his naked body spans the entire sofa, its dark skin is highlighted and muted where light reflects or is absorbed. A body at once hard and at perfect ease. His crossed ankles give him an air of nonchalance. An oversized white towel is under his buttocks and spills onto the floor. Enoch's smile is uncertain, fearful of a rebuff; the muscles of his stomach pulse faintly.

James says, 'And I'll say to Jack Warner . . .'

Enoch frowns and moves a warning finger to his lips. He shakes his head slightly too. The tip of his cock is stuck in the folds of the towel, causing it to round into a backward letter 'C.'

There doesn't seem to be enough air in the room for James. He runs his tongue over his teeth, considering possibilities. The gesture increases the tension. They are looking directly into one another's eyes. Enoch's 'C' pulses once, twice; it frees itself and begins to straighten. The room is stifling.

James's cock prods the yellow towel as though in response to a call. He tastes his own lips. And takes air through his mouth. Words would be stupid; instead, he tips his head quizzically.

Enoch smiles assent. The smile is nothing more than friendly.

James unpinches the fingers at his waist and his towel slides over his erection on the way to the floor. He can sense Enoch before he touches him. They will be late for the party; it is only a matter of how late.

It is not possible to know absolutely which one initiates the movement, whether James approaches or Enoch beckons. In actual fact, each initiates, each reacts.

James sits on the edge of the sofa, on a small patch that has been offered on Enoch's towel. The tips of Jimmy's ears are flame red; he can hear his heart pulsing blood. The rhythm of arousal.

James wants to touch Enoch. It's only a question of where. Enoch raises his arms in a mock yawn, exposing his flank in the process. Curls of hair glisten under his arms. Along with his smile, the gesture is one of animal surrender, invitation. James would like to dip his fingers in those curls.

He starts to speak. Again Enoch halts him. The moment of separation seems eternal to James. They are frozen like lover-warriors on an heroic stele. In actual fact, James's advance has been stayed for a few seconds, as much to savor his brief decision as to delay it. Where to touch Enoch Moss is not an easy choice.

Enoch loops two fingers around the base of his member. It throbs to fullness. James does the same with his own cock and moves it closer to Enoch's. He leans down and touches tip to tip. He begins to make a honing movement with his penis on Enoch's, playfully, as though this were sword play, even though his brow is tightly drawn. Enoch is smiling.

Without any encouragement from Enoch, James follows a desire he hadn't acknowledged before. He opens his lips, closes his eyes, and licks the crown of Enoch's penis as though it were a snow cone. Why he has done this, he cannot know – rather, cannot explain. He can hear Enoch's heartbeat alternating with his own. The palm of Enoch's hand lightly touches the back of James's neck. No taste registers on James's tongue. As he bobs his head, a warm, salt savor forms. All at once he positions himself where he can ingest the cock whole. When it touches the back of his throat, he stops. He pulls his head up slowly and eases it down again. James's eyes look up at Enoch: they smile mischievously. It's as though he's pulled off a clever joke.

Enoch slides off the sofa, pulling himself away from James and rolling on top of him. They embrace and grasp, clutch and probe – the encounter is part wrestling match, part love match. It is an endurance contest as well: for nearly an hour James and Enoch will be attentive, intemperate lovers.

This is their farewell, this is their repayment of debts. But debt has little to do with the overwhelming rush of pleasure to which their senses have surrendered. There is freedom from time and place and self. Lines have been obliterated between knowledge and mystery, between consciousness and stupor, between desire and fulfillment. James had never imagined such an erasure of self to be possible.

Finally, Enoch kisses James – slowly and with fervor. There is an aftertaste of sorrow.

They roll away from each other on the carpet. Each stares at the ceiling.

'Feel funny about it?' James says.

'I don't want to admit it, but I'm going to miss you.'

'Shit, don't go *schmaltzy* on me, Moss.'

'Don't go hard-boiled on *me*, you little twerp.' Enoch pulls his legs straight up from the waist and then further back over his head; he somersaults backward and springs to his feet. As Enoch turns in the air, James believes he sees the woman in the flowered dress standing in the doorway to the bathroom. She is watching with her arms folded at her chest. When Enoch lands, she's gone.

*

It is a serious, New York stage actor send-off, which means a bunch of neurotics sitting around a large living room in an upper West Side apartment talking intensely about themselves and acting, and themselves. That's why Jimmy was reluctant to go. Enoch made it clear he had no choice. He simply had to face all the actors who were not going to Hollywood to make a movie with Kazan. James reminds himself to be modest and not to drink too much.

As he enters, he sees he's gotten lucky – Strasberg is there already, established room-center in a comfortable armchair: around him a throng of young actors, some of them at his feet, waiting for pearls; at his right hand, kneeling, her hair stroked by Strasberg, Julie Harris, who will play opposite James in *East of Eden*. This night Lee

Strasberg will hold forth: there will be no need – or room – for any other egos.

As he is seen, there is some applause, a few glasses raised in his direction, not enough of a fuss to warrant embarrassment. James clenches his fists above his head like a victorious boxer and takes a turn. Amanda comes up and plants a wet kiss on his cheek. At the same time she interlaces their fingers and squeezes very hard. 'I've got to be leaving early.' She looks over her shoulder at a light-skinned East Indian boy eating a salad.

James nods and says, 'Congratulations, babe. He shows promise.'

'He's my new dialect coach. The show wants me to sound more authentic.'

'His voice looks very authentic. Can I go over and examine his tongue?'

'Will I see you before you leave?'

'Flying out tomorrow afternoon. Late.'

'I'll call you in the morning. Maybe bring over some strudel.'

James opens his arms wide and squeezes Amanda Archer *née* Boyce very tightly. He would like to hurt her gently.

She expels air in gasps. When he releases her, she bends back at the waist. 'You're a looney. Tomorrow?'

'Sure. Your maharajah looks hurt and lonely.'

James doesn't want to interrupt Strasberg, who nods his welcome. Julie Harris blows him a kiss. 'The biggest mistake you can make,' Strasberg is advising, tapping Julie's temple, 'is to get it in your heads' – he glances up at James – 'that you're doing the Cain and Abel story. Certain death, believe me. *East of Eden* is not Cain and Abel.' He wiggles back in his chair waiting to be asked why it would be certain death.

Jimmy, whose chin is cradled in his hands, is more concerned with how he's being perceived by the guests than curious about Strasberg's advice. Julie asks obediently, 'Why, Lee? Why is it certain death?' The actors smile. James picks up the smile like a singer trying to fake the words of the anthem.

Strasberg is oblivious to her sarcasm. 'Because, sweetheart, it leads directly to Arthur Murray.' Again he expects to be prompted. When nobody asks *Why Arthur Murray?* he says, 'Those footprints on the floor. You think they teach you to dance?' He moves his shoes arhythmically into an imaginary pattern on the rug. 'Left, right, left-left, right. It's stepping, it's not dancing. So if Steinbeck only wrote the Cain and Abel story all over again, and you two just step on the Biblical footprints, you won't really be dancing. Even a movie audience will know this, believe me. They may not know they know, but something will tell them something's wrong. Who needs old Cain and Abel music? All you need is right here in your heart: if you can't dance to that, what have I been doing with you two all this time? Feh. Arthur Murray.' He throws his hands at the rug.

James makes believe he's jotting the words into a notebook. 'Can I quote you on that, Lee? "Feh. Arthur Murray?"'

Strasberg doesn't acknowledge the wisecrack: 'Steinbeck read his Genesis, certainly, but just as certainly he stuck it right back on the shelf. No, let me amend that. Bet you dollars to doughnuts he never looked at it at all. Approach a novel like a Bible story and it'll be . . .'

While Strasberg conjures another description of artistic failure, the students say, '. . . certain death.'

He doesn't smile. 'You laugh. Sure. But I'm right, believe me. Better you should read Freud than Genesis. A profoundly psychological tale. A boy wants his father's love desperately. What boy doesn't? No matter what Cal does, he can't earn that love.' He's lecturing Dean directly. 'How do you earn love? With this perfect brother around, the first-born, the one with the birth-right. Primal stuff.' He turns to Harris. 'And the girl who is drawn to the rejected boy. She wants to save him, to do something useful with her love. The perfect brother, what need does he have of a sacrificing woman?' Strasberg touches Julie's hair.

It's impressive how much Strasberg knows about this story, what background an actor needs to approach the material.

'But enough, I'm prattling. I know this, though, even if the experience turns you inside out, you two are going to learn a great deal about yourselves and your craft.'

'Why inside out, Lee?' James is looking at his own clasped hands.

'Because of the things you'll have to work out. Think about it.

Oh, you know.' He indicates it might be unwise to discuss it publicly.

James misses the cue. 'I don't see getting turned inside out. After all, it's just another role. New problems to solve, but "inside out," I don't see it . . .' James shrugs.

'First movie, lots of pressure. You'll see.' Strasberg clears his throat.

'Come on, Lee. Do you think I'm not ready? So why "inside out"?'

Strasberg considers and makes a decision, suggested by a you-asked-for-it gesture. 'Did you want your father's love? When you were growing up?'

James slides down to the floor, landing softly on his knees. He stares upward into Strasberg's unblinking eyes. He says, 'My father's dead.'

'Before he died?'

'He's been dead as long as I can remember.'

Strasberg tilts his head and brings his fingers to his upper lip, considering whether or not to press the boy on the accuracy of his statements. He starts to speak, but decides against it.

'Do you feel he cheated you?' The voice comes from behind. Everyone turns. It's Elia Kazan. No one had seen him enter.

Before James has a chance to respond, Strasberg raises his arms as though to stop traffic. 'Whoa. Whoa, there, Kazan. This is supposed to be a send-off, a shindig.'

'That's not what I've been hearing. I heard talk about how Dean here was supposed to play Cal Trask. Correct me if I'm mistaken.' From the set of his face, especially the pull of the dark brows that have blended into a single line, it's hard to believe that Kazan is anything but disturbed. His tone belies the impression.

Kazan's presence, the tension in the air, draws people from elsewhere in the vast apartment. This could be a memorable moment in American theater, something to tell the children about someday – Strasberg and Kazan in conflict.

In the manner of a eulogizer rather than an accuser, Strasberg says, 'Behold, here is the new force behind the silver screen. Modest, unassuming, virtually invisible, but there's no one in the business who doesn't recognize Hollywood's latest miracle man.' Strasberg's foxy eyes move from face to face. James, who has been protected from Kazan's probing question, has no idea that Strasberg is actually running interference for him.

Kazan says to the audience, 'If you leave Broadway, even for a few weeks, Lee feels you've betrayed him for some corrupt foreign power. God forbid you should use your talent and also make a little money.' The tone remains perfectly poised between insult and spoof.

'Of course there are those of us remember Gadge from another time, from the Group Theater' – still in respectful, reminiscing tone – 'a time when he couldn't get out of his own way on a stage. Every year fewer and fewer people can remember his Eddie Fuselli in *Golden Boy*, so he can rewrite history and convince people he wasn't really so awful. Remember, Gadge?'

James interrupts: 'Wasn't Marty Goldglass in that production?'

Strasberg says, 'Marty? Maybe he did props. But film, I don't know. Kazan here wants us to think only of . . .' Kazan tries to speak, but Strasberg holds up a warning finger. 'So let's talk film. Even though he has personally tried to destroy all existing prints, some of us still cannot forget his early silver-screen roles.'

'Beware, beware the green-eyed monster.'

'Jealousy, hell. Has anyone here ever seen a Warner Brothers opus called *City for Conquest?*' No one responds. 'What's wrong with you people? Why did you wait so long to be born? Okay, I'll describe it for you. If I may?' He bends toward Kazan for permission.

Kazan downs the rest of his drink and shrugs. What choice does he have?

'In this masterpiece, Mr. Kazan plays Googi, yet another gangster – so what else is new. He had what Hollywood in those days called "a city look." Down at the Group we weren't so discreet – right, Gadge? – they were Wop roles and Jewboys, but at Warner's it was "a city look." And Kazan had it. Still does. Look at that scowl: how'd you like to run into that in a dark alley? So in *City for Conquest*, a fight movie, he plays this guy with "a city look" to Cagney's Irish pug. In his big scene, he comes strolling into Cagney's dressing room with a dozen chorus girls on each arm . . .'

'This humble man isn't capable of exaggeration.'

'. . . every girl is a head taller than he is. And he announces, "I'm from down on Delancey Street." And you know what?' Strasberg waits for an answer.

'You know what the real point of this story is?' asks Kazan without waiting for an answer. 'It's that Lee would have given his eye teeth to play the ladies' man and say he was from Delancey Street for a hundred-fifty smackers a week, and in Depression dollars.'

Without acknowledging that Kazan has spoken, Strasberg says, 'And for his earnest little performance, you know what the critics called him?' He waits three beats. '"The Proletarian Thunderbolt." This man. This man, who as a director has almost single handedly legitimized Warner Brothers with serious movies, serious acting, serious scripts, was once their "proletarian thunderbolt." Such a transformation the world hasn't seen since Dr. Jekyll. Take a bow.'

There is quiet giggling and gentle applause.

Kazan refill his glass and isn't sure whether or not to let matters rest. He speaks before he's finished sipping: 'Oy-yoy-yoy. So much envy. Overwhelming resentment.' Kazan is imitating Strasberg perfectly – the lingering pauses, the quizzical trill at the end of questions, the sweeping hand gestures and neck jerks. 'And why such resentment, you might wonder. Only one thing as far as I can figure. Height. Or rather lack of same.' Strasberg leans away as though slipping a punch. 'Short as *I* am, I'm still half an inch taller than the King of Broadway.'

Strasberg throws both hands at Kazan. 'You were wearing Adler elevators that time. I'm every bit as tall as you are. Taller even.'

'Or could it possibly be the abject failure of his own film career? "Career" may be something of an overstatement. A debut so inauspicious, shall we say, that even a Googi still sticks in his craw.'

'Admit it, you were wearing elevators.'

'See how he wants to change the subject. I want to talk acting, now he's talking shoes.'

'So let's settle it. Let's measure right now.'

'That only means you're the one who's wearing heels tonight.'

Theirs are the bickering tones and postures of two small Semitic men, half-playing at being malicious and enjoying themselves immensely.

Kazan says, 'Still I believe I'm taller. Stand up.'

'Not now. I'm too comfortable.'

'Now he's too comfortable. So you want me to tell them about the test you did for *Body and Soul*. Or do you want the honor?'

'Do you honestly believe that if I really wanted to play Jules's father in *Body and Soul*, I couldn't have had the part? Let's be serious now, Gadge.'

'So I'll tell it.'

'Fine. You're in the Hollywood myth business anyway. So tell your version of reality.' Strasberg passes his hand across his face as though clearing away smoke.

'S'true. Rossen really wanted Lee, probably because it wouldn't have taken much makeup for him to look like Garfield's old man. So he flies him out for a test. It's a formality. Rossen really wants him. Okay, they set up. An early scene, Garfield is a kid and he's just come back to the store – he's got this big shiner he's trying to hide from his father. Lee's the father; he's supposed to play the scene with a slight Italian accent. No big deal. So Rossen sets up, cameras roll, they run an actor in the front door and . . . You know what? Stanislavsky here won't read. "It's not Jules," he says. "It's a stand-in," Rossen says. "I can't play to a stand-in," Lee says.

'Rossen tells him Julie's not in town, he's in New York. Rossen says it doesn't matter who plays the kid, it's Lee they're testing, the camera will be on him for close-ups. And this *schmeggeggi* says he still can't play the scene. Why? Because he's only ready to play Julie's father.'

Strasberg shakes his head. No, he won't yet risk speaking in his own defense.

'You know the upshot? Rossen says, "Listen, Lee, you're out here, so why not just shoot the scene even without Jules." And you know what our friend here says?'

Strasberg loves to hear Kazan tell this story. He stifles laughter with a frown.

Kazan looks at him a long time. 'The line is famous. They still quote it out there. Yes they do, Lee, believe me. Strasberg pulls himself up to his full height – insufficient as it may be – and says, quote, "I don't even know this kid, how can I be his fucking father," unquote.' The line is supposed to get a howl, it gets smiles because the crowd is so loyal to Strasberg.

Kazan takes another sip. 'So they go to Eduardo Ciannelli, who's not so particular and can play anybody's fucking father for a pay-check.'

Strasberg hits himself softly on top of the head with his fist. 'So you see how my career was completely ruined. I came back to New York in utter disgrace. Such a failure. Oh shame, oh shame.'

Jules Harris rubs Strasberg's knee.

'Maybe,' Strasberg says as though it's an unpleasant discovery, 'maybe that's why I've sent all these crazy actors out to Hollywood. All my Method people going out there to drive everybody in Hollywood nuts. You kids are Lee Strasberg's revenge.'

'Listen, if the shoe fits.'

'Again with the shoes?'

Kazan points his chin at Julie Harris. 'With you, sweetheart, I know what to expect. You've already worked with Clurman, Zinnemann. Strasberg hasn't had his hands on you long enough to make you impossible to direct. This other one . . .' – meaning Dean – '. . . who knows?'

'I know,' Strasberg says.

'So tell me. He's more temperamental than Brando? Less? About the same?'

James enjoys being discussed as though he weren't present.

'If you're asking, "Will he play a scene in a vegetable store with a father he hasn't ever met before?" I'd seriously advise against it.'

'The thing I have noticed, though, is that he's one of the quiet ones. That always worries me. Especially when he still refuses to answer the sixty-four dollar question.'

Jimmy licks his lips: 'Which is . . .?' He has one eye closed and his head is cocked.

'Which *was* . . . "Did you want your father's love when he was alive?"' Although the soft smile doesn't leave Kazan's face, his dark eyes are insistent.

'Are you asking how my Cal Trask will play against Massey's Adam?'

215

'It *is* the motive force in the story. It drives everything.'

'You want me to tell you what I'd do to have my father love me?'

'Careful,' Strasberg warns, 'until you sign the contract.'

'Don't worry, he's signed. He's my Cal Trask come hell or high water.'

'So what do you want, for me to spill my guts about my old man?'

'We'll have plenty of time for that. In private. We'll talk.'

'Private? Hah. We're actors. There is no "private" for us. Everything's public. Everything's fair game to be bent to our will and used.' James stands and pulls his shirt out of his pants. He loosens his belt and begins to unbutton his pants. He enjoys watching the eyes widening around him. *What the hell is this guy up to?* He pulls his pants and striped underwear down on the right side. 'Never let it be said Jimmy Dean hides anything. Emergency appendectomy.' He traces the scar with his pinky. 'Damned near died. Doctor Walter Groves. Grant County Hospital. August 22, 1943. See, there's nothing I ever hide. So what's the question on the table – How much did I want my father's love? – why would I want to duck it? He died when I was twelve. Did he love me? I think so. I can't say he didn't. But I can't really remember him that clearly. You know what's a better question – How do you know if anyone ever loves you? Ever?' The intensity in his voice gives his words a resonance that intrigues Kazan.

James folds his shirt in his pants and, holding everyone's attention as he backs toward the piano, says, 'To know how to love – for that I'd give more than Cain ever offered the Lord, more than the Wise Men gave baby Jesus.' With his foot, he slides a small throw rug away from the piano and against the wall. 'More even than Jesus himself . . .'

People watch in wonder as he comes back from the buffet table with a salt-shaker and pours salt on the floor in small circles. 'More than Cal Trask can possibly offer Raymond Massey . . .' He whispers to the piano player, whose slow arpeggio matches Jimmy's airplane spin on tiptoe into the first steps of half-tempo soft-shoe. A dance he learned in the class Goldglass arranged for him.

He sings, 'Nothing I won't give up for love . . . Nothing I'll ever hold back . . . because I want to give Him . . .' He looks to heaven, 'All of me. Yes, why not take all of me . . .' He's launched in his song. James is looking down at his feet now and flapping his arms with natural ease. He winks at the piano player, who keeps perfect time with James's slow soft-shoe. The crowd loves it.

'Can't you see, I'm no good without you. Take my lips, I'll never use them.' He makes his arms appear to want to fly off. 'Take my arms, I want to lose them . . .' He dances silently through the rest of the chorus until coming to the last line, which he sings: 'You took the part that once was my heart, so why not take all . . . of . . . me.'

Some observers applaud, but the performance does not end. James's soft-shoe is classically delicate. He holds his rump high in the air, his shoulders hunched with his palms down and flat, his fingers curled like a typist's. In the second chorus, which he does not sing, his dancing becomes more confident. He does another airplane spin on tiptoe and descends to a rolling walk in small circles. The room is so silent, the scratch of salt on the floor sounds like a drummer's brush.

James is starting to perspire and breathe hard, but he maintains the soft-shoe dancer's special suaveness. 'Have you noticed . . .' he says to the crowd gathered around, '. . . that some of the . . . finest songs have . . . the stupidest lyrics?'

They nod, he dances. Enoch becomes his straight man: 'What songs you talking about, man?' This is Energines material.

'A song like this one . . . "All of Me" . . . it's an old standard we hardly ever listen to.' At a wink from James, Enoch comes forward and begins dancing a slow-time step alongside. 'By the way, everyone, let me introduce my colleague, Mr. Enoch Moss. We've been through thick and thin together.'

Enoch bows. 'I've been through thick, he's been through thin.'

Jimmy sings '"Take my lips. I want to lose them." My God, talk about . . . crazy lyrics. What kind of face is that without lips?'

Enoch says, 'A very yoo-gly face, if you ask me.'

'Matter of fact, Enoch, if he lost his lips . . . how could you understand anything he was singing about?'

'"Xactly. And who'd be interested in someone *sans* lips?'

'Actually . . . after this guy loses his lips, you couldn't understand . . . a damned thing he's singing.'

'That's right, man!'

'So when he's singing about having his arm chopped off, you couldn't understand a word.'

Enoch likes this part: 'Preee-cisely. He'd be singing, "Ake ay ars, ay ant oo ooze 'em."' He shrugs, 'Who could tell what the hell that means?'

The laughs come in just the right places. James and Enoch have the same thrill of invention they had when they first worked on this bit.

'Grizzly, isn't it, man, this guy's begging to be mutilated all because he lost this girl.'

'You know, Jimmy, I wonder what they do with all the lopped-off parts?'

'The arms, the lips? Freeze 'em, I guess. Throw 'em in a meat locker.' He sings, 'Your goodbye left me with eyes that cry.'

'Where them tears goin' to run? Down that weird, lipless face.'

'And he can't even dry them off – he's got no damned hands!'

People are laughing all the more for trying to stifle their laughter. These two Energines are a hit. Shame Amanda has left.

James sings, 'How can I go on, dear, without you . . .?'

'Jeez, he can't even dress himself. Can't even wipe his . . .'

'*You* took the part that once was my heart . . .'

'You're not telling me there's this great big hole in his chest too!'

'That's not the worst of it, Enoch. The girl took it away with her!'

'That's truly dis-gust-ing.'

'Imagine this. The gal's driving to L.A. in a big, shiny convertible. Whizzing through Maumee, Ohio. Cop pulls her over. Says, "Let's see your driver's license." She opens the glove compartment, and you know what falls out . . .?'

'Yup. Right out of Edgar Allan Poe. This giant heart . . . tha-thump . . . tha-thump . . . tha-thump . . .'

Enoch goes down on one knee: James sits on the upright one. They spread their arms and sing together: '. . . soooo-WHY-NOT-TAKE-ALL-OF-ME.'

Whistles. Applause. Enoch and Jimmy bow and run into the kitchen. The pianist plays them off and pounds a final chord.

Later in the evening, Jimmy and Julie sit alone on the sofa. She is holding a tall glass with a small amount of champagne in two hands. 'I thought it was terrific, the way you handled that.'

He empties his glass. 'What *that* is that?'

'Before, when Kazan was digging at you.'

'Was that digging? I didn't even notice.'

'C'mon, you don't have to be Mr. Cool with me. We're going to spend months together on this project. How about we make them honest months?' Her smile is sadly candid.

'You want to know the truth?'

'That's what I thought I was saying.'

'Well.' He looks into her eyes for a sign. 'I'm scared. Don't know if I'm up to months of Kazan.'

Julie Harris closes her eyes and expels air. 'I'm so glad to hear you say it. I am too.'

'Uh-oh. And you've already got a name out there. Those people eat guys like me with their caviar and crackers. What is it that scares you?'

'The role. I don't have the key to Abra at all. I think, "What if it doesn't come?" and it scares me to death.'

'Have you talked to Kazan about it?'

'No. Have you?'

'Not yet, but that's not what scares me.'

'What then?'

'It'll sound dumb.'

'No dumber than losing your lips.'

'Probably not.'

'So tell me yours. I told you mine.'

'You'll hate me for it.'

'Try me.'

'I don't like the way I look on the screen.'

She laughs in an unladylike spasm. 'Don't tease me, Jimmy.'

It becomes clear from his sideways glance that he has not been teasing. 'I can't even bear to see myself in close-ups. There's something retarded in my eyes, my slack jaw. If I try to make the look go away, it only gets worse. You know Kazan's in love with close-ups.'

She realizes that he's serious and it turns her skepticism into dismay. 'Jimmy.' She starts over, lowering her voice: 'Probably we're all too critical about our looks on film, but you, my God, you have a face the camera'll love. I don't understand how . . .'

'I shouldn't have said anything . . .'

'No. You should have if it bothers you, but, listen, from my point of view – from any woman's point of view – your looks are incredible.'

Julie will remember this curious admission by James long after he is gone. His biographers will come to her and ask for a telling moment, a revelation, in their work together on *East of Eden*. She never repeats this conversation. She never realizes, however, that on the eve of starring in his first movie, James Dean was only worried about his face and not at all about any of the acting challenges.

In a small sitting room, Strasberg and Kazan rest side by side on a velvet settee. Two small, bitter friends. They speak to one another softly while looking straight ahead. Kazan says, 'So what can you tell me about this Dean?'

'I thought it was all signed, sealed, and delivered?'

'It is. Still, what do you really think?'

'Lightning in a bottle. He could even make you a famous director.'

'Fun-ny.'

'A word of advice. Stay away from any of that stuff about his father. It's tricky, what with the subject matter of your story, it could be a . . .'

'I know all about it. The father's not dead. Jack Warner did a check into the family. It's the mother.'

Strasberg cocks his head, 'A family check? That Warner's a real prick. So why did you . . .?'

Kazan shrugs: 'Because I'm a meddling bastard.'

'So what's the story with the father?'

'Nothing. He's a dentist or something in California.'

'Remember, lightning in a bottle. But if you take the lid off: poof, it's gone.'

'So why didn't you come clean about the kid?'

'What are you saying?'

'Because you want me to send him back here, to you, untouched by human hands. Am I right or am I right?'

'Fat chance of that.'

'Believe me, Lee, I send them back. I sent Brando back.'

'For what, a week?'

'Don't you think I want a fresh supply of great New York actors? But no matter what I tell them, they don't want to go. It's like guys on a chain gang who don't want to escape.'

'Except in Hollywood the chain is made of orchids.'

'Orchids? Why orchids?'

'Orchids. That's the image that comes to my mind. The Hollywood orchid chain. They have no idea how . . .'

Led by Julie and James, a throng of young actors enters the room. They move like the posse approaching the prison. Dean says, 'All right, you two. You've got us ready to kill each other. This thing's got to be settled. Stand up.'

Kazan shakes his head.

Strasberg says, 'See. He refuses. That's all you need to know.'

'In socks, I'll do it. Not with a cheater.'

'If I take off the shoes, you'll say I'm wearing elevator socks.'

Somehow Julie gets Kazan to his feet while Jimmy kneels and unties Strasberg's shoes. It takes longer than it should to get them standing back-to-back in stockinged feet, but eventually they stand, stretching their bodies upward like two grade-school kids. Students, admirers, friends, all the guests at the party have gathered around, exhorting their champion.

It's not possible to tell with the naked eye which one is taller: it varies depending on who outstretches the other. Harris calls for something straight to lay across the tops of their heads. Someone passes a bent soup-ladle forward. 'Sure,' Kazan says, 'he'd like nothing better than that.' A walking stick, perfectly straight, replaces the ladle.

Julie hands it to James and announces, 'Jimmy's going to be the judge.' There's applause and a roll by the pianist.

James raises the stick to both heads. It bobs momentarily in favor of Kazan. Strasberg raises up. It levels. 'Feet on the floor. He's cheating,' Kazan says.

'*He's* cheating. It's an old Delancey Street trick – a cheater accusing.'

'Somebody check their heels,' James orders.

Julie kneels on the floor and grabs ankles. 'Okay. Do it.'

The cane quivers and bobs. James says cautiously, 'Well . . . by my weathered eye . . . I'd say . . . we have what looks pretty much like . . . a draw. What do you all think?'

There is much uncertain muttering, approval, disapproval, and doubt.

'Be it known throughout the kingdom, then, that neither Lee Strasberg nor Elia Kazan is of greater stature than the other. It is so declared on this night, the 23rd of . . .'

'It's after midnight.'

'. . . the 24th of April, the Year of Our Lord 1954, and so shall it ever be true. All in favor, say aye.' The apartment echoes with 'Ayes.' 'The "Ayes" have it.' He makes a pious face and the sign of the cross in mock benediction. 'May we all, Jew and Gentile alike, stage and film, Broadway and Hollywood, accept the shortcomings – no pun intended – of one another and go forward in peace and prosperity.' The pianist plays a hymn-like chord. 'A-men.'

The crowd sings: 'A-men.'

Enoch says, 'Especially the prosperity part.'

*

He's the only one who steps off the train at the West Fourth Street station. That's so unusual on a Saturday night that he looks up and down the platform just to be on the safe side. The station is poorly lit, but he sees a man in the bright change booth up ahead. As he walks toward it, a roar builds in the tunnel behind him, and a train pulls up at the opposite platform.

James looks at the people sitting in the cars. Other lives. Passing him by unknown, unknowing. Lives as valid as his, every bit as important. No, he rejects that idea with a laugh.

He waves at the man in the booth, who sits in a half-doze waiting for his shift to expire. The clock behind him shows 1:18.

At the top of the stairs, a bum holds a cupped hand at his chest. The man's eyes are half closed.

James shows emptiness with his hands. He only has a couple of bucks.

The air on Sixth Avenue is damp and cool. James pulls his shirt collar up around his neck. He looks extraordinarily lonely.

Two dollars will go a long way in Chumley's. He can watch the chess players, taunt the radicals, listen to Mrs. Chumley talk about cats and her old speak-easy, nurse his drinks until closing. On good nights, Timmy Mac, the bartender, an ex-fighter, tells terrific stories about boxers Jimmy thinks he's heard of.

The Village is ready for bed. Lovers stroll home in pairs. Street artists pack away their paintings. Cooks and waiters, musicians and merchants, seek buses and cars. Writers urge their typewriters onwards in second storey windows: poets tempt the muse yet again. James notices a boy in a beret standing on the far corner; he whistles shrilly as James turns into Waverly Place. There's something unusual about the whistle, but not foreboding.

James walks over the broken, irregular pavement looking down at his feet, the next step and the next. As he turns on to Charles, a street narrower and darker by half, the foreboding comes, but now Chumley's is only yards away.

The voice and the glint of a blade come from behind a tree. 'In the alley.' The voice is hoarse, almost voiceless.

James is stock still.

'The alley. Get in there.'

It isn't truly an alley: rather, a narrow walkway between two brownstones. It's barely possible for him to back into the opening without his shoulders touching brick on either side.

Before he sees the face, James sees the knife: a long switchblade. His stomach tightens automatically: he can feel the scar tingle. But his concern at this moment is only for his face. Kazan loves close-ups. He brings his open hands up to his cheeks.

'The money.'

James sees his assailant then. A middle-aged white man with swollen features. Desperate eyes.

'Give me your money.' He shows James the knife at chest level.

The words are out before James can consider their effect: 'I'll give you half.'

'What?'

'I'll give you half.'

223

The eyes register confusion. The laugh is gruff, a crude surprise. It blends into the word 'Ha-half?'

'You need some money. I can see that. But I need some for myself. So I'll give you half.'

'Hah. Yeah, we all got needs. Never heard such a thing – "I'll give you half." Okay, give me half.'

'Problem is I only have two bucks . . .'

'. . . listen, wise ass . . .'

'Wait. Listen. The bartender in there knows me. He'll lend me twenty. I'll give you ten.'

'Eleven.'

'Sure. Eleven. Come on in. I'll buy you a drink.'

The mugger considers. He laughs again. 'This is the craziest fucking thing I've ever done.'

'Makes two of us.'

11. East of Warners

EAST OF EDEN: screenplay by Paul Osborn; based on the novel by John Steinbeck; cinematography by Ted McCord; art direction by James Basevi and Malcolm Bert; musical direction by Leonard Rosenman; produced and directed by Elia Kazan for Warner Brothers.

Cal Trask	*James Dean*
Abra	*Julie Harris*
Adam Trask	*Raymond Massey*
Aron Trask	*Richard Davalos*
Kate	*Jo Van Fleet*
Sam	*Burl Ives*
Will	*Albert Dekker*

Page thirty-eight of the shooting script: The Trask kitchen. The father, Adam, is making his wayward son, Caleb, read aloud from the Bible. Cal, rebellious, refuses to read with conviction.

Adam: You have no repentance. You're bad through and through.
Cal: You're right. I am bad. I knew that for a long time.
Adam: I didn't mean that, Cal. I spoke in anger.
Cal: It's the truth. Aron's the good one. I guess there's just a certain amount of good and bad you get from your parents, and I got the . . .

Adam: That's not true. Cal, listen to me. You can make of yourself anything you want. It's up to you. A man has a choice. That's where he's different from an animal. You don't listen.

Cal: My mother. (Examines father's face for a reaction.) She's not dead and gone to heaven. Is she?

Adam: Why do you ask that?

Cal: She's not dead at all. She's alive.

Adam: What makes you think so?

Cal: I heard from a guy. I don't know his name. He was just passing through. How come you told Aron and me she died?

Adam: I thought it would save you pain.

Cal: Pain.

James Dean says the word as though he were the first human ever to feel it.

Kazan hooks James's arm as he passes in the Warners commissary. James's sandwich and chocolate milk slide perilously across his tray. Kazan gestures *sit* and makes room. 'You didn't get the soup?' It's an accusation in the form of a question, a New Yorkism James used to enjoy. 'For some reason the soup is terrific in this place. I hope no one tells Jack about it. He'll probably have someone taken to task.'

Even before he's fully seated, words spill out of James. 'Gadge. It's Massey. I just can't seem to play a decent scene with the man. I – just – can't.' James gives his complaint a reinforcing deliberation. 'It's not just for me, it's the picture I'm thinking about.' Kazan goes down for another spoonful of pea soup. 'Hell, I'm happy with what you've let me do. It's just that I can't get anything going with him.'

Kazan shrugs. James takes it for a lack of concern; it is meant also to minimize James's apprehension.

'Don't get me wrong, I know he's been at the top since Caesar was a pup.'

'Hector.'

'What?'

'Since *Hector* was a pup.'

'Whoever was a pup. The point is, he's nothing but a face for me. He tries to give me anger, you know what it is?' Kazan refuses to look up. 'He curls his lip. That's the signal for anger. Doubt? He narrows one eye and tips his head. How can you play anything authentic with someone like that? How, Gadge? Tell me and I'll do it.'

'Just exactly the way you're doing it.'

'Yeah, sure.' James slaps his chest looking for a cigarette; he has none and unwraps his sandwich instead. 'I'm telling you, Gadge, he gives me nothing. Zippo.' James makes a zero with his thumb and forefinger and waves it near Kazan's soup.

'That's why,' Kazan says, 'I wanted him for the role. If the God of the Old Testament could act, who do you think he'd be, Laurence Olivier or Raymond Massey?'

Upset as he is, James smiles and begins to see the point.

'He doesn't understand your Cal. Couldn't in a million years. You're just not on the same wavelength and never will be. I want him wooden, for Christ's sake, not just acting wooden, but a wooden actor. I want him to miss everything about you. This is the God of the Old Testament we're talking about. That God really does curl his lip and narrow an eye.'

'And it's working?' This is James's attempt to extract a compliment.

'Believe me, it's working fine. You just keep coming at him as hard as you can. He'll keep missing the point. And we're all in business.'

'And yesterday, the Bible scene, it worked? I felt incredibly frustrated when I got home.'

'How many cameras was I shooting with?'

'Three I counted.'

'Tell me, why three?'

'I guess a close-up on each, and a long shot for both of us at the table.'

'So?' Kazan presents his hand like a merchant awaiting payment.

'To cover all bases?'

Kazan scratches the bulb of his nose with a knuckle. He's considering how much he wants to tell James. 'In the original script you had five scenes alone with Massey. Have you noticed in each rewrite since then we either knock the scene out or bring in other characters. We ended up with one scene with just the two of you, and yesterday was it. I haven't seen the rushes yet, but I'd like – that is, I'm inclined depending on what I see – to go with alternating close-ups, reaction shots, of each of you. Make you more independent of each other. So where you said in the fourth or fifth take, "My mother. She's not dead and gone to heaven, is she? She's not dead at all,' I wanted only you on the screen so it looks like you're talking to yourself. It's your accusation, if you see what I mean. I want you to be independent of him. I want you *really* not to connect. Then. Then we can cut to his close-up, to his line.'

'Where he says, "I thought it would save you pain"?'

'Right. I want the audience to see you struggling with yourself even more than with him.'

James bites into his sandwich and speaks with his mouth full. 'I got to admit, there are times when he looks at me and it goes right through me. I get the same feeling I have with my old man.'

'I thought you said your father was dead.'

'He is. The feelings are the same as I used to get.'

Kazan looks across the commissary. Winton has been calling the publicity department repeatedly, and one of the calls had finally been put through to Kazan, who believed the man's story but told the voice on the other end he could do nothing to help him make contact. Kazan touches James's wrist: 'You know what I loved? That take you did when Julie gets out of bed.'

James knows the scene and his reaction. Abra has said, 'I've got to put something on'; Cal manages to look utterly innocent and at the same time devilish enough so the camera can tell he wants to take a peek. Kazan has left the camera on him the entire time. James knows how good he was for those moments. He says, 'I don't know, I thought that whole thing was a little too arch.'

'Jesus, Jimmy, spare me.' Kazan does not say, *Don't pull that modesty bullshit on me.* 'It's tough enough being good even for a few seconds, so don't undermine yourself with false modesty. You were very fine, let's leave it at that.' James sets his eyes on Kazan; Kazan matches his gaze. Each is seeking a safe place in the heart of the other.

James's smile is confessional and disarming; Kazan's aspect remains stern. 'Look, Jimmy, we don't have to play games. This movie, whether I can pull it off completely or not, is going to give your career a real leg up – at the least – so just keep reaching in and coming up with the good stuff. Next big one's the stroll with your mother? You got your lines?'

'Hell no, Gadge, I'm too big a star to bother about something as trivial as lines.'

'I'm going to get another bowl. You want one?'

'No. Thanks. I've got to sit for publicity stills in twenty minutes.'

'Don't look too brooding in them. They'll think everyone from New York is Brando.'

*

He must have been sweating because he feels very clammy and cool; his cheek and arm adhere to the pillow and sheet. It isn't fear that stuns him awake; it's something more, something that will come to him if he doesn't panic, doesn't move. He lies stock still, his eyes rounding the room, trying to make the unfamiliar friendly. The clock points 2:05. Funny, but when they were on location up in Mendocino he slept like a baby; back here he has yet to sleep through the night. It's not the camera fright he mentioned to Julie. This is subtle, erosive, more like a cliff face nibbled from below for ages and then suddenly collapsing into the water. The word *collapse* frightens him more than any other. He lies perfectly still for a long while, cold in his perspiration.

There are two elements of collapse: the undermining force from below, or more likely from within; the unbearable, top-heavy weight that cannot be sustained. A tic flutters under his right eye; he perceives it as an acting gesture he's cultivating, in fact it's cultivating him.

If his expression at that moment could be transferred to film, a careful observer would not see the self-contained young American iconoclast destined to become a symbol for youth all over the world. He wears the face of doubt and torment. But it's not Cal Trask, the troubled persona he has been carrying for the past six weeks: this is the authentic face of personal pain. He believes some understanding, some relief at least, will come if he does not move a hair.

The collapse he senses and fears will not occur tonight. The anxiety eases with time – 2:11, and it has receded once again; it is an ache only. By 2:20 it is not even an ache anymore but a weariness of the soul, something that will pass with the right sort of rest – a fishing trip, a motorcycle tour – with a friend when the picture's done. This is a necessary untruth. He doesn't have a friend. Only Lem Craig comes to mind. 'Tell me who?' he says.

He doesn't answer. No one does.

So he waits, stock still – 2:28. In half sleep he asks, 'What the hell's the matter?'

The answer doesn't come in words but he will remember it in words: *I'm tired. Of having to be you. It will only get worse.*

James smiles sorrowfully – or perhaps dreams he does. 'Being me? That's not the end of the world.'

The phone rings from a great distance. He expects someone else to answer it. It rings a second time, a third, coming closer. He has the memory of being afraid to move. Fortunately he does not have to. The telephone half rings then stops.

He can hear the surf beating from 300 yards away, slower than his heart, faster than his breath. There will be no final collapse, there is only ebb and flow, ebb and . . . The telephone sounds harshly. He rolls a full turn across his mattress and grabs the phone before a second ring. His lips are glued with dried spittle. He says, 'Mmm?'

Silence on the other end. Breathing and the soft throated sound of pre-speech.

'Come on. Don't mess with me.'

'Jimmy.' It's not a question.

'Yes.'

'Hello Jimmy Dean. Welcome to Hollywood.'

He knows the voice, its timbre and tone, its reluctance. He's confused and intrigued by its peculiar lack of accent, its stage-standard training. He knows he knows this woman. 'So how're you doing, baby?'

'Not as well as you, that's for sure. But well enough.'

'You know it's almost 3 A.M.'

'Had to work up the courage.'

'Listen, I'd like to cook up a few more hours sleep. Could we do this in about . . .?'

'You don't know who this is, do you?'

231

James is sure it'll come to him. He says, 'Sure I do. I do. It's just you woke me up like that.'

'You don't. You have no idea.'

'Look, I'm hanging up.'

'Who is it then?'

'I've got to . . .' He touches the receiver down. As he does, he hears, 'Ramon is dead.' He pulls it up immediately. Disconnected.

He waits for the phone to ring again. Looking upward through the blinds, he imagines the sun coming up. It isn't. He rubs his hands slowly over his face, touching the tips of his fingers to his eyes, under them. Fortunately they aren't shooting today; he knows he looks terrible. He stares at the phone trying to prompt it to ring. Only then does he go behind Yazzy's voice to her message. *Ramon is dead.*

Is it accusation or simple fact? Accusation, no doubt. By the time he drifts toward sleep, her message has been transformed into *someone killed my brother.*

While he's showering, he looks into the mirror and does a passable Cagney. Stiffening his upper lip, dropping his shoulders and swaying slightly, he pokes the air with his razor and sneers at his own image: 'I know you did it, I know you killed my brudder. And you better say your prayers, cause I'm gonna kill you . . . you an' all them other dirty rats.'

The phone rings at 10:05. He assumes she's decided to make a fresh start. He picks it up after the second ring: 'Lem Craig's Service Station. No offense large or small we can't make worse.'

Confused silence on the other end: 'Mr. Dean?'

Confused silence on his end: 'Speaking.'

'I'm so glad. This is Arlene Grossbard, Mr. Warner's secretary.'

'Oh, sure.'

'Mr. Warner wanted to speak with you today. He wondered if you could possibly drop by at 11:30.'

'Hmmm. I'm going to have to check with my secretary.'

His response confuses her. 'It's rather important.'

'I don't doubt it. Mr. Jack Warner his own self. It's got to be important. Let's do this, then, my dear. I'll have my secretary give you a call in a little while. Let you know when I can make it. How's that?'

'Mr. Dean. He's free at 11:30. He would very much like to see you then.'

'Won't he be in all day? Or is he off to the races? Playing polo maybe?'

'Mr. Warner will be here at 11:30 and hopes to see you then.' Her voice is firm, a teacher who will toss late homework into the trash can.

Still he can't capitulate: 'And where exactly is Mr. Jack's office?'

'Second floor of the Administration building. Mr. Dean.' Her tone says, *You know exactly where it is. Grow up.* Before he can frustrate her further she adds, 'See you then.' Her cheerfulness has topped him. James puts the phone down softly with a pang of admiration for a true professional.

James thinks about his meeting with Jack L. as he lifts the moist towel off the leather seat of his M.G.–T.F. sports convertible. It is the same color as the avocados lying in bushel baskets at the roadside stands. The door on the driver's side is dented a little above the curb; James has had the car two and a half weeks. It isn't completely paid for.

The morning air is very still; James rushes through it to produce a breeze that comes in his adjustable windshield and blows his hair back and up, giving him the look of a suddenly awakened devil. The road snakes eastward through Thousand Oaks; some of the 'esses' are so severe he can barely get the M.G. up to 65 before having to brake in a turn. Still, he loves the squeal of rubber as he leans into a bend and the feeling of lightness in the outside wheels. He never feels more invincible than when he puts himself in jeopardy. Kazan senses this and has put him at risk often in the film. The speed, the sense of danger, these chase out any semblance of last night's fear. He is, if anything, more alive than he was yesterday, or the day before that.

He comes to a screeching halt before the long, low wooden building that is the Warners commissary. As intended, his parking gets the attention of extras in World War I uniforms, the Indian braves, African tribesmen, misshapen people in circus costumes. As he parks with a squeal, an elephant being led to Soundstage C trumpets and drags his handler a few paces off course.

'Sorry, Jumbo,' James shouts. He slams the door of his prize crisply and enters the commissary. His car is in the space reserved for 'Oscar Bernard – Comptroller.'

It is still early for lunch: there are more people dressed in normal clothes than in costumes. That will change when the soundstages break for lunch. James goes to the counter for coffee. 'Hot and black, Gracie. And sometime today, please.'

Gracie looks grandmotherly – hair in a bun, pink cheeks, wide face softened by kind blue eyes and pale lips. 'Black as your heart, as hot as you think you are in bed, but only as fast as this big old ass can move from there to here.'

'Oh, Gracie, why aren't you twenty-one?'

'I am. Three times.' She hands him his coffee. 'Slick down your hair, you look wild.'

'I am wild.' James runs his fingers through it while he looks for a seat near a window from which to admire his car.

'Here's the baby you wanted to look at. Not crazy about parting with her, though.'

James looks up, blinks and slowly recognizes someone he knows but cannot name until he sees the camera in the man's hands. 'Hi, Gus. Want a coffee?'

'Yeah. I'll get it. Take a look at this, but be careful.'

Gus Clement is the cameraman of the second unit. Then James remembers. Clement has a Hasselblad he said he'd be willing to sell. James turns it over in his hands. He holds the viewer to his eye and focuses on his M.G. A girl dressed as a trapeze artiste walks past in high heels: James follows her movement in the lens. The globes of her rump meet the backs of her legs in jellied arcs; he lines them up in the cross hairs and watches them wobble away.

'So what do you think of her?' says Clement, an old silent-movie player whose knowledge of photography salvaged the ruin of his career.

'Nice piece of work.' James starts his slow and usually winning smile. 'Tell me about her.'

Clement mocks: 'Nice piece of work. Hah. It's a Hasselblad. The best.'

James hold the camera up with renewed admiration. 'Nobody can touch the Germans for this sort of thing.'

'It's not German, Hasselblad.'

James remembers Lem Craig's Düsseldorf story very clearly: 'You sure?'

'Sure I'm sure. Hasselblad's Swedish. The lenses, they're usually Zeiss, that's German, but Hasselblad's Swedish. Everyone who knows cameras knows that.'

'Funny, I was told German. So tell me about it.'

'Not much to tell. Got her in '48. She's their first S.L.R. . . .'

'S.L.R.?'

'Single Lens Reflex. They've never made the system any better. This is the first model with interchangeable lenses and magazines. But I'm going to keep the other lenses; I'll just give you this .35. Starting out, you've got no need for a whole bunch of fancy stuff. If you discover you need them, you just pick 'em up.'

'How come you're selling?'

'They just came out with a Super Wide – the 1000F Series, I think. She's got a ninety degree angle of view. I do a lot of big nature stuff up in the Sierras.'

'So why shouldn't I just buy the Super Wide?'

'It's for pros. A greenhorn like you wouldn't have the faintest clue how to use it. This would be a great break-in camera.'

'What'd you pay for her?'

'Why would I tell you that? It's what I'm asking that matters.'

'Okay, lay it on me.'

'Four hundred bucks.'

'You're kidding.' James registers true shock. 'It's a used camera, for Christ's sake.'

'It's a Hasselblad. They're like great paintings. They accrue.'

'I'll give you three hundred.'

'I ain't here to haggle. I'm asking a fair price, believe me.'

'Well.'

The two men drink their coffee. Clement clears his throat. James looks out to his car.

'Let's say I buy it. Will you throw in some lessons how to use it?'

'Sure. But if you want the truth, the way you make any camera your own, you shoot hundreds of rolls and you make every mistake in the world with it. You learn from mistakes. Actually, there are no *mistakes*, if you know what I mean. Anything someone tells you about "how to shoot good pictures" is bullshit. But, sure, I'll show you how to load, the speeds, the stops.'

'Then I guess we got a deal.'

'Fine.'

The two men raise their cups. James says, 'To the brothers Warner, whose benevolence makes all things possible.'

'Listen, if you want to call them the smartest kikes in this town, sure. Or the ballsiest. But "benevolence," forget it. Not that I begrudge them anything they got: God knows, they earned it. But, Jesus, they're established as the top studio – let's say one of the top – and the nickel and diming never ends. So don't tell me about the Warners and their benevolence.'

James had no such intention.

'You forget, I knew them when they started in the twenties. There were four of them. There's a kind of guy, when he's around, you take your wallet into the shower with you, well you could say that about any of them. And there were *four* of them. A school, like barracudas. Hollywood didn't have a chance. Al, Harry, Sam and Jack. As bastards they were in a class by themselves, even by Hollywood standards. Harry's at least mellowed a little. I worked for them in the silents. Just a baggy-pants, knock-about comic. I told Al about talkies, told him it was the smart way to go. Everyone thinks it was such a big gamble, but they were going down the tubes anyway. They had to do something.'

'So *you* saved Warner Brothers?'

Clement pretends to think: 'I don't brag about it, but, yeah, I guess basically I'm the guy who saved Warners.'

'And transformed the movie business.'

'Yeah. And transformed the movie business.'

James fondles the camera. His eye wanders over the parking lot, his mind ranges further. Across the commissary he sees her. Clement is speaking from miles away. For some reason, James does not want to speak with her; he's satisfied with the steady exchange of gaze, with the knowing expression on her sweet face.

If she works at the studio, she must do something interesting, not just a secretary, something creative. A dialogue coach or something like that. A film cutter. She looks so confident and earnest.

Her brown eyes, expressive, intelligent, benign, are a match for his. Her smile comes slowly, flickers sidewise, and fades sorrowfully. She is young even in middle age. James cannot be certain if the flowered print dress and light sweater she wears are exactly the ones he's noticed before. It doesn't matter; their affinity is consoling and hopeful, the closest thing to love he's felt as an adult.

Clement's words break the connection: '. . . the prick of all pricks. He's the one who'll fuck you over good given half a chance. Seen him do it to his own brothers.' Clement chuckles to himself. 'In some strange, perverted way I admire the guy.'

Clement's crudity now offends James; it hadn't before. James says, 'That how you survived too?'

'No, I'm different. I lasted because I'm an ass-kisser.' There's a note of mocking pride in his tone.

'You trying to tell me there's only two ways to make it out here – prick or ass-kisser?'

Clement takes a moment to consider. 'Yup. That's about it.'

'What about just having talent?'

Again consideration. 'Talent's just about the worst thing you can have. That gets people pissed off. Everyone'll be gunning for you – the talents and the no-talents. No, my motto is "talent don't last, kissin' do."'

'Man. And I thought I was bleak. You make me look like a goddamned Pollyanna.'

'Well, Polly, let me tell you a little Hollywood story. After my first marriage broke up, I shared an apartment with Monk Meyers. The name mean anything?'

James shakes his head.

'He was the greatest stuntman ever in the history of this town. He's the guy who went over walls in prison movies, leapt off bridges and moving trains. You name it, if no one else wanted to touch it, Monk would give it a try. He invented the flame-suit and knew how to get trampled under stampeding horses. If you don't believe how good the man was, just ask some of the old-timers.' Clement's indignation flares. 'One night we're running late on an Indian massacre, shooting a night raid with floodlights and Monk is supposed to jump off a cliff onto a bareback horse. The lights spook the horse, Monk misses real bad. Broken back, worse than anyone figures. Paralyzed for life . . .'

James looks beyond Clement to where his mother had been. She isn't there, but he catches a glimpse of her in the parking lot. She looks back and either waves or touches a wisp of hair.

'. . . discovers that the accident took place after midnight. Turns out Monk's union card had expired that midnight. Would you believe that Jack L. contested the insurance coverage! Not because he'd have to pay – the insurance company was liable – but because he didn't want his rates going up. Meyers was forced to settle for a twentieth of what he should have got. Here's a guy who gave the studio thirty years, and he ends up living in a wheelchair and getting by on charity. But the part that really gets me is right over there . . .' Clement points to a plaque on the entrance wall of the commissary. 'You ought to take a look. Says, "To the dedication and sacrifice of Edwin 'Monk' Meyers: Without people like him Warner Brothers would be a loveless place. Jack L. Warner." Imagine! – "would be *lov*less." You know why they say working here is like fucking a porcupine?'

James smiles.

'Because it's a hundred pricks against one.'

James snorts a laugh.

Clement taps the camera. 'You can pay me later on this.'

As he's about to leave the commissary, Jimmy spots Kazan at a corner table. He walks over, conscious of walking in a defensive slouch, as Cal does. Kazan raises a single eyebrow. 'You didn't get the soup?'

'Gadge, I don't really like soup.'

'But this is terrific soup.'

*

James wanders up the stairs and through the doors that are replicas of the Roxy Theater in New York. Jack Warner's office isn't merely *on* the second floor, it *is* the second floor.

James approaches Arlene Grossbard's sweeping art deco desk in his darkest 'New York Method actor' mood. He stands on one leg and rubs his chin and mumbles, 'Mr. Dean to see Mr. Warner.'

Miss Grossbard smiles politely at this adolescent: 'Mr. Warner will be pleased. Go right in.'

James had hoped his deliberate lateness would be a hindrance. Apparently not.

Warner's oval teakwood desk is fifty feet from the door, a distance furnished with an array of Oriental rugs, low tables and cushioned chairs, and hundreds of photographs of Warner Brothers stars. The back lot of the studio is framed in a wall of high windows behind Jack Warner. Standing in an aura of luminescence, he looks down on a small-town Main Street, a pier in a European fishing village, a circus tent with ferris wheel and roller coaster – this set is being used in *East of Eden* – the steps of a State Capitol, a western boom town with oil rigs and saloons. The world according to Jack L. Warner.

At a distance and silhouetted as he is, Warner seems tall. As he approaches and begins to come into focus, he shrinks a bit. When he offers his hand, he is actually shorter than Jimmy.

'We should have gotten together long before this, young man. Gadge has been giving me wonderful reports.' Two things about Warner strike James: the cultivated richness of his voice; the slim mustache that doesn't appear to move while he speaks.

'Glad he's happy, J.L.' James had been planning to use the initials all morning.

'Happy? He's swallowed a canary. A cup of something? Tea?' James shakes his head and sinks low into a soft sofa. Warner sits tall in a high-backed chair. 'And you know Mr. Kazan is a perfectionist, not given to superlatives. So tell me, you're still ensconced in no-man's land?' Warner has been bothered by James's living in North Beach. He wants him living much closer to the studio.

'The folks out there might take exception to "no-man's land."'

'I'm sure it's beautiful. It's just too much of a trek to Soundstage B. Something could happen, we could lose time.'

James puts on his glasses to indicate seriousness. 'Where are you living these days, J.L.?'

'Ah. *Touché*. So. Are you happy with us? Are they treating you all right?'

'The work's what matters. Seems to be going okay.'

'Better than okay by all reports.' Warner leaves a silence during which James is supposed to wonder why he's there. He does but refuses to ask. 'I'm the sort of person who wants to get to know our emerging stars better, especially someone I hope to have with us for a good long while.'

James smiles, rubs his chin, and says nothing.

'It's time, isn't it, to think about our next project.'

'Not a little premature?'

'I own horses, Mr. Dean, and when I have a good one who's in prime condition, I race him.'

'Just like that?'

'Just like that. Any particular project you're interested in?'

This is the perfect time to mention Enoch. 'Well, yes, there is something. I've been reading books about the real Billy the Kid. The true story's never been told, not in a realistic way.'

Warner has been shaking his head slightly since James mentioned Billy the Kid. 'It's not prudent to come right back in another Western. They'd type you and bury you maybe forever.'

'*East of Eden* isn't a Western. It's more a Bible story.'

'If you've been shooting up in Salinas, to me that's a Western. But down the line, if you become the comet Publicity thinks you'll be, we could consider it.' He takes a leather notebook out of his breast pocket and writes. 'If I put an idea in my little black book, it's like it's written in my heart. I'll have some Development people look into it.' He writes and closes the book as though something important has been accomplished. 'As a matter of fact, Publicity has been urging me to talk to you. They tell me you're not the most cooperative fellow.'

'I'm out here to act not to pose.'

'This is true, you're an artist first, a very good one or I wouldn't be wasting my time with you. But you are more, you're a Warner Brothers artist. That's contractual. And I'm charged with the very great responsibility of providing the American public – whose tastes and expectations I am devoted to satisfying – with entertainment of the very highest order. This, I'm sure you will agree, is a very great responsibility. And if you look at the activity going on out that window . . .' – he points to the back lot, the soundstages – '. . . at these incredible talents . . .' he indicates the photos.

240

James picks out Cagney, Bogart, and Garfield; Bette Davis, Barbara Stanwyck, Olivia de Havilland – '. . . you'll agree we're not doing such a bad job. It is my devout wish, Jimmy, that you will join this pantheon of Warner stars.'

James scans Paul Muni, Al Jolson, Mary Astor, Gary Cooper, Ingrid Bergman, Leslie Howard, Fredric March.

'Do you know what makes great moving pictures possible?'

'Actors.'

'Absolutely. Incredible actors like these, of course. But more. Something very simple. Box . . . office . . . receipts. In other words, all those quarters and half-dollars Americans will pay to see Jimmy Dean as whatever character he plays. What makes them want to see you? Talent? I'll grant you that, yes, talent. And . . .'

James considers interrupting.

Warner raises a finger: '. . . *And.* Everything our Publicity Department tells America that makes America want to see this new phenomenon, this James Dean. Those are not just pictures of artists on the wall, young man, those are stars in the heavens. We're in the astrology business. So. Here's what I propose: you take care of the acting part and let me find a niche up in the sky for you. If for some nutty reason, you don't want that niche, I suggest you take a closer look at your contract.' Warner is beaming, eyes sparkling; he appears to be making a joke. 'Your "full and willing cooperation" clause.' There's not a trace of humor.

'So who do I kiss first, the babies or the horses?'

'Starlets. Date some of our starlets. Be seen around town with them. We'll get the photos. Distribute to the columns, plant the items. Don't look so unhappy, it's not like we're pulling teeth. Most young fellows in your position would kill for this. Know what I mean?' Jack Warner winks wickedly and touches James's knee. 'And everyone benefits, that's the beauty. The girls, they're like you: good kids whose careers, too, would get a boost. For this they will be extremely grateful. And the studio, too. It's not a great deal to ask, young man.'

'No, not really, I guess. Except . . .'

'Except what?'

'Except that I'm engaged to be married.'

241

'When? Who? Is she one of ours?'

'We haven't exactly set the date.'

'Good, good. We can explain things to her. I'll sit down person-ally and explain the situation if you'd like . . .'

'Problem is she's very jealous. Hot tempered. Mexican.'

All Warner can think of is, *The skin, how dark?* He says, 'She'll come in, we'll talk. Publicity had some ideas about releasing this film. You're from a small town, right? Indiana, someplace?'

'Someplace, Indiana.'

'They wanted to send you back home with one of our beautiful new girls and premiere it out there. There's a lot of mileage in some-thing like that. I okayed it, but with this marriage story, I don't know. There's time to see how things work out. Maybe with the Harris girl. The two new stars of *East of Eden*, it makes sense. She, what's her background?'

'Julie? I don't honestly know.'

'Is she from a small town too? It doesn't matter, that's for Publicity.' He digs out his black book and writes.

James cannot resist. 'Why can't I just go home with my fiancée? No one back there's ever seen her.'

'No, no, the Harris girl is the way we should go if we decide . . .' He continues to write.

With a smirk on his face, James looks at more photos: John Barrymore, Joan Crawford, Walter Huston, Edward G. Robinson, Douglas Fairbanks, Jr., Marlene Dietrich. He has to squint to make out a photo further away. Rin Tin Tin.

Warner stands first. 'Good. I'm glad we had this little talk. You'll make yourself available for interviews. Publicity will contact you later today. Put yourself in their hands: they know their business.' He taps James's shoulder reassuringly. 'Are you shooting today?'

'It's just the forming of the posse to catch the rustlers. I'm not in that scene.' Said deadpan.

Warner picks up something, thinks, and says, 'You're a bit of a wag, aren't you?'

James opens his arms: 'What can I say?'

'That's good. It means you're clever. You'll be fine with inter-viewers once you've gone over your contract carefully.'

'You know, Mr. Warner, I just remembered – there *is* something I wanted . . .'

Warner touches his shoulder again. 'Anything to keep a young star happy.'

'There's an actor in New York. I did a "Philco Playhouse" with him, and . . .'

Warner makes a stop sign with his hand. 'I understand your loyalty, believe me.' He leaves out the *but*. 'I've been in this business almost forty years, never once did I discover a "close friend" I could really use.'

'This actor is different, I can assure . . .'

Stop sign. 'To show my good faith. Give the name to Arlene on the way out. I'll have someone take a look.' But Jack L. Warner does not write Enoch Moss's name in his black book.

*

'Gadge. How about I stand on that high ground and watch her passing? Maybe follow her from tree to tree and then just come down and walk alongside. Like a school kid, almost like I'm trying to court her. What do you think?'

It's a good idea. Kazan doesn't answer. The first two takes were flat, flatter than the rehearsals. The problems has to be Jack Warner's presence on the set.

James woke up at 3 A.M. with a sense of physical dread. Here was the scene he knew would make or break the movie – where he walks alongside the mother who abandoned him as an infant, a mother turned whore who is now a wealthy Madame. Uncertainty and anxiety were normal as he approached any important scene but never before this level of self-doubt. He knew what provoked it; he did not want to know what provoked it.

Warner's presence has the opposite effect on him than on the others – it makes him combative, as though he has something to prove.

Before the third take, James whispers to Jo Van Fleet and Kazan: 'I was in the men's room yesterday and he' – James indicates Warner with his eyes – 'came in to piss right next to me. His weenie would fit into a thimble.' He indicates the tip of his pinkie and puts his other hand up in an oath.

The scene will be shot from a double track, one from Jimmy's side, one from Jo's and then pieced and intertwined. The shooting schedule allows half a day for the two and a half minutes. Before they move to their spots, James says to Jo, 'Clear out your bookcase, here comes your Oscar.'

'Okay,' Gadge calls through cupped hands, 'let's go for the whole damn thing. Camera two, stay on Dean. One, you're on Jo, but use some judgment. Quiet everybody, aaannd . . . action.'

Jo Van Fleet, costumed in period crimson velvet, a white ruffled blouse, red bonnet, starts to move forward from a distance along the path toward the camera. Screen left on the high ground above her, James, all in white, scoots from behind a tree to the cover of another tree; his movement is as much of the stalked as the stalker. Van Fleet is exactly the age Mildred would have been. At precisely the moment Kazan starts to signal him to run down the slope and trail his mother, James stumbles down, seemingly drawn by her force. He trails her for a long while. Kazan gives him his head. Van Fleet, unlooking, knows he's there.

He is coy, adoring, scared. She is curious. James pulls abreast, matching her cadence. Somehow they are bonded. She says, without turning toward him, 'What does Cal stand for?'

His hands are deep in his pockets. He sneaks a look at her: 'Caleb. It's in the Bible.'

'What's your brother's name?'

'Aron. That's in the Bible too.'

'What's he look like?' Her voice is hard; her interest tender.

'Well, he looks like you.' He wants to please.

'Well, is he like me?' Her *well* is impatient, almost self-contemptuous.

'No. He's good.' Three words delivered brilliantly: they at once distinguish Cal from Aron, bind Cal to his mother, and insult her.

Jo's laugh is immediate, carnal. 'How's Adam? How's your father?'

'I don't want to talk about him.'

'Oh you don't, huh?'

'No.'

They walk. A field of force between them draws and repels.

'Aren't you afraid to come around here . . .?'

James's face, his entire person, is ready to say no: 'Yeah. I am, I am, no. Kind of . . .'

'What do you want, just to look at me?'

'I want – five thousand dollars.' He states his request as a question that surprises even him. In fact, in this single page of dialogue there's been the true, unadorned, unanticipated speech of two human beings overheard.

The scene is the high point of the film. Although he has to shoot it again in segments from other angles, Kazan knows he has magic in the can. Van Fleet will win the 1955 Academy Award for Best Supporting Actress. James will be nominated as Best Actor.

Jack Warner has slipped away unnoticed well before the shoot is finished.

*

The phone rings in James Dean's apartment. He picks the entire telephone off the floor and puts it on his chest, where he lets it ring again. He sweetens his voice; he has expectations. 'I sure hope it's you.'

The caller hangs up. That encourages James. In a minute it rings again. James says, 'It is you.'

'Ramon is dead.'

James waits, perhaps out of respect for the dead. 'How? When?'

'Suicide.'

'How? When?'

'Last week. Shot himself.'

'We should talk. I want to see you.'

'Why?'

'Because there's all we never had. We should at least . . .'

'At least what? Ramon kills himself and you don't even say you're sorry, don't have any guilt.'

'I do.' He didn't. 'That's why we should meet.'

'He's dead, and you say, "We should meet." You are a very strange *hombre*.' Her new voice has a peculiar shifting of inflections he cannot unravel because he's never heard anything quite like it. 'You never even say, "I'm sorry he's dead." You don't ask me how I got your number. Nothing, just, "We should meet."'

This woman could be crazy. 'Tell me about Ramon. The details of it.'

'Nothing to tell. You showed him how it's done, remember?'

'With a gun?'

'Yes, with a gun.'

'Not right in front of you.'

'That was the rottenest thing, when you did that to me. My heart stopped.'

'It wasn't intended for you. Ramon was the one it was meant for.'

'And I? I was just an innocent bystander?'

'He slashed me, if you remember. Thought it'd throw a scare into him.'

'It's me you scared to death.'

'Sorry.'

'You sound like a little kid.'

'Listen, I can help you through this. I *want* to help you through this.'

'He left a note.'

'What'd it say?'

'It didn't make any sense. He mentioned you.'

'How?'

'He said . . .' This she has memorized. '". . . that crazy white kid would have been better for you, but he was not yet man enough." He talked about you. Couldn't get over what you did.' Her voice has become emotional. 'I don't miss him. He got impossible to live with, the last year. I just wanted to tell you, to maybe hear a little remorse from you. But now you're James Dean, movie star, too important to feel sorry for a . . .' Her sob sounds like a snicker.

'Don't, Yazzy. I can't say I liked the guy, but I would never want something like this for . . .'

'So you're sorry for what you did?'

'To you, sure.'

'And you feel true remorse.'

'Yes.'

'And guilty?'

'Yes,' he lies.

She giggles. 'Good.'

Jimmy cocks his head and looks at the receiver. Her reaction is befuddling. He hears her laughter break the bounds of restraint. Yazzy is almost breathless when she says, 'I wanted to do this in person, but I wasn't confident enough. The phone was better. It worked, didn't it?'

James is confused.

'I couldn't see you again until I got even with you. Well, not really *even,* but just to get you to fall for it.'

He's less confused. 'I guess I fell for it, all right.'

'Not hide or hair of him for six months. Maybe someone shot him, but I think he went home.'

'How'd you get my number.'

'Easy. We work at the same place. I've been watching some of the shooting. You're still the best kid in the class.'

'I want to see you. Tomorrow?'

'I'm not sure.' Her coyness spreads like honey.

'I can find you through Personnel.'

'No you can't. You don't know my new name.' The click is muted.

That next morning James calls Chick Murray, head of Warners Security, with a description of Eusabia Gomez as he remembers her. Twenty minutes later a return call tells him, 'She could be Carmen Reyes. She did take acting classes at U.C.L.A. Lives, Cavalcade Apartments 1510 North Wilshire. Under contract since December '53. Appeared in three shorts and two features – *Murder in Rio* and *Blossoms of Santa Rosa,* that last one hasn't been released yet. The only problem with your description is that this girl's a red-head, but you know . . .'

'Sure. Thanks, Chick.'

James has three, no, two dozen red roses sent to Carmen Reyes's apartment. He leaves the card unsigned.

12. Not Home at Home

REBEL WITHOUT A CAUSE: screenplay by Stewart Stern; based on Irving Shulman's adaptation of a story by Nicholas Ray; cinematography by Ernest Haller; art direction by Malcolm Bert; musical direction by Leonard Rosenman; directed by Nicholas Ray; produced by David Weisbart for Warner Brothers.

Jim..*James Dean*
Judy...*Natalie Wood*
Plato..*Sal Mineo*
Jim's father..*Jim Backus*
Jim's mother..*Ann Doran*
Buzz...*Corey Allen*
Moose..*Nick Adams*
Goon..*Dennis Hopper*

Judy has not seen Jim since Buzz's death in the chickie-run. She looks out her bedroom window for his car coming into the driveway. She pulls the shade halfway down and walks out of the frame, appearing to go to bed. When he drives up, she's sitting under a tree.

In 1955 when the film was released, the company was having a problem with its WarnerColor printing process: there seemed to be a blue tinge to everything. The flaw helped give Rebel *its dark mood.*

James comes toward Natalie – his red jacket looks orange; her white coat is azure. His brown eyes are indigo.

Jim: Still pretty upset?
Judy: I'm just numb.
Jim: You know something. I woke up this morning. The sun was shining and it was nice. And I saw you. And I said to myself this is one terrific day . . . and it was . . . until . .

Dean speaks very deliberately: his character is not so much inarticulate as bone-weary. He nears Natalie, leans down and kisses her quickly, nervously, shyly. He turns his back to the camera, as though it was the camera he had kissed.

Judy: Why did you do that?
Jim: I felt like it.
Judy: Your lips are soft. (She stands and moves away from him.)
Jim: Where you going?
Judy: I don't know. We can't stay here.
Jim: I know one thing. I'm not going back in that zoo.
Judy: I'm never going back.
Jim: I know a place. An old deserted mansion. You want to go there with me? You can trust me, Judy.

J ames has been shooting the 'chickie-run' sequence in *Rebel* for the
past three days and has done a lot of the driving himself, which
is why he's slept in so late on this day off. He might have slept even
longer if he hadn't been wakened by the clink of pans and the insistent smell of onions frying. Then Yazzy trilling a Mexican song.

In the five weeks since Yazzy has moved into the North Beach
apartment, these things have happened: Carmen Reyes has been
signed to a three-year starlet's contract: she is working as a French
girl in *Paris Does Not Answer*, in which she has a page and a half of
dialogue and a death scene with Tab Hunter – the death is his; she
has just about worn Jimmy out with her cooking.

James stands in the doorway wearing pink pajama bottoms and
the bewilderment of enduring sleep. Yazzy knows he's there but
continues beating her eggs and singing. Over her thin robe she
wears a striped apron tied tightly in the small of her back. She sways
imperceptibly to her own music: James cannot separate the rhythm
of the dance from her wrist movements. It is cooking: it is performance. They've not made love for two days.

She allows him to watch, to receive the pulsing signal. Eventually
she turns with surprise that is not surprise. Her eyes question his. As
sexual performer and temptress, there is nothing Stanislavsky could
have taught her. Eusabia Gomez has the power to be different
women according to whim, all of them erotic in disparate and dis-
similar ways. She can be whore and virgin; teacher and student;
sister, mother, daughter, friend and fan, all and each by sudden and

mysterious turns. Once she decides what erotic aura she will slip on, James Dean lapses into helplessness. He is a little afraid of her too. Of her power.

Her eyes meet his. 'I wanted to surprise you with breakfast. Why aren't you asleep?' Her voice rich with concern. Other than the suggestion of a pout, there is no overt sexual suggestion. James is aroused.

She turns back to her eggs. There is something about the way her long, muscular neck turns and the twist of her back and waist that excites him. An observer might only see a beautiful woman preparing eggs. But Yazzy Gomez can make what is not sexual into the opposite. Carmen Reyes can also do it on camera.

They make love twice in the kitchen. Once on the floor, once on the table while feeding each other peppered eggs.

There's no reason for Jimmy to leave the house today. It's a surprise when he says, 'Benny's coming over. We're going up to Riverside.' Riverside is the speed track, forty minutes east of L.A.

Benny is Benny Ungar, the studio's stunt driver. In his time, Ungar has choreographed chases and raced everything from motorcycles to Sherman tanks at Warners. He's already got Jimmy averaging 85 m.p.h. around Riverside's oval. Today Jimmy is to try the complicated sports car layout behind the grandstand for the first time. The kid seems to be able to handle pure speed pretty well, but sports car racing is brake, turn, shift: rhythm, timing, judgment, and, like all racing, guts. He's driving his new silver Arnott Coventry-Climax, one of only twenty-five produced the previous year.

Never once has Yazzy tried to dissuade him or even warn him about driving too fast. She finds his thrill-seeking thrilling. She says, 'I've got a script to work on. Seafood tonight?' If she wasn't willing to let him leave with Benny, the same sentence would have been an irresistible invitation to a sexual snack.

The day is sunny but very dry and with a sweet land breeze. Too beautiful to be the day Jimmy Dean is killed.

Ungar shades his eyes and points ahead to the small, temporary grandstand, the hay bales and striped pylons. 'The trick on this course is to always stay to the right of obstructions until you hit the

backside, then let the orange arrows guide you. You'll be all alone
out there, so take a slow turn around the course first . . .' Ungar
hops out of the passenger seat. '. . . just to acquaint yourself . . . to
get the feel of the layout.'

'You're deserting?'

'I've got a family. After you pass me again, I'll throw you a signal.
That's when you open her up if you feel comfortable. I'll be timing
you.' Ungar smacks Jimmy hard on the top of his blue helmet. 'Just
remember, you got no roll bar, so don't try to set any land records.'

'God's my roll bar.' His voice throbs with movie bravado.

Jimmy pulls down his goggles and jumps the car into first: the
wheels kick up dirt and gravel. Ben Ungar steps back and covers his
eyes. The silver car glints in the sun, its motor changing pitch with
every shift of gear. It screams into the first hairpin.

Ungar likes what he hears – hums and groans and screams as
Jimmy shifts, speeds, and slows. Ungar knows Jimmy is a promising
driver, maybe even a good one – for a celebrity. James, for his part,
envisions driving the twelve-hour race at Sebring in a year or two.

Photography and racing. James isn't aware that he loves them for
the same reason. Photography stops time: racing devours it – either
way, James is in control, or believes he is. Both discoveries he owes
to crazy Lem Craig, but he never acknowledges the debt.

He is driving the trial lap much faster than he should, not only to
impress Ungar but to feel the machine's traction on the straights, the
sense of drag, and the pull of the suspension on the hairpins. To
thrill at the rush of wind over and around the car, and to know that
he is still not really going all-out. 'Man. I *love* this shit!' he shouts to
the wind. And he truly does. He drives directly at a pylon, brakes
once, twice, with his heel, pops the clutch and downgears, cuts the
wheel to the left and hard back to the right, hits the gas as the car
picks up speed, and moves instantaneously through fourth to fifth.
'Love it. God!'

He slows as he approaches Ungar again. Ungar holds up his stop-
watch. Like a Warner Brothers bomber pilot, James flashes a
dramatic thumbs up. He's smiling one of his least ambiguous smiles.

The Coventry explodes away from Ungar. If it screamed on the
trial lap, it is in torment this time, running the gamut of engine

emotions through each hairpin. James is at once part of the machine and its master. Ungar once told him, 'When it's the way it should be, you're the car, the car is you. The only thing you want to control is the course. The course, she'll tell you when she wants it. Like good screwing – smooth, smooth, thrust. But remember, you're the one on top.' James laughed in a low register: Ungar didn't even smile. But James remembers the lines like good dialogue.

The Coventry is gurgling and vibrating as James roars through the turns and accelerates into the straights. His forearms ache; his shoulders and upper back are knotted; his right leg, the braking one, feels as though it's asleep. He's not in shape for an extended race.

He comes out of the double 'S' on the far side of the course, throws the stick into fourth for the longest straightaway on the course. Into fifth and the quivering speedometer breaks 100. The blur of terrain, the whine of the engine, put James Dean in a state of near ecstasy. He certainly sees the large orange pylon ahead: it is, in fact, the sole focus of his being. But he must not brake or gear down too far from it: that's how fractions of seconds are pared. He concentrates on the cone and the diminishing distance; concentrating too much, it turns out. Brake, clutch, down-gear: brake again, release clutch. The pylon is closing like mad, and James . . . has . . . no . . . idea . . . no remembrance . . . of the course. Left or right? He demands a decision of his brain, but that brain does not know, can't believe it ever knew. Right? Right? Left? No, right.

His arms pull the wheel first one way then the other, then both ways. He's forgotten to brake. Benny Ungar sees the crash before it happens and is on the run to a spot where he expects the car to end up. It's almost half a mile away.

The Coventry wails through the pylon, sending the heavy cone back over the car with a rubbery thud. The car begins to fishtail and kick up dust in its wake. Jimmy realizes he must fight the wheel and taps the brake while trying to regain control, but he cannot straighten the line. Then his foot stomps to the floor, there is no brake. He jerks the hand-brake – proud of his presence of mind – and the car slows just a little: he smells the brake pads burning.

Ahead the end of the grandstand. To the right a storage pile of hay bales. James leans to the right and gets the Coventry's rear to come around slightly. He'll miss the grandstand and hopes the hay will cushion the crash. He pulls mightily on the hand-brake and hears metal on metal. He closes his eyes and crosses his face with his arms just before impact. He hears a *whooosh*, a crystalline *craa-aack*, and is thrown violently forward against the steering wheel. Pain burns his elbows and his kneecaps; the belt across his waist takes the air out of him. The rest is silence and darkness and the pungency of dried grass.

The distant voice is Ungar's: 'You okay, kid?'

James thinks he is responding: he's only thinking responses.

'Here. Let me get some of this crap off you.'

The darkness flickers. It lightens as Ungar tosses the bales out of the Coventry and off James.

James is dappled by sunlight. And confused. And in pain.

'It happens,' Ungar consoles. 'I should have taken a few laps with you. You froze. Unfamiliar with the course. Could have happened to anyone.'

James is ashamed.

'I think,' says Benny, 'we're going to have to re-stage a crash over at my place. Insurance won't touch this thing out here.' He indicates the body of the Coventry, but James is still too stunned to see its fiber-glass skin webbed with cracks from radiator to tail-light. Ruined. And not yet paid for.

James's left elbow is splintered, but he opts to float on and through the pain – the shooting of *Rebel* won't be finished for weeks, and he won't delay it.

'You okay?'

'Woozy.'

'Slide over. Let's see if we can get this out of here.'

To Yazzy, James seems nothing more than sullen. She's seen him like this when he was unhappy with his work: she assumes the driving didn't go well. After one failed attempt to get his interest, she decides to let him lay quietly on the mattress, his knees pulled to his chest, his left arm cradled in his right hand. The sky is as red as a stop light. The tide is out. She tiptoes through the kitchen and out to the beach.

*

'I have been trying. I told Warner about him, and he said he'd give him a test. He wrote his name down, promised he'd get in touch and fly him out. It's funny Enoch hasn't heard. When Warner writes it in his book, it's a done deal.' James has convinced himself what he is saying is true.

Amanda is calling because she's just discovered that Warners has bought the rights to *Fight Of His Life*. 'I know you're trying, but if they bought it, it's the perfect set up. The two of you have already done the thing.'

James sings, 'Let-ters, we get letters.'

'It's different now. They're starting to use Negro actors.'

'For *Green Pastures* maybe.'

'That kid in *Blackboard Jungle*, he was incredible. And remember, boxing movies are always box office. They must have had something in mind if they bought the rights. So just see what they have planned for the script.'

'I'll do that, of course I'll do that. How'd you and Enoch like to come out for a visit anyway? I'll get the studio to fly you.'

'You got that kind of influence?'

He doesn't. 'Jack Warner loves me.'

'That'd be swell. I'll ask Enoch. He's sort of down, Jim.'

'The trip'll pick him up. And you can meet Yazzy.'

'You get yourself a dog?'

'Yazzy's my love. My truest love.'

'You mean your latest, truest love.'

'Don't be snide. It's unbecoming.'

'Are you taking vocabulary lessons?'

After inquiring at Development and Publicity about *Fight Of His Life*, after talking to some of the writers and directors without learning a thing, Jim decided to go to the person who knew everything that happened at Warners.

He approaches her desk with his face covered by two dozen white tea roses.

Arlene Grossbard pretends the flowers are not for her: 'They're very beautiful.'

'Here.' He offers them like a child.

'Oh, my. They're lovely. But . . . it isn't my . . . But . . . why?'

'Because I'd like a truce.'

'A truce? I didn't know there was a war.'

'Well, mending fences, then.'

'This is very swell mending.' She holds the roses at arm's length for reappraisal. 'Let me get a vase.'

As she arranges the flowers on her desk, James says, 'I read something in *Variety* about a drama I once did on T.V., *Fight Of His Life*. It said the studio had bought the rights. I was just wondering what plans we had for it. I'm kind of nostalgic about the material. Mr. Warner asked me if I had some ideas about another project . . .'

Arlene Grossbard knows precisely what property Warner has in mind next for James Dean, but she repeats the title: '*Fight Of His Life?* Mmmmm.' She also knows nothing's been mentioned about the acquisition in *Variety*. She stands and opens a filing cabinet, extracting a folder. 'Here. Yes, we have acquired, but no action taken, nothing pending. It's the sort of property that can sit for years. You realize, I hope, that three-quarters of our acquisitions never get finalized.' She watches James's face go through some serious thinking. 'Does this mean you'd like your flowers back?'

He doesn't seem to hear. He snaps out of thought with a laugh. 'Course not. They really *are* a peace offering.'

In the commissary, he sits down with Gus Clement. The talk is of photography, which James has temporarily deserted in favor of racing. 'If you buy the best camera in the world, you should use it or at least lend it to someone who will.' Clement says with disappointment.

'I'll get back to it, don't worry. Hey, tell me something. Why would a studio buy a property and never even make the picture?'

'Depends.'

'On what?'

'Million things. They could buy it because the subject's hot or they got an actor in mind and one or the other just goes flat. Maybe they never get the script right. All sorts of things. The real surprise is that any picture ever gets made. Why'd you ask?'

'They bought a T.V. drama I was in and I was interested. Attached, I guess.'

'Not *Fight Of His Life?*'

'You saw it?'

'No. But I heard about it.' Clement raises his eyebrows. 'It's not going to be made.'

'How'd you know?'

'They got this black actor over at Metro who they think might catch on with white audiences. Sidney Porter, or something like that.'

'You mean they just bought it to keep Metro from having it?'

'Or maybe to get a little leverage for something else they got in mind. Who knows, maybe one day he'll get unhappy over there and they'll be able to woo him here with that script. But you can bet *Fight Of His Life* isn't going to be made while we're pissing in this pond.'

'I'll be damned.'

'They do it all the time, Jimmy me lad. It's called the movie business. But believe me, that's nothing compared to the real crap that's been going on around here. You interested?'

James doesn't say no.

'This one is so exquisitely machiavellian, someone should record it for posterity.' Clement could see by Jimmy's expression he didn't understand 'exquisitely machiavellian.' 'Remember I told you Jack was the rottenest of all the brothers: well, even I didn't know how sneaky he could be – even by Hollywood standards.' His voice becomes thick with conspiracy. Then he chuckles: ' Really, I still can't believe this.' Clement shakes his head with admiration.

'Gus, I'm hooked. Reel me in.'

'Jack has been humiliating Harry for years. Harry's wanted out of here for a good long time now, but he'd kill himself before he'd sell his half of the company to Jack. So word comes to Harry via a broker there's a serious buyer out there, a money man named Semenko: a Russian, a Pole, a mystery man, a guy who's stepped in plenty of times when studios have been in trouble. Semenko and his people and Harry and his people negotiate for six months before the deal goes through. They signed the final papers three weeks ago.'

James has heard something about financial goings on at the top. It didn't affect his work, so he gave it little mind.

'So, like I said, the deal's done . . . Hi, Natty.'

Natalie Wood, who is Jimmy's girl in *Rebel*, and Nick Adams, who plays a punk named Moose, approach the table with coffee cups.

Clement slides over: 'Have you guys met Jimmy?'

Natalie says, 'Face looks familiar.'

Adams says, 'Isn't he that new country singer?'

James howls, 'Mah bleedin' har-art will tell on yoooo.'

'I think we're about to make a big mistake,' says Wood, unsure of whether or not to sit down.

'It might be amusing,' says Adams, sitting.

'I'm telling Jimmy a Warners story. *The* Warners story. About selling his share of the company.'

'I didn't know that,' Wood says.

'Yeah, a few weeks ago, Anyway . . .' Clement focuses on James. '. . . a week, no more than ten days after Harry sells to Semenko, Semenko turns around and sells his half of the company to . . .?'

James draws his eyebrows down, indicating an unwillingness to believe. 'Jack Warner?'

'You got it. Jack L. set the whole thing up. He knew Harry'd never sell to him, at least not at the same price he'd sell to a stranger, so he arranged for an independent buyer. I'm sure he had to pay Semenko handsomely for his services, but still it was worth it. But tell me that isn't the nastiest piece of family business you ever heard.'

James mutters, 'His own brother, Jesus.'

'That's what makes the guy King of the Nether World. Nothing he won't do, no tactic he won't use to get what he wants. He's absolutely . . .' Clement doesn't know exactly how to describe Jack L. Warner. '. . . absolutely . . . Biblical.'

'Biblical?' Wood is mildly offended.

'Jacob and Esau. Cain and Abel.'

Adams adds, 'Sodom and Gomorrah.'

James says, 'So Jack owns the whole shooting match now?'

'Right down to the spoon in Natty's coffee. If it was hard working here before, it's going to get brutal.'

Adams says, 'So is he gonna change the name of the place?'

'To what?'

'Warner Brother.'

'Wouldn't be surprised,' James says. 'But why's he hate his brother so much?'

'That's the point. He doesn't hate him.' Clement sips some coffee. 'Hate's a passion. You can't live with a consuming hate. This is cold, calculated stuff. This is wanting, taking, having, manipulating – the stuff he does to everyone, and he doesn't hate all of us. But if you really want to know, you can ask him. He's sitting right over there. And you know the guy who's with him? Semenko himself.'

Clement indicates they are seated behind Jimmy. James turns and sees two balding men in intense conversation: they wear duplicate blue suits. The anger about Enoch and *Fight Of His Life* stirs within him.

James stands and takes a ten dollar bill out of his pocket. He approaches their table fingering the bill, his breath shallow, his teeth on edge. He plants himself between them, his thighs against the table. Warner looks up, recognizes him, smiles, but does not say a word.

'I wonder if either of you gentlemen have change of ten.' He rubs his nose with a knuckle – the part calls for a self-conscious gesture – and offers the ten dollars pinched between two fingers.

'Jimmy. We're talking business here.' Warner's tone is that of an irritable father.

'This *is* business. I'm willing to pay a fee if you change this for me. Money, gentlemen, real money to be made here.' He lets the bill flutter onto the table between them.

'Jim-my.' This is a warning.

'Look, I'm willing to pay for your services. Here.' Now he is tossing a handful of dollar bills in the air. 'Come on, gentlemen. there's money to be made here.' He drops coins on the table, on the floor. 'Come on, you're money men. Let's see what you'll do for money.' Still more coins.

Jack Warner stands.

James holds his empty hands in front of Warner's face. 'I guess I'd better get out. I got no more value.'

◆   *

'We can't exactly offer this young man the key to the city. Mostly because we aren't a city and because no one in Fairmount locks any doors. Don't need keys. Everything's open, son, just the way it always was, especially the hearts of everyone here today. What we can give you, though, is certain knowledge that whatever the future holds, Jimmy Dean is always welcome in this town – and you didn't have to become a Hollywood star to warrant it either.'

Judge Carr isn't really a judge. He's been Mayor, running unopposed, since Hoover was president. The Carr family is the largest landholder in the county and owns most of the Fairmount Security Bank. The eldest Carr boy is always named Judd and called Judge by everyone: it's logical, inevitable actually, that he be the civic leader of the community. Jimmy never liked this Judge because he always demanded special treatment at Hardy's: he also happened to be the cheapest bastard Jimmy had to deal with.

'But we must appreciate the return of our prodigal son in a manner . . .'

Cameras click continually. A Warners photographer shoots publicity shots that will be in dozens of Midwestern newspapers. Manny Monk, head flack in Warners Publicity Department, is in charge of promotional arrangements. The *Indianapolis Standard* and the *Kokomo Banner* have photographers and reporters on the scene. The studio hasn't sent Natalie Wood. They did offer to send Carmen Reyes, but James rejected that without telling Yazzy.

As Carr lectures the crowd from the steps of the Town Hall, James covers his eyes from the sun's glare and scans Fairmount's faces. Almost every face is identifiable but peculiarly unfamiliar.

'. . . something is bred into the bone in this honest American town that . . .'

The breeze, ripe with cutting and gathering grain smells, wafts toward him on warm air. Instead of embracing him, welcoming him home truly, they isolate him.

Two teenage girls wearing green 'Quaker' jackets wave to James and titter. One is Brett Collins's youngest sister – he can't remember her name; the other looks like . . . he discovers he has no idea. He raises his eyebrows at them and winks in recognition.

In spite of the fact that Ortense's smile beams satisfaction directly at him, Jimmy feels a rush of embarrassment wash over him. When he lived here, no one really saw him. Now their looks are searching for someone who isn't there. Why can't they . . .?

'. . . a plain farm boy whose Fairmount roots have taken hold in a soil that . . .'

They've changed. Because he has changed – something has changed. He has distinguished himself, separated himself, left Fairmount completely to them: he cannot return and act as though he is of them. Standing on the steps of the Town Hall, being praised for his modesty, for his loyalty to Fairmount, separates him further, alienates him. Here is a role he has no idea how to play. If he has begun to feel like an impostor in these first hours, how can he survive three days of feeling fraudulent? How can he face the class reunion tonight? The premiere of *Rebel* at the theater? Friends with whom he has nothing in common anymore, pretending their lives hadn't forked. Manny Monk and the photographers are borrowing this town as a backdrop. He has an urge to get away, leave tonight, drive back to L.A. Or New York. He does not allow himself to consider Lem Craig.

'. . . the boy out of Fairmount, but they can never take Fairmount out of the boy. So, Mr. Dean, just so you are never far from Fairmount, Indiana, wherever your career and travels may take you, it is my pleasure, my honor, to present you with this beautiful cut-glass decanter, the creation of Fairmount's own Maude Slocum, containing one pound of Fairmount 'black gold,' the richest soil on God's earth.' Carr holds the frosted urn high above his head. There is applause.

Carr hands the token to James. Manny Monk runs up the steps with his photographer and poses the two men. Cameras click.

'And this official scroll signed by myself and the town council, making you . . .' He reads, '". . . Fairmount, Indiana's first citizen, her finest representative, and goodwill ambassador to the world beyond her borders." That means, Jimmy, if Hollywood would like to compensate us in any way for stealing you away, you have the authority – should I say, obligation? – to make the deal. Heh. Heh.' No one in the crowd laughs. Judge Carr hands the document to James and waits for the cameras.

*

'Suits me just fine, Ten-ten, if you'd just leave it off the hook.' James gnaws on a cold rib, feeling halfway comfortable in Fairmount for the first time.

Marcus, not Ortense, responds: 'You're joshing. She'd just as soon lose her ear than lose her telephone. Same thing, now I think about it.'

Ortense returns to the table. 'Just folks being naturally curious. Mostly wanting to know if they can be helpful.'

'Sure,' Marcus says. 'Help him figure out what to do with some of his cash.'

'Marcus, that's not funny.'

'Didn't mean it to be.' He wipes his chin with a checkered towel.

Ortense stares angrily at her husband. He works to avoid her gaze.

'Wish you two'd come to the reunion tonight.'

'It's not for fogeys like us.'

'Marcus, what's wrong with you anyway? Haven't been yourself since Jimboy arrived. Everything you say is crazy. Are you nervous, or something? Don't you listen to him. Got nothing to do with being fogeys.'

'So why not come then?'

'Because it's *your* class reunion. A night with your friends. Not for us to horn in on what should be your big night.'

'Doesn't want the old biddies to gossip.'

'Mar-cus.' Yet another warning.

James considers telling Ortense about the feelings he had on the Town Hall steps. 'What if I insisted you come with me.'

'That's what she wants – to be talked into it.'

'No, Jimboy, it's for the young people.'

'What'd I tell you? Not for old fogeys.'

The phone rings. Ortense's voice is sweet in the distance.

'How's Lem doing?' James tries to sound politely curious.

'Mmmmmm,' Marcus says. 'Hear all sorts of stuff about him. Got caught driving drunk a few times. Wrecked a couple of cars. People say he's a Peeping Tom. No one's actually caught him doing anything God-awful, but you get the feeling it's only a matter of time. Know what I mean?'

'Still at Hardy's?'

'Yup. And still a good man with a machine.'

Ortense hangs up and returns to the table. 'Claudia Klegg. Wants to drop off a couple of *Look* magazines with your picture in it for you to sign.'

Marcus says, 'And you told her "sure."'

'Of course I did. Jimboy hasn't gotten so snooty he won't do a simple favor.'

Marcus waits for James to correct Ortense. James says, 'I'm the same modest, unassuming kid I've always been. Ain't I, Marcus?'

'Same wise ass, too.'

*

The new gym at Fairmount High School is not completely new. The old wall leading in from the main hall, on one end, and the locker rooms, at the other, were left standing. The new gym is almost double in length and twenty feet higher. The old entranceway is covered with photos of Quaker athletes, championship banners, plaques, trophies and medals: it's a somber remnant of an old time thrown into stark relief by the bright lights and smooth texture of the new construction. A small stage has been set up beneath the raised basket at the far end of the gym; on it a swing band plays 'Sentimental Journey.' Above the bandstand a huge green-on-white banner reads, WELCOME HOME, JIMMY.

Cafeteria tables have been set in a row to form a dais. Draped tables offer punch bowls and potato chips and pretzels, trays of fresh vegetables and crackers with cheddar cheese.

Most of the people in the large space – almost 200 of them – huddle close to the old gym wall, more comfortable with the school they knew than the one it has become: safer gathered in the past. They are remarkably subdued: those who speak, speak in hushed tones.

Only James wears a white dinner jacket and black tie. He leans against a trophy case, sipping a cup of punch that needs a good lacing. The no-man's land that surrounds him is the result of old friends holding back. No one seems to be in charge. Photographers record the awkward interlude. It's up to him to push away from the wall, to get out there and mix. He tells himself he will after one more sip.

He hears a hubbub in the main hallway, male voices building in intensity. Then, more specifically, 'Where is he? Where's the Rebel? Where's the star?'

A small group of young men led by Lem Craig in a shiny under-sized black tuxedo bursts through the crowd. James recognizes Horse Johnstone and Brett Collins, behind Lem, who stops at the entrance, points at Jimmy, and bellows, 'There he is. Seize the prisoner.' Brett, Horse and two others guys come forward: James steps toward them, expecting to be clapped on the back. But Horse ducks under him, pins his knees together and hoists him in the air. Immediately Brett and one of the other guys are beneath him too, and he's bobbing awkwardly on their shoulders, then higher on many upstretched palms. He looks down at Lem's glistening face, that crazy tooth highlighting a crazier smile. Their eyes lock – James's are curious, searching; Lem's burn with fever, 'You ready, J.D.?'

'C'mon. Lem. We don't need . . .'

Too late. Lem Craig picks the large silver ladle out of the punch bowl and, using it as a marching scepter, leads the group toward the bandstand. 'Hey,' he demands, 'let's hear "Fairmount Forever."' The band stands and begins the school song. Lem has taken the micro-phone: 'Let's all hail the conquering hero. One, two, three – HAIL!' Not everyone has caught the spirit Lem is willing on them. 'No, no. This time with some good ol' Fairmount pride. One . . . two . . . three . . . HAIL! That's better.' He starts to sing, praise to thee, our Quaker pride . . . on Quaker history we stand astride . . . C'mon everybody . . . SING! It's a damn reunion not a wake.'

Lem says something to the band and it breaks into the school fight song. Then, with scepter raised, he leads the group holding James aloft around the table. The band strings out behind the marchers. The guests fall in with the revellers, all singing the fight song. By an overt act of will, Lem has changed the mood from reserved to riotous.

Lem, strutting, leads the parade around the gym. Then out into the main hall. Past the principal's office. Through the cafeteria. In the front door of the chemistry lab and out the rear. Into and around the music room. James, aloft, is pumped up and down in time to the rhythm of the music. Lem gapes back over his shoulder at James – his expression part Pied Piper, part rat. Flashbulbs pop continually. In the most famous picture, James seems about to tumble off the supporting hands and shoulders; his body corkscrews away from the camera; his hands are in front of his face, at once seeking to hide his identity and trying to help him regain his balance. One eye is visible and conveys a shy man's call for help. To the females who see the photo he looks vulnerable, extremely lovable. Years hence there will be a disagreement, even a law suit, over which photographer actually took the photo.

When James is finally dropped at the seat of honor, at a table in front of center stage, beneath the podium, his discomfort is palpable: surprisingly no one acknowledges it. He downs an entire glass of punch. People he knows but does not recognize – composite faces drawn by a police artist – float before his eyes. His efforts to focus and recall are undermined by a wavering dizziness bordering on nausea, as though a dentist were putting him under. He hears his own hollow voice under another voice even more hollow. It's Mr. Ebinger, the principal, at the microphone behind him. James hears the voice doubly – as true voice and as an echo off the far wall.

All eyes in the room are on him, on the speaker above him, on him again.

'. . . every time we got in the car and crossed the state line, my Great Aunt Effie – even when she was in her nineties – used to sniff and say, "The air's different. Cain't breathe normal. We . . ."' Everyone in the gym has heard Ebinger's Great Aunt Effie story often enough to shout out the punch line – '". . . must've left Indiana."' This time it's not politeness that restrains them – they're not really listening. They're trying to get Jimmy's attention; or coming over crouched low to the floor to whisper a remembrance. He is lightheaded and still sweating heavily. Someone must have laced the punch after all.

He knows the smiling face coming toward him. It's Jenna, bent low and trying to be invisible. All eyes follow her. Jimmy gets half out of his seat to meet her. Ebinger's words arch over him: '. . . who only five short years ago graced these halls . . .'

Jenna's face without a doubt, but flatter and wider. Her hair is short and straight, her forehead much more prominent. She kneels on one knee at his feet, offering a cheek to be kissed. He sees everyone watching as he bends; he closes his eyes and breathes deeply when he kisses her. She smells of soap.

'Got here late,' she whispers. 'Just wanted to say how glad I am for you.'

Ebinger says, '. . . mind it a bit as long as . . .' He raises a warning finger and looks directly at James. '. . . as long as you don't forget your roots.' He utters the word in pure Indiananese – *ruts*.

James whispers, 'Sit here. We'll make room.'

'Can't. You know I wrote to you, didn't get an answer. I'm sure you were busy.' Jenna knows she's chattering and can't help it. 'I'm here with Gregg,' She looks back over her shoulder.

He looks where she looks.

'You didn't notice?' Her voice is accusative.

He's confused. *Notice what? Gregg?* Jenna stands taller and touches her stomach. She's extremely pregnant. 'Oh that's great, Jenna.'

'My second. Kyle's almost two.'

'Two. Gee. Great. I never got any word. I would have . . .'

'We'll stop by later. Everyone's watching. I just wanted to say how terrific I feel for you, your success. It's so great for you.' There's a lost look in her eyes. She offers her cheek to be kissed. He kisses her lips. A kiss he remembers.

'. . . they say California might fall into the Pacific Ocean one of these days. Let's hope the young man we're honoring tonight has the good fortune to be right here in Fairmount – on solid ground . . .' – he taps the stage with his heel – '. . . when the fated day arrives. In other words, that he'll never be a stranger to the folks who care about him. Maybe he'll give us some sort of pledge . . .'

'See you later, Jimmy. Want you to meet Gregg. I think you're going to have to say something.'

James hadn't thought.

'. . . our guest of honor tonight . . . feel a strong sense of local pride . . . our own James Byron – yes, that's his middle name – Dean.'

Applause. Around him people begin to stand. Everyone is looking at him, beaming with proprietary pride and expectation. He must speak, he must offer them something in return.

He's recently read Edna Ferber's *Giant*, the novel Jack Warner had sent to him. The character he's likely to play, Jett Rink, too drunk to make a speech during the grand opening of his lavish hotel, collapses on the platform. Art has reminded him what not to do in life. He releases his third glass of punch, stands, and walks to the microphone with hunched shoulders and averted eyes. He hears waves of applause coming from behind him. Modesty is the requisite posture. When he turns to face the crowd, the glare of lights, some of them flashbulbs, cause him to stagger.

He holds a protective hand up to ward off the applause, the glare, trying to find a face he can talk to. He sees Manny Monk's bald head. Monk is signalling him to smile. He sees Jenna holding hands with Gregg. Miss Flagg, the librarian, whispering to her deaf mother.

He says, 'Thanks. Thank you.' The microphone lets out a cry that Mr. Ebinger rushes forward to correct by lowering the microphone a few inches. James continues to scan faces. He sees Brett Collins again, this time looking forty, settled and content, alongside a plump woman he takes for Brett's mother. *No, can't be. It's Cora Lang. He married Cora.*

He seeks Lem Craig's mad face in the crowd. Lem, the only truly familiar person he's discovered in Fairmount. He looks slowly, carefully. Each person basks in the gaze of the celebrity, but there is no Lem Craig. *Gone. The bastard.*

James sees her then. Perhaps her aura has drawn his attention. She sits alone at a table along the wall about halfway back. There is no glare around her, only soft light. She nods at him. Her smile, always quizzical, is mostly approval, but it also reflects his doubts, his isolation, the erosion no one else has noticed. She is there to help, will always be there to help. She fans herself slowly with a folded sheet of paper, the evening's program.

James looks only at her. The applause has begun to diminish. He can bring her face into focus as in a film close-up. Her hair is short and lightening to gray; fine lines web her eyes and have thickened around the corners of her lips. There is a palpable sadness. The applause has stopped. She hasn't escaped the erosion of life, but there is satisfaction too. Most assuredly there is satisfaction.

James feels an infusion of dignity move from her to him. He'll be able to do this perilous thing now. There is a silence in the room deeper than soundlessness. James feels the weight of it, its taut expectation. He looks at his mother again.

His words are soft. For her. 'You've never left me.' His pauses are thoughtful, solemn. 'I never left you either.' He is looking toward Mildred Wilson in a shy manner the audience finds curious at first. They begin to sense his inspiration is coming from an invisible source.

'You always believed in giving me the freedom to be myself. Not any old self. But the truest self I could be, the one you believed in. I tried for that – I wasn't always perfect, but I tried for that. I can't tell you how grateful I am to you for that.' James is unaware that the words he intends for her are being taken as high compliments about the people of Fairmount.

'I've never felt I left you. It was more your leaving me, although I realize now just how wrong I was.' He considers his words and shakes his head. 'Kids can be crazy, thinking only of themselves sometimes. The important thing is that those things pass and we can always get back together again. Always.'

Mildred stops fanning herself. She bows her head.

'And we'll stay together for a good long while, I hope.'

Brett Collins calls from the dimness. 'Sure we will, Jimmy.' Other voices second the sentiment. Others applaud. The distractions make him aware of his double message.

'You know, we all have to leave eventually, one way or another. It's usually only a question of whether it's a choice or not.' That's a line from *Giant*. 'You probably won't believe this but when I was a senior playing *Hamlet* here, I almost changed the "To be or not to be" speech. I wanted to say, "To leave or not to leave, that is the question." And that *is* the question. Funny thing is that in the end, leaving, staying, coming back – it doesn't seem to make such a big difference . . . it all pretty much comes to the same thing.'

Most of the listeners have a vague sense that they've been insulted. They deny the possibility.

James ends with the only sentence he had even half-planned: 'There are really two Fairmounts – the one you can always come back to, to get some friendship and a good meal, and the other Fairmount, the one you carry with you no matter where you go – the Fairmount in your heart.'

Many of his listeners now have the impression a part of them will go with him when he leaves, that they are part of his genius. He has made them feel that their care has produced this bounty.

'So,' James offers his slow, self-conscious smile, 'I guess that's it. Let's have some music.' He breaks away from the microphone.

The music – 'Back Home Again in Indiana' – cannot be heard above the applause of the crowd. His friends come forward to congratulate him. This time he resists being placed on their shoulders. When he looks for her, his mother has gone. He hasn't seen Lem Craig since the wild parade through Fairmount High.

*

When only a handful of the gathering remain, James is tipped back on a stool on the bandstand playing bongos, a bleary-eyed member of a bleary-eyed trio. Paul Newlin is on piano, Digger Bean is on bass, and they're playing a rhumba version of the Quaker fight song. James has a lighted cigarette in his ear; his glasses sit low on his nose, his white jacket is on the floor, shirt stuck to his body, collar open, bow tie undone and hanging down his chest. This, too, will become a famous photograph of James Dean's homecoming.

Manny Monk excuses himself from two Fairmount businessmen and whispers in Jimmy's ear, 'It's after one, kid, and you got a really big day tomorrow. Farm shots in the morning, two luncheons, the premiere. Don't mean to sound like your mother or anything, but . . .'

James looks up at Manny with murder in his eyes.

While he drives Marcus's pick-up home, Jimmy tries to make her materialize again. He pats the passenger seat to encourage her; he drives slowly and watches the roadside expectantly. He is certain she will reappear.

A cloud covers the moon as he pulls up to the barn. He hears Ginger nicker and kick the stall. Two cows low and bump the side of the barn. He walks to the old storeroom, where Marcus now keeps extra oats. It is covered with a grain-flecked blanket. He rolls it outside under its wrap. James pulls the blanket off the Whizzer: the moon, too, sheds its cover.

The cycle is in perfect condition. James smiles his gratefulness to Marcus. He bounces the back wheel lightly to get a sense of its buoyancy and to loosen things up in general. The Whizzer feels perfect in his hands. He throws a leg over the seat and straddles his bike. The choke slides easily – Marcus has oiled it. He throws his weight into a kick start: the motor almost turns over. He moves the choke in a quarter inch and jumps the starter. The Whizzer growls alive and purrs contentedly. Dear Marcus.

James rolls down the dirt driveway and gears into second. At the road, he heads west: moist night air rushes past him and billows his evening jacket. He is moving through a dream terrain of his own shaping. At the Kokomo Turnpike, he recalls his mad drives with Lem Craig and considers heading north to the all-night diner. Lem might be there. He heads south, back toward Fairmount.

No traffic, open highway. He smooths the Whizzer into high gear and eases the speed upward gradually. The pale headlight illuminates almost nothing. He cannot read the darkened speedometer but it feels like 60. He bends low over the bar and brings his elbows in to his body to lower wind resistance. His glasses press the bridge of his nose. Speed is still his temptress.

The eyes appear as very distant lights. The deer is actually no more than 100 feet ahead. James is not even aware of veering to the right: rather, he is aware of a force guiding his hand slightly that way. The cycle dips as he passes within inches of the animal. He overcompensates coming out of the dip and sends the Whizzer into a series of decreasing bends before he straightens and slows.

He's about a mile north of Hardy's Texaco when he pulls his cycle to the shoulder of the road. The ground rises and dips beneath him.

He glides to a stop, using his shiny shoes to slow himself. The Whizzer wobbles on its stand as he jumps off and throws himself on the wet grass. On his back, he scans the stars. He knows almost nothing of Dippers or Bears or Belts or Sisters, but he sees designs everywhere in the Oriental carpet lying over Earth. He closes first one eye and then the other: all the star-designs jump back and forth.

He rolls onto his side. His cheek finds a perfect niche in a slight depression in the ground. So does his chin and jaw and the back of his head. It seems to him that this Indiana earth has been sculpted perfectly to his face. The idea becomes more attractive the more he thinks about it.

He plans to drive on to Hardy's and turn off to County 633.

It surprises him to see an overhead light in the garage bay. As he nears, he sees another light. Unsteady, flickering. He recognizes the flames just before he pulls into the station. As he runs to the office, the fire spews from a metal trash can beside the cash register. Newspapers mostly. So intent is he on trying to extinguish the blaze, he doesn't acknowledge the blood splattered over the broken plate-glass window behind the desk. He tries to stomp out the flame, but it is too strong. He takes off his white jacket and wraps it around the base of the can. Awkwardly, he moves it toward the door, down the low step, and out away from the gas pumps. He watches for a moment as embers leap in the air and blow toward the peaceful town. No need to call the firehouse.

Then the blood. The shattered window. He begins to anticipate what he doesn't want to anticipate. Blood runs down the cracked glass behind the desk. Clumps of hair and fragments of tissue stick to the glass.

James sees the wheels of the upturned chair first, then the folded tuxedo jacket and the cuff of a ruffled shirt sleeve.

The muzzle of an army rifle is in Lem's other hand. Only inches from his chin. It is impossible to look at the face because of the horror just above it. The top of Lem Craig's head has been torn away. The blood. The cranium blown off his face and dashed against the window. James looks at the brainless hole as his nausea mounts. The body of Lem Craig has one shoe off; the big toe has pulled the trigger. The sock on the floor is insultingly white.

On the office desk along with the repair bills he has not completed, Lem Craig has put a copy of the evening's program for J.D.'s homecoming. It covers a larger photograph. He pulls it free. It is James lying in a coffin; there is a trace of a smirk on his face: although the eyes are closed, the lids appear to flutter. James crumples the photograph and puts it in his pocket.

Then he sees the childish scrawl on lined paper. He assumes it's an explanation, a justification. He is struck by the fact that he's never before seen Lem Craig's handwriting. There is no date on it. It begins. 'Dear Reader:' It doesn't make any sense.

Dear Reader:

We're all proud as punch of old J.D. But I don't believe any of us are really surprised he made such a big splash. You'd have to be blind not to tell from the get-go he had that certain something. On a stage, your eyes just went right to him. Like a magnet. That's what they're always talking about isn't it? Star attraction? I won't say it was me who kept him from quitting acting in school but we used to have lots of serious talks about it. If he wins an Oscar or something, I expect him to send a part of it here – the toes or something.

He writes me about once a week telling me what the life is really like out there – stuff about stars and starlets he really wants kept quiet. It sure is a crazy world. I write him about the goings and comings at the station but it's hard to make changing spark plugs and tires sound interesting. He's got to be eating his heart out over what he's missing here but he hides it awfully well. It'll be hard for him to leave after his visit's over. Hah. Hah.

J.D. used to date my sister. She kids and says he was a dud. That's just my sister though. He probably could have got lots of dates but he concentrated on the artistic side of things. He was a lot more arty than the other kids that's for sure. But there was not anything fruity about him. He played basketball and baseball. Not much football I don't think.

I was the one who showed him about photography and I taught him about music too. I'm not angry that he became a

273

big Hollywood star. I'm not angry about J.D. at all. I'm glad for him.

James puts the letter in his pocket.

With difficulty, he steals another look at the head, at the dispersed brain and bone and hair. He's forgotten the number of the police station. James dials 'O.'

He looks around the office. Why the fire? To cremate himself. He wanted to cremate Hardy's Texaco, too.

James walks outside and waits for someone – the Sheriff's car, an ambulance.

He walks to the trash can and adds the photograph and the 'Dear Reader' letter to the flames. They burn, curl and disappear. He unbuttons his fly and pisses on the fire. He looks at the stars. It's as possible to live as to die.

13. Saved by The Dream

GIANT: screenplay by Fred Guiol and Ivan Moffat; based on the novel by Edna Ferber; cinematography William C. Mellor; production design by Boris Leven; costumes by Marjorie Best and Moss Mabry; musical score by Dimitri Tiomkin; directed by George Stevens; produced by George Stevens and Henry Ginsberg for Warner Brothers.

Leslie Lynnton Benedict..*Elizabeth Taylor*
Bick Benedict...*Rock Hudson*
Jett Rink..*James Dean*
Luz Benedict.....................................*Mercedes McCambridge*
Angel Obregon..*Sal Mineo*
Jordan Benedict III..*Dennis Hopper*
Luz Benedict II...*Carroll Baker*
Vashto Snythe..*Jane Withers*
Uncle Bawley..*Chill Wills*

Luz Benedict has willed Jett Rink a boggy piece of land known as Buffalo Waller. It has little apparent value, but it does break the contiguity of the vast Benedict spread, so Bick calls Jett into his office to buy the land from him. No one says no to Bick Benedict, least of all an ignorant wrangler like Jett Rink.

Bick's lawyer and his ranch managers are also in the room. The lawyer does most of the talking: 'Well now, to get right down to the point, Mr. Rink. (James's cheek flutters – no one has ever called Jett "Mr. Rink.") We're prepared to place in your hands, in cash, the sum of twelve hundred dollars.'

Jett slumps in a chair, playing with a short lariat, curling and uncurling the serpentine rope. He looks at the money Bick slaps down on the edge of his desk and whistles softly. 'Boy.' He looks to heaven and then around the room.

Lawyer: Twelve hundred dollars, which any gentleman here will be happy to tell you is twice the value of the land.

Voices off
camera say:
{
That's a lot of money, Jett.
What're you going to do with all of it.
You're in the chips now, boy.
It's all yours.
Sure is.
}

Jett: I don't know what to say, heh, heh. She sure was a fine lady.

Voices:
{
Sure was.
Hallelujah.
Amen.
}

Jett: I want you to know that I appreciate her gen . . gen'ros-ity . . . (He slurs the word rather than mispronounce it.) . . . and yours too, Bick, and y'all. I sure want to thank you for it. (James politely lets gratefulness run its course. Then there is a sudden and complete change of character: rather, the emergence of a deeper, truer character.) You know something, Bick. I don't know what it just might be a good idea to gamble along . . .

Bick: (Surprised.) How'd you mean?

Jett: Just gamble along. Just keep what she give me. I'm senti-mental too. Bick. (James grabs his hat off the floor and stands.) I think it's good to gamble along with her. I know that land ain't worth much but then someday I just might up and put my own fence around it – call it Little Reata. (He swings his rope deftly and makes it jump into a loose knot. At the door he turns and smooths his hand through the air at waist height.) See ya.

The party at Ciro's is Brando's idea. It is supposed to be in honor of Jimmy, a send-off to Texas for location shooting on *Giant*. It is, of course, Marlon's party to himself. He is trying to prove that he can drink five Old Fashioneds in less than two minutes without touching any of the glasses with his hands.

The waiter is lining up the drinks on the table. 'Watch the technique,' Brando says. 'The trick's high intensity sucking.' He leers. 'Sometimes I amaze myself and suck up the cherries and the orange slices too. Once in New York I sucked so hard the damn glass caved in.'

'Tell me this,' Jimmy says, not fully aware of what's going on.

Brando assumes the subject will be the vacuuming of Old Fashioneds: 'Ye-ess.'

'Stevens, the director. Is he a good guy to talk to about developing a character?'

Brando, bending from the waist to sip the surface of Old Fashioned number one, splutters and coughs. 'Does the character happen to have a redwood forest growing out his ass?'

Jimmy is confused.

'This isn't Kazan you're talking about, man. George Stevens shoots scenery. He's C.B. DeMille, for Christ's sake – epic, epic, epic. He'd take longer to shoot the Creation than God took to make it. And stop trying to screw up my concentration.'

Brando puts his open right hand on his chest and smiles. It appears to be a gesture of extreme modesty, but that's not possible.

In reality he is holding his tie and lapels from falling into the drinks. 'Time me, Jimmy. Give me thirty-second intervals.'

James looks at his watch. 'Ready. Get set.' Brando bends into position. 'Go!'

Brando draws off the surface of the first glass: then, by puckering his lips, he siphons the liquid right to the bottom. He's halfway down number two when James calls, 'Thirty seconds.'

Brando finishes two and moves on to three with the entire restaurant watching. He stops, laughs to the ceiling and shouts, 'Stell-aaaah.'

The third glass is drained more quickly. And a fourth.

'One-minute-thirty.'

Brando slows to add a bit of drama to the contest. When he finishes the final drink, he bites the glass and raises up with it between his teeth. His arms are wide, requesting applause. He gets it. Brando bows low to each corner of the room.

James hasn't looked up, 'Two minutes.'

A little later, when the alcohol has reddened Brando's face and bathed him in perspiration, James leans in close and says, 'Didn't he win an Oscar for *Shane*? And just two years ago for . . . for that really sad Clift movie?'

'Didn't who?'

'Stevens. I think he won an Oscar twice.'

'Once. *Place in the Sun*. But that just proves my point, sweetheart. Didn't say it was a bad thing he didn't know shit about acting. While he's framing the mountains in the background, he leaves you alone to figure out what you want to do. Then you just try to outact the scenery, and he ends up with a beautiful and a well-acted film and everybody's happy. You'll hold your own with him, kid.'

James looks across at Yazzy and at that moment decides not to fly her down to Texas. If he is unsure about how to play Jett Rink, and if Stevens won't be of much help, he doesn't want her there to witness the result.

He had never come so close to shooting – one week – without having a strategy. That's not to say he usually had a character down pat – that was never the case – but he always had a way in, a psychological insight, a series of gestures, something. With Jett Rink, nothing has captured his imagination. Nothing except the nub of an absurd association with Winton Dean.

The notion starts to become an idea after he calls Edna Ferber in New York. There is much about her he does not know. He doesn't know she had turned seventy. He doesn't know she wrote *Saratoga Trunk* and *Show Boat*, and he's forgotten she wrote *Dinner At Eight*. On the basis of *Giant*, he assumes she lives in Texas.

'I'd like to speak to Miz Edna Ferber, please.' He isn't close yet to Jett's creaky drawl.

'This is she.'

Her good grammar and upper-class tone surprises him. James feels he is speaking with aristocracy. 'Miz Ferber, My name's Jimmy Dean, and I'm gonna be Jett R . . .'

'Of course, Mr. Dean. I've heard wonderful things about you. I think you'll be an excellent Jett.' She had seen neither of his movies. 'I look forward to seeing you sometime in Marfa.'

James is confused. He doesn't know what 'Marfa' is and assumes it's the name of her ranch. He says nothing for a while. She senses his confusion. 'That's the site they're using for the film. The location. Right on the Mexican border, and I'm ashamed to say I've never even been in the area. Unless you count Brownsville, which is close enough I guess. I'll be down for a brief visit.'

'I was wondering, Miz Ferber . . .' He's being his most charming. '. . . wondering if I might talk with you before that. Maybe meet at some place convenient . . . or something.'

Without hesitation: 'I really don't see how.'

'You see, I want to make sure I get Jett exactly right.'

'Your "right" or my "right"?'

'Jett Rink "right," ma'am.'

'You might do better to talk to those fellows who wrote the screenplay. Their Jett isn't completely recognizable to me. Apart from that, my problem is, Mr. Dean, that there are many, many words for me to write and not nearly enough time in which to write them.'

James has never fully recognized or understood the demands of time on art. His talent didn't really work that way – when he needed something, it was there. He never considered the extent to which a writer is urged and oppressed by the clock. He says with a plaint in his voice, 'I've been thinking a great deal about Jett, Miz Ferber.'

'I would hope so.'

'And I've been thinking, I mean, he strikes me as a single-minded sort of guy.'

'Hah.'

'Why'd you laugh?' Had it been a laugh exactly?

'Would you say the snake in the Garden was single-minded?'

'I sure would.'

'Well, that's the single-mindedness of our Mr. Rink.'

'But what's the source of his . . . snakiness?'

'Hmm. I guess I'd say spite.'

And that was it. A single word. A locus for all his random, and even contradictory, impulses about Jett Rink. 'Spite.' He says the word dreamily, as though he wished it had more syllables.

For her part, Miss Ferber leaves a silence.

'That's a good deal of help right there. Spite. I sure do look forward to seeing you in Marfa. I do indeed.' His accent slips across the Texas border.

'Well, then. 'Til Marfa.'

'Thank you, ma'am.'

'You're welcome, suh.'

James takes courage from the conversation. He begins to shape his Jett Rink differently from any other character he's ever played. If Rink is the Snake in the Garden, the *Inner Man, Outer Man* interplay does not apply, or doesn't apply in the same old way. He'll play him as the irreducible essence of a single human urge – spite.

When he dreams, his unconscious mind ranges freely through the garden of human desires, looking for traps and deceptions and hidden dangers. When he wakes, he perceives, in indistinct outline, the countenance of Winton Dean. Winton creeps into his thoughts more and more, always associated vaguely with Jett Rink. It's not that James had ever attributed spite to his father – if anything, it's James who's the spiteful one – but there is a hard, dry, narrowness about the man he associates with Jett's hard-scrabble will. He remembers the look on Winton's face when Mildred told him she was going to learn to drive a car – a ferret gnawing at his own paw.

By midweek he is thinking about nothing but Jett, spite, Winton Dean. He does not call Winton at that point: he merely knows he will. He needs to make a specific, physical connection with Jett first.

James slides off his half of the mattress, making sure not to wake Yazzy. They have not touched one another since the night in Ciro's.

He moves to the kitchen stiff-backed, his knees locked. It is the beginning of Jett Rink's walk. He enters Jett Rink through his amble. The stiff, side-to-side movement shaped by a life spent dealing with unyielding forces – the sun, the wind, the hard earth, years on horseback. It is very much Winton's walk at the outset. When it's finished, it is modified substantially. He adds the cowhand's pigeon toes, the bowlegs and flat ass, and the defensive curl of a stomach wound, but the essentially stiff-bodied movement of an alert animal picking its way over hostile terrain – that much is consciously Winton.

When he calls Winton, he hopes Rhea will answer. She does. He hears the stateliness that has come into her voice. She repeats, 'Dean residence.' In the background Peewee iterates. 'Dean, Dean, Dean . . .'

James's voice is sweetly sinister: 'They're showing *La Grande Illusion* at the Granada tonight. You free?'

'Jimmy. Oh, I knew you'd call. I've been telling Winton, "The boy's going to call, I just know it." And you did. He's going to be so thrilled, I can't tell you. He's so proud of you.'

'I'm calling you, too, Rhea.'

'Oh, I know that, dear. Are you really coming by?'

'Well, not tonight. But I would like Winton to call me.'

'He's been calling.' There is no accusation.

'I've been a big dummy, Rhea. There's stuff I had to work out.' This is, and is not, an apology.

As the conversation rambles, Rhea wants to know about some of the actors in *East of Eden* and *Rebel Without a Cause*. It's Raymond Massey, in particular, she's curious about. 'Long as I can remember, I've had a crush on that man. What is he really like, Jimmy?'

'A great actor. A true gentleman.'

'Oh, I knew it. I could tell.'

'Well, you were right.'

James feels cleansed after he hangs up. He wants Winton back in his life but wants him on his terms.

Winton phones that evening. His voice sounds older: it has been chastened by his son's withdrawal. Winton works the word 'son' into the conversation more than he ever has: 'I knew you'd call me, son. Knew you had some things to work out in your career, but I knew you'd call, son, sooner or later. Told Rhea that a dozen times.'

'I'm going off to Texas for about a month or so, maybe more, and I'm going to be wanting you down there with me. You interested?' A chastened Winton could be helpful to Jett Rink.

'Sure I'm interested, son. But getting away. I don't know. There's the lab . . .'

'I'm talking about working for me.'

'Working? A father doesn't work for his own son. Doesn't do it to be paid, I mean.'

'I'm not talking about a handout. I need someone to take care of the business side of things. Someone I can trust. Just to stand between me and all the people who . . . well you know.'

Winton does not know in any specific way, but he is grateful for the genuine need he perceives. But there is also the discomfort of a man being paid by his own son. 'I'd be glad to help you, but the paying part doesn't seem at all right.'

'I need an answer. I'm leaving soon.'

'Maybe I can get away from the lab for a time.'

'Fine, but I'm going to need to know definitely.'

'How about we try it for a week or two? See how it works out?'

'I'm leaving Saturday. Early. Call me tomorrow night.'

'I will. I will. I knew you'd call. Son.'

*

The trucks and vans of the film crew, the bus that drove out the guests, reporters, and photographers, are parked behind the camera set-ups. The lighting reflectors and sound equipment are mounted near the tower and water pump Jett has built at Buffalo Waller. He's also put in an oil-drilling rig and built a small house. He has named Luz Benedict's final gift 'Little Reata.'

Today's scene is intended to establish the unstated, unconscious relationship between Jett Rink and Leslie Benedict, Bick's wife. Leslie, returning from a visit to the community of poor Mexican families on her husband's ranch, is driving past Jett's property at a distance. Jett spots her, climbs the tower and fires his rifle to attract her attention. When she drives up to Little Reata, he invites her in for tea, which he has only stocked in the vain hope that one day this very unlikelihood might happen.

Stevens has learned to stay away from Jimmy before a scene and to give him his head during it. So have most of the technicians. Winton is the last person Jimmy speaks to: he tells him to drive his car back to Marfa to have it washed. He feels Winton's presence would inhibit him today. Among the guests in the shade of the tent erected as a defense against the burning wind is Edna Ferber, sipping a cup of pineapple juice. Even though Rock Hudson's Bick is significantly absent from this shot, Hudson is there to entertain Miss Ferber and to show the press that harmony prevails among the cast.

Hudson does not like Dean. The dislike takes the form of cracks about the Method, but its source is the unmistakable contempt Dean shows for Hudson's work.

When Stevens calls 'Places,' Jimmy turns his back partially on the crew, the press and invited guests. He unzips his fly. This action is not called for in the script: the scene's supposed to start with a close-up of Jett drinking water from a running pipe. Jimmy Dean starts to piss. In view of everyone. The arc of his water kicks up some dust and settles some.

Rock Hudson mumbles, 'Jerk.'

Ferber taps her chin thoughtfully with the cup, trying to comprehend.

Stevens smiles narrowly. He's got four more weeks of this. He knows that however infantile Dean's behaviour has been, it has helped give him a Jett Rink who walks and talks like Ferber's unschooled cowherd, not a glamour boy in rough clothes. He's never worked with a young star so willing to sublimate ego to truth. When a reporter asked him the best way to handle James Dean, he said, 'At a great distance.'

James has convinced himself that the act of urinating is a

necessary demonstration, to himself as well as to the others, that he is in the mind and skin of Jett Rink. It is truly that. It is also the posturing of an adolescent ass.

James shakes himself dry, zips up his jeans and takes his mark without raising his eyes off the ground. Stevens gets the shot he wants – Jett sipping water and spotting Elizabeth driving by – in the second take. He shoots it again to be safe.

The scene inviting Leslie in for tea will take the rest of the day. It's a short tracking shot. In it, she steps out of her car and walks with him to the porch. He has his rifle stretched across his shoulders, holding the barrel and the stock in each fist. His walk is shy and mincing, the most relaxed this lonely, insecure man can be. In her presence there is not the slightest indication of his spitefulness. She is a loving, civilizing influence, even on a Jett Rink.

Stevens says, 'Let's walk through the whole thing once or twice, all the way into the house. Just for the movements, the dialogue, the sight lines.'

Elizabeth takes James's arm. 'We're satisfied with our readings, George,' she says. 'It's straightforward. He adores me from afar – as Lord knows, he should. And now, out of the blue, I'm in his house. Naturally he falls all over himself trying to please me. Right, Jett?'

He acts so flustered, he can hardly speak: 'Ah . . . ah . . . I guess so, Miz Leslie, ma'am.'

Stevens is ready to shoot the scene two hours later. In the meantime, Elizabeth has passed some pleasantries with Rock and Edna Ferber in the tent. Stevens has come by to be sociable. James has grabbed his Hasselblad and taken close-ups of Jett's dog and some of the pumping and drilling equipment.

When called back to their marks, the sun has moved but the lighting has altered only slightly. When Elizabeth steps out of the dusty car, there is a look of polite discomfort on her face. Her clothes are windblown, especially her straw bonnet, but she looks ravishing.

Jett says, 'Howdy, Miss Leslie.'

'How are you?' Taylor strikes a nice balance between tact and curiosity.

'I'm doing pretty good.'

She looks around at his work. 'Made some improvements.'

The undercurrents – what is left unsaid, or said ambiguously – between Jett and Leslie, and to a surprising extent between Jim and Elizabeth, will make the scene a classic. The animal attraction between them is so completely repressed, so utterly denied, by their words and their postures, it becomes even more of a presence.

They are at the porch. He scratches at the step with his toe, 'Do you like it?' Jett opens the door and she enters.

Leslie says, 'Looks good.'

'It ain't much yet but coming right along.' He's overcome by a faint whiff of Leslie Benedict's hair. James's words are unclear, as Jett's would have been in the circumstances, more muddled than in either of his earlier films.

Leslie sits. 'You know, I wouldn't have believed it.'

'Believed what?'

'Truthfully, I wouldn't have expected this sort of house to be one of your virtues.'

He is abashed as only the truly reticent can be by any compliment, even a back-handed one. 'That's the first time I was ever accused of having any of that.' Sound barely picks up his voice.

'It really is nice, Jett. Real nice.'

'Well. Someday I'm gonna have a place that no one'll be ashamed of.' He reaches nervously for the sole teacup.

*

The Porsche 550 Spyder is too new to race, too tight, not 'giving' enough, as Jim calls it. All week until the late-night fogs roll in, he races into the valleys and up the mountain passes, getting the feel of the sweetest machine he's ever driven, letting the car get the feel of him. At these moments James Dean loves his Spyder more than any person in the world, and loves it in precisely the same way, with tactile satisfaction and the anticipation of an indefinable fulfillment. Pure speed, sensual and dangerous, is the Spyder's promise: she is low and sleek and silver and seductive. James has had the number 130 painted in black on the doors and the hood and the words 'Little Bastard' etched in red on the cowling.

The plan to drive to Salinas is foolish, but almost everything he's done for the fourteen months he's been in Hollywood has been crazy to some degree. Three deeply intense performances, a great deal of praise, a new $100,000-a-year contract from Jack L., and the feeling of power and detachment that comes from floating on the rising tide of fame. It had been his year: next year would be even better. No matter that he sleeps four to five hours a night, wakes with black rings under his eyes, and reaches for a Chesterfield immediately, the first of sixty each day.

He's been reading a troubling new script, *No Help Forthcoming*, about a young psychiatrist who is pushed to the brink of insanity by the death of his wife in an automobile accident. Thrown into hopeless despondency, he resorts to more and more extreme cures. Under the influence of a voodoo priestess he begins to take delusion-inducing potions until they make him think he was driving the car that killed his wife. He hasn't finished the script but has dreamt about it vividly each of the last three nights.

The plan is to drive the Spyder 300 miles up to Salinas airport on Friday afternoon, sleep over, and drive the car in a competition. James had wanted a tune-up race at Riverside immediately after the return from Marfa, but George Stevens asked him to wait until the banquet scenes that would complete *Giant* were in the can. James agreed, although some of the driving he's done after leaving the studio is as dangerous as anything he'd see on a racecourse.

All that remains on *Giant* is for him to loop the end of his drunken speech at the banquet. The audio quality on the original was poor: James has agreed to do it immediately on his return from Salinas.

Benny Ungar will be up at Salinas to help, but he can't get away on Friday. He'll fly up Saturday morning. James's passenger for the drive is Rolf Weutherich, a mechanic from Heilbronn, Germany, whose knowledge of Porsche engines is encyclopedic but whose knowledge of English is not.

That morning at Competition Motors, Rolf had to install seat belts in order to meet race requirements. Fine-tuning the motor took so long, however, he only had time to anchor a belt on the driver's side. He puts an extra belt in his tool case in the trunk in the unlikely event he has time to install it up in Salinas.

James tosses his red jacket behind the seat and clips a pair of shaded lenses over his glasses. He drives down Cahuenga and over to Ventura to get on the freeway. The low windshield keeps the breeze at their hairlines. It's not easy to talk over the rush of air.

'Where's your seat belt?'

'No time.'

'What do you mean "no time"?'

'Only your side.'

'Hell, Rolf, that's not fair.' James throws off his seat belt with a flourish. 'If you die, I die.' Rolf does not understand but waggles no-no with a finger. James says. 'Belts are real uncomfortable for me when I'm not in a race.'

The inland route up to Salinas is as beautiful as the coastal, but scenery is not Jimmy's concern. It's longer and has far less traffic so he can push the Spyder's motor into racing readiness. On State 99, the ridge road through the mountains, he puts the car through turns and gear shifts and hard braking. Rolf sits with an ear cocked, listening to the musical scales of the motor. There is no stretch of straight road where James can really let her out until the long descent out of the mountains in southern Kern County. After a burst to 100 m.p.h. he steadies at 80.

The highway patrol car comes from the other direction, passing the silver racer without flashing a light. James checks the side mirror as he brings down the speed to 65. The patrol car diminishes in the glass, its tail-lights do not flash red. James is satisfied and brings it up again. 'How'd you get interested in cars?' he hollers to Rolf.

'In the Luftwaffe.'

'You worked on German planes?'

'Flew.'

'You flew for the Nazis?'

'Luftwaffe.'

James hasn't seen the police car cross the divider and head north after the speeding Porsche.

'Bombers or fighter planes?'

'Never killed. I. Never.'

The patrol car has closed on James and flashes its overhead lights.

He still hasn't noticed. The trailing car wails its siren. 'Oh shit.' His thoughts are of the problems this will cause at the studio. Fortunately, he's got his license and registration in the glove compartment. He pulls over and takes off his glasses.

The patrolman is tall and seems immense from James's low vantage. 'Little Bastard? How come Little Bastard?'

'Just trying to be clever, I guess.'

'Have any idea why I pulled you over?'

'Guess I was goin' a little too quick, officer.'

'About 20 m.p.h. too quick.' He steps back. 'This a 550 Spyder?'

'Uh huh.'

'First time I ever saw one of these dolls in the flesh.'

James sees an opening: 'We're running her in a 25-lap up in Salinas.'

'Don't say?'

'She's so smooth it's almost impossible to tell how fast you're going.'

'Had to floor mine to catch up with you.'

'Didn't notice. I truly didn't.'

'Let's see your license and registration.' James senses something kindly in his tone and hopes he'll get lucky, get away with a warning.

The patrolman asks James to sign the speeding ticket on the line that reads. *I promise to appear at time and place above indicated.* That would be two weeks hence at the Justice Court in Lamont, California.

'I know your "Little Bastard" wants to run away,' says the patrolman, 'but try to hold her down.'

'Promise.' Boy scout salute.

James buys Rolf lunch in a truckers diner at Famosa. Afterward, the terrain becomes flat and arid; oil lamps dot the landscape, tumbleweed blows in a whistling wind. He could almost be back in Marfa. On 466 he opens the Spyder up again and easily brings the speedometer needle to 110 m.p.h. James is pleased, but the light car is unsteady in the gusts of wind. Rolf listens and knows exactly which spark plug he's going to have to gap again before the race.

A little after 5:30 P.M. – four hours after they'd left L.A., two hours after Jimmy received the ticket – the Spyder speeds west on

466. Jimmy vaguely remembers a fork up ahead where 41 divides and heads inland because he once took it by mistake and stayed on it for an hour before discovering he was headed away from Monterey. The sun is low and glinting directly at him. The tinted glasses make the landscape seem darker than the soft reds and purples that precede the California twilight. He slows to 65.

'Thank you, Jamie,' she says.

James does not want to turn to her for fear of seeing Rolf.

'I like it so much better when you're careful in the car,' she says. 'We may get there a little later, but at least we know we'll get there in one piece,' she says. 'It can be tricky this time of day,' she says. Her voice has the smartness of southern Indiana. He hears it more clearly than ever before. He reaches over and touches the back of her gloved hand.

She slips off the glove and places his hand in her palm. Her skin is smooth and tough. She squeezes affectionately.

Ahead, moving toward the intersection just before the Route 41 fork, a black-and-white 1950 Ford Tudor. Mostly black. It stops at the intersection and rolls cautiously out onto the main highway. The driver, a student at Cal Poly, does not see the low silver racer because it reflects the lowering sun in the same manner as the road.

Through his dark glasses, James sees only the whitened lower portion of the Ford. He thinks it is stippling on the road, maybe a spot where a can of paint has spilled. Or perhaps he is thinking about nothing whatever, as when he crashed at Riverside.

Fortunately, Mildred sees everything clearly, sees a possible collision developing. 'Jamie,' her voice is calm, more cautionary than alarming. Her second 'Jamie,' is on edge but not panic-ridden. The crash is a certainty: neither driver is yet fully aware of the other car.

James feels Mildred's strong hand on top of his on the steering wheel. She is pulling to the right. He resists her steady strength and turns to look at her: as he does he sees the Ford directly in front of him and immediately yields to her pull. Her hand never leaves his. He may, he may just . . . miss the rear of the Ford. At the moment of impact, he closes his eyes.

There is no crash. When he looks again, he is headed off the road toward a barbed-wire fence. He pulls hard back to the left, runs across the highway and rolls up on the rocky earth beyond the shoulder. The car bounces wildly before it regains the shoulder and then the road. He pumps the brake as the Spyder zig-zags this way and that. It straightens and slows. 'I never saw it, I swear. Never. But I'm sure glad you did.'

He hears high-pitched curses in German.

*

James Dean's body, or rather his fractured and shattered remains, is sent by ambulance to the War Memorial Hospital in Paso Robles. The neck has been broken; the skull has been fractured; there are numerous and severe internal injuries. Killed immediately upon impact. The time on the death certificate from the coroner of San Luis Obispo County is 5:45 P.M. – the correct time is actually eleven minutes earlier – and the chief cause of death determined to be the broken neck. The coroner made the least complicated choice.

The body is taken to Kuehl's Funeral Home, where under the harsh light of the embalming room Martin Kuehl tries to make the bashed-in forehead and left cheekbone acceptable. James has not been in an embalming room since Mosbacher's with Lem Craig. Although there is little blood left in the body, the arterial system holds the embalming fluid. But before any reconstruction can proceed, Kuehl has to pull hundreds of small shards of glass out of every square inch of face and scalp. By daylight on Saturday, Kuehl has injected enough gel by syringe to give the forehead the suggestion of a dome. The cheekbone would not stay put, however: so he places the head sideways on the pillow. The face requires three layers of make-up.

The hearse from Paso Robles takes the coastal highway down to the Los Angeles airport. Winton is there to accept the casket and accompany it back to Fairmount.

*

Two days later, a memorial service is held in a church on the Warners back lot that has appeared in films for over a decade.

Jimmy's Hollywood friends and colleagues have been invited. All the seats are filled, people line the walls and are packed in the rear.

The small chapel is decorated and lighted as for a film. Only the first five rows of pews are real: the others are temporary benches set behind balsa and plywood copies of pew dividers. The assembled fall to a hush when Jack L. Warner walks through a side door and steps behind a podium placed in front of the altar. He waits for the silence to become respectful and takes a folded sheet of paper out of his jacket pocket. A script.

From the first word, his voice has a ring of authority: 'Death.' The word, uttered with finality, gets the consideration Jack Warner intends. He repeats – 'Death . . . is a robber. A robber of dreams, of hopes, of possibilities. A sneak thief who skulks and prowls and takes our most precious possessions. And last Friday it came and robbed this studio of James Dean.

'When Death stole James Dean from us, I never felt more powerless, for it stole from his family and friends a remarkable young man. A boy, really. Which is something too easy to forget. Full of the excesses of youth, of its uncompromising purity, of its wild, untamed appetites.

'He came to us unheralded, as is the case with so many of the unique ones. I sensed something quite special in him during a long conversation about film-making which we had in my office. James saw the panoply of Warner Brothers stars clustered on the walls of my office and wondered out loud if he could ever achieve their elevation, their brightness. I laughed and said, "Of course you can young man." And I meant exactly what I said.

'My mother, who was a very wise, a very practical woman, used to tell my brothers and myself that anything worth doing was worth doing right. That phrase might have become this studio's slogan. The sense of pride in one's work, the commitment to excellence, they are virtues that seem to be disappearing from our world these days.

'But James Dean had them. And if anything positive can possibly come out of this loss, it is the idea that since we do not know what the future holds for any of us, we must do our best work today, and the next day, and for however many days we are allotted. If we do that, James Dean will look down on our efforts with that enigmatic smile he had, and we will bring some tears and some laughter to anyone who sees a Warner Brothers picture.

'I read in an astrology book recently' – he means 'astronomy' but misreads the word – 'that there is a new theory about the stars in the heavens. They say that stars get old and die just like people do. Maybe that's true in the universe, but at Warner Brothers that's not how it is. Here an actor may pass away, even a very young one stolen before his lustre has become its brightest, but his star will shine forever, or at least as long as there is celluloid, a projector, and a silver screen.'

Jack Warner folds his eulogy neatly and slides it back inside his jacket pocket. He does not bow his head. He looks to Arlene Grossbard for an idea of what to do. She signals him to invite others to come forward and pay homage to James Dean.

Carmen Reyes very much wanted to say goodbye to Jimmy, but Manny Monk took her aside as she came in the chapel and told her Mr. Warner thought it might be enough just to be seen today.

Martin Goldglass waits and then feels moved to step to the altar. 'I've played so many parts in my life,' he says softly, 'it's hard not to slip into a role here. I just want to tell you about the first time I met Jimmy Dean. He simply showed up one morning at my office at U.C.L.A. begging to get into my drama class. I said, "Beginners or Advanced?" and he said, "Both."'

A breath of laughter circles the chapel.

'That was Jimmy. At the same time the purity of a beginner and one of the most advanced and subtle actors I've ever seen. I had no idea he wasn't even enrolled at U.C.L.A., that he just walked in off the street and insisted on taking courses. I noticed he was carrying a small book. It was this,' Goldglass holds up a thin volume. 'Stanislavsky, *An Actor Prepares*. I said to myself, "It's probably just a prop to try to impress me." It wasn't. He knew the book cold: it was his testament. What he didn't know was that these Russian words scribbled . . .' He opens to the title page, '. . . in the front are in Stanislavsky's own hand. I asked to borrow it.

'I never returned it. I kept meaning to, but I forgot. If this book was the source of Jimmy Dean's brilliance, I guess I wanted to keep it in case some of its magic might rub off.' The admission unburdens Goldglass and his voice cracks.

'Anyway. Now I will send it to his family back in Indiana.' He takes a step. 'Oh. Here's what Stanislavsky wrote above his signature. Jimmy was never able to read it. "Dear Friend. A life in art is the most difficult pathway, full of nettles and pit-falls and frightening ghosts. It is for the courageous, perhaps for the foolhardy, but once it beckons, the pilgrim must follow. It may lead to destruction, it may lead to Paradise, it may lead nowhere. That does not matter.'"